Dear Reader,

One morning over a decade ago I walked into my office as I'd done a thousand times before. But that morning something was in my office that every publisher dreams about but few publishers get to experience, something that literally changed the future of our company and shook the very foundations of the publishing industry. What caught my eye as I threw my coat across the chair was not the proposal resting in my in-box—I see those every day. No, what grabbed my attention immediately was the title of the proposal: *Left Behind: A Novel of the Earth's Last Days.*

What a great title, I thought to myself. *But can the content deliver?* I jumped on that proposal and pushed every button at our publishing house to get the deal done and the book to market. The rest is history and still making history—a series of novels that has sold an astonishing 62 million copies and will sell millions more. The last seven books all have been #1 best-sellers on the *New York Times, USA Today, Publishers Weekly*, and *Wall Street Journal* lists.

Why do I write this here? Because I want you to know, dear reader, that recently I had a very similar experience—a real déjà vu. Not many months ago my fiction director, Becky Nesbitt, sent me a proposal for a new novel by an author named Joel Rosenberg. I walked into my office one morning and there it was—something every publisher dreams about but few get to experience, something I now believe can once again shake up the publishing industry. This time it wasn't the title that caught my eye, nor was it Becky's note that told me to lock the door until I'd finished reading the proposal; it was the manuscript's first two sentences, which read:

> *Boris Stuchenko would be dead in less than nineteen minutes.*
> *And he had no idea why.*

What a great opening, I thought to myself. *But can the rest of the book deliver?* Deliver it did! I sat down with that manuscript, and was instantly propelled into a ride I'll never forget. Becky and I jumped on that proposal and pushed every button at our publishing house to get the deal done and the book to market. Now it's your turn. Fasten your seat belt because this is not just a page-turner, it's a page-churner. You'll churn through the pages with the same heart-stopping intensity of viewing a great thriller movie for the first time. When you get to the end, you'll be a different person than you were at the beginning.

I have the same gut feeling about this novel as I did about *Left Behind*. That novel is a thrill ride bringing to life the prophecies of the book of Revelation. The book you hold in your hand is the same kind of thrill ride, but bringing to life the biblical prophecies leading up to the events of Revelation. So turn the page, and enjoy the ride of your life. Where you're going, there's no turning back.

Ron Beers
Publisher

PRAISE FOR *THE EZEKIEL OPTION*

★ ★ ★

New York Times best seller
USA Today best seller
Publishers Weekly best seller
Christian Booksellers Association best seller

★ ★ ★

"If you only read one novel this year, this is it! *The Ezekiel Option* is brilliantly conceived and flawlessly executed—one of the most exciting political thrillers I've ever read. I literally could not put it down. **LIKE AN EPISODE OF 24 WITH A SUPERNATURAL TWIST.** Rosenberg has become one of the most entertaining and thought-provoking novelists of our day. Regardless of your political views, you've got to read his stuff."

★ **RUSH LIMBAUGH,** #1 *New York Times* best-selling author

"Joel Rosenberg is one of my favorite novelists of all time. . . . *THE EZEKIEL OPTION* **IS ANOTHER OUTSTANDING BOOK.** . . . What's so eerie about all Rosenberg's novels is that he brings them to life with modern events."

★ **SEAN HANNITY,** #1 *New York Times* best-selling author of *Let Freedom Ring* and *Deliver Us from Evil*

"Joel C. Rosenberg is a masterful storyteller, a true friend of Israel and of the Jewish people. He understands the real problems and threats in the Middle East better than any American novelist I know and turns it into a chilling, prescient, and unforgettable read."

★ **NATAN SHARANSKY,** former deputy prime minister of Israel and *New York Times* best-selling author of *The Case for Democracy*

"RIPPED FROM THE HEADLINES—NEXT YEAR'S HEADLINES."

★ *Washington Times*

"Eerily prophetic . . . unsettling and scary . . . Rosenberg documents his plot with extensive research. . . . A fast-paced story with action from beginning to end."

★ *Dallas Morning News*

"Another page-turner."

★ WORLD magazine

"*THE EZEKIEL OPTION* IS PERFECT IN EVERY WAY . . . exciting, fascinating, well-written, character driven, and above all, it is plausible. It will keep you on the edge of your seat and never let you go. This is a very powerful book."

★ *Kingston (Mass) Observer*

"Get ready for one of the most riveting reading experiences of your life. This book is too good to put down! . . . This heart-pounding end-times thriller is so close to what's happening in the world even as you read that it will hold you captive until the very end."

★ Crossings Book Club

"Better written and more complex than *Left Behind*, to which it will inevitably be compared."

★ *Publishers Weekly*

"Absolutely fantastic! A must read! . . . THE EVENTS THAT TAKE PLACE IN THIS BOOK ARE ALL TOO PLAUSIBLE, and fans of action thrillers will find themselves thoroughly immersed in the story line so much that they will not be able to put the book down until the last page is turned."

★ HARRIETT KLAUSNER, #1 Amazon.com reviewer

"*The Ezekiel Option* is provocative . . . compelling . . . a roller-coaster ride through Washington, Iran, Russia, and Israel."

★ ONEJERUSALEM.org

"Another direct hit on the dangers of a troubled world . . . Joel Rosenberg again displays an uncanny eye for global realities along with his powerful storytelling ability—and a sense of the pressing spiritual challenges of our time. *The Ezekiel Option* is bound for well-deserved best-seller status."

★ RALPH PETERS, author of *Beyond Iraq: Postmodern War and Peace* and *New Glory: Expanding America's Global Supremacy*

"I was hooked on this book from the first two sentences. . . . *The Ezekiel Option* stands alone for a tension-filled reading experience. The characters are well drawn and the dialogue is crisp in this contemporary novel. . . . THE TENSION FOR THE READER GROWS WITH EACH PAGE UNTIL YOU REACH A POINT OF NO RETURN—where you have to complete the book in that sitting, even if you stay up until the wee hours of the morning."

★ FaithfulReader.com

THE EZEKIEL OPTION

THE EZEKIEL OPTION

JOEL C. ROSENBERG

Tyndale House
Publishers, Inc.,
Carol Stream,
Illinois

Visit Tyndale's exciting Web site at www.tyndale.com

TYNDALE is a registered trademark of Tyndale House Publishers, Inc.

Tyndale's quill logo is a trademark of Tyndale House Publishers, Inc.

The Ezekiel Option

Designed by Dean H. Renninger

Scripture taken from the *New American Standard Bible*, © 1960, 1962, 1963, 1968, 1971, 1972, 1973, 1975, 1977 by The Lockman Foundation. Used by permission.

This novel is a work of fiction. Names, characters, places, and incidents either are the product of the author's imagination or are used fictitiously. Any resemblance to actual events, locales, organizations, or persons, living or dead, is entirely coincidental and beyond the intent of either the author or publisher.

Library of Congress Cataloging-in-Publication Data

Rosenberg, Joel C., date.
  The Ezekiel option : a novel / Joel C. Rosenberg.
    p. cm.
  ISBN-13: 978-1-4143-0343-7
  ISBN-10: 1-4143-0343-2
  ISBN-13: 978-1-4143-0344-4 (pbk.)
  ISBN-10: 1-4143-0344-0 (pbk.)
  I. Title
  PS3618.O832E97 2005
  813'.6—dc22   2005005315

Printed in the United States of America

11   10   09   08   07   06
7   6   5   4   3   2   1

This book is dedicated to the Rosenberg family,

who escaped czarist persecution of the Jews in Russia

in the early years of the twentieth century;

and to my parents, Len and Mary Rosenberg,

who taught me by their love and example

the true meaning of faith and freedom.

CAST OF CHARACTERS

★ ★ ★

THE PRESIDENT OF THE UNITED STATES
- James "Mac" MacPherson

THE VICE PRESIDENT OF THE UNITED STATES
- William Harvard Oaks

THE PRINCIPALS
- Marsha Kirkpatrick, *National Security Advisor*
- Jack Mitchell, *Director of Central Intelligence*
- Burt Trainor, *Secretary of Defense*
- Nick Warner, *Secretary of State*

SENIOR ADMINISTRATION OFFICIALS
- Jon Bennett, *Senior Advisor to the President*
- Bob Corsetti, *White House Chief of Staff*
- Ken Costello, *Undersecretary of State for Political Affairs*
- Erin McCoy, *Senior Advisor to the President, on loan from the CIA*
- Indira Rajiv, *Director of the NAMESTAN Desk, CIA*
- Chuck Murray, *White House Press Secretary*

ISRAELI LEADERS
- David Doron, *Prime Minister of Israel*
- Dr. Eliezer Mordechai, *Former head of Mossad*

RUSSIAN LEADERS
- Grigoriy Vadim, *President of the Russian Federation*
- Aleksandr Golitsyn, *Russian Foreign Minister*
- Andrei Zyuganov, *Director of Presidential Administration (Chief of Staff)*
- Sergei Ilyushkin, *Deputy Speaker of the Duma; Protégé of Vladimir Zhirinovsky*

AL-NAKBAH LEADERS
- Yuri Gogolov, *Russian Cofounder of Al-Nakbah Terrorist Movement*
- Mohammed Jibril, *Iranian Cofounder of Al-Nakbah*

OTHERS
- Mustafa Al-Hassani, *President of Iraq*
- Ruth Bennett, *Mother of Jon Bennett*
- Salvador Lucente, *European Union Foreign Minister*
- Ibrahim Sa'id, *Palestinian Prime Minister*
- Ifshahan Kharrazi, *President of Iran*

AUTHOR'S NOTE

★ ★ ★

The journey that follows is fiction.

The prophecy upon which it is based is true.

The cryptic vision of a Hebrew scribe—writing twenty-five centuries ago—foretold one of the most horrific periods in the future of mankind.

Yet even today it remains one of man's great unsolved mysteries.

Its central premise was once discussed in a speech before the U.S. Congress, and was believed to be both true and increasingly close at hand by one of America's greatest presidents.

Its central characters surface throughout history, in the Tanakh and the book of Revelation, in the journals of Marco Polo and the writings of Voltaire, in the Dead Sea Scrolls and the histories of Josephus, in the works of Russian authors like Nikolai Vasilevich Gogol, and in the writings of Nobel Prize winners like Elie Wiesel and Isaac Bashevis Singer.

How soon will this prophecy come to pass? Some believe that even now there are signs that the board is being set, that the great game is about to begin. Some believe that among those signs are the fall of Saddam Hussein and the death of Yasser Arafat.

Winston Churchill once called Russia "a riddle wrapped in a mystery inside an enigma."

It is unlikely that he understood the full magnitude of what he was saying. But it is here that our story begins.

Joel C. Rosenberg
Moscow, Russia
September 2004

The most important failure was one of imagination.

We do not believe leaders understood the gravity of the threat.

★

THE 9/11 COMMISSION REPORT:
Final Report of the National Commission
on Terrorist Attacks upon the United States

Things fall apart; the centre cannot hold;

Mere anarchy is loosed upon the world,

The blood-dimmed tide is loosed, and everywhere

The ceremony of innocence is drowned;

The best lack all convictions, while the worst

Are full of passionate intensity.

★

W.B. YEATS
The Second Coming

1

TUESDAY, JULY 29 – 3:16 P.M. – 52 MILES SOUTHEAST OF MANHATTAN

Boris Stuchenko would be dead in less than nineteen minutes.

And he had no idea why.

The fifty-three-year-old self-made billionaire had a long list of enemies; of this he had no doubt. Business competitors. Political rivals. Mistresses too numerous to count.

But this made no sense. Was it really a hit? Was he really the target? Or was the president and CEO of Lukoil—Russia's largest oil company— simply in the wrong place at the wrong time for the first time in his life?

Stuchenko gripped the leather armrests. He couldn't see the terrorists. At least one was behind him, back in business or economy class. But he didn't dare turn and look.

He wasn't even supposed to be on this flight. As the richest man in Russia, he never flew commercial. His fleet of private jets, including a gleaming new Gulfstream V, was the envy of the Russian oligarchs.

But over the past eighteen months, he'd become obsessed with buying Aeroflot, Russia's aging airline—her jets, her routes, her infrastructure— and turning the much-ridiculed "Aero-*flop*" into a world-class competitor. To seal the deal with the Wall Street crowd, his strategists were positioning him as a man of the people, willing to fly one of the most troubled airlines on the planet before turning her into a profit-making superpower.

Now all that was about to change.

Stuchenko tried to slow his breathing and focus his thoughts. Two hijackers were in the cockpit. He'd seen them go in. But now the door was shut, and the pilots' screams had long since been silenced.

Out of the corner of his eye he could see two badly beaten flight attendants, huddled and shivering on the floor in the forward galley. Their hands and mouths were bound with duct tape. Their swollen eyes darted from face to face, silently pleading for help from anyone in the first-class cabin.

No one moved.

They were so young and innocent, the kind of exquisite and courteous Russian women around which he could have rebuilt this airline. He'd flirted with one for half the flight. But now Stuchenko refused even to make eye contact. The women had the air of hunted animals, and he wanted nothing to do with them.

What kind of man was he? He couldn't sit here like a coward.

Stuchenko had served his time in the Red Army. He'd fought in Afghanistan in the eighties against bin Laden and his demons. He'd been trained in hand-to-hand combat. And he'd have the element of surprise. Especially if he could enlist the help of his two top aides, sitting in the row behind him.

The cockpit wasn't sealed shut. The terrorists had jammed the lock. He'd seen them do it. He'd seen them come in and out, and the door had swung easily every time.

A quick glance to his right confirmed that no one was coming up the aisle. He reached for his fountain pen and wrote quickly in German on the napkin beside him. His aides knew German, but it was unlikely the terrorists did.

"We must storm the cabin, like the Americans did on 9/11," he wrote. "We have no choice. We must retake the plane, or die. Cough if you're with me."

He set down the pen, crumpled the napkin in his right hand, then slipped it back between the seats, hoping one of them would see it and take it.

One did. The napkin slid from his fingers. He waited.

He could hear the muffled cries of children behind him, but mostly there was an eerie quiet, save for the roar of the jet engines. The acrid stench of gunpowder still hung in the air. For the life of him he couldn't imagine how they'd gotten weapons on board. But he could see the results. On the floor ahead of him lay his personal bodyguard, a pool of crimson growing around his head.

The young air-traffic controller tried to stay calm.

"Aeroflot six-six-one-seven heavy, once again, this is New York Center; acknowledge."

Still no response.

"Aeroflot six-six-one-seven, this is New York Center. Execute immediate course change to three-four-five—repeat, three-four-five—and acknowledge, over."

Again, no response.

The controller took a deep breath and scanned his instruments again. He'd only been on the job for a year, but he'd been well trained. The jumbo jet was inbound from Moscow and scheduled to land at JFK within the half hour. But instead of heading into a landing pattern, the plane had banked sharply to the southwest, bypassed New York City, and refused to acknowledge his radio instructions.

He picked up the phone and dialed his supervisor.

Seconds later, his call was relayed to the FAA's operations center in Virginia.

No, the transponder was still on, he told the watch officer.

Yes, it appeared to be transmitting properly.

No, the jet had not squawked 7500, the international hijacking code. Or 7600, for radio malfunction. Or 7700, for a general emergency.

No, the pilots had not flashed an *HJK* text message for a hijacking in progress.

No, there was no evidence of depressurization.

Or reports of a fire or shots on board.

But something was seriously wrong.

The FAA watch officer now speed-dialed NORAD. He was patched through to the North East Air Defense Sector at Griffiss Air Force Base in Rome, New York, and explained the situation. The NEADS commander didn't hesitate. He scrambled fighter jets out of the 119th Fighter Squadron in Atlantic City and the 121st out of Andrews Air Force Base in Maryland, then called the National Military Command Center at the Pentagon.

Moving at 550 miles an hour—with clear skies, unlimited visibility, and no headwinds—Aeroflot 6617 was now less than two hundred miles from Washington, D.C.

The briefing wasn't going well.

President James "Mac" MacPherson had just begun a meeting with his Council of Economic Advisors. The first-quarter growth numbers were dismal. The second-quarter estimates were worse. The recovery had stalled. Unemployment was climbing, and his approval ratings were slipping.

But the instant Secret Service Agent Jackie Sanchez burst into the Oval Office without warning, MacPherson knew the meeting was over.

Sanchez leaned in and whispered, "Mr. President, you need to come with me."

"Why? What's going on?"

"Right away, sir. I'm sorry. I'll brief you on the way."

MacPherson rose and apologized to his economic team. He started to gather his papers, but gave up as three more agents took up positions and rushed him toward the door.

"Gambit's moving," Sanchez said into her wrist-mounted radio.

"What's going on?" MacPherson demanded.

"Mr. President, NORAD is presently tracking a Russian passenger jet headed for D.C. Probable hijacking. Possible suicide mission. ETA about fourteen minutes. NMCC has initiated Noble Eagle, and they're waiting for you, sir."

MacPherson hurried through a set of steel blast doors and down three flights of stairs to the Presidential Emergency Operations Center, a nuclear-bomb-proof communications bunker deep underneath the White House.

"Julie and the girls?"

"They're being airlifted to Mount Weather, sir, along with the VP's wife."

"Where's the vice president?"

"Checkmate is inbound to the White House. Should be here in a few minutes."

"What about the Speaker?"

"En route to New York for a fund-raiser, Mr. President. We've re-routed his plane and are giving him a fighter escort out of the northeast corridor. House and Senate leadership are all being secured. The Hill is being evacuated as we speak, and the army is deploying triple-A batteries around the Capitol, the Pentagon, and Langley."

"And your guys?"

"We're good, sir. I've got Avengers and Stingers on the roof. We've got two F-16s scrambled out of Andrews flying CAP and four more about to go up."

The president entered the PEOC, where National Security Advisor Marsha Kirkpatrick and White House Chief of Staff Bob Corsetti were already working the phones along with another dozen military aides and Press Secretary Chuck Murray.

"Where are we?" asked MacPherson as he took a seat at the head of the conference table.

"Mr. President, NMCC just initiated the air threat conference," said Kirkpatrick. "We've got all the relevant agencies on secure audio and video. The VP is still a few minutes out. The SecDef is choppering to the Pentagon and should be in place shortly. Right now I need you to speak with General Charlie Briggs—four star, air force, commander at NORAD. He's on one of the secure feeds."

"What've we got, General?" asked MacPherson.

"Sir, on the far left screen you can see the radar track of the Russian jet."

"That's real time?"

"Yes, sir—they're 163 miles outside of D.C. In a moment we'll have live video feeds from the F-16s involved in the intercept."

"Who's up there?" MacPherson asked.

"Two F-16s out of the 119th in Atlantic City, Mr. President."

MacPherson watched another video screen flicker to life. He could now see the two F-16s roaring in behind the Russian jet, moving faster

than the speed of sound, and could overhear the pilots as they communi-
cated with their commanders.

"NEADS, this is Devil One-One, in half-mile trail behind the airliner," came the voice of the lead U.S. fighter pilot, thirty thousand feet
above the coast of Delaware.

"Devil One-One, this is NEADS Command," replied the two-star
general from NORAD's Continental Region at Tyndall Air Force Base in
Panama City, Florida. "You are authorized to switch to Guard frequency
and begin communications with the Russian jumbo."

"Roger that, sir."

MacPherson heard the F-16 pilot attempting to reach the Russian
pilots on the standard frequency all aircraft were required to monitor.
"Aeroflot six-six-one-seven, this is a United States Air Force F-16 off your
left wing, transmitting on Guard."

There was no answer.

"Six-six-one-seven, again, this is a United States Air Force F-16 off
your left wing. Acknowledge."

Nothing.

"Six-six-one-seven, this is Devil One-One, transmitting on Guard,
two-four-three-point-zero, and one-two-one-point-five. If you can hear
me, acknowledge with a wing rock, over."

There was nothing but the hiss of static.

"Devil One-One, this is CONR Command. Son, can you see into the
cockpit?"

"Negative, CONR. No frost. No signs of depressurization. But the
sun's pretty hot up here. We're getting a wicked glare off the Russian's
windshield. Devil One-Two, this is Devil One-One. Do you have a line of
sight into the cockpit from your side?"

The second F-16—positioned off the right wing of the Russian jet—
tried to maneuver for a better look.

"Negative, Devil One-One. Can't really tell."

The two-star in Panama City came on again. "Devil One-One, what
about the passenger windows? Any movement inside?"

"Negative, sir. All the shades are pulled down on this side. Can't see a
thing."

His wingman fared no better.

"Roger that, Devil One-One," came the word from Panama City. "Try the flares."

"Copy that, CONR. Stand by one."

The lead F-16 now banked away from the Russian's left wing, then roared forward, pulling in front of the Russian by about half a mile.

Devil 12 banked right, slowed a bit, then pulled in behind the Russian jumbo.

Sixty seconds later, the lead fighter jet released a barrage of sizzling, red-hot flares. They were typically used as decoys to confuse heat-seeking missiles. Now they were trying to catch the attention of anyone who might be alive inside the Aeroflot cockpit.

Again the F-16s attempted radio contact.

Again there was nothing but hiss and static.

President MacPherson's stomach tightened. He caught the eye of his chief of staff, then looked back at the radar track. Aeroflot 6617 was now only 109 miles outside of the nation's capital and coming in at nearly the speed of sound.

The plan was almost set.

Stuchenko reached his hand back to receive one last crumpled note from his aides in the first-class seats behind him. His hands trembled. He glanced to his right, listened carefully, but saw and heard no one as he opened the napkin under the protection of his fold-out tray.

"We know there are two in the cockpit," it read. "But what about behind us? Where's #3? Is there a fourth? more? We must know before we move."

Stuchenko was furious. They wanted *him* to turn around? They wanted *him* to look back to find the other terrorists? Wasn't he *their* boss? Why didn't *they* turn around? But Stuchenko knew full well why not. They were as terrified as he was. Everyone on the plane had been ordered not to move, not to stand, not to go to the bathroom, not to turn around. To disobey was suicide. But what other choice did they have?

Stuchenko closed his eyes, straining to hear any sign of trouble. But aside from all the crying children, all he could hear now was his PR agent rubbing worry beads and mumbling some sort of prayer over and over again.

What a fool, thought Stuchenko. *The idiot is going to get us all killed.*

Stuchenko tried to breathe, tried to steel himself.

If he had to die, he would die like a man.

☆　　☆　　☆

Marsha Kirkpatrick put the question directly.

"Mr. President, are you ready to order this plane shot down?"

MacPherson hesitated to say no out loud. Instead he began firing off questions.

"Are any U.S. marshals on board?"

"No," said Kirkpatrick. "There aren't enough marshals for every flight, and this route has never been a problem."

"What about Russian marshals?"

"We're not sure yet. Aeroflot is supposed to fax the flight manifest to the FBI's field office in Moscow, but nothing has come in yet."

"Is there any possibility that passengers on board might be able to overtake the hijackers?"

"Perhaps," Kirkpatrick conceded. "But there isn't much time, and if the flight gets within fifty miles of Washington, the situation will get infinitely more dangerous."

"Why?"

"Because the plane would have to be shot down over land, sir. That puts the lives of innocent people on the ground at risk."

MacPherson struggled to think clearly. "Is there any other way to stop the plane?"

"Unlikely," Kirkpatrick said. "Mr. President, you should be under no illusions. If Chechen rebels are in control of the aircraft, they are likely on a kamikaze mission, and there will be no negotiations."

MacPherson looked up at the radar track.

The jet was now less than one hundred miles from D.C.

The two F-16s took up flanking positions behind the jet. Each carried two AIM-120 air-to-air missiles, and two AIM-9 Sidewinder heat-seeking missiles. Each was also armed with a front-mounted, 20 mm cannon loaded with five hundred rounds of ammunition.

MacPherson knew the pilots had trained for this moment. But it had never happened. Not yet. U.S. fighter jets had never shot down an unarmed civilian jetliner over Washington or anywhere else. And certainly not a civilian jetliner owned by Russia.

White House Press Secretary Chuck Murray put down his cell phone and began turning on a bank of television sets on the far wall of the PEOC. Every cable news channel and all four broadcast networks now had the story.

MacPherson could feel his chest constricting and reached for a glass of water.

Defense Secretary Burt Trainor had arrived at the Pentagon and was now linked in by a secure video feed. Trainor had run two wars for this president. A highly decorated Vietnam vet, he had previously served as the CEO of General Motors and had been named *Black Enterprise* magazine's "Leader of the Decade." He'd been a close personal friend of James and Julie MacPherson for more than twenty years. He had earned MacPherson's trust. Now Trainor needed the president's decision.

"Mr. President—," Trainor began, but MacPherson shook his head.

"What's the fail-safe point?" the president asked.

"Thirty miles, sir. But—"

"No, not yet," the president shot back.

MacPherson knew Trainor was fighting to keep his instincts in check. But he didn't care. He wasn't ready. "Marsha?"

"Yes, Mr. President."

"You got that manifest for me?"

"We just got a partial copy, sir."

"Partial? Why?"

"I don't know, sir. We're checking."

MacPherson was furious, but he had to maintain focus. He was running out of time. "Whom would I be shooting down?" he asked the national security advisor.

Kirkpatrick seemed to hesitate, so MacPherson asked again. *"Who is on this plane?"*

Kirkpatrick swallowed hard. "Sir, we count 173 civilian passengers on board. Sixty-three families. Forty-one children."

"God have mercy," said the president.

"There're more complications, sir. Three members of the Russian Duma are on board. They're scheduled for meetings today and tomorrow at the U.N., then here in Washington later in the week."

MacPherson looked to Bob Corsetti, his chief of staff and senior political advisor, who shook his head slowly, too stunned to say anything.

Kirkpatrick continued. "Also on board is Boris Stuchenko, president and CEO of Lukoil, as well as several members of his board of directors and top aides. They're on their way to a series of meetings on Wall Street."

"Anyone else I should know about?" MacPherson demanded.

"We believe several members of the Moscow Ballet may also be on the flight."

"Get the secretary of state on the phone," MacPherson said to his chief of staff.

Aeroflot 6617 was now just seventy-five miles from Washington.

Stuchenko knew this was it.

Carefully, quietly, he unbuckled his seat belt. The instant he gave the word, they would storm the cockpit. He gave them a one-in-three chance of successfully wresting control of the plane. How they'd land the enormous craft was another matter entirely. But he could only worry about so much at a time.

Stuchenko wiped his hands on the pants of his custom-tailored French suit. He shifted forward to the edge of his seat, then quickly turned his head for the look he'd been dreading.

But it was then that his heart stopped. He was staring into a silencer. Five shots later, his assistants were dead. He never heard the sixth shot.

MacPherson closed his eyes.

To blow a Russian passenger jet out of the sky would have unprecedented global ramifications. But so, too, would a decision not to defend the American capital.

What worried him most was the law of unintended consequences.

Relations with Moscow were already strained. The war in Iraq. Moscow's ties to Tehran. The rising anti-American sentiment among the ultra-nationalists in the State Duma. A sharp rise in anti-Semitic attacks throughout Russia. All exacerbated by falling oil and gas prices that were dragging down Russia's economy and causing the worst Russian unemployment since the collapse of the Soviet Empire.

On a personal level, MacPherson and Russian president Grigoriy Vadim liked each other a great deal. The two had developed a professional bond of trust over the past few years. But a question kept churning in MacPherson's gut: though U.S.-Russian rapprochement had taken years to build, how quickly could it be destroyed?

The president looked up and ordered General Briggs to have his fighters buzz the Russian jet to try to divert its course. Moments later, he watched the lead F-16 perform a "head butt"—flying directly at the front windshield of the Russian jumbo jet at Mach 1.2, then pulling up and away at the last possible moment.

It was a supersonic game of chicken. And the Russians didn't blink.

His heart racing, MacPherson then ordered the F-16s to fire their machine guns near the cockpit of the Russian jumbo. It was a last-ditch effort to convince the hijackers he would not let them reach Washington. But again, whoever was inside did not flinch.

The plane banked westward, boosted its power, and began its descent. Aeroflot 6617 was now just fifty miles from the White House.

MacPherson pressed his team harder.

"What about cell phones?" the president asked. "Can we establish contact with the hijacker—or anyone else on the plane—using a passenger's cell phone?"

"I'm afraid not, sir," Kirkpatrick said. "The FBI has been trying, without success. It's too late for any further attempts."

"The secretary of state is online, sir," an aide announced.

MacPherson turned to Nick Warner on the video feed from Foggy Bottom. "Nick, have we been able to get President Vadim on the hotline?"

"Not yet, Mr. President," Warner responded. The Russian leader was currently in the Black Sea resort of Sochi, but thus far direct contact had not been possible, and the Russian Foreign Ministry was keeping quiet until it had specific instructions from Vadim.

MacPherson weighed his options. They were dwindling fast.

Now sixty-three, the president was no stranger to combat. A former navy pilot, MacPherson had flown F-4 Phantoms over Vietnam in the last years of the conflict. He'd downed three enemy planes during his tour and narrowly survived after his own plane had crashed in the Sea of Japan. As commander in chief, he believed his presidency was a quest to protect the American people and bring peace to a troubled world. But the price had been steep.

MacPherson had sent U.S. forces into harm's way numerous times over the past several years to wage war against the radical Islamic jihadists who, if given the chance, would launch attacks of almost unimaginable proportions against the American people. Scores of U.S. servicemen and servicewomen had died thus far, and many more had been wounded. MacPherson himself had almost been killed during a kamikaze attack in Denver. He'd lost one of his top counterterrorism operatives in a gun battle with Islamic militants in Jerusalem, and his first secretary of state and thirty-four American diplomats and security personnel had died in a suicide bombing attack in Gaza.

Not a day went by when he didn't count the cost. Was he doing the right thing? Was he honoring th165e memories of the dead by creating a safer, more secure world?

He was trying, and there had been good news.

The Taliban was dead, and Afghanistan was quiet.

Iraq, too, was largely pacified—finally—and, despite all the hardships, had a democratically elected government as well. Saddam Hussein's regime was dead and buried. The vast majority of U.S. and coalition troops were finally out of Iraq. And the new government, while still working to firmly establish its legitimacy, was—for now, at least—peaceful, only lightly armed, and friendly to American interests.

What's more, Yasser Arafat was dead. A moderate, democratically elected Palestinian prime minister was in power. An interim Israeli-Palestinian peace agreement—MacPherson's baby—was bearing fruit, and a final status agreement could very possibly be completed by the end of the summer. In fact, if the Russians would sign off on the deal, a signing ceremony at the White House could occur as soon as the fall.

Now all that was at risk.

MacPherson and his chief of staff stepped to the side of the room. "Tell me you're seeing something I'm not, Bob," MacPherson said, praying for a miracle.

Bob Corsetti was the man who had persuaded him to enter politics almost fifteen years before. It was Corsetti who had gotten him elected— and reelected—governor of Colorado. It was Corsetti who had managed his presidential campaign and served as his only White House chief of staff. MacPherson relied on Corsetti to see around corners and compensate for his blind spots. They were almost brothers at this point, and though MacPherson had paid him well, he knew Corsetti, ten years his junior, would have done it all for free.

"I'm afraid I'm not, Mr. President. It's clearly an aggressive profile. Everything's been done by the book. But you don't have a choice. You need to take this guy out fast."

The president said nothing. He turned to look again at the radar track. The Russian jet was now just thirty-five miles out and coming in red-hot. Corsetti was right. He was out of options and out of time.

"God forgive me," MacPherson said.

The president finally gave the order to Defense Secretary Trainor.

On the monitor, MacPherson saw Trainor pick up a phone and say into it, "It's a go. Repeat, mission is a go."

"That's affirmative," came the response from Panama City on another monitor.

All eyes turned to the live video feed coming in from the lead F-16.

"Devil One-One," said the two-star in Panama City. "POTUS declares the target is hostile. You are cleared to engage."

"CONR Command, do I understand you right? . . . Target is hostile? . . . You want me to engage? You want me to fire on an unarmed civilian jetliner?"

MacPherson could hear the tremor in the flight leader's voice.

He shot a hard look to his national security advisor. It was the president's job—not a pilot's—to wrestle through the moral justification of a call like this. The commander in chief had just issued an order. Why wasn't it being obeyed?

The Aeroflot jet was now twenty-five miles out.

Marsha Kirkpatrick picked up the open line to NORAD just as another voice came over the intercom.

"Devil One-One, this is General Briggs at NORAD. Son, you are ordered to take this Russian jet down. *Repeat, take the target down.*"

For a moment, there was nothing but silence.

"I can't, sir."

It was the voice of the lead pilot.

"I'm sorry, sir. . . . I . . . I just can't do it. . . . It's not right."

MacPherson saw Kirkpatrick gasp and instinctively cover her mouth with her hands. Chuck Murray was ashen.

"General Briggs," MacPherson said, grabbing the phone from Kirkpatrick, "this is the president of the United States. The capital of the country is under attack. I am ordering you to take that plane down *now.*"

"Yes, sir. I'm on it, sir."

Aeroflot 6617 was now only fourteen miles out and picking up speed.

"Devil One-One, this is General Briggs at NORAD. Peel off immediately. Devil One-Two, do you have a shot? I repeat, do you have a shot?"

Silence.

"Devil One-Two, do you have a shot?"

"Roger that, General."

"Then take it, son—before ten thousand people die."

"Roger that, sir."

All eyes in the PEOC were glued to the video feed coming in from the second F-16. The fighter jet maneuvered into position behind the Russian jumbo.

MacPherson glanced at the TV monitors. Every network now had its own images of the Russian jet screaming down the Potomac River and two F-16s in hot pursuit.

They were chilling, mesmerizing pictures, and MacPherson had no doubt they had the power to set the world on fire.

"Sir, I have radar lock. . . . I have tone. . . ."

The planes were now just eight miles from the White House.

"Fox two!"

An AIM-9 Sidewinder air-to-air missile suddenly exploded from the right side of the F-16. The missile streaked through the morning sky. It sliced into the Russian plane's fuselage, and then, in a fraction of a second, Aeroflot 6617 erupted in a massive fireball that would alter the course of human events forever.

2

★ ★
★

Jon Bennett told himself he had no reason to be anxious.

He had cut hundreds of deals over the years, and he was ready for this one. He'd thought through every angle and considered every scenario. He was ready for every possible objection. A front-page profile in the *New York Times* had once described him as "one of the youngest and most successful deal makers on Wall Street."

So why was he chewing antacids like candy?

True, Bennett was no longer on Wall Street. Now a senior White House advisor, he was the chief architect of the administration's "Oil-for-Peace" initiative and was on the verge of wrapping up a treaty that would forever change the destiny of every Muslim, Jew, and Christian in the Middle East.

Nor was he so young. At almost forty-four, Bennett realized that life on the political bullet train was beginning to take its toll. His short, dark hair was going gray at the temples. His grayish green eyes needed glasses when he read or worked on the computer. At six feet tall and 190 pounds, he was still in good shape, in part because of his obsession with running three to four miles every morning. But he still suffered from severe, chronic pain in both of his shoulders that no amount of medication seemed sufficient to extinguish—ever-present souvenirs of a terrorist attack that had nearly cost him his life.

Such, he concluded, were the fringe benefits of "serving at the pleasure of the president" in the new age of terror.

Bennett stared out over the city of his youth from the outdoor café on the tenth floor of the Ararat Park Hyatt, one of Moscow's most expensive and prestigious luxury hotels. From here he could see the redbrick towers and pale yellow administration buildings of the Kremlin, the four onion-domed Russian Orthodox churches within the Kremlin compound, and the massive State Historical Museum guarding Red Square.

Looking due west, he could see the imposing gray granite of the State Duma, the lower house of the Russian parliament, and almost directly below him was the famed Bolshoi Theatre, now dark and closed for the night.

In the distance a storm was brewing. But it was summer, and even at this late hour, Moscow was very much alive. Traffic was heavy. There was music in the air. Stylish young couples strolled down the main thoroughfare, laughing and holding hands under the streetlamps, making out and heading for the ubiquitous, all-night casinos that now dominated this city that was once the mecca of Marxism.

Most of Russia was still dirt poor and suffering a near Depression-era economy. But Moscow—the *new* Moscow—was a hedonistic epicenter.

Gone were the days of drab storefronts and empty shelves. The new Moscow was awash in dazzling colors and pulsating neon. The world's ritziest shops and boutiques battled for the best real estate on the city's biggest boulevards. Tiffany's. Chanel. Versace. Zegna. Ralph Lauren. Benetton.

Everything was for sale in the new Moscow.

Drugs. Sex. Booze. Of every variety.

But something didn't fit. Russia's nouveau riche—the jet-setters clogging Moscow's streets with their brand-new Mercedeses and Porsches and Audis and Beemers—were not distinguished gray couples who'd built a fortune over a lifetime. Many were Gen Xers. Some were worth hundreds of millions, and the number of Russian *billionaires* was rising annually.

It wasn't all drug and casino and *mafiya* money. But much of it was.

There were also the new oligarchs, Communist bureaucrats who woke up one day after the collapse of the Gorbachev regime and decided to become gangster-capitalists, looting newly "privatized" companies and gunning down anyone who got in their way. How long could such a system survive?

✩ ✩ ✩

Bennett checked his watch.

She was late. He tried to keep his mind off her, at least for now.

So much about this city had changed, and not all for the better, he mused.

From the age of six until his thirteenth birthday, he had been a latch-key kid in the vortex of the Evil Empire. His late father, Sol Bennett, had been the Moscow bureau chief for the *New York Times*, winning a Pulitzer along the way and earning two other nominations during some of the coldest years of the Cold War. Bennett's mother, Ruth—now retired and living outside of Orlando—had taught English literature to children of State Department employees assigned to the U.S. Embassy.

Even when the Bennetts weren't officially on the clock, they still kept a grueling schedule, and typically it did not include time with their only son in the cramped, two-bedroom flat across the river from Gorky Park to which their mail was delivered. Embassy functions, dinner parties, university lectures, concerts, and evenings at the ballet were routine, as were weekend trips to Soviet and Warsaw Pact cities, shopping in Paris, and even an occasional romantic getaway on the Black Sea. There were sources to cultivate, appearances to keep. Far from finding it burdensome, Sol and Ruth Bennett relished their fast-track lives even as their son began to resent it all.

In those precious, formative years when a boy learns to read, learns to fish, discovers the world, discovers himself, discovers girls, and becomes a man, Jonathan Meyers Bennett found himself isolated and alone. What's more, he was eight time zones away from his childhood companions in New York, without siblings or cousins or even many friends in a city where darkness pervaded a man's day and his soul.

His saving grace was a Russian nanny, to whose flat he went after school to do his homework, have dinner, and fall asleep on her couch. She was a frumpy, flat-faced Russian woman with beefy arms and warm eyes and the worst teeth he'd ever seen. Widowed at a young age, this *babushka* named Naina (nai-*ee*-na) seemed to him at least a hundred years old at the time, though she was actually only in her fifties. She had no hope of learning English, or owning a car, or teaching him any of the things he wanted to know. Still, in her own way she loved him, and he knew it, and every time he thought of her death from stomach cancer, it still brought a lump to his throat.

She would have been proud of him, he told himself. His Russian was a bit rusty after all this time, but he hadn't turned out too badly after all.

Naina, of course, would not have measured success like he did. She'd lived a hard and simple life, without a passport or a desire to use one. The woman barely knew how to read. She owned only one book—her great-grandmother's tattered New Testament, printed before the murder of the czar and the Communist revolution—and she had tried to teach little "Jon-Jon" only one enduring lesson during all the winters they'd huddled together, trying to stay warm on a pensioner's income.

"Blazhenny mirotvortsy, ibo oni budut nazvanny det'mi Bozhyimi," she'd said again and again until he could repeat it in Russian.

Blessed are the peacemakers, for they shall be called sons of God.

The muscles in Bennett's face tightened.

Naina Markovna Petrovsky had been the first woman besides his mother—perhaps including his mother—who had ever really loved him. And as he looked over the crowded streets of Moscow now, Bennett would have given anything to talk with her one more time, to tell her that her prayers had been answered. Not only had he become a peacemaker among men, he had finally made his peace with God.

The night air was warm and sultry.

Bennett's once-starched white collar was now damp and wilted. His face and the back of his neck were covered with perspiration. He slid off his jacket and draped it over the back of a wrought-iron patio chair beside him, then pulled a handkerchief from his pocket and wiped his face and forehead dry.

The storm was approaching. Thunder crashed nearby. The winds off the Moskva River were beginning to pick up. He folded the handkerchief and slipped it back into his pocket. He took a sip from an icy-cold bottle of mineral water, tried to steady his nerves, and then saw her car pull up under the portico directly below.

It had been almost seven years since Erin McCoy had first taken his breath away. Yet just seeing her emerge from the black sedan brought back a rush of emotions all over again.

Bennett had been the senior vice president and chief investment strategist of Global Strategix, known to insiders as GSX, the company started by James MacPherson in his pre-politics days. Impressed with McCoy's Wharton MBA and her experience at the World Bank, Bennett had first hired her as a research assistant. Two years later, he promoted her to run the GSX London office.

With her playful Southern accent and honed geopolitical instincts, she was a good manager and an impressive market analyst. People seemed to gravitate to this woman. Her relaxed, optimistic, almost breezy manner contrasted sharply with his dark intensity. She possessed a nearly photographic memory that consistently put her a step ahead of her colleagues, yet she never seemed to betray the slightest trace of arrogance or ambition. Nor, of course, had she ever given any indication that she was actually an undercover operative of the Central Intelligence Agency.

Even after the president told Bennett that he had personally assigned McCoy to infiltrate GSX and watch Bennett's back as he developed his oil deal with the Israelis and Palestinians, Bennett still had had trouble believing it. *Would he have still hired her and paid her $200,000 a year plus stock options and bonuses if he'd known about her double life?* It was a question he had thought about a great deal in the years since he'd learned the truth about McCoy and been drafted into government service himself. Never a big fan of the CIA, a somewhat jaundiced view he no doubt had picked up from his father, Bennett nevertheless wanted to believe the answer was yes.

Now thirty-four, Erin McCoy had become the most trusted member of his staff. She'd traveled with his team to twenty-three countries, and she'd been at his side through three years of grueling negotiations with the Israelis and Palestinians and through every wrenching day of the final status negotiations, for which they were now back in Moscow.

It was Bennett who had first seen the economic and political implications of the discovery of huge reserves of oil and natural gas in and around the Dead Sea and off the coasts of Israel and Gaza. It was Bennett who had persuaded his superiors at GSX to invest a cool $1 billion into a joint Israeli-Palestinian petroleum company known as Medexco to build the pumping stations, offshore drilling platforms, refineries, and other infra-structure necessary to bring such reserves to market. And it was Bennett who had drafted for the president a plan to turn his oil deal into a peace deal that just might be capable of ending decades of hostilities.

But it was McCoy's command of Middle Eastern politics, her almost encyclopedic understanding of the key regional players, and her near-flawless Arabic that had helped turn Bennett's and MacPherson's Oil-for-Peace vision into a reality far beyond what either of them had ever hoped for, dreamed of, or imagined.

The Israelis and Palestinians, it turned out, were sitting on petroleum reserves rivaled only by the Saudis and Iraqis. Almost overnight, Medexco, a once unheard-of company, had become a force rivaling all of the world's major petroleum companies. What's more, every Israeli and Palestinian citizen now owned shares of the publicly traded behemoth, giving each of them a tangible, lucrative stake in the peace and prosperity quickly spreading across the region.

Bennett stared back at the floodlights illuminating the Kremlin walls and felt a chill run through his body. It was hard to picture what his life would have looked like had he not met Erin McCoy.

Indeed, it was hard to believe he would have lived this long.

The tap startled him.

"Remember me?" Erin smiled.

Bennett forgot to say yes. He put his arms around her and kissed her. He sensed her surprise, but only for a moment, and she kissed him back.

When they finally came up for air, Bennett began fishing something out of his briefcase. "I've got something for you. Happy Birthday."

The surprise on her face had been worth the wait.

"It's not till next week," McCoy protested.

"So shoot me." He smiled.

She smiled back as he handed her a small, cylindrical package, exqui-sitely wrapped, though not—obviously—by him.

The winds were picking up now. The temperature began to drop as the storm drew nearer.

"Should we go back in?" she asked, suddenly shivering in the same black formal gown she'd worn earlier to an embassy reception. Bennett took his tuxedo jacket off the chair and put it around her. She was right, of course. They were exhausted, jet-lagged. They needed a good night's rest. But not quite yet.

"In a moment," he said, "after you open it."

McCoy began to unwrap the package. It was about the size of a small thermos. Bennett watched her slender fingers carefully removing the gift paper, conscious again of how nervous he felt.

Suddenly McCoy held the *matryoshka* doll in her hands. It was hand carved and hand painted, and McCoy's eyes seemed to dance. "It's beautiful," she said. "How did you do it? Did you get this today? I didn't . . ."

Bennett put a finger to her lips, and she grew quiet.

"Open it," he whispered.

She played along, holding the base firmly while twisting the top section to the right. She'd only held one of the famed Russian "nesting" dolls—a doll within a doll within a doll—once before, at Jon's mother's house in Orlando, and she'd loved it. But every time they had come to Moscow for the peace talks, they had been too busy to buy one.

Bennett watched her open each of the dolls, carefully setting the larger pieces down on the table beside them. As she got closer to the center, he could feel his heart racing, and by the time she got down to the last section, he was down on one knee.

McCoy's breath caught as her eyes drank in the sight of the stunning two-carat diamond ring, sparkling amid the brilliant flashes of lightning all around them. It was resting on a small piece of blue velvet, nestled in the smallest doll, and for a moment she seemed too stunned to reach out and touch it.

"Erin Christina McCoy," Bennett began, his eyes blurring with tears. He couldn't believe how fast his heart was beating. "I know I don't deserve you. I know you could do better than me, but every day I thank God that you came along and rescued me, and I shudder to think where I'd be today if you hadn't."

Her bottom lip was quivering. Her hands were trembling.

"God knows I'm slow," he continued. "I should have done this a long time ago. But I need you, Erin, and I never thought I needed anyone. I love you. And now I'm asking you—will you marry me?"

Another bolt of lightning crackled nearby. Thunder boomed overhead. The storm was upon them, and as McCoy began to nod her head and cry, it started to rain. Soon it was coming down in sheets. Bennett hesitated for a moment, not sure what to do. Then he rose off his knee, held her in his arms, and asked, "Is that a yes?"

McCoy began to laugh and lifted her head to look into his eyes. *"Yes, yes, yes."*

Bennett exhaled and broke out in a smile.

He slipped the ring on her finger. They held each other tightly. And then Bennett took her hands and prayed, thanking God for loving him enough to bring this beautiful, amazing woman into his life, and asking for the grace to love her like she deserved.

The two began to kiss. They were laughing and dancing and the rain kept coming. Bennett took out a spare, clean handkerchief and tried in vain to wipe away her tears. Never before had he felt happiness like this.

And then, simultaneously, their pagers went off.

3
★ ★
★

"Mr. Bennett?"

"Speaking."

"This is the White House operator. Please hold for the president."

Bennett pressed the satellite phone to his ear, trying to hear over the *whoosh-whoosh* of windshield wipers on high speed.

At the wheel of their bulletproof Lincoln Town Car was an agent from the State Department's Diplomatic Security Service. It was well past midnight local time as they zigzagged through side streets, trying to bypass the main thoroughfares of Moscow.

Here, away from the casinos and the nightclubs, all was quiet. Not a soul could be seen in any direction. Fierce winds howled through empty canyons of darkened office buildings and department stores. Driving sheets of rain pelted their small convoy. McCoy cranked up the rear air conditioning in an attempt to keep the windows from fogging up completely, but to no avail.

Almost twenty minutes had passed since Marsha Kirkpatrick had briefed them on the Aeroflot crisis and said the president would be calling. Bennett and McCoy were both numb, the joy of their engagement suddenly washed away. All they could think about now was how close their government and their friends had just come to being annihilated.

It made no sense. There'd been no warnings, no increase in terrorist "chatter." And Bennett had no doubt he was about to be asked questions for which he had no answers.

Ahead of them was a sedan with two heavily armed DSS agents. Behind them was a black Chevy Suburban with four more agents.

Several years earlier, Bennett and McCoy had been attacked in Jerusalem by members of the terrorist group known as Al-Nakbah. Since then, this was what his life had become—no longer his own, thought Bennett. Other people shopped for his food. Security personnel tested his mail for anthrax and explosives. He couldn't go out to the drugstore—much less on a date with McCoy—without agents tagging along, packing Uzis.

His old Wall Street friends envied the glamour of his new life. The West Wing office. Flights on *Air Force One*. Weekends at Camp David. Never-ending front-page and network news coverage. The guarantee of making tens of millions a year the minute he left Washington and returned to Manhattan. But they had no idea.

Bennett's BlackBerry beeped again. McCoy looked over his shoulder as they read the latest flash traffic from the Situation Room.

U.S. military forces and embassies worldwide were at THREATCON DELTA, the highest state of readiness, lest more attacks were coming.

Local fire crews in Maryland were battling more than two dozen blazes caused by falling debris from the Russian jet. FBI agents and investigators from the National Transportation Safety Board were surveying the wreckage, strewn out over mile after mile of the Potomac River. The FAA had imposed a full ground stop across the eastern seaboard, forcing hundreds of planes to reroute to the Midwest and Canada. The National Security Council, meanwhile, had been meeting behind closed doors for the last forty-five minutes, and White House Press Secretary Chuck Murray had just announced that the president would address the nation within the hour.

"Jon? That you?"

"It is, Mr. President. Erin's right next to me."

"You guys OK?"

"We're fine, sir. And you?"

"We may not be through the worst of it," said MacPherson, his voice a bit husky.

"You had no choice, Mr. President. People will see that."

"I hope you're right, Jon."

Bennett hoped so too. From what Kirkpatrick had told them, there was no question the Russian jet had to be shot down. The alternative was unthinkable. But he worried that Pandora's box had just been opened.

Americans were in no mood for another war.

The country had been badly divided over Iraq. To Bennett, Saddam Hussein and his sons had represented a real and rising threat to U.S. national security and to world peace. They'd invaded Iran and Kuwait. They'd attacked Israel and Saudi Arabia. They'd variously threatened Jordan, Turkey, and the Gulf states. They'd funded Palestinian suicide bombers. They'd harbored, trained, or conspired with terrorists like Abu Nidal and the terrorist organization Al-Qaeda. They'd used weapons of mass destruction on their own people and had filled scores of mass graves. They'd tortured political prisoners by the tens of thousands. They'd defied the international community for years and had vowed to wage jihad against the West. Yet fewer than half of Americans now believed the war against Iraq had been just.

NATO, too, was a house divided. The governments of Germany and France, for example, certainly hadn't seen Iraq as part of an "Axis of Evil." Nor had most Europeans. To the contrary, they increasingly saw Americans as the aggressors. Even more disturbing was a poll taken by the European Union that found that a stunning 60 percent of Europeans believed that Israel was the greatest threat to world peace, with the United States and North Korea tied for second.

Such trends struck many of his colleagues as bizarre, but to Bennett they were beginning to make sense. The world was experiencing what he called "global schizophrenia." People were increasingly divided not so much along geographical lines as along moral and cultural lines, by how they defined right and wrong, good and evil.

As Europe grew more secular, Judeo-Christian concepts of morality were evaporating, and with them, the essential ideological underpinnings of the NATO alliance. What troubled Bennett was not whether NATO could hold together in its present form but when Brussels would make a formal break with the U.S.

McCoy said it was the pessimist in him, his dark side. Maybe she was right. Her faith was stronger than his. She had a confidence about the future he simply didn't possess. Not yet, anyway.

To her, the glass was half full. The Middle East was moving toward peace and prosperity. Why be so pessimistic about the Socialist and pacifist forces rising throughout the E.U.?

But Bennett felt the glass was not only half empty but about to be ripped from their hands. He considered himself a strategic optimist but a tactical pessimist. Sure, in the long run everything would turn out fine, in his life and in the world. But tomorrow could be a disaster. The breaking news from Washington just proved his point.

"Where are you right now?" MacPherson asked.

Bennett used his sleeve to wipe fog off his window and peered out to get his bearings. They were coming around the corner toward the American Embassy, a postmodern, concrete-and-glass, ten-story structure overlooking the river and the Russian White House. A Marine guard saluted and opened the massive steel gate leading to an underground parking garage.

"We're pulling into the embassy right now, sir."

"Good. Put me on speaker. I want to talk to McCoy as well."

When Bennett did, the president greeted McCoy and got down to business. He assigned Bennett to be the primary liaison to the Russian government in opening up a joint investigation into the hijacking and in making sure the tensions between Moscow and Washington weren't allowed to spin out of control. He tasked McCoy with ensuring close cooperation between Langley's Moscow Station, the FBI's local field office, and Britain's MI6.

"What about Ambassador Richardson?" Bennett asked.

"Stan's a good man, Jon, but he's only been there for, what, six months?"

"Eight, actually."

"Even still. Look, you're the highest-ranking American official there right now. I want you running the show until we can get the secretary of state in there."

Bennett was flattered but not convinced the president was right. "The secretary's still in Beijing?"

"He is. I just talked to him. He can fly to Moscow if President Vadim will receive him. But so far Vadim won't take my calls."

Bennett was stunned. "What are you talking about? Why not?"

"Good question. I've called twice. They wouldn't put me through."

"Who'd you talk to?"

"Andrei," said MacPherson, referring to Andrei Zyuganov, the Russian president's chief of staff and someone with whom Bennett and McCoy had worked closely for the past few years. "They're rushing Vadim back from the Black Sea," MacPherson continued. "Andrei said they'd be at the Kremlin by midnight, Moscow time."

McCoy looked at her watch. "That was half an hour ago."

"No kidding," said the president. "CIA says Vadim's plane landed forty minutes ago. The motorcade got him back to his office twenty minutes ago. I just called back. Andrei wouldn't put me through. He said Vadim was in an emergency meeting."

"Have you tried the foreign minister?"

"Not yet. The SecState is trying from Beijing. But you should try, too."

"I will. Erin and I are supposed to meet him for dinner Thursday night."

"Let me know what happens. And you two watch your backs over there."

4

WEDNESDAY, JULY 30 – 12:44 A.M. – U.S. EMBASSY, MOSCOW

An embassy official greeted Bennett and McCoy.

"Mr. Bennett, Ms. McCoy, you're cleared for access to the Bubble."

Part boardroom, part war room, "the Bubble" was one of the most expensive rooms in the Moscow embassy compound—and the most exclusive. It could be accessed by only a handful of senior officials with top-secret clearance, and only after undergoing a rigorous security protocol.

The embassy official used a key to operate a special elevator that ferried them to the building's top floor. In the elevator, the official gave each of them a security access card with a strap attached. "Show this to the guard up top," he said. "Then it goes around your neck. You'll need to wear it at all times."

As they came off the elevator, they showed their passes to the armed Marine guard who stopped them. After scrutinizing their passes and consulting a database, the guard escorted them to a two-foot-thick vault door and asked them to hand over all electronic devices.

The official swiped a key card through a magnetic reader beside the door and directed them to submit to a retinal scan.

Bennett walked over and looked directly at the small LCD screen. A dim light flickered within as a nearly invisible laser passed over the surface of his eye and back again. Then it was McCoy's turn.

Finally the huge door opened.

Inside, they walked across a ramp, through an air lock, and through a second door that was covered on both sides with sound-absorbent foam panels. The windowless room known as the Bubble was located in the center of the building and was literally suspended in midair, hanging from the roof by hundreds of steel cables effectively detaching the room from the rest of the embassy. Much like a professional music studio, the room was impenetrable by external sounds or vibrations of any kind. It was also carefully shielded from the prying eyes and listening ears of the Russian security services.

The room itself was octagonal in structure. It featured a low ceiling, recessed lighting, dark wood paneling, thick blue carpeting, and a massive, octagonal mahogany conference table. The Bubble was also equipped with state-of-the-art communications technology. Satellite and fiber-optic lines installed and maintained by the NSA provided direct, encrypted phone, e-mail, and instant-messaging access to all the power centers in Washington, NATO, and U.S. embassies worldwide. A series of cameras and large-screen monitors allowed for videoconferencing. Banks of televisions provided a real-time window on the world, and a half-dozen laptops linked to classified databases run by the State Department, CIA, DIA, and the FBI.

The phone rang. Bennett grabbed it first.

"Jon Bennett."

"Johnny, it's Mom. I just heard the news. This is terrible."

Bennett froze. This couldn't be happening. Not now.

"Mom, I'm right in the . . . I can't . . . this is not a good time. I'm sorry."

It was as if she wasn't listening to a word he was saying.

"I called the White House and made them put me through to you, wherever you are. Are you and Erin OK? Did you ask her? What did she say?"

He glanced at McCoy, but she was consumed with another call. He glanced at the clocks on the wall. "Mom? Listen. I love you. I can't talk. Not now. I—"

"Just tell me if you—"

"I did. She said yes. We'll tell you all about it—but not right now. I've got to go. I'm sorry." And he hung up, guilt gnawing at his stomach. She always seemed to pick the worst possible moment to call him.

Was it because he rarely took the time to call her?

Bennett shut that thought down quickly and shifted gears.

He picked the phone back up and called the private cell-phone number of Russian foreign minister Aleksandr Golitsyn.

"*Da?*" came the voice at the other end.

"Mr. Foreign Minister, it's Jon Bennett."

"This is not a good time, Mr. Bennett."

"I have no doubt, but it's urgent that I speak with you. President MacPherson is trying to call President Vadim, and we seem to be running into some interference. I know you can help me make this happen."

There was a long pause.

"I am afraid, Mr. Bennett, that will not be possible."

Bennett had never heard Aleksandr Golitsyn so much as raise his voice. Even in the most difficult discussions over the Iraq war, the NATO expansion talks, or the Israeli-Palestinian peace talks, the foreign minister had a gift for being calm, cool, and collected. But the man on the other end of this line was livid. He was controlled, of course—he wasn't screaming or shouting curses—but Bennett doubted Golitsyn's message could have been any more clear if the two were standing face-to-face.

"Aleks, talk to me. You and I both know—"

"Mr. Bennett, I do not think you appreciate the gravity of the situation. This is not a simple car accident. The United States of America has just shot down a plane carrying innocent Russian civilians."

Not all of them were innocent, Bennett wanted to say, but he held his tongue.

"My government sees this as a grave development that threatens to rupture the relations between our two countries."

Bennett's mind reeled. He desperately motioned McCoy to slide a notebook and a pen over to him. He began to scribble down Golitsyn's words. *Innocent. Grave. Rupture.* This was diplomatspeak for *firestorm.* And Golitsyn wasn't done.

The foreign minister went on to tell Bennett that a visit to Moscow by the U.S. secretary of state "would not be helpful at this moment," and that the Kremlin's participation in the Israeli-Palestinian peace talks would be "postponed" until further notice.

Bennett expected Golitsyn to be grieving over the loss of his fellow countrymen. But how could Golitsyn be angry? This wasn't Mac-Pherson's fault. If an American plane had tried to attack Moscow, Vadim would have done precisely the same thing. Hadn't the Kremlin once ordered poison gas pumped into a Moscow theater to prevent Chechens from blowing the place up? Nearly fifty terrorists had died, along with 129 hostages. Had the U.S. cut off relations with Moscow? Of course not. How, then, could an act of self-defense threaten to rupture relations now?

More to the point, thought Bennett, how was he supposed to prevent tensions from spinning out of control if Vadim refused even to take MacPherson's call?

5

★ ★
★

Was it possible? Was it time?

Dr. Eliezer Mordechai stared out the window into the darkness, but there was nothing to see. No moon. No diamonds glittering in the night sky.

Inside the luxuriously appointed yet unmarked U.S. State Department executive jet, the cabin lights were dimmed. But there was no way he could sleep.

He wished it were not the dead of night. He wanted to see it for himself. Even in broad daylight there wouldn't be much to see at thirty thousand feet—just raw, ugly desert stretching for hundreds of miles in every direction. But that didn't make his desire any less intense.

His hands were cold and clammy. He checked his watch, then looked back out the window. In less than two minutes, he'd be entering Iraqi airspace. It wasn't the first time, of course. Just the first time it was legal.

Eli Mordechai was a man who had seen just about everything in his eight decades on the planet. Wars and rumors of wars. Revolutions and earthquakes. Famines and persecution. And the miraculous rebirth of the modern State of Israel.

But nothing had prepared him for this.

Within the hour he would be on the ground in Iraq. At dawn he would awaken in a state whose army was once the world's fourth largest,

though now it was a mere shadow of its former self. By Thursday afternoon he would be breaking bread with Mustafa Al-Hassani, the new
president of Iraq, touring the palace and the new capital, and sharing a
helicopter ride over the Kirkuk oil fields that were transforming this
nation's destiny.

All of it defied the imagination.

Yael, God rest her soul, would have loved this trip, he knew. The
ninth granddaughter of Iraqi Jews, his wife would have savored the irony
of returning to the soil from which her family had been driven. She also
would have enjoyed the intrigue of traveling with him for once in his
shadowy career, this time from Tel Aviv to Istanbul, then to Cairo,
then around the Arabian Peninsula before approaching the birthplace
of civilization.

Yael would have enjoyed meandering down aromatic alleyways, and
peeking into spice shops, and bargaining for bags of coffee and rice to take
back home to her friends, flush with stories that she had actually been to
the "old country" and lived to tell about it. What's more, she would have
liked to see where her husband had worked in the early years of his career
in the Mossad, Israel's elite intelligence agency.

How many nights had she lain awake begging God for his safety as
he'd slipped in and out of this republic of fear, buying sources, running
agents, playing his deadly games? Why had she put up with any of it? Why
had he made her?

It was no life for a woman of her talent and beauty—long, endless
nights of loneliness and the dread that he might never come home. She
had deserved so much more, and the regret he now felt for not giving it to
her stabbed at his heart.

They had been together for nearly fifty years, and still she was a mystery. They had not been blessed with children or, for most of their lives,
any measure of wealth—that had come more recently and, sadly, only after her death. For five decades they had had only each other, and the years
had fused them together until she finished his sentences and he finished
her soup. If only she had lived long enough to see the changes God had
brought about in his life.

At the beginning of their courtship, they'd had nothing in common but their love for each other. He was an only child, born in Tobolsk, Siberia, on May 28, 1930. She was born in Haifa, Israel, on August 9, 1939.

Her grandparents had escaped Baghdad in 1923, made their way to Istanbul and then to Damascus, and eventually had passed through Beirut before making their way into Palestine in the long, hard winter of 1931. His family had escaped from the Soviet Union in the spring of 1941 through central Asia, Afghanistan, Iran, and Iraq, before finally arriving in Palestine in the fall of 1945.

Hers had been a merchant family, opening grocery stores in northern Israel and the Galilee during the British Mandate. His had been a family of intellectuals.

Though his father, Vladimir, had been a highly educated man and an aspiring rabbi and had suffered terrible persecution in Tobolsk, he had eagerly fought in Israel's War of Independence in 1948 before becoming a professor of Russian studies at Jerusalem's Hebrew University. Mordechai's mother, Miriam, earned two degrees from Hebrew University and taught nursing to young women drafted into the Israeli Defense Forces.

And then one day while Mordechai was away at IDF boot camp, his parents were killed during a terrorist bombing of a Jerusalem restaurant. In one cruel moment in time, all that he had was ripped away from him forever. He was an orphan. He was alone—without a family, without hope, without an anchor for his soul. Yet when he closed his eyes, even all these years later, he still found it hard to be angry. What man had meant for evil, God had used for good.

For across the street from the bombed-out restaurant was a grocery store. It was owned by a man with seven sons and five daughters, and one of those daughters was named Yael. Mordechai could still picture her face the first time he laid eyes on her, as she came over to help sweep up the charred debris. He could still see her turning her head and catching his eye as he stood in the burned-out doorway, tears streaming down his face. And he could still remember that still, soft voice as she introduced herself, apologized for his loss, and held his hand as he wept.

She had been only fourteen, but in that instant, somewhere deep inside of him, he knew they were destined to be married, and for a split second he began to suspect that perhaps God was not capricious and cruel.

Perhaps God was more tender than Mordechai knew, taking one family away but giving him another. It was an instinct that would eventually prove to be true, the first of many such instincts that would be borne out over time.

And suddenly he was overcome by a longing to finish this race, to see his precious Yael once again and fall into her arms and hold her for eternity.

"Dr. Mordechai?"

The hushed voice of a female military aide startled him.

"Yes—sorry—what is it?"

"Just wanted you to know we'll be landing in about fifteen minutes," she whispered in Hebrew.

"Thank you," said Mordechai, wiping his eyes and trying to gather his thoughts.

"Can I bring you something before we touch down?"

"Yes, thank you, that would be very kind. Do you have any hot tea?"

"Of course."

"And a little sweetener, if that is not too much trouble."

"No trouble at all, sir."

Mordechai thanked the young woman again, and she headed back to the galley. He choked back his emotions and tried to refocus on the task at hand.

Again he glanced at his watch. They had just entered Iraqi airspace. They were in. It seemed hard to believe to an old warrior like Mordechai.

It had taken longer and cost more in blood and treasure than anyone had expected, but incredibly, Iraq was now free. What's more—sitting atop some of the largest oil reserves in the world and no longer held hostage to the demands of the insatiable dictator Saddam Hussein—she was poised to become a global economic superpower.

The White House could barely contain its optimism. A peaceful, prosperous, democratic Iraq—combined with a historic final status agreement between the Israelis and Palestinians—would forever transform the modern Middle East, the American president and his top advisors believed.

But Mordechai had his doubts. Iraq, in his judgment, was the last place democratic capitalism was likely to flourish. Something evil lived under these sands, and every molecule in his body sensed that the evil here was regrouping, preparing to strike.

How soon? He couldn't say. Was it possible Iraq would be tranquil for a season? Perhaps, he conceded. But it could never last. Anyone who thought it could, even a man of President MacPherson's stature and experience, was fooling himself.

Still, Mordechai reminded himself, that was all a headache for another day. For now, he—a Jew from Siberia—was about to witness the heart of darkness up close and personal for himself. But why? How?

He had been director of the Israeli Mossad's Arab Desk from 1976 to 1984. He had personally planned the bombing of Iraq's Osirik nuclear reactor. He had gone on to serve as director of the Mossad's Nuclear Desk from 1985 to 1987, and as full director of the Mossad from 1988 to 1996. He had been a senior advisor to every Israeli prime minister since Golda Meir, and—despite his misgivings—he had spent the last several years informally advising the White House on its latest Middle East peace initiative.

How could Mustafa Al-Hassani allow such a man into his country, much less into his own palace? Had Iraq really changed that much?

6

★ ★
★

Russians awoke Wednesday to wall-to-wall coverage.

The downing of Aeroflot 6617 dominated not just the front pages of every major newspaper in Russia but hours of special coverage on Russia's radio and TV networks.

News of Boris Stuchenko's death caused the Russian stock market to plunge more than 12 percent at the opening bell. Markets in Asia and Europe moved down sharply, as did the New York Stock Exchange and NASDAQ. Oil prices—down sharply over the past year with Israeli and Palestinian reserves flooding the market and the prospect of Iraqi oil coming fully on line—suddenly reversed course, jumping almost four dollars overnight to $24.23 a barrel, a new twelve-month high.

But it was the deaths of the children aboard the Aeroflot jet that lit Russia's emotional fuse, much as it had after the school massacre in Beslan in September of 2004. Except that then they had blamed the Chechen radicals for the attack and then-president Putin for botching the rescue. Now they blamed the president of the United States, and emotions were raw.

By noon, tens of thousands of angry demonstrators filled Red Square. As the rains passed and temperatures began to rise, mobs surrounded the American Embassy as well, denouncing the United States and calling for some kind of retaliation. By midafternoon, anti-American protests were under way in every city across Russia's eleven time zones.

Government officials wasted no time getting into the action. Deputy Speaker Sergei Ilyushkin took the floor of the Russian parliament and delivered a blistering speech railing against the "ugly Americans" and the "criminal Zionist conspiracy to subvert Mother Russia from within." He demanded that President Vadim withdraw the Russian ambassador from Washington and expel all Americans from Russian soil.

Bennett wasn't sure what to think.

Watching Sergei Ilyushkin make a fool of himself on worldwide television was a luxury he couldn't afford, but it was hard to tear himself away from such a delicious spectacle. How this guy had ever become the second most powerful member of the Russian political system had never ceased to amaze him, but for now Bennett had more pressing matters on his plate. He muted the monitors and asked McCoy to bring him up to speed on what she'd gathered so far.

McCoy began by explaining that after much foot-dragging by Russian authorities, the FBI and CIA had finally obtained complete copies of the flight manifest from Aeroflot and had reviewed them for possible suspects. So far, however, none of the names on the manifest had shown up on any U.S., British, Russian, or Interpol watch lists. McCoy promised they'd have more information in a few hours, but Bennett privately wondered just how much time they had before the Russian "street" reached the boiling point.

McCoy continued by noting how odd it was that a plane with so many VIPs aboard could be so vulnerable to hijacking. Contrary to the initial information given to the president the previous night, there had, in fact, been armed guards aboard the Russian airliner. Some were protecting the three members of the Duma. Some worked for Boris Stuchenko and his Lukoil board. In fact, by McCoy's count, no fewer than eight bodyguards were on the flight. Moscow airport security tapes showed each of the bodyguards going through proper procedures to bring the weapons aboard, so what had gone wrong?

"Could the guards themselves have been part of the plot?" asked Bennett.

"That's what I'm wondering," said McCoy. "I've got a team at Langley reviewing the files on each of these guys as we speak, but there's something else that's strange."

"What's that?" asked Bennett.

"Doesn't it seem odd that the pilots never squawked an emergency—not to air-traffic control in New York, not to Aeroflot flight operations back in Moscow? Not a single emergency call was placed by anyone on the flight. No one used the onboard air phones. No one seems even to have used a cell phone. Wouldn't you think if there'd been a struggle with eight armed men battling a group of would-be hijackers, someone would have gotten the word out?"

Bennett nodded. But McCoy wasn't done. She had a list of other possible suspects besides the guards. It included Chechen separatists, various factions of the Russian mafia, and Al-Nakbah, the radical Islamic terror network that for the past several years had been fashioning itself as the global successor to Al-Qaeda.

And Langley did have one interesting lead.

Freshly translated NSA intercepts of cell-phone calls between known Chechen rebel base camps indicated that two senior Chechen leaders had been planning to go to Moscow ten days before the attack over Washington. Their whereabouts at the moment were unknown, but the two men were believed to have extensive experience with explosives and were rumored to be planning some kind of mega-terror attack inside the Russian capital for late summer.

"Were these men capable of hijacking a Russian airliner?" Bennett asked.

McCoy conceded that the analysts back at the CIA and FBI weren't sure. Neither was she. But assuming they were, wouldn't the men have been spotted by Russian security at the airport prior to boarding?

"Something doesn't fit," McCoy said, sipping her coffee. "I mean, let's say it was these two Chechens. And let's say that somehow they got past airport security. And let's say they really did overpower all those security guards—or were somehow in cahoots with them. Even if all that were true, wouldn't you expect Chechen terrorists to fly that plane into the Kremlin, rather than into the White House? The Chechens don't have a beef with us. They're trying to take out Vadim's government, not ours. In the last eighteen months, Chechen terrorists have been responsible for three assassination attempts against Vadim, two subway bombings near the Kremlin, and, of course, the recent kidnapping and beheading of Vadim's deputy press secretary."

"I thought Al-Nakbah claimed responsibility for the latest kidnapping," said Bennett.

"Responsibility, yes," said McCoy. "But as far as we can tell, the operation was run by the Chechens."

"Fair enough, but doesn't this seem like an Al-Nakbah operation to you?" said Bennett.

"The guys at Langley are leaning against any involvement by Al-Nakbah."

Bennett shook his head. "I didn't ask what they think. I want to know what you think."

McCoy hesitated. "I don't know, Jon. I guess in some respects the Aeroflot attack resembles the Al-Nakbah operation against the president a few years back. . . ."

"That's the first thing that came to my mind too—The Last Jihad," Bennett said, citing the Iraqi code name for the airborne attack near Denver that had almost cost MacPherson his life. The attack had been a key element of Saddam Hussein's plan to decapitate the U.S., NATO, and Saudi and Israeli governments almost simultaneously.

"Me, too, Jon, but for crying out loud—we've captured or killed almost all of Al-Nakbah's leadership and shock troops over the past few years. At this point, I'm not sure they'd even have the resources to pull off a job like this."

"To take over a single plane?"

"Jon, it's not as easy to hijack a jet as it was on 9/11 or when Saddam ordered the hit on MacPherson. Things have changed."

"I know, but, Erin, come on; you've seen Al-Nakbah operate. They've certainly got motive—revenge, blowing up the peace process—"

McCoy cut him off. "Jon, think about it. It doesn't make sense."

"Why not?"

"Look, Al-Nakbah's day-to-day operations are run by a guy named Mohammed Jibril, right?"

"Right. So?"

"So first, Jibril was once a senior operative in Iranian intelligence. Second, we still believe he has close ties to the regime in Tehran, and, so far as we can tell, Jibril does the Ayatollah's bidding when Tehran doesn't want to leave any fingerprints. Third, Jibril's partner in crime, don't forget, is Yuri Gogolov, the former Russian special forces commander turned strategist for the Russian Fascist movement. The FBI actually believe Gogolov founded the Al-Nakbah network."

"But Al-Nakbah has tried to take down Vadim before," Bennett broke in. "That's the reason Gogolov got involved with Jibril in the first place."

"True. But don't forget, Tehran wants a strategic alliance with Moscow, and Moscow couldn't be happier to oblige. The fact is, the two countries have never been closer than they are today. Since the breakup of the Soviet Union, Russia has sold hundreds of billions of dollars' worth of arms to Iran—tanks, missiles, submarines, you name it. The Russians are also helping Iran build no less than five nuclear plants, despite intense international pressure to stop."

"And despite the fact that gas in Iran costs six cents a gallon."

"Well, that's just it," said McCoy. "They've got huge reserves of oil and natural gas. There's absolutely no need for Iran to develop nuclear power, unless it's to convert the spent fuel into highly enriched uranium in order to produce nuclear weapons—which is exactly what we suspect is happening, with Russian collusion."

"So what are you saying?"

"I'm saying, add it all up. Moscow and Tehran are building a strategic alliance. They've been working on it for two decades while the world has focused its attention elsewhere, and Gogolov and Jibril are right at the heart of it all. Why in the world would Iran suddenly bite the hand that arms it? Why would they authorize Gogolov and Jibril to take out a *Russian* airliner? It just doesn't make sense."

McCoy had a point. She often did. And Bennett loved to see her mind at work, processing the data and looking for connections and relationships no one else could see. Even when she was wrong she had a way of sounding right. But she wasn't often wrong. He'd learned that the hard way.

She once predicted that Libya would cry uncle after Saddam's regime was toppled, giving up her weapons of mass destruction in return for an end to economic sanctions and the ability to start selling oil again. Bennett had told her she was crazy and had bet her a thousand dollars that Khadaffi would never cut such a deal with the U.S. or the U.N. as long as he was alive. But McCoy had been right. Bennett's only consolation was that she let him pay off his debt to her by taking her out to dinner at the most expensive restaurants in whatever city to which their never-ending shuttle diplomacy took them.

Bennett stared into his coffee. He couldn't even remember how many cups he'd had since midnight, or how many aspirin and antacids he'd downed. His head was still throbbing. His entire body ached. He desperately needed sleep, as did McCoy, and for a moment, he let his mind drift from the conversation, important though it was.

He wanted time alone with McCoy, time to make some initial plans for the wedding and time to talk about their future beyond government. They needed to get off this political bullet train before it killed them. Working for the White House was starting to feel more like a prison sentence than an act of public service. They'd both done their time. It was time to get out and start a life of their own.

But how? Bennett had hoped to announce his resignation as soon as a final status agreement was agreed to by the Israelis and Palestinians, and by the "Quartet"—the U.S., Russia, the E.U., and the U.N., the four major facilitators of the peace process. He had thought that would be a matter of weeks. But now everything for which Bennett and McCoy had been working for the past three years was suddenly at risk.

The Russians were putting the peace talks on hold. For how long? Without their cooperation it would be difficult, if not impossible, to nail down a final deal. How exactly were they supposed to secure the Kremlin's sign-off on the final language of the treaty if Vadim refused to even pick up the phone and take the president's call?

The phone rang. It was the director of Central Intelligence for McCoy.

Bennett silently ran through his options. Until he made contact with either Vadim or his senior staff, there wasn't much else he could do. So he picked up the phone and dialed Russian foreign minister Aleksandr Golitsyn's private cell phone for the third time in the past three hours. There was no answer.

"Mr. Foreign Minister, it's Jon Bennett again. I'd appreciate anything you can do to open up direct talks between our two presidents again.

Please call me back, regardless of the hour. Also, I'm sitting here with Erin, and we'd like to confirm our dinner meeting tomorrow night. Please let me know. Thanks."

Bennett fought the almost overwhelming urge to curse. He was growing restless and desperate. Someone out there had attacked the United States and, for all he knew, was planning to do it again, perhaps in the next days or even hours. At this point neither he nor McCoy had any idea who they were or how to stop them, and the Russians were treating them like the enemy.

Mordechai sipped a cup of hot tea and looked at his watch.

In a few hours he would leave his richly appointed room to meet President Al-Hassani.

He paged through the briefing book the Israeli Foreign Ministry had prepared for him. Much of the material was based on sources he himself had developed over the years. But a few stories in the appendix did catch his eye.

BABYLON IS BEING REBUILT

TO LURE TOURISTS AND BUILD IRAQI MORALE

Philadelphia Inquirer, October 10, 1986

NEBUCHADNEZZAR'S REVENGE:

IRAQ FLEXES ITS MUSCLES

BY REBUILDING BABYLON

San Francisco Chronicle, April 30, 1989

NEW BABYLON IS STALLED

BY A MODERN UPHEAVAL

New York Times, October 11, 1990

To these were added newer stories from the past few months describing Iraq's startling plans to move its capital to Babylon. "Baghdad was Saddam's capital, and we are trying to forget Saddam," one unnamed senior Iraqi official had told the *Washington Post*. "Babylon was the heart of our ancient empire, and she is the soul of our future."

Mordechai doubted the Mossad analysts back in Jerusalem had any idea of the significance of such articles, much less the events they described. To his former colleagues such stories were mere curiosities. But to him, they were evidence of a Rubicon crossed.

Perhaps their ignorance was not their fault. They were young and brash, as he had once been. They were so sure they understood the world in all its complexities when, in fact, they were missing the dawn of its horrific last days.

There was a time he hadn't understood the importance of such developments either. How could he expect others to understand without knowing what he knew?

It was Yael who had first become fascinated by ancient Hebrew prophecies after taking a few courses on biblical archeology. Her professor had claimed that prophecies were sort of supernatural puzzles, riddles that, once decoded, could explain the mysteries of the universe and allow mankind to peer into the future.

Mordechai had dismissed her interest, at first, as another one of her many hobbies—"the trivial pursuit of all things Jewish," he used to say.

But the more he learned, the more intrigued he became. Yael began to talk about passages like Jeremiah 31:8—"Behold, I am bringing them from the north country, and I will gather them from the remote parts of the earth"—predicting the return of the Jewish people to the land of Israel from all over the world, including "the north country," like Russia, from which Mordechai's family had escaped. She began showing him passages like Ezekiel 36 and 37, predicting the rebirth of the Jewish State of Israel from the ashes of the Holocaust, thousands of years before any of it happened.

And one day she had come across a series of prophecies predicting the eventual rise of ancient Babylon from the sands of Iraq, the rise of Babylon as a fearsome and terrifying global power and a mortal threat to the Jewish people and the peace of mankind. And suddenly Mordechai's interest was no longer casual and personal. It was immediate and professional.

Could prophecy actually help him as the head of the Mossad to predict the future?

Mordechai's parents had been atheists. They had neither known nor cared what the ancient Scriptures had to say about the past, much less the future. *Had they been wrong? Was the Bible somehow relevant to a modern life?*

Here he was, en route to Babylon.

And no longer was the rebuilding of this ancient city merely the pet project of a demonic despot or some kind of Middle Eastern EPCOT Center.

Nor was this massive undertaking stalled any longer by a lack of funds.

To the contrary, Mordechai realized, the newly pacified, post-Saddam Iraq was about to reemerge as a giant of the oil-producing world. Trillions of dollars would soon flood into the barren crescent of the Tigris and Euphrates. And when that happened, how long would it take for the once and future power known as Babylon to rise like a phoenix from the ashes, just as the ancient Hebrew prophets had foretold?

7

THURSDAY, JULY 31 – 10:19 A.M. – RIYADH, SAUDI ARABIA

"*Wahid* to *Mohandis*, do you copy?"

"Go ahead, *Wahid*."

"I have a visual on the target. He is inbound to your location."

"How long?"

"Three minutes."

"Very good, *Wahid*. All units, stand by."

It was Ibrahim Sa'id's first visit as Palestinian prime minister.

And the world was watching.

Ever since the Saudis had extended an invitation to the late Yasser Arafat's successor, rumors had been swirling that perhaps the royal family was considering reestablishing diplomatic relations with the Palestinian government. In recent years, Saudi leaders had heatedly denounced the Palestinians for signing an interim peace agreement with Israel and forming the Medexco joint venture with a Russian Jew named Dmitri Galishnikov that had created an oil and gas behemoth rivaling their own.

Others speculated that the Saudi royals merely wanted a face-to-face showdown with a man routinely denounced in the Saudi media as a "traitor" and "Zionist conspirator."

Either way, Ibrahim Sa'id believed the invitation alone was a significant development, and he had accepted without reservation. Now, gazing out the window on the half-hour drive from King Khalid International Airport to the five-star Al Faisaliah Hotel in downtown Riyadh in a gorgeous new Rolls-Royce sent by the foreign minister, Sa'id steeled himself for the conversation that lay ahead.

It was time for the Saudis to rein in their Wahabbi mullahs, who preached hatred and violence.

It was time to stop funding Al-Nakbah and any other terrorist group still on their payroll.

It was time for the Saudis to either invite Palestine and Israel into OPEC or help disband the cartel altogether.

And it was time for the Saudis to join Egypt, Jordan, and the Palestinians in signing a formal peace agreement with Israel, exchanging ambassadors and building economic and cultural bridges between their peoples.

This was the only way to ensure regional stability and keep the radicals at bay, and it was long overdue. But he could only imagine the icy reception that lay ahead.

Long before becoming the Palestinian prime minister, Sa'id had made his fortune in the Persian Gulf as the founder and CEO of the Palestinian Petroleum Group. He understood the politics of the Gulf, and he had no illusions about the Saudi leaders. They were not interested in peace. They were not even interested in power, per se. They were obsessed with wealth, and they would do whatever it took to protect what they had and expand it beyond measure.

Sa'id and his advisors had pored over Arafat's personal files over the past several years since his death. They knew almost to the dollar how much money the Saudis had been pumping into Arafat's coffers to pay suicide bombers, and buy weapons from Iran, and keep Arafat's widow surviving in Paris on $1.7 million a month.

But the stunning discovery of black gold in Israel and the Palestinian Authority had turned nearly every Muslim, Christian, and Jew in both countries into a multimillionaire. Suddenly the Palestinian government didn't need Saudi money. Suddenly the Palestinian prime minister was a big player on the world political and economic stage. And suddenly the Saudis wanted to talk.

☆　☆　☆

"*Ithnan* to *Mohandis*."

"Go ahead, *Ithnan*."

"Target is passing me."

"Copy that. All units stand by. Two minutes—I repeat—two minutes."

☆　☆　☆

His gamble was not without risks.

But Sa'id, now sixty-three, had always been a risk taker. Born dirt poor in a West Bank refugee camp, the youngest of six children, this quiet, unassuming, owlish entrepreneur now had everything a man could want. He was married to a beautiful, satisfying wife who had borne him four sons. He was the richest Palestinian in the world and was now leading his people out of the deserts of despair into a future so many Arab leaders had long promised but never delivered.

Early in the process of negotiating the Oil-for-Peace deal, Jon Bennett had asked Sa'id how it was possible that a moderate Ramallah Muslim would even consider doing business with a bunch of secular Israelis and an evangelical American president, given the history of the region.

His answer had intrigued both Bennett and McCoy.

"Vaclav Havel once said, 'The real test of a man is not when he plays the role that he wants for himself but when he plays the role destiny has for him.' I believe that, Jonathan, or I would not be here today.

"I grew up a stranger in a strange land—my own. Occupied by the Babylonians and the Persians, the Egyptians and the Ottomans, the British and the Jordanians, and now the Israelis. My father was a real estate agent. What can I say? He was right. The three rules of real estate are location, location, location. I always wondered, what is the big fuss about? Why are we all fighting about land that has so little intrinsic value? If you want to fight about something, you know, fight about the Gulf. Where there is gas. Where there is oil. Where there is wealth. To me, that made more sense.

"But, of course, the battle for the Holy Land has always been the hottest here—in *this* place, on *this* land, in *these* hills, in *this* city—even before we discovered oil and gas. Why? I have never been able to explain it. But I have come to believe that there's something supernatural at work here, Jonathan. Unseen forces are at work—angels and demons, powers of darkness and light—that move quietly and mysteriously, like the wind.

"You cannot see the wind, but you can see its effects. So it is with these unseen forces battling for control of this land. They are real, and they are alive, and they are shaping events here, turning some men into heroes and others into fanatics. And I believe they are locked in some kind of cosmic, winner-take-all battle that is yet to be decided. I don't pretend to understand it. But I believe it, because I live here, and I know this is not a normal place.

"And do not ask me how, but something inside of me tells me that good will triumph over evil. That this oil deal is going to go through. That we are going to help people become richer than they've ever imagined. That we are going to help people see the value of working together in a common market, for the sake of their children, even if they and their parents and their parents' parents have been at war for generations.

"Look at the French and the Germans. Look at the Japanese and the Koreans. They all used to hate each other. They fought wars of annihilation to wipe each other off the face of the earth. And now they live in peace. Why can the Palestinians and Israelis not do that? There is no reason. And I have this dream that the time to do it is now."

Bennett had thought about that, then looked straight into Sa'id's eyes and asked, "And if we all die in the process of trying to make it work, what will you say then?"

McCoy had winced at Bennett's bluntness, but Sa'id did not blink at all.

"At least," he said, "I can say I died on the side of the angels."

The motorcade was less than ten minutes from the palace.

Sa'id gazed out the window at the conundrum that was Riyadh—some of the world's oldest and largest and most beautiful mosques stood alongside some of the world's sleekest and most expensive skyscrapers—when something caught his eye. It was coming in fast from the right. It was a huge truck, an oil tanker of some kind, running a red light and barreling through the intersection ahead.

The lead car in Sa'id's motorcade tried to swerve, but it was too late.

The sedan hit the side of the eighteen-wheeler at almost seventy miles an hour. The fireball that erupted could be seen and heard throughout the capital as two more security cars plowed into the tanker right behind the first.

Sa'id could feel the searing heat from the enormous explosion. For a moment he was convinced he was going to die as well. The driver of their Rolls-Royce slammed on the brakes and spun into a 180-degree turn as machine-gun fire erupted from all sides.

"Left, left, go left!" shouted Sa'id's lead bodyguard, but two vans suddenly pulled into the alley, cutting off their best way of escape.

The driver again slammed on the brakes, sending Sa'id crashing into the partition dividing the front and back seats and shattering the glass in the process.

"Emerald Palace, this is White Tiger—*we are under attack.*"

"Say again, White Tiger?"

"I repeat, we are under attack two blocks south of the King Abdul Aziz Centre. Requesting immediate backup and air-extraction team, over."

But waiting for help to arrive wasn't a serious option, and they all knew it.

Hooded men jumped from the vans and began charging them, firing machine guns as they ran. Round after round smashed into the bullet-proof glass. The men were less than twenty yards away and coming fast.

Three Mercedes SUVs screeched to a stop nearby. A dozen Saudi security agents jumped out and returned fire, but Sa'id knew it wasn't enough.

"Go back, go back!" Sa'id yelled to his driver, his face covered with blood.

The driver threw the car into reverse. He gunned the engine and peeled down another side street.

The armored Rolls-Royce flew around a corner.

Neither the driver nor the occupants saw the trap coming. In a garbage can on the curb were fifty pounds of plastic explosives, linked by a short orange detonation cord to a small green cell phone just waiting for a call.

When it came, the force of the massive explosion blew out the windows of the Rolls and flipped the car onto its side, where it, too, exploded, killing everyone inside.

8

★ ★
★

"Dr. Mordechai, welcome to Babylon."

The two men met at the front entrance to the presidential palace and greeted each other with a simple handshake. What struck Mordechai first was how remarkably fit the new Iraqi president was for a man of seventy-four. He had intensely dark eyes, a long and weathered face, and a salt-and-pepper beard, but though he wore the traditional white robes of the region, Mordechai knew this was no ordinary Arab ruler.

Mustafa Al-Hassani was widely considered the intellectual grandfather of the Iraqi freedom forces. For decades—by day—he had been a beloved professor of Arab literature and poetry at one of the most prestigious universities in Baghdad. But by night he had steadily emerged as one of the shrewdest political strategists in the modern Middle East. He had conceived a vision of what Iraq could be without Saddam. It burned within him. He had vowed not to rest until a new regime was born, and then he set about to build a movement worthy of his dreams.

So on a cold, dark night in the winter of 1979, Al-Hassani had gathered three fellow professors at his home. Over thick, dark coffee and sweet cakes and pastries, he explained his plan. Each of the men signed on immediately, and together they founded the Iraqi National Alliance. The INA would serve as an underground agitator for free speech, freedom of the press, and free elections. It would identify, recruit, and train a network of like-minded students and professors throughout Iraq—a force dedicated to the proposition of overthrowing the Ba'ath Party. It would make contact with Iraqi exiles and dissidents in London, Paris, and even the U.S. If possible, it would accept money from the CIA and British intelligence. And it would plan for the right moment to strike.

During the 1980s, as the Iran-Iraq war raged and Saddam looked invincible, Al-Hassani published three books of what appeared to be ancient Babylonian poetry. In fact they were coded manifestos providing detailed instructions to those interested in a democratic revolution on how to find copies of the Magna Carta and Declaration of Independence hidden in Iraq's public libraries, and how to form cell groups and banned book clubs to study the lives and methods of revolutionaries in other countries.

Each of Al-Hassani's books became a runaway black market best seller in outlying cities like Mosul and Kirkuk and Al Najaf. But when one thin volume of the trilogy and a handwritten copy of the key to decoding it wound up in the hands of Saddam's son Uday in Baghdad, Al-Hassani's cover as a professor was blown. On a bitter cold night in the winter of 1989, Al-Hassani was arrested by the secret police and thrown into one of Saddam's gulags known as Abu Ghraib. There he was tortured without mercy for three straight years. He fully expected to be executed, but then something happened that would change the course of history. The United States Marines stormed the prison one day, and Mustafa Al-Hassani was suddenly a free man in an Iraq no longer controlled by Saddam Hussein.

Within months of his release, Al-Hassani was named a member of Iraq's provisional government. He ran for Parliament in the country's first democratic elections, where he not only won but was soon elected by his peers to serve as the speaker of the parliament. And then, following the tragic assassination of Iraq's first president, Al-Hassani suddenly found himself serving as the country's new leader. It was the dream he had refused to stop dreaming all those years in prison, and now—incredibly—it was real.

"Come, come, my friend; follow me," Al-Hassani insisted.

Mordechai did as he was told.

"I happen to know this is not your first time in my country," the Iraqi continued. "The files I have been reading from Saddam's Mukhabbarat intelligence agency have been quite fascinating, more like a novel than real life. From what I gather, you have spent quite a bit of time criss-crossing through this land. But I suspect this is your first time to Babylon, and certainly your first time inside one of our great palaces. Please tell me I am not wrong."

Mordechai couldn't help but laugh. The man had done his homework. He would love to get a look at those files, and he'd love to know what else Al-Hassani knew about him, but at this point there was no point denying the basic facts.

"It has been many years, but you are correct, Your Excellency," Mordechai said. "I have been to your country before, but it was never my privilege to step foot in any of your impressive palaces."

"I am relieved," Al-Hassani said with a smile, "though for today I will not ask you if you were ever in our Osirik nuclear reactor before it suffered such an untimely accident."

Relieved, Mordechai wondered why this man hadn't been appointed the country's president from the outset. He was as charming as he was shrewd.

"Are you fond of roasted lamb?" the Iraqi asked.

"One of my favorites," Mordechai assured him.

"Good, then our files are *indeed* accurate."

The two men laughed again, and Al-Hassani led the way from the foyer to his personal office inside the presidential palace.

Mordechai had never seen such opulence.

The vaulted ceilings of the palace were covered in pure gold. So were the pillars running down each side of the hallway leading into the heart of the mammoth building. Even the doorknobs and light switches were made of pure gold.

"Saddam Hussein—may Allah torment his soul—did one useful thing in his lifetime," said Al-Hassani without emotion. "In 1978 he began re-building the ancient city of Babylon on its original site. He did so, of course, against the counsel of all of his highly paid archeological advisors who insisted it would be a sin to build on top of the remains of the great capital without more time to excavate and explore. But Saddam was, shall we say, unencumbered by the advice of lesser mortals than he."

Mordechai smiled at the understatement of the evening.

"So the palace we are walking through," Al-Hassani continued, "is literally located in the heart of the legendary city, alongside the Euphrates River, which you will be able to see from my office. Down the hill is the great palace of Nebuchadnezzar—my personal favorite—and, of course, the Guest House, where you are staying. In a moment I shall show you a model of the city as we envision it will look when it is completely restored."

They continued walking down corridors the length of football fields, lined on each side with marble pillars and with diamond chandeliers hanging overhead.

"We have been working on the plans for the past several months. They depart somewhat from what Saddam wanted to accomplish, because he never envisioned the city as the actual political and commercial center of the country. I do. Saddam ran out of money after launching his foolish invasion of Iran, then his foolish invasion of Kuwait. Then, of course, came the U.N. oil embargo and two wars with the Americans, and Babylon just sat here waiting, not quite deserted, but only barely rebuilt."

"Which is where you enter the picture," noted Mordechai.

"That is true," Al-Hassani beamed. "I look at what is left of Baghdad after the war, and I can't help but think of it as the capital of Saddam, a city of our sordid, ugly recent past. When I look at Babylon, on the other hand, I see not just a testament to Iraq's glorious history but a symbol of our glorious future. I want the citizens of the new Iraq to be proud of their heritage and excited by what lies ahead. That is why I moved the government here and made Babylon our new capital. Yes, it was an enormous expense, and yes, it was a logistical nightmare. But I could not just allow this great city to rot in the sun—unused, unseen, unappreciated. Whatever else you say about Saddam, you must say he was an aberration of history. But Babylon *is* history. Babylon is who we are—and who we will become."

Al-Hassani stopped in one of the courtyards, lush with palm trees and other vegetation.

"We are not content to be second-rate actors on the world stage, Dr. Mordechai. Like you Jews, we long to resurrect our holy city and make her the envy of the world. And we believe that all the prerequisites for rapid economic growth are in place. I want Babylon to become the new epicenter of international commerce and tourism, and I will do whatever it takes to succeed.

"We don't begrudge what you Jews are doing now that you've discovered oil. Indeed, we applaud it. You are making the deserts bloom like never before. You are attracting trade and tourists, and you are quickly becoming the envy of the world. Why should my people not aspire to the same, or more? Like the great tower of Babel of old, who knows what the race of men can do when their resources are as limitless as their dreams?"

The two men approached the end of the hallway and passed an enormous mural, commissioned by Saddam, depicting King Nebuchadnezzar leading the armies of Babylon to capture Israel and destroy Jerusalem. The craftsmanship was extraordinary. The message was clear.

Mordechai was tempted to ask Al-Hassani when the mural was coming down, when a spirit of cooperation—if not outright friendship—might begin between their two countries. But he decided against it. It was not just that the request was inappropriate to discuss on a first visit, even for an old maverick spymaster like himself. It was that Mordechai already knew the answer, and just the thought of what lay ahead made him shudder with fear.

9
★ ★
★

The death of Ibrahim Sa'id hit Bennett and McCoy hard.

Since first meeting him in the earliest days of the Oil-for-Peace negotiations, they had grown to love his quick mind and gentle spirit. He was a
generous man, generous with his time and his trust, and they had enjoyed
spending time with him and his family in his sprawling home in the hills
overlooking Jericho.

McCoy had once likened Sa'id to one of America's founding fathers,
and in many ways the comparison was accurate. He had pledged his life,
his fortune, and his sacred honor to build a Palestinian democracy, and for
it he had paid the ultimate price.

"Salaam, this is Jon Bennett," he said, choking back his emotions as he
spoke to Sa'id's eldest son by phone. "I just heard the news—I can't begin
to tell you how sorry I am, how sorry Erin and I both are. You know we
loved your father very much."

The young man, just fourteen, could barely respond. He was clearly in
shock, and Bennett could hear his mother sobbing in the background.

McCoy, meanwhile, called Dmitri Galishnikov and his wife.

It was Galishnikov, a Russian Jewish émigré to Israel, who had nearly
twenty years earlier founded a small petroleum company called Medexco
and proceeded to create a joint venture with the Palestinian Petroleum
Group, founded by Sa'id. There weren't a whole lot of Russian Jews

forming business partnerships with Palestinian Muslims back then. Certainly not any others trying to strike oil.

But with Bennett and McCoy at their side, Galishnikov and Sa'id had done the impossible, landing themselves on the covers of *Time*, *Forbes*, *Business Week*, and *The Economist* and fundamentally changing the economic and political dynamic of the Middle East. And now the radicals were taking their revenge.

When McCoy finally hung up the phone, she buried her face in Bennett's chest and wept. How many times over the past few years had they seen friends killed by the jihadists? How much more could they take?

For Bennett, it was yet another reason to leave the White House and carve out a new life. He held Erin in his arms, trying to comfort her. Despite all they'd been through, he could still count on one hand the number of times he'd ever seen her actually cry. The first was the night he'd been shot by Al-Nakbah terrorists in Dr. Mordechai's house in Jerusalem. The most recent was just Tuesday night when he had proposed. This was not a woman prone to displays of emotion. Whether that was innate or her CIA training, he wasn't quite sure, but it made the few times he'd seen it happen all the more memorable, if for no other reason than it seemed to indicate that she increasingly trusted him with the things that mattered most to her.

Bennett gently stroked her hair and forced back tears of his own.

He, too, needed time to grieve. But time was not a luxury he had at the moment. He had calls to make to Israeli prime minister David Doron and the speaker of the Palestinian parliament. He was still waiting on return phone calls from Russian foreign minister Aleksandr Golitsyn and E.U. foreign minister Salvador Lucente.

He had to stay focused. First the attack on Washington, now Sa'id. Assuming President MacPherson himself had been the specific target of the Aeroflot hijacking, did that mean Israeli prime minister David Doron would be next?

News of the Sa'id assassination rocked the White House.

President MacPherson grieved the loss of his friend. He had known Ibrahim Sa'id for years. He considered him a kindred spirit in the war on terror and the long march toward freedom in the Middle East. And now he was gone. The loss felt from his absence would be incalculable.

It was too early in the morning to talk to the press in person, so the president went to the Oval Office to draft a statement. "Like the late Egyptian president Anwar Sadat and the late Iraqi president, my friend and colleague Ibrahim Sa'id has become another martyr for peace," MacPherson wrote in longhand. "But like these other Arab heroes, Prime Minister Sa'id's death will not be in vain. In the past few minutes I have spoken to senior members of the Palestinian leadership, as well as to the Saudi government and to several of our allies in Europe. I have assured all of them that the United States will do everything in our power to help hunt down those responsible for this act of barbarism and bring them to justice. The peace process will go on. America's commitment to peace and security in the Middle East will never waver."

When he was finished, he sent the draft to the Press Office and was joined by National Security Advisor Marsha Kirkpatrick, Director of Central Intelligence Jack Mitchell, and White House Chief of Staff Bob Corsetti. There was more troubling news.

"Mr. President," the DCI began, "I know we've got enough going on this morning, but we've just learned that President Vadim has ordered several elite military units into the heart of Moscow, ostensibly to assist with crowd control. Deputy Speaker Sergei Ilyushkin is scheduled to hold a nationally televised press conference at the Duma in a few hours, followed by an anti-American rally in Red Square. He's expected to draw over a hundred thousand people, and Vadim's people apparently want to make sure there isn't any trouble. Checkpoints are up on all the highways leading into Moscow, and security is being beefed up around our embassy."

"Are our people at risk?"

"We don't believe so, Mr. President," answered Kirkpatrick. "The Moscow police seem to have things in hand. Typical protest stuff—people holding signs, shouting anti-American slogans, that kind of thing. A college student burned you in effigy a little while ago. Unfortunately, that video is likely to pop up on cable news any minute."

That said, Kirkpatrick assured the president this wasn't Tehran circa

1979. The Russians weren't radical Islamic jihadists. They weren't going to storm the embassy and take Americans hostage for 444 days.

Still, there was no question that events were taking a turn for the worse.

☆   ☆   ☆

Ruth Bennett was stunned by the news.

Ibrahim Sa'id was dead? It couldn't be true. She *knew* him.

Jon and Erin had introduced her to Prime Minister Sa'id at the State of the Union address three years before. She'd had dinner with Sa'id and his wife at a White House state dinner just last year. Ever since, she'd followed every development in the peace process, clipping any article that mentioned Jon or Erin and arranging them all in a scrapbook she hoped to one day give her grandchildren.

And for a moment, she panicked, desperately trying to remember where Jon and Erin were at the moment. *Had they been with Sa'id? Could they be dead?*

The very thought seemed to suck the life out of her. She was already a widow. She'd lived through the near death of her only son and her daughter-in-law-to-be so many times she didn't think she could take it again.

Clicking on the light beside her bed, she groped for her glasses and ran downstairs to check her calendar. *No, thank God. They weren't in Saudi Arabia. They were in Moscow. Which meant they were safe.*

10

St. Basil's Cathedral was the symbol of Russia.

Construction had begun on the magnificent monument in 1555 upon the order of Czar Ivan IV (aka "Ivan the Terrible") to commemorate the Russian conquest of the Khanate of Kazan.

Built in the heart of Moscow, on the edge of Red Square, the basic structure was completed six years later, though additions and improvements were constantly under way. The onion domes, for example, weren't added until 1583. They weren't painted the brilliant colors visible today until 1670. The Central Chapel of the Intercession, the ninth of the nine chapels, wasn't built for another two centuries.

Nearly five centuries after its auspicious beginnings, it was not only a magnet for tourists, it was the icon of an empire. But like so much of Russian history, St. Basil's story was stained in blood. It was said, for example, that Ivan was so struck by the cathedral's splendor that he ordered the eyes of the architect who had designed it to be gouged out so that the man could never again create something so beautiful. Directly in front of the cathedral's south side was a small, circular stone platform known as *Lobnoe Mesto*. It was from here that the czars used to address the people when they were not having them executed on the same dais. And it was here that Sergei Ilyushkin could now be found, in full rant.

☆ ☆ ☆

Bennett sat alone in the Bubble.

McCoy was for the moment busy with something elsewhere in the embassy compound, leaving Bennett with some rare time to himself. He found himself unable to take his eyes off the bank of television monitors on the far wall of the conference room. One was tuned to RTR, a major Russian network. The others showed CNN International, Sky News, and the BBC, respectively. All covered Ilyushkin's speech live, though for the moment all the sets were on mute.

Sergei Ilyushkin had risen quickly through Russia's post-Putin political scene. Now deputy speaker of the Russian parliament, he constantly lamented the collapse of the Soviet Empire and blasted the Kremlin's "limp-wristed, weak-willed, cowardly foreign policy" in the face of "American aggression and expansionism." He warned that falling world oil prices were making the "Yankee imperialists" stronger while devastating the oil-dependent Russian economy, destroying jobs and incomes, and adding to the pervasive image of Russian weakness in Washington, London, Paris, and Berlin. What's more, he seemed to make it his mission in life to blame Russia's problems on the "dirty Jews and their Zionist coconspirators."

As he watched Ilyushkin preaching through the powerful sound system—the Kremlin and Lenin's Tomb to his left, the GUM Department Store to his right—Bennett could see his dark eyes darting from face to face, flashing with rage. His face was beet red. Thick veins bulged from his throat and neck. His hair was tousled, his tie askew. His shirt was drenched in sweat and opened several buttons down, revealing a chest full of hair. It was not a pretty picture, but it was a compelling one. The crowds were listening, and they were growing.

Even without the sound Bennett felt the hair on the back of his neck stand up. Ilyushkin struck Bennett more like a drunken fan at a Russian hockey game than one of the highest-ranking members of the Russian legislature. He was speaking so fast, so furiously, you could see the spit coming out of his mouth.

Bennett scanned the quotes running across the bottom of the screen via the BBC's electronic ticker tape. *"Ilyushkin demands Vadim expel all*

Americans from 'sacred Russian soil' . . . warns Vadim to recall the Russian ambassador from Washington 'or face the wrath of the Russian people' . . . denounces MacPherson administration as 'cold-blooded murderers' . . . says U.S. represents the world's 'new Roman imperialists' who 'kill with impunity' and see Russians as 'second-class citizens' worthy only of 'target practice.' . . . "

It was vintage Ilyushkin, but what worried Bennett was the size and reaction of the enormous crowds. They were drinking it in and chanting for more.

Sergei Ilyushkin might look like a fool, but he was no novice. A disciple of the late Vladimir Zhirinovsky, a man once known throughout Western diplomatic circles as Mad Vlad, he had been well schooled in the seductive art of political propaganda by one of history's underappreciated masters.

Bennett still vividly remembered the 1994 *Time* magazine cover story on Zhirinovsky entitled "Rising Czar," describing Zhirinovsky as a rabid anti-Semite and dangerous demagogue who "threatened to restore Russia's imperial borders, annex Alaska, invade Turkey, repartition Poland, give Germany 'another Chernobyl,' turn Kazakhstan into a 'scorched desert' and 'employ large fans to blow radioactive waste across the Baltics.' "

Ilyushkin embraced Zhirinovsky's vision, and then some.

Both men had been born in Alma-Ata, central Asia, in the spring of 1946. They'd grown up side by side and in many ways were inseparable. Both graduated from Moscow State University in 1969. Both served in the Red Army until 1973. Both served for a time in Soviet military intelligence. After getting out of the military, both had gone to law school and become lawyers before becoming politically active. Together they had launched the woefully misnamed Liberal Democratic Party of Russia, or LDPR, just as the Soviet Union was breaking up.

Badly underestimated by Western intelligence agencies, including the CIA, Zhirinovsky had roared out of nowhere in 1991 to run for president and stunned the world by placing third, behind Boris Yeltsin and Nikolai Ryzhkov. By 1994, the LDPR had Washington and NATO in near-panic mode after it captured 25 percent of the vote and Zhirinovsky was made deputy speaker of the Duma.

As a senior Russian government official—and a constant thorn in

President Yeltsin's side—Zhirinovsky had quickly struck up a close friendship with Saddam Hussein, regularly traveling to Baghdad until it fell. But it was Adolf Hitler he seemed to most admire.

Over the years, Zhirinovksy counted German and Austrian neo-Nazis as pals. He denounced the U.S. Congress as "Israeli-occupied territory." He urged the Russian government to "set aside places [on] . . . Russian territory to deport this small but troublesome tribe [known as the Jews]," effectively calling for Jews to be rounded up in new concentration camps in order for Russian society "to survive."

What's more, he vowed to execute at least one hundred thousand political prisoners the moment he took office, even as he remained one of the highest-ranking leaders in Russia.

Shortly after the regime change in Iraq, however, Zhirinovsky mysteriously disappeared and was eventually presumed dead by Russian authorities. Ilyushkin, his deputy and thus the ranking member of the LDPR in the Duma, assumed Zhirinovsky's position as deputy speaker of the Russian parliament and soon proved himself an equally radical—yet far more effective—politician.

For years it had been unclear where the LDPR got its funding. Ilyushkin was proving to be a prodigious fund-raiser of late, but it had long been rumored that the KGB and Soviet military intelligence had provided the initial seed money to get the party off the ground and fuel Zhirinovsky's and Ilyushkin's political ambitions. The CIA had never been able to nail it down for sure, but according to McCoy, it wasn't implausible.

Put simply, Zhirinovsky had been the KGB's man. Part of his platform was to hire a total of *one million* agents to serve in the KGB (now known as the *Federal'naya Sluzhba Bezopasnosti*, or FSB) the minute he was elected president. That, in part, was how they had recruited perhaps their most deadly ally—Yuri Gogolov, the former commander of the elite Russian military force known as *Spetsnatz* who was now believed to be recruiting disaffected Russian military and intelligence officers to support the Zhirinovsky-Ilyushkin political platform.

In addition to pledging to rebuild Russia's intelligence capabilities, Zhirinovsky, Ilyushkin, and Gogolov vowed to buy all the guns, tanks, ships, and planes the country could possibly afford as soon as the LDPR swept into office. They promised to raise military pay, buy new uniforms, and rebuild the famed Russian cavalry units of the nineteenth and early twentieth centuries. What's more, they pledged to scrap or simply disregard all the arms treaties with the U.S. in order to rebuild Russia's strategic nuclear forces until they were the best in the world.

None of this was conclusive proof that Zhirinovsky had been bought and paid for by the KGB and the Red Army. But it was close. Zhirinovsky was their biggest fan, and they were his.

Ilyushkin and Gogolov, not surprisingly, had picked right up where Zhirinovsky left off. The LDPR was now the second-biggest political party in the entire country—just behind Vadim's own Russian Unity Party—and without question the most dangerous. Avowed Fascists, they hated the U.S. They hated Jews. They vowed to rebuild Mother Russia, restore her glory, and bring back the czar. And now they were center stage.

Bennett turned up the sound to find the voice of a young British reporter translating Ilyushkin's speech.

"We have all witnessed yet another act of American barbarism—will it ever end?" bellowed Ilyushkin. *"In the 1980s, the Americans shot down an unarmed Iranian airliner over the Persian Gulf. In the 1990s, they bombed an aspirin factory in Sudan. And the Chinese Embassy in Kosovo. Then came Afghanistan and Iraq. And now, because Putin and Vadim said nothing, did nothing—because we have allowed the arrogance of the Americans to go unchecked—it has come to this.*

"Innocent Russians are dead. Women and children are dead. The Americans refuse even to apologize. The American president won't even pick up the phone and say he is sorry, or offer compensation to our grieving families. Will we do nothing?"

"*NO!*" the crowd roared.

"Will we bow before American masters and cower like whipped dogs?"

"*NO!*" the crowd roared again.

"Will we allow Russian weakness to invite more aggression, or let the Jews who run America and Israel and the world banking system suck the lifeblood out of our economy and leave Russian workers without jobs, without homes, without food?"

"Nyet, nyet, nyet, nyet," came the fervent chants.

Bennett didn't need to wait for that translation.

"One million wealthy, while 150 million are in chains. This is what Putin and Vadim have brought you. Weakness. Shame. Poverty. Corruption. I know you are sick of it. You are frightened. You are angry. They call me an extremist. That is OK. If that is what we need to prevent the Americans and the Jews from stealing our country, then let us be extreme. We have tried it their way," Ilyuskhin continued, his arms raised to the sky. *"Now I ask you: give me a chance. That is all I ask. Can I do worse than they have? Can you honestly believe that I would do worse than Yeltsin, Putin, and Vadim? I love this country, as you do. I love Russia more than anything on earth. And when I am done, she will be great again. I promise you that. When I am done, Mother Russia will live again. She will be respected, and she will be feared."*

The crowd erupted, surging toward the platform where Ilyuskhin paced like a man possessed. Sky News now had wide shots of Red Square and the adjoining streets.

A banner scrolling across the bottom of the screen said the LDPR estimated the crowd at four hundred thousand. The Moscow police put it closer to a quarter of a million. But the discrepancies didn't matter. Television and radio crews were beaming the speech to homes all across Russia and the former Soviet republics and to viewers around the world, all of whom now knew a firestorm was building in Moscow.

President Mustafa Al-Hassani turned off the television.

Mordechai tried desperately to control his emotions. He had just seen the horrifying coverage from Saudi Arabia.

How could Ibrahim Sa'id be dead?

It wasn't possible. They had just had dinner together near Tel Aviv at the home of the U.S. ambassador to Israel a few nights before. They'd sat on the veranda at sunset, overlooking the glistening Mediterranean, smoking cigars, and strategizing ways of bringing the Saudis to the table. They'd stared out at mile after mile of offshore drilling platforms and marveled at the success of Medexco and toasted a future that just seventy-two hours ago had seemed so pregnant with possibilities.

How few brave ones there were left, thought Mordechai. *How few were willing to do more than merely hope for peace.* Without Sa'id, there would never have been a joint venture between PPG and Medexco; nor, of course, would there ever have been an Oil-for-Peace agreement with Israel. *Could either survive his death?*

"Do you think it is all connected?" asked Al-Hassani.

The question jarred Mordechai back into the moment.

In his shock and grief, the question had not yet crossed Mordechai's mind. Could the Aeroflot hijacking and the assassination of the Palestinian prime minister be connected? There was no evidence, beyond the timing. Not yet, anyway. But did he really believe in mere coincidence? He did not.

If the events were connected, then someone was trying to blow up the peace process. But who? And where would they strike next? Mordechai forced himself to become an analyst again, to push back his roiling emotions, start processing what few facts he had, and begin looking for connections, however remote or obscure.

"Perhaps," said Mordechai.

"*Perhaps?*" Al-Hassani scoffed. "There is no question they are connected, nor who is behind it."

"Who?" asked Mordechai.

"I expected more from a former head of the Mossad."

"*Who?*" Mordechai pressed again.

"Iran, of course."

Mordechai was taken aback by the intensity of Al-Hassani's conviction. Was he right? Did he know something Mordechai didn't? Or was he trying to settle a score with an old enemy?

"The mullahs in Iran issued a *fatwah* against Sa'id the minute he signed the interim agreement with us," Mordechai cautiously conceded. "But why blow up a Russian jetliner?"

Al-Hassani shook his head. "Need I remind you, Dr. Mordechai, that it was the Iranians who invented chess, that they are masters of plotting ten, fifteen moves ahead?"

"You think these are the opening moves of a larger Iranian game?"

"Come now, Dr. Mordechai. For the last two decades, the Iranians have been trying to build nuclear weapons. They have been buying the latest weaponry from Moscow. They have been planting sleeper cells in Oman and fomenting terror and instability in Yemen and Somalia and Ethiopia and Eritrea. They have built strategic alliances with Sudan and Syria. And I do not have to tell you how much they spent bankrolling Hezbollah in Lebanon, and Hamas and Islamic Jihad in Gaza and the West Bank."

"Yes, but to what end?"

"You cannot see it for yourself?"

"I came to hear your views, Mr. President, not my own."

"Then let me be perfectly clear: Step by step, Iran is surrounding the

Arabian Peninsula, surrounding Israel, Iraq, and Saudi Arabia. The mullahs want your land, they want our oil, and they want the Islamic holy sites of Mecca and Medina, which the Saudis presently control. Step by step they are preparing to rebuild the Persian Empire. It is only a matter of time before they strike."

"So why hijack an Aeroflot jet?" Mordechai asked again.

"Perhaps to distract the Americans. Perhaps to decapitate them. It is too soon to say for certain. But mark my words, you will not find Iran's fingerprints on this hijacking. Not directly. They are too clever for that. Do you remember a few years back when the Libyans were caught planning an assassination of the Saudi royal family?"

"Of course."

"Do you really think the Libyans care that much about who runs Saudi Arabia? Of course not. It had all the earmarks of an Iranian operation. The Iranian mullahs are Shi'ites. The mullahs hate the Saudi royal family. They have been plotting the downfall of the House of Saud for years. Why? Because the royals are Sunni Muslims, which means they are apostates in the eyes of the mullahs. The Saudis are, by their very presence, desecrating the Islamic holy sites and polluting sacred Islamic soil. And if that were not bad enough, the Saudis are in bed with the Great Satan—the Americans—selling them cheap oil and, until recently, basing infidel forces on Muslim lands. I have no doubt the mullahs offered the Libyans money—or weapons—to assassinate the Saudi royals, so long as the operation could not be traced back to Iran."

Mordechai pondered that for a moment, then asked, "Can you prove that?"

"Do I have a smoking gun?" asked Al-Hassani. "No, not yet. But the circumstantial evidence of an intensifying alliance between Tehran and Tripoli is mounting. I know the White House thinks Libya's decision to give up its weapons of mass destruction was a masterstroke of American diplomacy. But I do not believe it for a moment. It turns out that almost all of Libya's WMD programs were run by the Iranians. One team of weapons inspectors inside Libya found evidence of nearly one hundred signed contracts between Iranian companies and the Libyan government to build chemical, biological, and nuclear weapons facilities, as well as to build conventional weapons systems. They even found a previously unknown Scud missile factory, built entirely by Iran. Believe me, Dr. Mordechai, the Libyans hate us. They hate the Saudis. And they are not too happy about you, either."

The two shared a laugh. "It is a tough neighborhood," said Mordechai.

"It is indeed. But look, the Iranian-Libyan connection is just part of Tehran's grand design. The mullahs are also trying to forge a strategic alliance with Turkey. Last year Iran signed a security pact with Turkey. The year before, they signed a major bilateral trade deal together. Not long before, they signed a landmark energy deal in which Iran agreed to sell $20 billion worth of natural gas to Turkey over the next ten years. Now, given the fact that Turkey imports nearly all of its energy needs—and Iran has just become the second-largest supplier of natural gas to Turkey after Russia—what kind of leverage do you think Russia and Iran now have over the Turkish government?"

Mordechai took a sip of coffee.

"Did you read the Reuters interview with Turkish president Kuzemir?" Al-Hassani continued.

Mordechai hated to concede he had not, but he had no choice.

"Understandable, of course; it just hit the wires," Al-Hassani insisted, as though eager to spare his new Israeli friend any embarrassment. "I will have one of my aides get you a copy, but for now let me summarize it for you. The Turkish president said that while he is sympathetic to every country's right of self-defense, 'blowing an unarmed civilian jetliner out of the sky could be considered by some an act of war.' Then he called for an investigation, conducted by the U.N., to avoid any 'appearance of impropriety.'"

That cannot be right, thought Mordechai. Was a major NATO ally suggesting the U.S. might be guilty of a crime, a cover-up, and an act of war?

"Do not misunderstand me," Al-Hassani added. "I would not be concerned by Nargil Kuzemir. You will not find a more inconsequential man running such an important country. But I guarantee you he did not wake up this morning and say to himself, 'I think I will slit my throat with the Americans.' That is not like him. He is incapable of an original thought. Someone is squeezing him."

"Iran?"

"Of course; who else?"

"OK, let us say you are right," said Mordechai. "The central question still remains—why would Iran risk its relationship with Moscow by hijacking a Russian jet full of civilians? It just does not make sense."

"Why not?" Al-Hassani pushed back. "Suppose the mullahs *are* behind the attack—not directly, but through Al-Nakbah. Is Iran taking any heat for it? Of course not. No one is even talking about who hijacked the plane. They are all talking about who shot the plane down. The Russians are furious with Washington, not Tehran. And it is not only the Russians. The whole world is furious at the MacPherson administration over this. Which begs the question: is the U.S. suddenly in a stronger position to confront the next member of the Axis of Evil—Iran? Of course not. Just the opposite. There is absolutely no political will in the United States to deal with the Iranians, even as they move ever closer to completing their nuclear weapons and unveiling their plot to seize the Arabian Peninsula."

Mordechai's pulse quickened. *Was this why he had been summoned? Was Al-Hassani suggesting Iraq and Israel work together somehow to block the rise of a new Persian Empire?* On the face of it, the idea seemed impossible. But a week ago if someone had asked him the chances of a former Israeli spy chief being invited by the Iraqi head of state to discuss the Iranian problem, he would have said that was impossible too. Yet here he was, in the city whose very name conjured images of the end of days.

There was no question Al-Hassani was trying to open a back channel to Jerusalem. The question now was just how far the Iraqi leader wanted to go. Mordechai was about to ask when one of Al-Hassani's aides stepped into the room and whispered in the president's ear.

Al-Hassani abruptly stood and held out his hand.

"You have been most kind to come all this way, Dr. Mordechai. I have enjoyed our conversation immensely, and I hope you have found it helpful as well. My colleague here will take you on the tour of Babylon. And I hope you and I have the opportunity to meet again in the near future."

Mordechai was stunned. They were just getting started.

"Please, please, my friend, do not be offended," Al-Hassani insisted. "You understand that neither your interests nor mine are served by the two of us being seen together. You arrived under the cover of darkness, and you shall depart the same way. But rest assured that you will not, by any means, leave empty-handed. I have left a gift for you back at the Guest House—for you and your prime minister."

Then Al-Hassani lowered his voice, almost to a whisper. "I trust neither of you will be disappointed."

And with that, the inscrutable Iraqi leader turned and walked out a side door, leaving Mordechai bewildered and alone.

12

★ ★
★

Bennett dashed off an e-mail to McCoy's BlackBerry.

"*e—did you see it?*"

"*what?*"

"*ilyushkin . . . how worried should i be?*"

"*you've got enough to worry about without adding that nut to your list.*"

Bennett wasn't so sure. "*i don't know. . . . have you really listened to this guy?*"

"*i'm more worried about this resolution the libyans are planning to introduce at the u.n. . . . did you get ken costello's flash traffic?*"

"*something just came in—haven't read it yet.*"

"*you'd better.*"

"*all right, hold on.*"

Bennett checked his new mail. Sure enough, there was an urgent message from Kenneth R. Costello, undersecretary of state for political affairs. A former ambassador to the European Union and deputy ambassador to the United Nations, Costello was the administration's leading authority on matters involving the U.N. and E.U. As such, he'd become a key asset in building international support for the Oil-for-Peace deal and was thus a man whose judgment Bennett trusted enormously.

But the latest news from Costello was not good.

> FLASH TRAFFIC <
(Priority One/EYES ONLY)

Sources at the U.N. tell me Libya will introduce a resolution on Monday condemning the U.S. for shooting down
Aeroflot 6617 "without sufficient provocation" and for
"massacring 173 innocent men, women, and children." Not
clear if Moscow is behind the Libyan move, but President
Vadim will likely be supportive, at least in principle. No
word on whether other countries are involved in the draft-
ing. END. KRC, UndSecPolAf.

XXXX310714-09:06ET-WASHDCXXXX <

Bennett rubbed his eyes. This was just what he needed on top of
everything else.

A new message from McCoy popped up.

"think it can pass?"

"doubt it," Bennett wrote back. *"libya doesn't have the clout to push it
through."*

"but you're still getting an ulcer just thinking about it, aren't you?"

McCoy knew him too well. Bennett changed the subject.

"any news on the chechen angle?"

"still working on it—my boss is driving me like a slave."

"guy sounds like a jerk," Bennett wrote back, smiling.

*"you don't know the half of it. . . . thinks he's a real hotshot . . . used to work
on wall street . . . you know the type."*

"i say dump him like a junk bond and run off with me."

"elope?"

"absolutely—scuba in aruba, anyone?"

"name the time and the flight—i'll be there. :)"

"don't tempt me."

"soon enough, my love."

It couldn't possibly be soon enough, thought Bennett. He leaned back and
closed his eyes. There was nothing he would love more than to cut loose
and marry this girl right then and there. They were more than in love.
They were best friends. He'd never believed in long engagements anyway.

Was forty-eight hours long enough?

☆   ☆   ☆

Mordechai was seething.

For the last several hours he had been forced to endure a mind-numbing series of lectures by various Iraqi "experts" on the history of Babylon, amid blazing July temperatures. He had suffered through a concert of Iraqi folk songs and some of the ugliest belly dancers he had ever seen. He had been forced to hold his tongue while some assistant-to-the-deputy-director-of-whatever had been his tour guide, a young man unable or unwilling to answer any but a handful of his questions about Babylon's past, present, or future.

And he was still furious at the way Mustafa Al-Hassani had so abruptly ended their meeting. Had the entire trip been a waste of time? Why exactly had he been summoned in the first place if only to be handled so rudely?

Light-headed and slightly nauseated, Mordechai wiped the sweat from his forehead with his handkerchief and sank back into the plush leather seats of the royal blue Mercedes. Then he took a swig of bottled water and signaled his driver to take him back to the Guest House, eager to pack his bags and get back to Israel.

As he stared out the window at the heat distortion on the horizon, it occurred to him that everything in this city seemed distorted, like a mirage.

Had Yael not taught him Jeremiah's prophecy that the Babylon of the future would not only be the epicenter of evil but "a golden cup in the hand of the Lord, intoxicating all the earth" and driving the nations mad? What a fool he'd been to expect anything else.

Yael.

Just the thought of her triggered an unquenchable thirst to be with her, to hold her hand again and gaze into her beautiful brown eyes and tell her that he loved her. And that he was sorry.

Soon enough, he reminded himself. Soon they would walk together hand in hand through the streets of Jerusalem—streets paved with gold, streets filled with laughter instead of fear. Soon they would be together again, and not because of anything they had done but because God in His mercy had opened their eyes to the truths of prophecy and His precious gift of salvation.

But how close he had been to missing it all.

Mordechai had been sixty-two before he'd ever even read Micah's prophecy that the Messiah would be born in Bethlehem. Or Isaiah's prophecies that the Messiah would be born of a virgin, minister in Galilee, and be tortured and killed as a "guilt offering" for the sins of mankind. Amazingly, Isaiah also wrote that the Messiah would not remain in the grave but would rise again and "prolong His days." How had he missed for so long King David's prophecy that the Messiah's hands and feet would be pierced and that His enemies would cast lots for His clothing and mock Him unmercifully? Or Daniel's prophecy that the Messiah would be killed before the destruction of Jerusalem and the Second Temple in AD 70? Or Zechariah's prophecy that men would look upon the Messiah "whom they have pierced; and they will mourn for Him, as one mourns for an only son, and they will weep bitterly over Him, like the bitter weeping over a firstborn"?

It was Yael who had first connected the dots, who had both understood and truly believed that the messianic prophecies all pointed to Jesus of Nazareth. It was Yael who first began to read the New Testament for herself and soon fell in love with the person of Jesus—His love and compassion and supernatural power. And every day Mordechai lived with the shame of getting so angry at her, of accusing her of betraying him and betraying the Jewish people by becoming a follower of Jesus as Messiah.

More than a decade had passed, and he still felt the shame of ever having feared that his wife's new faith might cost him his career if any of his colleagues found out. And though he knew God had forgiven him, he was still not sure he could ever forgive himself for letting her die of cancer without ever taking her faith seriously.

It was the gaping chasm in his soul caused by her death—the unshakable sadness and loneliness he felt every day—that had forced him into the spiritual journey he had for so long resisted. Was there *any* hope of seeing the woman he loved again? Was there really a heaven? Was Yael really there? And if so, how could he know—beyond the shadow of a doubt—that he could go there too? Was the God of Abraham, Isaac, and Jacob also a God of second chances, a God who would let him see his precious

Yael one day, that he might ask for her forgiveness and tell her how much he loved her?

And three months to the day after her death, Mordechai had gotten down on his knees in the privacy of their large, empty home and surrendered. The evidence was overwhelming, and it demanded a verdict. Jesus had to be the Messiah. Yael had been humble enough to admit it was true. Finally, in his anguish, he was too.

There was just one problem—he was the head of the Israeli Mossad at the time. In his world, becoming a Jewish believer in Jesus was tantamount to treason. It would take years of prayer and study of the Scriptures before he would finally be able to turn such fears about his country and career over to the Lord. But now a new anxiety was rising in his soul: the gnawing, unshakable instinct that grave new threats lay just over the horizon.

13

★ ★
★

The car pulled up to the Guest House.

Mordechai got out, thanked his driver, and took the elevator to his spacious suite on the third floor, grateful for the blast of chilled air that greeted him upon entry.

It dawned on him suddenly that he was no longer angry with Al-Hassani. Not like he had been, at least. Contact had been made. If that's all Al-Hassani could handle for now, why should he be so dismissive? Had any Israeli had such high-level contact with an Iraqi leader since the prophet Daniel? Not that he could remember. Perhaps such a relationship would prove useful in the future.

And then he saw it.

Resting on the center of his royal blue silk bedspread was a large box. It was wrapped in emerald green gift paper that bore exquisite, hand-painted images of the Hanging Gardens of Babylon. The package was topped by a large bow.

What was it? What did it mean?

Mordechai closed his eyes for a moment and tried to replay his conversation with Al-Hassani in his mind. The assassination of Sa'id. The Libyans. Iran. Turkey's veiled threat against the U.S. What was he missing?

And then it came to him.

In his anger, he had heard the words but hadn't truly registered them.

Hadn't Al-Hassani insisted that he would go away neither "empty-handed" nor "disappointed"?

Was this what he had meant? Should he open the box? Perhaps it would be better to wait and let someone on the prime minister's staff open it and evaluate its contents.

He was daydreaming, of course.

There was no way they could run off, like in the movies. Everything they had worked for was on the line, and they had to keep their eyes on the ball.

But it was at times like this that Bennett resented where he was. He hadn't sought this job. He'd never wanted to be a "point man for peace." He'd been drafted by a president to whom he couldn't say no, and now he was in too deep for an easy exit.

Or was he? He had money—$22 million and change socked away from his years at GSX. It couldn't buy him happiness, but it could buy him a change of pace. Maybe it was time to enjoy it for once in his life. Maybe it was time to lavish it on the woman who'd swept him off his feet.

Bennett was suddenly overcome with the desire to be with Erin, to hear her voice, even for a moment, to talk about their wedding, their honeymoon, their lives beyond the White House. He tried to imagine the look she would have the moment he told her how much he had stashed away and that she could spend it on anything she wanted—houses, travel, the horse farm near Winchester she was always talking about buying someday.

Whatever she wanted, he would give it to her. He didn't care how much it cost. All he wanted to do was make her happy, and knowing she couldn't care less about money made him want to spend it on her all the more.

Bennett grabbed the phone to give her a call when an instant message popped up on the screen. It was from Aleksandr Golitsyn's private account.

"Jonathan, is that you? We need to talk."

It was only the second contact Bennett or anyone in the White House or State Department had had with any top official in Moscow in nearly two days. He couldn't afford to ignore it. But was it really Aleksandr Golitsyn, the foreign minister?

The message was in English. The cursor was blinking. Someone was waiting.

Bennett started with the obvious. *"are we still on for dinner tonight at six?"*

"We were scheduled for eight o'clock, were we not, Jonathan?" came the reply.

It was formal, carefully typed—one of Golitsyn's trademarks—and whoever it was, he or she had gotten the time right.

"oh, right, eight—at marko's?" Bennett replied, still probing, now sending blind copies of each transmission to McCoy.

"Jonathan, please, you detest Marko's. It's time to check out the Red Garden."

Bennett pulled back from the screen.

It was true he hated the food at Marko's, though it was one of Moscow's elite restaurants, akin to The Palm in Washington. But the Red Garden? Golitsyn and Bennett had never been there. No one Bennett knew had ever been there. The Red Garden was a nightclub owned by Sergei Ilyushkin, a rendezvous for anti-American and anti-Semitic writers and activists and allegedly a house of ill repute. Golitsyn had spent his whole life fighting the very Fascists and corruption the Red Garden had come to represent. There was no way this was the Russian foreign minister, unless . . .

"i wouldn't be caught dead at the red garden," Bennett typed back. *"neither would the aleksandr golitsyn i know."*

Bennett waited. But there was no reply.

Was it a setup? Had something happened to Golitsyn? *Was* it Golitsyn?

A separate IM popped up from McCoy. *"you think it's really him?"* she asked.

"i don't know. . . . who else could have known about the specifics of our meeting tonight? . . . but something doesn't add up."

"why wouldn't he just call you by phone?"

"good question . . . maybe . . ."

But just then another IM from Golitsyn came in. *"Your Naina—may she rest in peace—brought you up well, Jonathan. FCFF."*

Bennett was stunned.

Only one other person in the world besides Erin and his parents knew the name Naina Petrovsky, or that she had passed away exactly six years ago to the day. Only Aleksandr Vasiliy Golitsyn.

Almost two years earlier, Bennett had told Golitsyn the story of the woman who had practically raised him like her own son. He had told his Kremlin colleague about Naina's passion for freedom and her lifelong fear of both the Communists and the Fascists. He remembered the conversation as if it had occurred just the night before.

They had been dining at Marko's. McCoy had worn a stunning black designer gown and diamond earrings Bennett had bought her at Tiffany's for her birthday. Golitsyn spent the evening warning them about the growing support for Ilyushkin and the LDPR. Bennett, meanwhile, had gotten violently ill on a bad piece of fish. It was the last time they'd ever stepped foot into Marko's, and that day Bennett had vowed never to do so again. Only Golitsyn could have known all that.

And then there was the instant message's closing—*FCFF*.

In the years before her death, whenever Naina had sent Bennett letters from Moscow, she had always signed them with the only English letters she knew, *FCFF*. It was her own little code with a young man she considered her son.

Fight the Communists; Fight the Fascists.

Bennett suddenly remembered how much Golitsyn had liked that anecdote. Ultimately, that is what had saved Russia in the early nineties, Golitsyn had said—a million little acts of dissent and defiance, including those of an elderly *babushka* few others in the world had ever heard of, much less known.

"so, my friend, it is you," Bennett wrote back. *"you had me worried."*

"My apologies, Jonathan, I did not mean to worry you, but I am not in a place where I can talk right now."

Bennett was struck by the anxious tone in Golitsyn's message.

"what's wrong, aleks?"

"I have only a few minutes. I have just come from a meeting with the head of the FSB. He believes Yuri Gogolov and Mohammed Jibril are back in Moscow and that Al-Nakbah may be behind the attack on Washington. He also believes

that Gogolov, Jibril, and their forces may be planning another attack, either on the U.S. directly or on an American target overseas."

Color drained from Bennett's face. The heretofore cryptic reference to the Red Garden suddenly made sense.

Yuri Gogolov—strategist for the LDPR. Mohammed Jibril—operational leader of Al-Nakbah. Both worked with and for Sergei Ilyushkin, the face of the Russian ultranationalist movement. Together they were planning another attack against the United States.

The instant message continued: *"Our top security officials now suspect that Gogolov and Jibril are working with someone within the Russian government, possibly here in the Kremlin itself."*

A mole? A traitor inside the Kremlin? The thought horrified Bennett, but it made sense. Without inside help, it would have been almost impossible for Al-Nakbah forces to penetrate flight 6617. The pieces were starting to fall into place.

"I am afraid that I cannot meet for dinner tonight," Aleksandr Golitsyn continued. *"But you must know three things. First, I am working to set up a meeting with you and President Vadim, probably tomorrow. Second, a manhunt for Gogolov and Jibril and their thugs is being planned at this very hour. Third, I will brief President Vadim's chief of staff and get back to you as soon as I have something solid.*

"In the meantime, I implore you—stay at the embassy. Do not go out. If Gogolov and Jibril are in the city, you and Erin are not safe."

14

★ ★
★

Bennett checked his watch.

Neither he nor McCoy, or any of the president's top advisors, had gotten much sleep in the past twenty-four hours, nor were they likely to anytime soon, and tensions were running high. Bennett and McCoy joined the president, huddled with his National Security Council in the White House Situation Room, via secure videoconference. It was the third emergency meeting in the last twelve hours, and National Security Advisor Marsha Kirkpatrick now briefed the president.

"Mr. President, based on the intel from Foreign Minister Golitsyn—sketchy though it was—we have beefed up forces on our borders. We've mobilized additional forces to safeguard airports, trains, ports, and power plants. We're coordinating leads with the FBI and the CIA counterterrorism center. And I just completed a conference call with over two hundred state and local law enforcement officials to brief them on the Al-Nakbah threat. At this point, I think the question is . . ."

A military aide knocked on the door of the Bubble.

McCoy slipped out of her seat to answer it. A moment later, she came back with a sealed envelope, which she handed to Bennett. He scanned the message inside and handed it back to her. This was the breakthrough they'd been working for since the crisis began.

Bennett cleared his throat and said, "Excuse me, Mr. President."

"What have you got, Jon?"

"We just heard from Foreign Minister Golitsyn again."

A hush came over the NSC.

"And?" said MacPherson.

"Nothing more on the threat, sir, but President Vadim is ready to talk. He's invited Erin and me to the Kremlin."

Bennett could see the president clench the arm of his chair.

"When?"

"He wants to meet in less than an hour—at nine o'clock sharp."

Yuri Gogolov carefully opened the manila envelope.

Inside was a photocopy of President Vadim's latest internal polling results, numbers so new Vadim himself hadn't even seen them yet. Three years earlier, Gogolov and Ilyushkin had paid handsomely to buy an ally inside the Kremlin. And now their investment was finally paying off.

Gogolov's pulse quickened as he scanned the data. Vadim's job-approval rating had dropped sixteen points in less than seventy-two hours. Only one in three registered voters felt "good" or "very good" about the job the embattled Russian leader was doing. Fifty-one percent of Russians now disapproved of Vadim's performance. The rest were undecided.

What's more, a stunning 71 percent of Russians believed Vadim should withdraw the Russian ambassador from Washington. And 65 percent believed Vadim should expel all Americans from Russian soil for at least one full year.

Gogolov could only imagine the look on Andrei Zyuganov's face when he'd first seen the numbers. As Vadim's chief of staff and senior political advisor, it would fall to Zyuganov to bring the bad news to the president of the Russian Federation. Gogolov just wished he could be in the room when it happened.

He flipped through a few more pages and found something even more intriguing. Zyuganov's political team was polling in the U.S., too, and the data were striking. President MacPherson's numbers were already down nine points. A mere 41 percent of Americans now approved of the job MacPherson was doing—the lowest since he came to office—while 48 percent disapproved and 11 percent remained undecided. And if that weren't enough, 62 percent of Americans now said they felt MacPherson was "too quick to use military force to resolve international conflicts" and "unwilling to exhaust all diplomatic possibilities."

Gogolov sipped his cup of hot *chai* and smiled to himself. *What would the numbers be when his little operation was complete?*

Mordechai was desperate.

He had tried calling Bennett for the past half hour. He'd tried paging and e-mailing him as well. Thus far, however, he had struck out, and he was quickly running out of time. Frantic, he called the Israeli Foreign Ministry.

"Miriam, this is Eli Mordechai," he said in breathless Hebrew to the aide who picked up his call. "I need to get through to Jonathan Bennett at the U.S. Embassy in Moscow. . . . Yes, it is an emergency. . . . I tried that. . . . Of course I tried that—that is why I need your help. . . . OK, call me back at this number as soon as you track him down. . . . Yes, I will be waiting in my room. . . . Thank you."

Mordechai set down his satellite phone and tried to steady his nerves. He glanced back at the open package on his bed and the stacks of opened files sitting all around him. It was a gold mine, an intelligence operative's dream. But what good would it do if he couldn't get the information into the right hands in time?

"This is CNN breaking news."

National Security Advisor Marsha Kirkpatrick grabbed the remote and turned up the sound. "Mr. President, you'd better see this."

MacPherson looked up to find a live report from the U.N. headquarters in Manhattan.

"CNN can now report that the French ambassador to the United Nations has just introduced a resolution before the U.N. Security Council condemning the United States government for shooting down a Russian airliner earlier this week, killing all 173 people on board, including 41 children.

"French officials are calling on the secretary general to convene an emergency

session of the Security Council tonight to bring the resolution to an immediate vote. Sources tell CNN that France already has all but three members of the Security Council behind their resolution. Great Britain and Poland are believed to be opposed, as is, of course, the United States. As of this hour, the Russian ambassador to the U.N. has refused to comment on the resolution, but everyone is expecting the Russian Federation to support the resolution.

"Now, there has been some confusion here in the last few hours. It was originally rumored that Libya would introduce this resolution. But CNN has learned that late last night, Salvador Lucente, the increasingly influential foreign minister for the European Union, suggested that for such a resolution to be taken seriously by the global community, it should actually be introduced by one of the permanent members of the Security Council and preferably by a major NATO ally. By this morning, French and Libyan officials had begun talks in New York and Paris, and—as we just reported—the two countries struck a deal only minutes ago."

The car phone rang.

Bennett didn't even look up. He was reviewing his notes for the Vadim meeting and trying to ignore the rocks and bottles being thrown at their motorcade as they raced through the streets of Moscow surrounded by a full Russian military escort.

McCoy checked the caller ID but didn't recognize the number. Still, she picked up the phone, if for no other reason than to keep it from bothering Bennett.

"Hello?"

"Erin, thank God it is you—this is Eli—I must talk to Jonathan."

"Dr. Mordechai, it's good to hear from you. But can he call you back? He's right in the middle of—"

"No, no, Erin, this is urgent. It is about his meeting with President Vadim."

McCoy was caught off guard. How could he possibly have known where they were heading? No one outside Vadim's office and the NSC knew. No one was supposed to know. McCoy wasn't sure what to say. She didn't want to lie to a man she respected so much, but she certainly wasn't authorized to confirm the meeting.

"Dr. Mordechai, really, I'm so sorry, but I can't—"

"Erin," Mordechai insisted, "please, I must talk to Jonathan before he talks to President Vadim."

Bennett could see the question in McCoy's eyes.

They had only a few minutes. He wasn't about to take a social call, even from his friend and mentor.

His eyes drifted to the phone in McCoy's left hand and the engagement ring sparkling on her finger. It was a spectacular two-carat diamond in an eighteen-carat-gold setting from Tiffany's. He'd bought the diamond itself on a business trip to Johannesburg years before. It hadn't been for anyone in particular at the time, just for "Mrs. Someday," and it had cost him only a third of what it would have cost retail in the States. Had he known at the time it was going to be for Erin McCoy, he'd have easily paid ten times that amount.

The band was a little large. They'd agreed to get it resized in London or Washington on their return trip. But McCoy didn't seem to mind in the least. Bennett had the sudden, almost irresistible urge to kiss her.

She could tell, and smiled. "Later," she whispered, pointing out the window.

They were pulling into the Kremlin through the Borovitskaya Tower gate. Bennett knew she was right. They were out of time, but that hardly made his desire go away.

"You promise?" he whispered back.

McCoy nodded, her eyes sparkling like the diamond on her hand. He would hold her to it. And she knew it. Yet she promised anyway. Why? What had he ever done to deserve someone like her?

Suddenly, McCoy hit the speaker button, snapping Bennett back to reality.

"Dr. Mordechai, it's Jon."

"Jonathan, thank the Lord it is you. Now listen carefully, both of you."

"We'd love to, but I'm afraid you've caught us at a bad time. Can we call you back in a few—"

"No, no, Jonathan, you do not understand. I am in Babylon, and I have struck oil, as it were. Last night, President Al-Hassani gave me a large wrapped box as a present. I was not going to open it. But then I thought . . ."

"Dr. Mordechai, we've got less than a minute."

"Yes, yes, I am sorry. I will be quick. Inside the box were copies of Saddam Hussein's personal files on his relationship over the years with Vladimir Zhirinovsky and Sergei Ilyushkin and the entire ultranationalist movement inside Russia. At first I had no idea why he would have given me such files. But I have been up all night studying them and . . ."

The motorcade was pulling through another heavily guarded gate inside the Kremlin grounds.

Mordechai's tone suddenly changed. "Jonathan, what if the target wasn't really Washington at all?"

Bennett shot McCoy a quizzical look. It was obvious she didn't get it either. Dr. Mordechai was perhaps the most brilliant man he knew. He loved the man like his own father. But he had neither the time for a Socratic dialogue nor the chutzpah to simply hang up on him midsentence.

"I'm not following."

The motorcade began descending into a secure, underground parking garage.

"What if the real target was Moscow?"

"What do you mean?"

"Let us just assume for a moment, for the sake of argument, that the Aeroflot jet *was* hijacked by Al-Nakbah. . . ." A flash of static garbled the connection. ". . . they could not possibly have believed the attack on the White House or the capital would be successful, right? They had to have known the president would order the plane shot down, right?"

McCoy took that one. "But if whoever planned the attack *knew* the plane would get shot down, why do it at all?"

"Ah," said Dr. Mordechai, "but what if *that* was the point?"

Bennett was almost out of time. "What if *what* was the point?" he pressed.

"What if the point of the attack was to prov—"

The call seemed to cut off. Bennett cursed, then shook his head and apologized. The bulletproof sedan came to a halt.

"Hello, hello?"

It was Mordechai's voice. They were still connected.

"We're still here, but we can barely hear you. Say that last part again."

"I said, what if the whole point of the attack was to provoke a political crisis in Moscow?"

"A diversion?" Bennett asked.

"No, a prelude."

"To what?"

"A coup."

15

Andrei Zyuganov entered from a side door.

He shook hands with Bennett and McCoy—firm, polite, nothing more—then led them from the waiting area into his spacious, well-appointed office near the center of the Kremlin. His executive assistant had already offered them coffee and been turned down. He did not make the offer again.

Barrel-chested with thick, sturdy legs and a rapid, purposeful gait, Zyuganov was nevertheless a small man, a good six or seven inches shorter than Bennett. Yet his very presence seemed to rearrange the molecules in the room.

At sixty-one, he was a man who possessed raw political power, and everything about him projected that simple reality, from his meticulously tailored clothing to the ubiquitous retinue of aides and security men scurrying around him to the rows of power photos lining his office walls.

Andrei and Vadim meeting in New York with the U.N. secretary general.

Andrei dining with Yeltsin and Clinton during the G8 summit in Denver.

Andrei as a young aide (still with a full head of hair) at Gorbachev's side at the Reykjavik summit with Reagan.

Andrei and Vadim greeting the Ayatollah Khomeini at a palace in Tehran.

This was a man who both understood the power he possessed and appreciated its trappings. So why, thought Bennett, did Andrei Zyuganov project such bitterness?

The son of Russian elites—his elderly father was once the chancellor of Moscow University, and his mother had been a highly regarded nuclear physicist—Zyuganov had always lived in comfort and had always been politically well connected. He was rumored to be a distant relative of Gennady Zyuganov, the longtime head of the Communist Party of Russia, the country's third-largest political party, though Andrei had never confirmed that. To the contrary, he insisted that he was a Democrat and had always positioned himself to work for reformers, so long as they were reformers on the rise.

Still, the man's face was etched with a permanent scowl. He squinted constantly, as though he might own glasses but was too vain to wear them. And, whether he meant to or not, he had a way of making people feel that though he would tolerate their presence, he was, in fact, thoroughly disgusted with them. Bennett had long ago concluded this was no act, and he had no doubt it was no theatrical performance today.

Nevertheless, Bennett had come to respect Andrei Zyuganov. He wasn't the kind of guy with whom you'd want to go out on the town for a drink. But the man knew what he wanted and pursued it aggressively. He could state his case, argue the fine print, and when necessary—but not a moment before—cut his losses and walk away from even the most important deal with his dignity and reputation intact.

"Andrei, thanks again for providing for the crowd-control forces around the embassy and for the police escort to get us here," Bennett began as Zyuganov straightened some papers on a desk the size of an aircraft carrier. "I doubt we could have made it here otherwise."

"The president wanted you here on time. That is how we do business."

Zyuganov picked up the phone on his desk, whispered something neither Bennett nor McCoy could make out, and then motioned toward French doors on their left. "President Vadim will see you now."

McCoy entered first.

The sight took her breath away, but it also made her sad. Of all the times she had been to the Kremlin, she had never been in the president's ceremonial office—the working residence, yes, in what was once the Soviet Council of Ministers Building, and the Great Kremlin Palace as well, built from 1838 to 1849 for Czar Nicholas the First as a monument to Russian history and the glory of the Russian military. But never here.

In the past, Vadim had always tried to keep their meetings relaxed and informal. Often it was just Vadim, Foreign Minister Aleksandr Golitsyn, Bennett, and her. Occasionally Zyuganov would be there as well. Several times E.U. foreign minister Salvador Lucente had joined them. Once Palestinian prime minister Sa'id had come for a two-day visit.

The press conferences and state functions were always held in the fanciest of settings, of course, but never the private meetings. Vadim, in fact, had once told her specially that he wanted to create a warmer, more intimate setting for the peace talks, something easily lost amid the Kremlin's opulent decor; white colonnades; dark gray marble floors; twenty-foot ceilings; and dozens of mounted swords, pistols, and paintings of the czars and their kin.

But clearly something had changed.

As they entered the elegant, pale green-and-white oval hall of the Senate Palace, adorned with enormous crystal chandeliers, the Russian flag and coat of arms, portraits of great Russian military generals, and one of the largest fireplaces she had ever seen, it became painfully clear to McCoy that all pretense of informality had been swept away.

They were not being ushered in to see an old friend and colleague, but into the presence of a man who suddenly felt a desperate need to reassert his relevance.

Vadim bade them sit, and they did.

He had always struck Bennett as a rather gentle man, particularly in contrast to Zyuganov's fierce intensity, but today all of that kindness had evaporated.

Vadim's dark blue eyes were icy, his pale Russian face brooding. He was about Bennett's height and weight, though fifteen years his senior, with close-cropped blond hair and a swimmer's build. He had, in fact, competed on the Soviet men's swim team during the 1976 Olympics and won a medal in one of the relays—though Bennett couldn't remember which—and he still swam at least an hour every morning before attending to his official duties.

Highly decorated as a major general in the Red Army, Vadim got out of the military in the early 1990s and went into politics not long after the collapse of the Soviet Union. Twice elected the mayor of St. Petersburg— first in a squeaker, then in a landslide—he was later handpicked by Vladimir Putin to be the Russian interior minister, then energy minister, then foreign minister, and eventually vice premier. Finally Putin appointed Vadim head of his party and heir to his political throne, and he had essentially been unchallenged ever since.

Foreign Minister Golitsyn nodded at them but did not smile. Zyuganov took out a fountain pen and opened a leather binder to take notes. No comments. No warmth. Nothing but silence and hard stares.

Bennett took the hint and began. "Mr. President, gentlemen, thank you for inviting Erin and me here tonight."

When Vadim said nothing, Bennett cleared his throat and continued.

"Let me begin by repeating what President MacPherson said during his televised address on Wednesday. He and the first lady would like to express their personal condolences to you, to the Russian people, and particularly to the families and friends of the innocent people who lost their lives in Tuesday's tragedy.

"Second, the president remains committed to the rapid return of all the bodies we are able to recover, as well as all personal effects and, of course, in time, the wreckage of the jet itself.

"Third, the president would like to work with your government to open a joint investigation into how this hijacking happened, who was responsible, what their intentions were—and may still be—and how further steps can be taken to prevent the future hijacking of Russian aircraft and to ensure the safety of Russians and all people entering the United States by air travel.

"Finally, President MacPherson would like to discuss with you whether an economic aid package of some kind might be helpful to assist the Russian people through a very difficult time. Of course, such packages are not the sole discretion of the president. They must be approved by our Congress. But I think you will find the American government and the American people very understanding of the challenges you and your country face at this difficult time."

This was where he was most likely to blow off his own foot, Bennett knew. He had argued strenuously in the NSC against raising the notion of an aid package. It was true that the Russian economy—overly dependent on oil and gas revenue and thus far resistant to diversification—was sinking fast. And it was also true that the U.S. had no interest in seeing a partner for peace such as Russia remain in such economic trouble for long. Still, the notion of offering economic aid amid such bilateral tensions struck Bennett as, at best, sending a mixed message, and at worst, downright impolitic. Nevertheless, the NSC—led by the president—had unanimously overruled him.

MacPherson wanted no ambiguity: the U.S. desired to work with Moscow toward peace and prosperity and would let nothing stand in its way.

Bennett wasn't so sure it would be read that way. And for a moment, the room was silent. McCoy shifted in her seat. Bennett tried to make eye contact with Golitsyn, but the man seemed determined not to return his gaze until his boss broke the ice.

There was almost palpable discomfort in these men. But it was more than that that made Bennett uneasy. Bennett couldn't put his finger on it, but a sense of foreboding seemed to be overtaking him.

"I must say," Vadim began, "that the offer of an American economic package to my country is so out of the question, so unhelpful at this moment, as to be curious why it would even be raised."

Bennett leaned forward to speak. Vadim held up his hand and continued. "Please—do not interrupt me, Mr. Bennett. You have stated your case. I will respond, briefly, candidly, and then allow you to return to your embassy."

Allow? thought Bennett. *How chivalrous.* He shook it off. He couldn't let himself get defensive. This wasn't personal; it was politics.

"The Russian people," Vadim continued, "are not in need of

patronizing handouts. They are in need of compensation for a wrong that has been done to them. And frankly, I must confess that I am curious why no mention was made of American compensation to victims of this crime."

Crime? Compensation? The words hit Bennett like a punch in the stomach. Was Vadim suggesting that self-defense was now a crime? Perhaps he was simply referring to the hijacking itself as a crime, which of course it was. But how would that make the U.S. government liable for compensation? Was this whole thing about money after all?

Bennett had no idea how to respond. Not only hadn't the NSC given him any guidance on the issue of compensation, the subject hadn't even come up.

Bennett's mandate was crystal clear: keep relations between the U.S. and Russia from derailing. To do so he had to stick with his talking points.

"President Vadim, I will certainly relay the question to my government, but I believe a discussion of compensation is premature. What is needed immediately is a joint investigation, with full cooperation between U.S. and Russian security and intelligence services. We need to know who the hijackers were, what they wanted, and how they were able to seize the plane," Bennett stressed.

"What evidence does the U.S. have that the plane *was* hijacked?" Vadim asked.

Bennett was floored. "Mr. President, I'm afraid I'm not quite sure what you're getting at."

"It is a simple question. Have you, for example, recovered the black box?"

"Not yet," Bennett admitted.

"Any of the flight-data recorders?"

"We're still looking."

"It has been almost four days."

"The wreckage stretches for miles."

"Have you recovered the bodies of the so-called hijackers or their weapons?"

So-called? Was this some kind of negotiating tactic, or was Vadim serious?

"We have recovered pieces of six handguns so far, all believed to have been carried by the various security details on the flight," said Bennett.

"But none that have been identified as belonging to these so-called hijackers?"

"The investigation is ongoing."

"I noticed a new story on the Associated Press wire, indicating that the Aeroflot flight crew was a last-minute substitution for the regular flight crew, and that this new crew regularly flew a direct route from Moscow to Washington Dulles, rather than to JFK," Vadim said. "The story seemed to suggest there is a bit of confusion over whether the pilot may have thought he was supposed to fly to Dulles, since that was his normal habit. Does your government believe this has any relevance?"

Bennett had no idea what he was talking about. He'd neither seen the story nor been briefed on it. But the whole notion was ludicrous. Flight plans were logged and programmed long before takeoff. Flight crews rarely made a mistake like this, and there was no way any pilot could have missed the message of the two F-16s.

Bennett felt his skin crawl. He had the sudden urge to cancel the meeting and get McCoy out of here, but protocol made him stay.

"What exactly are you suggesting, Mr. President?"

"I am simply asking questions, Mr. Bennett."

Bennett weighed his words carefully, but he had to respond. "I must tell you candidly, Mr. President, that your questions sound like veiled accusations, and I want to make sure I clearly convey to my government both the letter and the spirit of our conversation."

Vadim said nothing.

"Are you suggesting," Bennett continued, "that my government shot down an unarmed civilian passenger jet *without provocation?*"

Vadim leaned forward and set his hands on his desk. "I am suggesting nothing, Mr. Bennett. I am simply asking questions. But let us be candid. There are many in my country, and some in my own government, who believe your president has gotten—how shall we say?—a bit 'trigger happy' in recent years, even when the evidence for the use of military force is, well, let us just say a bit thin."

"That's a serious charge to make of a friend," Bennett said. He could feel the blood rising up the back of his neck. His ears burned. His face felt flushed.

"These are serious times," Vadim replied.

Keeping quiet wasn't his strong suit, but Bennett tried to hold his tongue anyway. Where was the friend he had known so long? How many hours had he and McCoy spent with Vadim, trying to make peace in the Middle East? Now the man was trying to extort cash out of the American people for a crime they hadn't committed. How was that possible? And what had happened to Golitsyn in the hours since his last e-mail? Why was nothing being said of the threat posed by Al-Nakbah, or the manhunt for Gogolov and Jibril?

Storm clouds had again gathered over the city, but rain was not expected until Sunday. From where he sat, Bennett could now see shadows moving through the gardens. His sense of unease was growing, and he glanced at McCoy. Did she feel it too?

Vadim motioned to Zyuganov, then whispered something in the man's ear. Zyuganov picked up one of the phones on Vadim's desk and punched a button to get an open line. It didn't work. He punched another button, then a third and a fourth.

And suddenly there was a high-pitched whistle piercing the quiet.

16

"Jon, get down."

Before he realized what was happening, McCoy grabbed his shirt and tie and pulled him to the floor, covering him with her body as a massive explosion rocked the building, sending chunks of plaster and concrete and shards of glass flying everywhere.

All power in the building suddenly went down, plunging them into darkness.

Soon flames engulfed the room, and the air filled with smoke.

Then came a second deafening explosion, and a third and a fourth. Bennett could barely see, but he could hear someone screaming in pain, and through the haze he thought he saw Golitsyn giving Vadim mouth-to-mouth as two bodyguards burst into the room.

Bennett could hear others shouting through the halls and over their radios for help. He could hear automatic gunfire in the courtyard, and then machine-gun rounds began ripping through the walls and furniture.

Agents dragged Vadim into Zyuganov's office, locked the three principals inside, and called for reinforcements.

Bennett felt a searing pain in his chest, but his first concern was for McCoy.

"Erin, you OK?"

"I'm fine, Jon," she whispered as she rolled off of him and scanned the room for a way of escape. "Just stay down."

McCoy reached for her Beretta.

It wasn't there, of course. For security reasons, she hadn't been allowed to bring it into the building. She grabbed her phone and tried to speed-dial the U.S. Embassy's emergency ops center, but there was no service. She reached for Bennett's satellite phone, but it was too damaged to use.

A half dozen more agents now rushed into the room, weapons drawn. They barricaded the two sets of French doors with as much furniture as they could find, then took up positions at the windows and opened fire at dozens of armed men who had appeared on the grounds.

Bennett and McCoy were ordered into a far corner, out of the line of fire. The news coming in over the agents' handheld radios was chaotic, but it was increasingly clear to McCoy that the compound was being overrun.

She could hear men screaming in pain and shouting curses at each other. Twice she heard someone shout for his colleagues to fall back as the building shook with more rounds of explosions. She could hear the rumbling of tanks in the streets, and she wondered whose side they were on.

Bennett covered his mouth with his hand.

He tried to keep the smoke and dust from filling his lungs. He began coughing violently. His hand was suddenly filled with bright red blood. He tried to call out but could barely breathe.

"*Erin . . .*"

McCoy carefully turned him over. It was as if his chest were on fire. The pain was excruciating. He saw McCoy recoil in horror. He moved his hand to his chest and felt his shirt soaked with blood. He wasn't sure if he'd been shot or had punctured a lung when she'd pushed him to the ground. All he knew for sure was that once again, Mordechai had been right.

The coup was under way.

Marine One lifted off from the south lawn of the White House.

The president sat just behind the lead pilot, with the First Lady at his side. Behind them were Chief of Staff Bob Corsetti and Secret Service Agent Jackie Sanchez.

As the chopper banked north, MacPherson waved to a group of on-lookers, then turned to a leather folder with their schedules and weekend call sheets.

Corsetti's phone rang first.

"This is a FOX News Special Report."

Marsha Kirkpatrick briefed Corsetti from the White House Situation Room on one phone as she took updates from Director Jack Mitchell at CIA on another. But for the moment the best information seemed to be coming from a FOX reporter broadcasting live from the roof of a hotel near the Kremlin.

The images were horrific. Hundreds of bodies lay in the streets. Tanks were on the move. Much of the city was on fire, and heavy machine-gun fire and explosions continued almost nonstop.

Kirkpatrick turned up the volume and put Corsetti on speakerphone.

"A feverish gun battle is under way in Moscow at this hour," the corre-spondent yelled as she crouched behind a brick wall. *"No word yet on the whereabouts or safety of President Vadim or his senior ministers. But I can tell you that many of the security forces brought in to protect the capital are actually leading the fight against the current regime.*

"Information is sketchy so far. Power and phone lines throughout the city have been cut off. All Russian radio and TV stations are off the air. We're operat-ing on generator power, but it's not clear at this point how long we'll be able to continue.

"Hold on. . . . I've just been handed . . . FOX News has just learned that the American Embassy has been attacked. . . . I repeat, the American Embassy in Moscow is under attack and is presently on fire. . . . We have unconfirmed reports that rocket-propelled grenades . . ."

The president came on the line. "Marsha, it's Mac."

Kirkpatrick grabbed the receiver and clicked off the speakerphone.

"Mr. President, the rebels have seized the airports. They've taken over the main terminals and are driving eighteen-wheelers across the runways to keep any planes from landing or taking off."

Agent Sanchez needed a decision—quickly.

"Mr. President, what would you like to do?"

"You think we should go back?" MacPherson asked.

"I do, sir."

"Bob, what about you?"

"I agree, Mr. President. Camp David is fine, but we're closer to the White House, and I think it sends the right message if you're there."

"Fine. Agent Sanchez, get us back on the ground. And, Bob, get on the line with State. I want Secretary Warner on a plane within the hour, headed back to D.C. He's obviously not going to Moscow, but there's no point leaving him in Beijing."

"You got it, sir."

Corsetti began working the phones while MacPherson turned his attention back to Kirkpatrick, still on the line. "Marsha, what do we know about Bennett and McCoy?"

"No word yet, sir."

"Were they still in Vadim's office?"

"So far as we know. But the situation is pretty chaotic at the moment, Mr. President. All but one of their DSS detail are confirmed dead. Bennett's driver is still in the parking garage but pinned down by heavy fire. And he hasn't been able to get through to Bennett or McCoy for the last half hour."

Through the night, McCoy could hear the gunfire getting closer.

Corridor by corridor. Office by office. No one could move. No one could sleep. She feared for Bennett's life. It wouldn't be long before he slipped into shock. He was losing too much blood.

McCoy gritted her teeth and tried to push away the fear of losing him. But that was impossible. She remembered the last time she had wondered whether she would lose the man she loved. Suddenly she was back at Dr. Mordechai's home in Jerusalem, kneeling over Bennett, desperately trying to stop the bleeding from two gunshot wounds he'd sustained from an Iraqi terrorist tied to Al-Nakbah.

Just like on that day, she could hear the thunder of gunfire crashing all around them. She could smell the gunpowder in the air. At that time, Bennett hadn't been a follower of Christ. She and Bennett hadn't even been dating. But she had loved him. From the moment she had met Jonathan Meyers Bennett, she had fallen in love with him. And the idea of not only losing him but letting him slip away into an eternity without Christ had been more than McCoy could bear.

She had begged God to save his body and his soul. And she had wept like she wept when both of her parents died, when she'd been left all alone in the world, without brothers or sisters or a family to call her own. God had answered both her prayers that day. Jon's eternal destiny was secure. But his body was once again in danger. And so she prayed for Jon again.

She wiped the tears from her eyes and the soot off the face of her watch.

It was just after four in the morning. As best she could tell, the rebels had blasted through the last defensive perimeter at the stairwells and elevators. McCoy knew the agents in the hallway were putting up fierce resistance. But by now it was obvious that they were outnumbered and outgunned. She had no idea how many agents loyal to the regime remained in fighting condition in the Kremlin compound, much less in this building. But unless Vadim's forces were able to mount a counterassault within the next few minutes, they were about to be overrun.

McCoy scanned the room, calculating their odds.

Of the nine agents barricaded in the office with them, four were down. Two lay dead of gunshots to the head and chest. Another had been blown to pieces in one of the early mortar attacks. A fourth lay writhing on the floor with an ugly wound to the right arm as two other agents fought to keep their comrade alive.

Her back pressed against the wall, McCoy stood up slowly, inched her way to the nearest shattered window, and peeked outside, only for an instant. Tracer bullets and flares lit up the night sky, thick with smoke.

Several nearby buildings were engulfed in flames. She could see no emergency equipment nearby, but she could see tanks—four of them— each of their turrets aimed directly at their floor.

These men were hunting Vadim, and McCoy had no doubt they would take down the entire building if they thought it necessary.

Another window shattered.

A flash bomb exploded a few yards from where McCoy stood. Again the room began to fill with smoke. The impact seemed to shake Bennett from his stupor. He was gasping for air and coughing violently.

The hallway suddenly erupted with automatic gunfire. The floors and walls shook violently as one grenade after another exploded on the other side of the French doors that locked them in. Two more agents went down. A third lay dying in front of her, badly burned by the explosion.

McCoy made her move.

She hit the deck and scrambled over spent shells and broken glass for a submachine gun and tossed an automatic pistol to Bennett. The remaining Russian agents didn't seem to care. They knew they were down to mere minutes. They had no hope of getting out of this room alive. The best they could do at this point was buy Vadim as much time as they could.

McCoy looked over at Bennett. He was in bad shape, but he would have to pull himself together enough to make a final stand. "Jon, grab that guy and follow me," McCoy shouted, pointing to one of the dead bodies a few feet from Bennett.

McCoy grabbed another dead agent by the lapels, dragged him to the inside wall near the hallway, dipped her hands in a pool of blood, and began smearing it all over her face and neck.

Bennett was obviously in intense pain. McCoy helped him pull the dead man to the wall and smear himself with the man's blood.

Then both sat with their backs to the wall, pulled the dead men onto their laps, and waited. They could hear people on the other side of the wall.

"They're attaching plastic explosives to each set of doors," McCoy whispered. "They'll be in here any second. You cover that side. I'll cover this side. Wait until at least three or four are in the room before you open fire."

"And then?" Bennett asked.

McCoy looked into his eyes. She could see how much pain he was in. It was everything she could do not to sob in his arms. He needed to be strong, for a few more minutes, at least. Which meant she had to be strong as well.

"And I'll see you in heaven, my love."

She leaned over and kissed him, her eyes blurred with tears. She could hear the sound of military helicopters approaching from the east. Their only hope was that the choppers brought a counterattack by forces loyal to Vadim.

Suddenly, the doors to their left and right exploded into a hundred pieces of burning wood and metal, followed by more flash bombs and tear gas.

Vadim's remaining protectors unleashed the last of their ammunition, but it was not enough. They were met by overwhelming force, and one by one they fell to the ground.

Gagging on the noxious fumes, unable to see, unable to aim, McCoy could wait no longer. There was no doubt the attackers were in the room now. She could hear their boots and the tinkle of spent shells hitting the floor as the rebels put the last of Vadim's forces out of their misery.

And then it was quiet. Eerily so.

"*Clear,*" one of the men shouted in Russian.

That was their cue, McCoy decided. Hidden behind two dead Russian agents, she knew she and Bennett had an element of surprise. It wouldn't be much. But they would not go down without a fight. She aimed toward the open room.

"*Now!*" she yelled.

17

★ ★
★

The room again erupted with gunfire.

A dead man on top of him, Bennett held the automatic pistol with both hands and began firing at shadows in the smoke.

He pivoted to the left—another shadow, another round—then turned back toward the center and pulled the trigger again and again until the gun stopped firing.

Though his eyes burned from the fumes, Bennett saw three men drop to the floor in rapid succession. His heart raced wildly as adrenaline surged through his system.

For an instant he forgot the searing pain in his chest, but he was not proud of what he'd just done. He was operating on pure instinct, the will to survive, but he had still taken human life, and suddenly he began to vomit.

"Forgive me, Lord Jesus. Help me. . . ."

And then it came.

A brilliant flash of white light.

Fire poured forth from a barrel across the room. Bennett tried to bury himself behind the corpse on his lap, but it was not enough. He cried out for McCoy.

And then all was quiet.

She knew instantly that Bennett was hit.

The second she heard her name.

She heard his pistol drop to the floor, then his cry of agony. She wanted to help him, to throw her body over his and take the bullets for him. But the best she could do for the moment was to turn to her left and aim at the man shooting at Bennett. She pulled the trigger and didn't let go, emptying the entire magazine at the man's chest.

Two bullets suddenly ripped through her own stomach.

McCoy tried to scream but couldn't. The machine gun dropped from her hands. She instinctively pulled into a fetal position. She couldn't think, couldn't breathe, couldn't move, and it suddenly dawned on her that if she didn't bleed to death, it would only be because she would suffocate first.

Ruth Bennett saw the horror unfolding on TV.

She called her son's cell phone. Like always, however, she got voice mail.

"Johnny, it's Mom—please call me—even for a moment. I just need to know you're OK. I love you."

She hung up and dialed a number she knew by heart: 202-456-1414.

"White House operator; may I help you?"

"This is Ruth Bennett. I need to know if Jon's OK," she said, her voice shaking.

"Mrs. Bennett, I'm afraid I don't have—"

"Then put me through to Bob Corsetti," she demanded.

"I'm afraid he's unavailable at the moment; can I—"

Ruth Bennett slammed down the phone and began to cry. All she wanted was to talk to her son. To know that he was safe. To tell him she loved him. *Was that really so hard? Wasn't a mother entitled to that much, at least?*

The smoke began to clear.

McCoy was breathing, but she didn't know how. Her eyes stung and filled with tears. Nevertheless, she counted eight—no, nine—heavily armed paratroopers standing about. But for the moment, at least, they didn't seem to be worried about her.

But what about Bennett? Was he still there? Was he still alive?

She couldn't turn her head. She couldn't move at all. Someone had gathered the weapons. She could see them laid out on the floor on the other side of the room. There was no way to reach them, of course, and they'd certainly been stripped of any remaining ammo.

A fire raged inside McCoy's stomach. She was soaked with sweat and blood and was shaking. She closed her eyes and tried to quiet her breathing.

"The Lord is my shepherd, I shall not want," she prayed quietly. *"He makes me lie down in green pastures; He leads me beside quiet waters. He restores . . ."*

She heard footsteps coming down the hall—two sets, maybe three. They were hard and purposeful and coming her way.

Using every ounce of energy she had left, she reopened her eyes and tried to focus. A shock of fear rippled through her body.

She was staring at the faces of Sergei Ilyushkin and Mohammed Jibril. She recognized Ilyushkin instantly, and she knew Jibril from CIA briefings and the FBI's Most Wanted List. She would have gasped out loud, but no sound came out.

Jibril's eyes were cold and lifeless. Ilyushkin's were wild with demonic delight. Neither spoke to her. Instead, both turned and crossed the room.

"Open that door," Ilyushkin ordered his men.

Within moments, President Vadim would be in these men's hands. So would control of ten thousand nuclear warheads.

Guilt consumed McCoy. Why hadn't she held her fire for these two?

It was foolishness, she knew. She and Bennett could never have retained the element of surprise that long, but still . . .

"He restores my soul; He guides me in the paths of . . ."

McCoy watched Jibril kick in the doors to Zyuganov's office. She knew what was coming next. Ilyushkin towered over his victims and taunted them.

McCoy kept praying softly.

"He guides me in the paths of righteousness for His name's sake. Even though I walk through the valley of the shadow of death, I fear no evil. . . ."

No one else said a word. Even the gunfire outside had stopped.

"Any last words?" Ilyushkin asked, his voice raw with vengeance.

". . . for You are with me; Your rod and Your staff, they comfort me. . . ."

The room was still.

All McCoy could hear was her own heart pounding wildly. She knew she and Bennett were next, if he was even still alive. That's just how revolutions were done—in Russia, anyway.

"Very well," said Ilyushkin with disgust. "I believe you all know Mohammed Jibril, at least by reputation. Mohammed, would you do the honors?"

"Of course," Jibril said in Russian. "It would be a pleasure."

Someone cried out, *"Oh no—please, no."*

McCoy couldn't see who it was. It sounded like Golitsyn.

"You prepare a table before me in the presence of my enemies; You have anointed my head with oil; my cup overflows. . . ."

"Turn around," Jibril grunted. "On your knees."

"Surely goodness and lovingkindness will follow me all the days of my life, and I will dwell in the house of the Lord forever."

Bennett heard Jibril chamber a round.

His mind was racing. Was there nothing he could do? Someone was talking—whispering, actually—though he couldn't make out the words.

It sounded like McCoy.

Bennett slowly turned back to the right despite the excruciating pain. McCoy's face was gray, her eyes at half-mast. She seemed barely conscious, but she was saying something. *What was it?*

The room shook with the explosion of the first round.

Bennett turned quickly to see who'd been shot, but two of Jibril's men stepped in behind Ilyushkin, blocking Bennett's view.

Then came the second round.

And then a third.

"Mr. President, you need to see this."

MacPherson was in the Oval Office, on the phone with Jack Mitchell at CIA, but there was something in the voice of his chief of staff that made him turn his head instantly.

He hung up and followed Corsetti into the chief of staff's adjoining office. Corsetti gestured toward the television on the far wall. And there, broadcast live to the whole world, was a Russian tank moving down Moscow's main thoroughfare, amid all the flames and carnage of the last two days.

It was Sunday evening in the Russian capital. The rebels claimed to have the upper hand, and few were disputing them.

But what had the world glued to their sets now was an elderly Russian woman, at least seventy or seventy-five years old. She was standing in the center of Tverskaya Boulevard, throwing rocks at a tank as it rumbled toward her, unyielding.

When the old woman ran out of rocks, she shook her fist at the tank, screaming at the top of her lungs, and suddenly, the tank stopped.

It tried to move right, but she moved right.

The tank feinted left, but she moved left.

The Oval Office was silent. MacPherson and Corsetti recalled the scene from Tiananmen Square in 1989 when a young Chinese man, determined to bring about democratic reforms in his blood-soaked country, faced off against a tank and thus the entire Communist government. Was it really happening again?

The rapid-fire patter of news anchors seemed to drift off midsentence, as each intuitively grasped that there was nothing they could say that would communicate more powerfully than the pictures they were beaming around the globe.

In a single moment, an old woman's defiance in the face of sheer barbarism seemed to capture the entire battle, its cost, its stakes.

The tank's turret popped open. A helmet-clad gunner emerged and began to scream back at the woman, who was still screaming at him.

Suddenly, the gunner drew his sidearm and pointed it at the woman's head.

MacPherson gasped. How could he just watch the murder of this innocent woman on television? He was the head of the world's only superpower. Wasn't there something he could do? Yet how could he do anything without risking all-out war with Russia?

A gunshot rang out. A puff of dust and smoke rose from the pavement to the right of the old woman as a bullet ricocheted into the street.

But the woman did not flinch.

Another gunshot to her left, closer this time, but still the woman did not flinch.

The gunner retreated into the tank. The turret closed. Again, the tank moved left, but the woman blocked its path. Then back to the right, but she held her ground.

MacPherson sat mesmerized. Words did not come. The office remained silent.

Thick, black smoke began to pour out of the tank's exhaust pipes and it began to move again, forward, toward the old woman. She took off her shoes and heaved them, one by one, with all her force, at the tank, now just ten yards away.

It would stop, right? It had to. These weren't monsters. Russia was a civilized country, emerging from a century of darkness.

But the tank did not stop.

Instead, it increased its speed, and before the world could think or react, it mowed down the old woman and with her, Russia's last line of defense.

18

★ ★
★

MacPherson gathered his team in the Situation Room.

CIA director Jack Mitchell began the latest briefing by explaining that ultranationalist rebels continued to battle with forces loyal to Vadim in five midsized cities in southeastern Russia and around several key Siberian oil towns. But for the most part, the data suggested the *putsch* was brilliantly conceived, almost flawlessly executed, and very near complete.

As of yet, no one had stepped forward to claim credit or declare himself the new czar of Russia. Still, there wasn't much doubt about who was behind the violence. Rumors had it that Sergei Ilyushkin's top advisors were making preparations for a nationally televised address by their supreme leader within the next several hours.

MacPherson put four questions on the table:

First, if Ilyushkin was the mastermind behind the coup, what might his immediate demands be? Second, what were his longer-term intentions? Third, what should be the administration's strategy to contain Ilyushkin? Fourth, were there any plausible scenarios for a surgical, preemptive strike to take out Ilyushkin and his allies and install an interim, pro-democracy, pro-Western regime?

Defense Secretary Burt Trainor responded to the last question first. "Mr. President, as sympathetic as I am to your desire to take Ilyushkin out, I'm afraid that does not appear to be an option at the moment. Based on the events of the past seventy-two hours, the man appears to have the support or sympathy of most of the Russian military's high command.

"I think we have to assume at this point that Ilyushkin has seized control of Russia's strategic nuclear forces. And, of course, his forces have surrounded not just the American Embassy but all of the NATO and other allied embassies. They control the fate of tens of thousands of Americans and other foreign nationals living, working, and studying inside Russia. And we believe they are holding Jon Bennett and Erin McCoy."

MacPherson turned to Marsha Kirkpatrick. "What are the scenarios by which we could launch missions to rescue Bennett and McCoy, as well as our embassy personnel?"

"I'm afraid there aren't any at the moment, Mr. President," Kirkpatrick responded. "In terms of the embassy, the Marines on the ground were able to get the fires out and are tending to the wounded. The staff have been working around the clock all weekend burning documents and destroying all critical communications equipment. At the same time, however, rebel forces have positioned antiaircraft batteries on the rooftops of every adjacent building. Even if we wanted to send in airborne forces right now, they would likely be shot down."

MacPherson leaned forward. "And Jon and Erin?"

"Sir, at the moment we don't have any good intel on where they are. We're not even sure they're alive. We do have one Kremlin source who escaped during the chaos. She says she saw Erin wounded but alive and being loaded into an ambulance. But we haven't been able to confirm that, and a check of local hospitals has turned up nothing."

MacPherson didn't want analysis. He wanted action, regardless of what the polls were telling him. "We can't just sit here and do nothing, people. The status quo is completely unacceptable, and I want detailed contingency plans on my desk by this afternoon. One for rescuing our embassy personnel. One for extracting Jon and Erin. And I want a full-scale plan for retaking the Kremlin. In the meantime, start by pre-positioning rapid-response strike forces at forward NATO bases, ready to carry out such plans on a moment's notice. Is that understood?"

MacPherson scanned the room so each of his principals could see the determination in his eyes. He could see the anxiety in theirs. The tension in the room was palpable, and he knew what everyone was thinking.

Was he really going to order U.S. forces into battle against a Fascist regime armed with nuclear weapons and obviously prepared to use devastating force?

Even he wasn't sure. But doing nothing was out of the question.

Jack Mitchell glanced at Corsetti, then back at the president. "Mr. President, you can count on the men and women of Central Intelligence to get you what you need as quickly and professionally as we possibly can. But I need us all to be crystal clear on one thing."

"What's that, Jack?"

"Sergei Ilyushkin is not simply a disciple of Vladimir Zhirinovsky. He's Adolf Hitler with thermonuclear warheads, and right now he's got ten thousand pointed at our heads."

Where was Erin? Was she alive?

That's all Bennett wanted to know. But whom was he going to ask? He had no idea where he was. He had no idea what day or even what month it was. His eyes and limbs felt like lead. Every part of his body ached. But all he could think about was Erin.

He tried to open his eyes, but he was slipping in and out of consciousness. The room was small, and the walls were bare and a disorienting bright orange. The paint smelled fresh. The bed was small, like a child's, forcing his feet to hang over the end. He realized he was wearing only a hospital gown. Two IV tubes were taped to his arm, and his hands were chained to the metal frame of the bed.

He tried to call out, but his mouth was dry and sticky, his lips chapped and raw.

How long had he been here?

Again his eyes felt heavy, and his head began to swim.

Erin? Where was Erin? Where was . . .

MacPherson knew he should head back to the Situation Room.

Ilyushkin's speech was set to begin in two minutes.

For Muscovites, it would air in prime time—9:00 p.m., Monday night, Moscow time—1:00 p.m. in Washington. But MacPherson knew it was not just 140 million Russians who were desperate to know about Sergei Ilyushkin and the regime that now controlled them. An anxious world waited as well.

With an enormous nuclear arsenal, the Russian Bear—however wounded, however weakened since her prime during the Cold War—was still a force with which to be reckoned. She could annihilate tens of millions of souls in the blink of an eye.

Was that Ilyushkin's plan? MacPherson wondered. *How closely did he intend to follow his mentor's playbook? How long did they have?*

Bennett was startled by someone barging through the door.

He had not seen or heard another human being since . . . *since when?* His mind was blank. The last thing he could remember was Mohammed Jibril executing the duly elected president of Russia, his foreign minister, and his chief of staff. *How long ago had that been?*

An orderly entered with a television on a cart, plugged it in, adjusted the picture, and then left as abruptly as he'd entered.

Bennett's mind reeled. He knew he must be a prisoner of the Sergei Ilyushkin regime. His life span had to be measured in days, if not hours. He couldn't remember eating. He couldn't remember talking. He could barely remember human contact of any kind.

And now they wanted him to watch television?

Bob Corsetti entered the Oval Office alone.

The president waved him in and glanced at the grandfather clock near the door. It was time to join the rest of the NSC in the Situation Room. But something was wrong. He could read it in Corsetti's strained expression.

"Something on your mind, Bob?" asked MacPherson.

"Mr. President, the others are worried," Corsetti began.

"They should be," MacPherson agreed.

"No, not just about Ilyushkin. They're worried about you."

MacPherson looked in his friend's eyes. They had known each other a long time. They had been through many battles together. Corsetti's counsel had won MacPherson two terms as governor of Colorado and two terms as president of the United States. So though MacPherson hated "constructive criticism" as much as any politician, he was, at least, willing to listen to a man with a track record of success.

"You guys afraid I'm going to take the country into a war we can't afford?"

"No, Mr. President," Corsetti said quietly, "into a war we can't win."

A test pattern appeared.

The signal was immediately picked up and simulcast by every broadcast and cable-news network in the U.S., as well as in most countries around the world. Then a digital clock appeared in the lower-left-hand corner of the screen, counting down from thirty seconds.

A hush settled over the Situation Room. Not since the Cuban missile crisis had the country been so close to war with Moscow.

Three, two, one . . .

The clock struck zero, and the picture faded in from black. On the screen was the new czar of Russia. But it was not—as expected—the face of Sergei Ilyushkin that a waiting world saw. It was, instead, the face of Yuri Gogolov.

19

★ ★
★

"Esteemed citizens of Russia and dear friends . . ."

Gogolov's eyes burned into the camera.

". . . today begins the resurrection of Mother Russia."

Eliezer Mordechai watched the speech on his computer.

He had no need of anyone translating the speech. He had been born in Siberia. He spoke Russian fluently. And the miracle of modern technology allowed him to download the broadcast directly from the Russian satellite feed.

Besides, there was something about being able to hear the cadence and rhythm of Gogolov's voice without a filter or middleman of any kind that seemed to provide an additional window into the man's soul.

"The new Russia seeks peace, not war. But she also demands justice, and she will not be deterred. Too long have the Russian people lived on the Titanic. *Too long have we known our ship of state was sinking even as we watched our leaders and their cronies emasculate our military and loot our national treasures.*

"Once we were the envy of the world, rich in culture, rich in history, the first to put a man into space. The world trembled in our presence. Today we are fast becoming a third-world country. In 1991, the year the Soviet Empire was allowed to fall apart, the average life expectancy for a Russian man was sixty-five years. Today it is fifty-nine—fifteen years below that of American men—and it continues to drop.

"Before 1991, no Russian went hungry. No Russian went without first-rate medical care. No one was abandoned. Everyone was cared for. Yet today, one in five Russians lives below the poverty line, earning an average of two hundred rubles a month—about thirty American dollars—not enough to survive on, much less live with dignity and respect. Why? What happened to us?"

Where was Ilyushkin? Mordechai wondered. *Why wasn't the man who had set this madness in motion seizing the spotlight?*

Mordechai's thoughts immediately flashed back to the files Al-Hassani had given him in Babylon just a few days before. According to documents in those files, Saddam Hussein had secretly paid Ilyushkin tens of millions of dollars to help Iraq circumvent international economic sanctions in what became known as the U.N. oil-for-food scandal. The documents specifically showed that Saddam wanted Ilyushkin to persuade Boris Stuchenko, then president of Lukoil, to buy embargoed Iraqi oil at cut-rate prices.

The plan was simple enough in concept: Stuchenko would resell the Iraqi oil on the global petroleum markets at a markup, thus making a fortune. Saddam would use the illegal proceeds to buy arms to prepare for another showdown with Washington. And Ilyushkin would use his share of the illicit profits to continue building an ultranationalist fifth column inside Russia in the hopes of one day taking over the Kremlin.

The files indicated that the scheme had been in operation since the early 1990s, and for most of the time it had worked like a charm—except for the fact that Saddam's regime had been toppled, Stuchenko was dead, and Ilyushkin was nowhere to be found.

Had Gogolov been paid off by Saddam as well? No, Saddam's correspondence with Ilyushkin and Zhirinovsky had never mentioned his name. How then had Gogolov climbed to the top of the greasy pole?

"What went wrong?" Gogolov continued, so calm, so dignified that he seemed more like an American CEO than a homicidal neo-Nazi. *"Are we without natural resources? Of course not. We are one of the biggest producers of oil and natural gas in the world. Are we without human resources? On the contrary, Russians are among the most educated and innovative people on the face of the earth. Then what has become of us?*

"I will tell you. Russia has been raped—devoured by men driven by greed insatiable and untamed. Take the late Grigoriy Vadim. Did you know our former

president had more than $23 billion stashed away in Swiss banks? Did you know that he was wholly bought and paid for by Boris Stuchenko, the Siberian oil baron for whom 'rampant corruption' is too mild a descriptor? It is true. But Stuchenko was getting restless. He did not like writing checks in the shadows. He wanted the world to know how big a player he was—head of Russia's largest oil company and owner of Russia's most corrupt politician. So Vadim and his forces paid two Chechen terrorists to have Stuchenko killed, and in so doing, they have set into motion a crisis with the United States that threatens to spin out of control.

"In due time, we will lay out the proof. We have much. We are gathering more. And you will be the first to know. But now you know why action had to be taken—now, this weekend, before it was too late. It was not pleasant. I do not pretend that it was. But it was necessary."

MacPherson couldn't believe what he was hearing.

Was any of it true? Had Vadim been on the take? Could he have conspired with Chechen terrorists to provoke a crisis with the U.S.? What would have been his motive?

The questions kept coming, but even as they did, the president found himself riveted by Gogolov's performance.

The man looked different from the grainy, slightly out-of-focus photos the FBI and CIA had of him. He seemed younger, in better shape, with a lean face, a sharp European nose, square jaw, and a thin, cruel smile. His golden hair was shorter, though not quite a crew cut, and his complexion was fairer, almost Aryan.

But those azure eyes were the same—intense and hypnotic—hidden though they were behind round, gold, wire-rimmed spectacles that almost made one forget that Gogolov was nothing more than a cold-blooded killer.

Ruth Bennett just stared at the television.

She could not remember a single time in all the years she had been coming to this beauty salon that it had been so quiet. It was usually a beehive of good gossip, and thus one of the few outings she looked forward to each month. But today was different. Everyone understood the stakes, and Ruth and the other ladies were glued to the set. What's more, they knew she had once lived in Moscow. They knew her son and future daughter-in-law were caught up in all this somehow. And when it was done, they would have a million questions, she had no doubt.

But what could she possibly tell them?

Who was this man Gogolov? What did he really want?

Something about his eyes, about the way he spoke, terrified her. And suddenly she was back in Moscow, newly married, caring for a baby, trying to survive in a city that seemed to hate Americans, in a country that openly threatened to bury them alive.

Her late husband, Sol, had loved their years in Russia. She had hated every minute—the parties, the constant travel, the constant fear that the KGB might be listening in on everything you said, the bone-chilling cold. Most of all she'd hated playing the "little woman," constantly leaving little Jon-Jon with some toothless nanny just to show up in public with her globe-trotting, chain-smoking, deadline-worshiping, emotional vacuum of a husband.

For what? To raise a son who resented everything about her?

She stared into Gogolov's soulless eyes, and her hands began to tremble. Call it a woman's intuition, a mother's instinct, a sixth sense. In that moment she knew this man was holding her son, and she knew she would never see him again.

☆ ☆ ☆

"Which brings me to the task at hand," said Gogolov.

"Due to the deaths of so many who fought for this liberation, the responsibility for rebuilding a new Russia falls to me. I did not ask for this task. But, however reluctantly, I have been persuaded to believe it is my destiny. Thus, I will devote all that I am to the task ahead. I will build a team around me of good and faithful servants of the people, men of honor and courage and unquestionable integrity. I will restore order in the streets and cleanse our capital from this stain of corruption.

"To begin with, I will order our security forces to round up those responsible, at home and abroad, for the rape of Russia, and I will not rest until justice has been done, nor will I ever forget those who have aided and abetted our enemies.

"As such, I hereby authorize the doubling of pay for every man and woman serving in our military and intelligence services. Those who have honored us, we shall honor. Moreover, I hereby announce a new initiative to modernize and expand our military. Over the next ten years, we will go from one million to three million active-duty personnel. We will also expand our intelligence and security services to a full one million officers over the same period. But we will do away with the draft. A new Russia demands a new military—a professional, motivated, highly trained force of the willing and the committed. We will recruit the best and the brightest Russia has to offer. We will pay them competitively. We will equip them with the latest technology.

"No longer will the United States be the world's policeman. No longer will Washington impose her will upon the rest of the world. No longer will she alone shape the world our children and grandchildren will inherit. I am, therefore, suspending relations with the United States, effective immediately. I have ordered our embassy in Washington to be shut down. I have ordered our ambassador to be recalled. I am also ordering all those holding a U.S. passport—including those working at the U.S. Embassy here in Moscow and in U.S. consulates throughout the Russian Federation—to leave Russian soil within the next seven days or risk imprisonment on suspicion of espionage.

"No other foreign citizens visiting or working in the Russian Federation will be affected. Indeed, in the days ahead I look forward to speaking by phone or in person with the leaders and ambassadors of Russia's friends and allies, beginning with members of the European Union with whom we see our future aligned.

"Have no doubt, sons and daughters of Mother Russia. I am aware that the responsibilities I have undertaken are enormous, and I do not take them lightly. But I do take them with confidence that our best days are ahead of us. Today is a historic day, my friends, the dawn of a new age, the birth of a new Russia—free, prosperous, rich, and strong, a Russia whose citizens are proud at home and have respect around the world—and I consider it my sacred duty to unite the people of Russia for this very purpose."

20

★ ★
★

The drugs were wearing off.

Bennett had tossed and turned for hours, unable to sleep yet unable to turn over, even onto his side, handcuffed as he was to the bed frame. Now the pain was excruciating, and he was alternately burning up with fever and chilled to the bone.

Since the end of the speech, Bennett's thoughts had toggled back and forth from worrying about Erin to worrying about Gogolov. For now he was consumed with the latter. *How had it come to this? How was it that the world's most wanted man now possessed the world's most dangerous weapons? And was Ilyushkin waiting somewhere in the wings? It didn't wash. Could he have been killed after leaving Vadim's office?*

Bennett tried to sit up but again felt the handcuffs cutting into his wrists. He stared at the bars of fluorescent lights on the ceiling, then closed his eyes and again tried to reconstruct the scene at the Kremlin.

He recalled Ilyushkin giving the gun to Jibril and Jibril telling Vadim, Golitsyn, and Zyuganov to turn around and kneel down. He had heard the gunshots—one, then another, then a third. Had there been four? He remembered only three. So who had walked out of that room alive?

Ilyushkin, he was suddenly convinced, had not.

Suddenly, Bennett heard voices and footsteps, and then keys. The door burst open. A guard unlocked his handcuffs.

"Get up," someone barked in English, pointing an automatic pistol at his face.

Two other guards forced him to dress at gunpoint. He was gagged, handcuffed again, wrapped with a blindfold, and led through what seemed like a labyrinth of hallways. He had no idea how long it had been since the last time he'd stood up, but the pain in his legs intensified.

His breathing was labored. With the gag in his mouth, he could barely draw enough air through his nose and was afraid he was about to suffocate or at least pass out.

After what seemed like ten or fifteen minutes, Bennett heard a door open and felt a blast of humidity. He was outside. Then he heard a car door open, and he was ordered into the backseat.

"What does Gogolov really want?" asked the president.

Marsha Kirkpatrick took off her half-glasses and leaned back in her chair.

MacPherson watched her as she considered the question. Six years in the White House as the national security advisor had taken its toll. MacPherson was actually surprised she'd stayed on this long.

"It's the worst-case scenario, Mr. President," she began. "Sergei Ilyushkin was the devil we knew. But I don't know what we're dealing with now. That was a very shrewd speech, and I suspect it went a long way toward calming a very anxious Russian citizenry. Gogolov hit all the populist angles while also staying true to the LDPR's nationalistic and pro-military objectives. He also sent a strong signal to Europe that he considers us the enemy, not them. That could complicate our lives enormously, depending on how Paris, Berlin, and Brussels react."

"You think he's trying to drive a wedge into NATO."

"No question about it. The question is *why*. Dividing NATO isn't an end in itself. It's a means. But to what? What does Yuri Gogolov want? Is he a true disciple of Zhirinovsky and Ilyushkin, something better, or something worse?"

"What could be worse?" asked the president.

Kirkpatrick paused for a moment, then said, "For one, Gogolov could have had Ilyushkin killed when he'd outlived his usefulness. And if that's the case, there's no telling what else he's capable of, including provoking a war with us."

Bennett finally felt the car slow down.

It entered what sounded like a parking garage or a tunnel of some kind. When the vehicle came to a complete stop, he was ordered to get out and start walking, a gun to his head, a guard holding each arm.

They trudged up a flight of stairs, went through a set of revolving doors, down a hallway, and stepped onto an elevator. No one spoke. The elevator rose for a long time. Bennett had little sensory data to go on. He suspected they were heading to the top floor of a large office building, or perhaps an apartment high-rise.

A bell rang, and the elevator door opened. He and his handlers got off, walked down another long hallway, and stopped. Now he could hear whispers. There were others around, and there was an echo.

For a fraction of a second he heard someone on a walkie-talkie, until it was abruptly turned off. Bennett cocked his head. He'd been here before. He recognized the ambient noise, the tone of the room. He ran through his mental Rolodex of all the places he'd been to in Moscow, trying to place it.

Suddenly Bennett's hands were uncuffed and he was roughly pushed down into a chair. His gag was removed, then his blindfold. He instinctively shielded his eyes, trying to adjust to such bright light.

It took a few moments.

When he looked up, he found himself in the presence of Yuri Gogolov.

He had been taken back to the Kremlin.

All thought of his own pain vanished immediately. Bennett had only one objective. He demanded to know where Erin was and to be taken to her immediately.

Gogolov took off his glasses to clean them. "You are in no position to make demands of me, Mr. Bennett. You will learn of her fate in due time."

Bennett's instinct was to lunge for Gogolov's throat. He wanted this man to suffer. He wanted this man to die a grisly, horrific death. But attacking Gogolov would do nothing to bring McCoy back to him. Indeed, if she was still alive, such a move could condemn her to certain death. And did he really think he would live through an attack on the new czar of Russia? The man was surrounded by bodyguards. Gogolov himself was trained to kill. He trained others to kill. Bennett would have no chance. It would be a suicide mission, and Bennett wasn't about to sacrifice himself for nothing.

With his makeup for television wiped away, Gogolov's face was even more pale in person, making his deep-set and almost hypnotic eyes all the more striking. His voice was soft and measured, his message concise.

"I would like you to write this down, Mr. Bennett, so there are no mistakes, no misunderstandings."

An aide stepped in and handed Bennett a pen and legal pad. His mind churning with conflicting thoughts and emotions, Bennett took them without question.

He was not used to feeling powerless. Back in Washington, the entire White House staff and State Department bureaucracy moved at his command. As the personal emissary of the president of the United States, he was given great honor and deference in capitals all over the globe. His motorcades stopped traffic. His speeches made headlines. Yet suddenly it was as if he were a slave in the presence of Pharaoh, as impotent as he was inconsequential. He began to feel numb.

"Take this down carefully," Gogolov began, utterly disinterested in Bennett's physical and psychological trauma. "In the pursuit of justice for those Russians who died aboard Aeroflot flight 6617, Russia expects reparations from the United States in the amount of $1 billion per passenger, as well as a formal American apology to the Russian people, passed by the Congress, signed by the president, and read aloud before the United Nations Security Council."

Bennett heard the words but was having trouble focusing. He wasn't used to taking dictation from Fascist dictators, and he had to force himself to record every word.

Gogolov waited for him to catch up, then continued. "If over the next twelve months the United States government can assure the Russian people—and the people of the world—that it means Russia no harm, the czar is open to reestablishing relations, albeit slowly.

"The new Russian Federation has no territorial designs or military ambitions with regard to the United States. Russia no longer believes in the efficacy of an East-West conflict. The times have changed. The world has changed. So long as the U.S. and her allies show no further hostility toward Russia and her allies—so long as Mother Russia's pursuit of her own economic and geopolitical interests is not interfered with—Washington need not be concerned with the government of Gogolov. After all, the Marxist-Leninist era is over. A new day has dawned, a day of unprecedented peace *and* prosperity for everyone of goodwill."

His right hand now cramped, Bennett finally finished writing and looked up.

"Now, as to your fiancée," Gogolov said without expression. "I am not unsympathetic to your love, Mr. Bennett. Miss McCoy was a beautiful young woman and a zealot for her country. But I am afraid she is no longer with us."

Bennett couldn't breathe.

He shook his head and felt the room begin to spin. He winced as shocks of intense pain now streaked through his body. He tried to suck in enough oxygen to keep from collapsing and keep him from breaking down and sobbing in front of this monster. He refused to give Gogolov the satisfaction.

No. He refused to believe she was dead.

They were lying. Gogolov was a liar. They were holding her hostage. He was using her as a bargaining chip. She was still alive, Bennett told himself again and again. *She had to be.* He couldn't live without her.

Gogolov signaled an aide, who brought over a rectangular velvet box, something in which a gold or diamond necklace might rest.

Bennett hesitated to open it. His hands began to shake.

"Take your time," Gogolov said gently. "I realize this is difficult."

The very sound of the man's voice nauseated Bennett.

Cautiously, Bennett opened the box, and his face went ashen. There, resting on velvet, was a severed bloody finger, still wearing his diamond engagement ring.

21

★ ★
★

Mohammed Jibril slipped into Tehran under the cover of darkness.

It had been almost a week since Gogolov's televised address and more than eighteen months since Jibril had been home. Everything had changed. He was now a top aide to the most dangerous man on earth, and he would be treated as such.

Iran's foreign minister met Jibril on the tarmac and whisked him into a bulletproof limousine. Flanked by three security vehicles, they drove to a nearby military base, where they boarded a waiting helicopter and were flown to the presidential retreat complex in the mountains overlooking the Iranian capital.

At daybreak, Jibril had breakfast with the ayatollah and Ifshahan Kharrazi, president of Iran, both of whom had already sent their greetings and congratulations for Jibril's new post and Gogolov's new government. Jibril began the meeting with the story of how he had masterminded the hijacking of Aeroflot 6617, conspiring with Andrei Zyuganov, President Vadim's chief of staff, to replace the copilot and Russian air marshals with men loyal to Al-Nakbah and to smuggle arms on board before takeoff. But this was just an appetizer.

The main course consisted of Czar Gogolov's suggestion that it was time to formalize the military alliance that had been developing between

Russia and Iran since the early 1990s and to show the Americans that a new global superpower was on the rise.

To that end, Jibril said, Gogolov was prepared to sell Tehran the twenty-five nuclear warheads they had been seeking for the better part of two decades.

No longer would the reactors at Bushehr and elsewhere be necessary. Nor would Iran's covert, subterranean nuclear research centers. Gogolov was willing to sell the warheads outright.

The price, of course, would be steep. There were also terms and conditions to which the ayatollah and the mullahs would have to agree without negotiation. But if a deal could be struck, the warheads could be in Tehran in fourteen days. They could be shipped by railway in standard freight cars, unlikely to attract attention. Russian technicians could then have the warheads attached to Iran's ballistic missiles, known as *Shahab*-3s—meaning "meteor" or "shooting star" in Farsi—by the end of September. And done properly, neither the Americans nor the Zionists would have a clue.

Still no word.

Ruth Bennett hung up the phone.

Somehow the White House staff always managed to sound pleasant, but they had to be getting annoyed by her calling three or four times a day. She didn't care.

Bennett was a man possessed.

He'd just been released from captivity and put aboard a State Department plane headed back to Washington. But thoughts of vengeance—not home—consumed him. Yuri Gogolov had stripped him of the only woman he'd ever had the courage to love. And for that he would pay.

Bennett stared out the window of the Gulfstream IV jet at the roiling North Atlantic, trying in vain not to think of Erin's severed finger in that box. Was she dead? Was she being tortured? Would he ever see her again? He knew he should pray, but he was seething with a rage that both frightened and inspired him.

Then suddenly he reached into his jacket pocket and tore up the letter of resignation he had planned to submit upon his return.

For weeks he'd been telling himself it was time to step down, settle down, become a husband, and get a life. Now everything had changed. If he was going to find a way to kill Gogolov, the last thing that made sense was to go back to Wall Street. He had all the military and intelligence resources he needed right where he was, a new DSS security team watching his back, and the ear of the president. He would stay at the White House and plot his revenge from there.

For starters, though, he needed to regain his strength, gather as much information as he could, and look for an opening he was sure would come. And there was something else. He picked up a satellite phone and dialed Orlando.

"*Mom?* It's Jon—they just let me go."

The fires in Moscow were now out.

A sense of order and calm was being restored throughout the capital and the country. For Russians, at least. For Americans it was a far different story.

By noon on Monday, August 11, all U.S. embassy and consulate officials were back in Washington, but thousands of American tourists, students, businessmen, and journalists continued to clog roads to Moscow's Sheremetyevo and Domodedovo airports, trying desperately to get on a flight out of Russia before the deadline was up.

News coverage showed European airports crammed with U.S. passengers with nothing but the luggage they could carry scrambling to arrange connecting flights to the States. There had been no time to pack up homes or apartments, much less ship any of it back home, and now there were reports that Russian mafia factions had begun looting those abandoned American residences and places of business.

But no one had any hint of the horror yet to come.

22
★ ★
★

Misdirection is an essential tool in the illusionist's arsenal.

And Gogolov was a master of the magician's black arts.

He began by summoning the ambassadors of France, Germany, Great Britain, Italy, Austria, and China, as well as the foreign minister of the European Union, for a special evening at the Kremlin. He did not tell them why.

As night fell over the capital, the honored guests arrived in their armor-plated limousines and were escorted to Gogolov's private dining room—an intimate, wood-paneled, candlelit chamber with a large round table for twelve, covered in white linens and hand-painted china dating back to the time of Czar Nicholas II.

"Mr. Foreign Minister, what an honor to finally meet you," Gogolov said as he greeted the E.U.'s Salvador Lucente, the first to arrive, with a warm handshake. "How is your wife, Esperanza?"

"She is well, thank you."

"And your son, Miguel—just turned twelve, did he not?"

"He did indeed, three days ago," Lucente responded, caught off guard by Gogolov's charm offensive. "You have been well briefed."

"Not at all; I have actually been tracking you for some time," Gogolov continued, his eyes locked on Lucente's. "You have had a remarkable career for such a young man. A degree in mathematics—summa cum laude—from the University of Barcelona. MBA and JD from Harvard. Doctorate from Oxford. Vice president of AT&T's operations in southern Europe before founding your own multibillion-dollar telecommunications company. Elected to the Spanish parliament in '97. Later the minister for industry, commerce, and tourism. Followed by labor minister. Then Spanish foreign minister before becoming deputy secretary-general of the Council of the European Union, and now this distinguished post. A renaissance man, to be sure; am I right?"

Lucente's experience proved not to be unique, as Gogolov surprised each of the arriving ambassadors with his detailed knowledge of their years in Moscow, their previous tours of duty, and their professional credentials, as well as the names of their wives and children.

When everyone was finally seated, Gogolov produced another surprise, introducing his own wife to a group that had no idea he was married, much less to a woman as beautiful as Natasha Gogolov. A round of applause welled up from the assembled guests, whereupon the host shocked them yet again.

"Finally," Gogolov said, raising a champagne glass for a toast, "I would like you all to meet my newly appointed foreign minister. . . ."

Pausing, Gogolov turned his eyes to a side door to which the gaze of everyone else in the room quickly followed. A moment later, several of the ambassadors gasped, then covered their mouths and looked quickly at Gogolov as if in fear of having offended him. But Gogolov only smiled. He not only enjoyed their shock, he had anticipated it. For the man who now stood at his side was a man few knew was still alive: Andrei Kanetsky Zyuganov.

Gogolov could almost hear the astonished thoughts of his guests. *How was this possible? Hadn't Zyuganov died the night of the coup? He had been President Vadim's chief of staff, a loyal senior advisor for nearly a decade. Had he been bought off by Gogolov and Jibril? Or had he been a mole in Vadim's operation since the very beginning?*

Everyone in the room was thinking the same thing. But no one had the nerve to verbalize it. They were not there to confront Gogolov. They were there to hear him out. And there was no question he now had their full attention.

☆ ☆ ☆

By the time dinner was over, the shock had worn off.

The ice had melted. Vodka and brandy flowed freely. The air was thick with the sweet aroma of Cuban cigars.

Gogolov stood and tapped his water goblet with a fork.

"Gentleman, Winston Churchill was right. Russia is a riddle, wrapped in a mystery, surrounded by an enigma. Nothing here is as it seems. In the last days you have witnessed the Second Russian Revolution, but unlike the first, Europe has nothing to fear.

"I am not the monster I am being portrayed as in the press. Do I share my comrades' love of Mother Russia, their revulsion for the weakness and corruption of the Vadim *junta*? Of course I do. Am I concerned about the eastward creep of NATO, that an American-led military and political and economic alliance advancing toward my borders could trigger unintended consequences? I would be lying to you if I said otherwise.

"But, gentlemen, let me put your minds at ease. I have no intention of firing nuclear missiles into Germany, seizing Poland, threatening the Baltics, or building enormous fans to blow radioactive waste toward EuroDisney. A big relief, no?"

The room chuckled with nervous laughter.

"I am not Vladimir Zhirinovsky—Mad Vlad, as you in the West used to call him. Nor am I Sergei Ilyushkin. I share neither their virtues nor their vices. These men were clients. That was all. It was business, not personal. But they are gone, and you are here, and a new opportunity lies before us."

Gogolov looked deep into the eyes of each man around the table as his left hand played with his wife's blonde locks.

"My friends, the new Russia will be a true citizen of the world and a member in good standing of the United Nations Security Council. Russia has needs, of course. Russia has interests, and she will pursue those interests as she sees fit. But what are those interests? Is Russia not part of Europe? Is her fate not linked with those of her fellow Europeans? Of course it is, and we want the strongest possible relationship with the European Union. Likewise, is Russia not part of Asia? Is her fate not linked with those of her fellow Asians? Again, the answer is yes. And we are committed to being a good neighbor with our Chinese and other Asian friends.

"What Russia is not—and never will be—is part of the Americas. My predecessor forgot this. He mortgaged Russia's moral and economic security in the vain attempt to strike deal after deal with the Americans. But where did it leave us? Are the Russian people better off today than they were before Grigoriy Vadim climbed in bed with the Americans? The answer, sadly, is obvious. But I would add that neither Europe nor Asia has been well served by tying your futures and your fortunes so closely to the Americans. It is Washington—not Moscow—that vetoes or ignores treaty after treaty and initiative after initiative that would favor both European and Asian interests. Am I right? Is that how the world should work?"

Gogolov scanned the room, looking for some flicker of identification in the eyes of those around his table. One by one, his guests displayed signs that he was getting through to them.

"Think about it, gentlemen. Those of us sitting here tonight represent nearly two billion people. *Two billion.* Together we are seven times the population of the United States. Now imagine—just for a moment—the peace and prosperity a common market of two billion consumers could create. Imagine the innovations such human capital could unleash. Imagine what we could do together if we began to explore our common interests, rather than blindly accepting this unipolar world in which we now find ourselves, a world dominated by—indeed *governed* by—the United States of America. I would submit to you that the United States has become like a new Roman Empire, a yoke around our necks that none of us was meant to bear."

Gogolov let his words sink in. But he was not yet finished.

He argued that "twenty-first-century American imperialism seems to know no bounds—Haiti, Somalia, Bosnia, Afghanistan, Iraq, Palestine; shall I go on?"

He suggested that Washington's so-called war on terror had become a showcase for American arrogance, an excuse to run roughshod over the U.N. and the World Court, and, further, was evidence of America's colonial designs on the oil fields of the Middle East.

And then he reminded the ambassadors that there was still no hard evidence that Aeroflot flight 6617 had actually been hijacked. He suggested that "significant questions regarding Washington's actions remain unanswered to the world's satisfaction."

He criticized Washington's refusal to allow Russian, German, or French companies to bid on contracts in a post-Saddam Iraq, despite the fact that Iraq still had an outstanding debt to Moscow alone of some $7 billion.

He pointed to Washington's opposition to Russia's and China's receiving full acceptance into the World Trade Organization, despite years of E.U. efforts to work through the remaining areas of disagreement.

What's more, he expressed deep disappointment with Washington's resistance to a wide array of European objectives, from signing the international global warming treaty to paying its full debt to the United Nations, now measured in the billions of dollars.

On each issue, Gogolov was struck by the warm response he received. This was going better than he had hoped. He did not want to overreach, but time was of the essence. He glanced for a moment at Zyuganov, who nodded discreetly, and decided to make his move.

"Gentlemen, before this evening is over, there is one other issue of common interest that I must raise."

A hush settled over the room.

"What you report back to your home governments about me and about this evening is your business, though as I mentioned during dinner I would like to meet with each of your presidents and prime ministers here in Moscow or in your capitals or wherever they so choose. And I am more than willing to travel anywhere necessary to make it clear the new Russia wants nothing but peace and prosperity for all nations of goodwill.

"But whatever you report back, I would ask you to make one thing abundantly clear. I speak now of an issue that has badly divided the world in recent years, but one of the utmost importance: the proliferation of weapons of mass destruction.

"You must know that the Russian people share your grave concerns about nuclear, chemical, and biological weapons falling into the wrong hands. Indeed, I *personally* share those concerns. I do not wish to see the spread of such weapons that could threaten our children, our economy, or our environment. But I will tell you quite candidly that I see hypocrisy in the American position, and it must be addressed.

"Soon I will outline my concern to the world community in an address to the United Nations. But in the meantime, let me simply say that I am deeply concerned about one country in the Middle East that without a doubt possesses weapons of mass destruction—including nuclear weapons—and the will to use them. You know of whom I speak, and it is not Iraq."

23
★ ★
★

Bennett sat outside the Oval Office.

He straightened his tie and chewed on another antacid. Meeting with the president of the United States no longer held the thrill it once had. All he could think of now was the last time he had been there with Erin and the sickness he felt over losing her.

When the president had called and asked him if he was up to stopping by, he had flat-out lied. *Of course, he'd be happy to.* The truth was he had no desire to be back in the White House, no desire to endure everyone's pity and "deepest condolences."

There was only one reason for showing up.

He needed this briefing. He needed to get back inside. No matter how much pain he was in, there was nothing he could accomplish sitting around his town house in Georgetown for the next few weeks.

It was his first trip back to Washington since just after the Fourth of July. Following a weekend biking and white-water-rafting trip in Colorado with old friends, he and Erin had come back to D.C. for a series of nonstop briefings at the White House, Langley, and Foggy Bottom before another lightning round of shuttle diplomacy in London, Brussels, Paris, and Moscow.

He remembered trying not to stare at her in the Oval Office, and he remembered everything she had worn. The light blue open-neck shirt under a new navy suit. Her favorite pearl necklace and earrings, the first gift he'd given her after they'd started dating. The Cartier watch. Her hair down and freshly cut. And, as always, Chanel No. 5.

He closed his eyes and could still smell it on her.

"Mr. Bennett, the president will see you now."

Startled out of his dreamworld, he opened his eyes to find an attractive young aide offering to take his arm and help him up. He waved her off and struggled to his feet as the door to the inner sanctum swung open.

The president stepped out and gave Bennett a bear hug.

Bennett winced, and MacPherson suddenly realized what he'd done.

"Jon, I'm so sorry. I didn't—"

"I'm fine, really, Mr. President," Bennett lied again, "just a little sore."

"Good. How long till we get you back full time?"

"Doc says a couple more weeks. But I can come in for daily briefings."

Bennett couldn't stand the idea of being out of the game so long. Events were moving too quickly.

But MacPherson shook his head. "No, no, you need your rest. How about if I send someone over to your place from Langley every afternoon to keep you up to speed?"

"Sir, you really don't need to—"

"Don't be ridiculous, Jon. We need to keep you in the loop, all right?"

"Yes, sir, Mr. President. I'd appreciate that. Thanks."

"Don't mention it," said MacPherson, waving him toward the door of the Oval Office. "Come on in. I've got some folks who'd like to catch up with you."

Bennett was immediately greeted by Vice President Bill Oaks, Bob Corsetti, Marsha Kirkpatrick, and Jack Mitchell. And now that he was here, he was actually glad to see them. This group had been through a great deal together. They'd become family, and though it remained unstated, he knew they shared his sense that their darkest hours might still lie ahead.

MacPherson directed Bennett and the others to the couches as he and the vice president took their usual chairs by the fireplace.

"Where are we on Golitsyn's warning about an imminent attack by Al-Nakbah?" the president asked. "Is there anything to that?"

"We're doing everything we can, but so far we've got no leads," said Kirkpatrick. "It's like chasing a ghost."

"Why haven't you gone public?" Bennett asked.

"We're still not entirely sure what we're dealing with," Kirkpatrick explained. "We're not picking up any chatter about a possible attack. None of our usual sources seem to know anything. So is the threat real, or is Gogolov playing with our heads?"

"That's a dangerous game," Bennett responded. "It would be a nightmare for this administration if Al-Nakbah hits us again and people found out we knew it was coming and didn't say anything."

"But that's just it, Jon, we *don't* know it's coming," Corsetti noted. "We've got one unconfirmed, unsubstantiated rumor. That's it."

Bennett wasn't satisfied, and he knew the president could see it in his eyes.

"I'm worried about the nightmare itself," MacPherson said calmly, "not about the public relations."

"I'm just saying—"

"Believe me, Jon, I know what you're saying. We've been around this thing a hundred times. Let's talk about your conversation with Gogolov."

Bennett's instinct was to argue, but he was too tired and in too much pain. That said, he wasn't sure what more he could tell them. He'd already had an exhaustive debriefing by the CIA and FBI at Ramstein Air Force Base in Germany before coming back to Washington. He'd turned in all the notes he'd taken in the Kremlin, and he was certain everyone in this room had not only read but memorized them by now.

Still, he was the only American official to have ever met Yuri Gogolov face-to-face, and in their shoes he guessed he'd have wanted to hear the story firsthand too.

He backed up a bit, telling them first about his and McCoy's meeting with Vadim, Golitsyn, and Zyuganov, and briefly described the coup. Then he fast-forwarded to the actual meeting with Gogolov and re-counted, word for word, Gogolov's message to the president.

"And that's when he gave you the box?" Kirkpatrick asked.

Bennett clouded over. The image of Erin's bloody finger was almost more than he could bear. He said nothing, just nodded.

Kirkpatrick looked at Mitchell, then to the president.

"Jon," MacPherson began, "give me your hand."

It was an odd request, but Bennett hadn't the energy to ask why. So he held out his hand, and when he did, the president set McCoy's engagement ring in his palm.

Bennett just stared at it, not sure what to say.

"Jon, what I am about to tell you . . ." The president paused a moment and cleared his throat.

Bennett slowly closed his fingers over the ring and pulled it toward him, then looked up at the president.

MacPherson composed himself and continued, "Well, it goes without saying that it's highly classified, and not to leave this room. Understood?"

Bennett nodded.

"It also runs the risk of raising false hope, which makes me hesitant to say anything. But you're a friend, and part of my inner circle, so I'm going to say it anyway, and I trust it will go no further. At least for now."

Again Bennett nodded.

The president looked to the director of Central Intelligence to finish what he could not.

"Jon, what the president is trying to say," said Jack Mitchell, "is that . . . the finger you saw wasn't Erin's."

Bennett felt his chest constrict.

"What? I don't . . . the ring was hers . . . it's the one I gave her. . . . I . . ."

"Yes, I know," Mitchell continued, "the ring is genuine, but the finger was not Erin's. When you landed at Ramstein and turned it over to my staff, we ran the fingerprint against everything in our database. If it was Erin's, we would have known immediately. We also tested the DNA. Believe me, it wasn't her."

"Then I don't . . . what are you saying?"

"There's a chance—a slight chance—that Erin is still alive."

Bennett could feel an injection of adrenaline surge into his system. But it was anger, not elation. "How long have you known this?" he asked, his eyes flashing.

"I got the word Tuesday afternoon."

"It took you two days to tell me? Who the—"

"Jack didn't tell you because I told him not to," MacPherson stepped in. "You needed sleep. We needed more data. That's what I've had Jack doing for the last forty-eight hours."

Bennett bit his tongue.

"I'm not trying to minimize what you're feeling right now, Jon," Mitchell continued. "But Erin McCoy is an officer of the Central Intelligence Agency. We recruited her. We trained her. We—I—sent her to work for you, at the president's direction. I put her at your side. I put her in Moscow. I know, it's not the same. I'm not saying it is. But she's one of our own, and we're doing everything we can to track her down and get her back safely.

"The fingerprint isn't our only clue. An eyewitness who was there the night of the coup says she saw a woman matching Erin's description being taken out of the Kremlin and loaded into an ambulance. We've got a satellite photo that shows an ambulance arriving around that same time."

"Do you have a photo of her alive?"

"No, unfortunately we don't. But I've got assets scouring every part of Moscow. Every hospital. Every clinic. Every hotel. Anywhere we can send human agents or direct our satellites, we're doing it. The president has ordered me to make finding her a top priority, but frankly, even if he hadn't, we'd be doing it anyway. I don't know what we're going to find. I can't tell you the outcome is going to be any different than what you thought it was a few minutes ago. But we're trying everything we can. I thought you deserved to know that."

The room was silent.

Just because it wasn't McCoy's finger didn't mean she wasn't dead, Bennett told himself. *And just because someone said they'd seen her being put into an ambulance, what did that really prove? Nothing.*

Bennett didn't think he had the emotional energy for another roller coaster. But neither did he have a choice. If there was even the thinnest chance Erin was alive, he had to pursue every lead. The question was how.

Not alone.

That much he knew for certain.

24

★ ★
★

Mordechai stared at the e-mail in his in-box.

He was not accustomed to communicating with the Israeli prime minister this way. But there was no mistaking the return address. This was a personal note from David Doron himself, sent through the e-mail account of his executive assistant.

"Eli—how are you, my friend? I hope all is well. My staff and I have reviewed your report on Operation Chunnel. A job very well done. I share your concern that the traffic, thus far, has been light, but this does not worry me. Now that the pipeline is built, the odds of its increased use are far better than they were, no? That said, I need something else—we've just learned that Gogolov held a private dinner meeting the other night with a number of key European and Asian ambassadors, including E.U.'s Lucente. No word on the evening's agenda or any action items, but I would greatly value your take on events unfolding in Moscow. What do you believe are GOG's objectives? How serious are they about provoking a confrontation with WH? Do you believe they have designs on the ME? SOI? When you're ready to brief me, let me know and we'll have lunch. —DD."

On one level, Mordechai was flattered, to be sure. He'd been out of the game for some time, and it felt good to be of some use again.

But one word jumped off the screen and grabbed him by the throat. *GOG.*

Why had Doron used it? What exactly did he mean by it?

Operation Chunnel made sense—that was the code word the Mossad had assigned to his trip to Iraq and his back-channel dealing with President Al-Hassani.

WH was the White House.

ME meant the Middle East.

SOI was the State of Israel.

But *GOG*? Did the prime minister realize what he was asking?

Mordechai quickly typed a reply.

"Dear Mr. Prime Minister—thank you so much for your note. I am well, and glad you found my report helpful. Let us hope you are right and Chunnel proves operational in both directions. That said, I am also honored by your latest request. I will give it some thought and get back to you soon. After all, have I ever turned down a free lunch? Forgive me, though. To what does 'GOG' refer? Guess I really am getting old. Faithfully, Eli."

He read it over several times.

Was he overreacting? Was he tipping his hand? He didn't think so. It sounded like a simple enough question. He just wasn't sure if he was ready for the answer. But he had to know, and before he could second-guess himself, Mordechai hit Send.

☆   ☆   ☆

Who was Yuri Gogolov?

For Bennett, the question burned in his gut night after night. To find and kill him, he had to know everything.

He knew what he was feeling was wrong. But he couldn't help the rage he felt at the monster who might have killed the woman he loved. Even if Erin was still alive—a hope he still did not allow himself to cling to— Gogolov had to die for what he'd done to her.

But how much did the U.S. government really know?

For the last several years, the FBI had ranked Gogolov at the top of its Most Wanted List. He was believed to be the founder, financier, and strategic godfather of Al-Nakbah. He had, therefore, been implicated in the attempt on the lives of Bennett, McCoy, and Dr. Mordechai in Jerusalem several years previously, as well as in the successful assassination of the U.S. secretary of state and the chairman of the Palestinian Authority in

Gaza City, an attack from which Bennett and McCoy had only narrowly escaped themselves.

Gogolov was believed to be the mastermind of a series of assassination attempts against the president of the United States and other NATO leaders over the past several years, aided by Mohammed Jibril, believed to be a senior member of Iranian intelligence.

But thus far, ironclad proof had been elusive. The case against Gogolov was largely circumstantial, and the physical evidence was underwhelming at best. Yet the U.S. government was convinced that Gogolov was extremely dangerous and had a long history of living up to his deadly reputation.

The financial resources available to Gogolov and Jibril were virtually unlimited. The breadth and depth of their network of allies and sources was beyond anything Bennett had ever seen before.

So how in the world was Bennett going to get to him? It wasn't just a matter of identifying where McCoy was being held—if she was even still alive. He needed to get inside these men's heads. He needed to understand who they were, what they wanted, how they operated, and what they might be planning next.

Bennett could set up base camp at Langley and pore over everything they had, but even this was not enough. As far as Bennett could tell, the CIA didn't know who they were up against any better than he did. Neither did the NSC.

Too many in the American intelligence establishment had a Western, modern, secular mind-set. They saw the world almost exclusively through political and economic lenses. But that obviously wasn't enough.

Bennett didn't quite know what to make of Jack Mitchell. He had the title. He had the corner office and the résumé to go with it. On paper, he was a president's dream candidate for CIA director. But in Bennett's estimation he possessed neither the intellectual nor spiritual bandwidth for the task that lay ahead.

On 9/11, when Al-Qaeda had hit the World Trade Center and the Pentagon, Jack Mitchell had been running the CIA's NAMESTAN desk, covering all of North Africa, the Middle East, and the "stans" (Pakistan, Afghanistan, and the former Soviet Central Asian republics). He'd been the director of Central Intelligence when Saddam and Al-Nakbah had launched Operation Last Jihad. And incredibly, he was still the DCI de-spite a Fascist coup in Moscow that was rapidly developing into the worst foreign-policy crisis in years.

Why hadn't Jack Mitchell seen any of these attacks coming?

Why hadn't he connected the dots?

How in the world had he been promoted to the agency's top slot?

And how had he remained?

Bennett knew the president's relationship with Mitchell went back years, and the president was nothing if not loyal to his friends. But so what?

Mitchell wasn't a bad man. He simply did not understand the enemy he was sworn to defeat.

The failure to anticipate the attacks of the past several years wasn't so much a failure of intelligence as it was a failure of imagination.

To misunderstand the nature and threat of evil was to risk being blindsided by it.

And to put it bluntly, Mitchell had been blindsided, time and time again.

Now the stakes were higher than ever. Evil was regrouping. Some-thing else was coming, something catastrophic. Bennett had no idea what. He just knew Jack Mitchell was not the man to ask.

Eli Mordechai was not a man accustomed to fear.

But it was fear he now felt. Doron's reply had finally arrived, and Mordechai's hand trembled as he clicked open the e-mail and began to read it.

"Eli—you are as sharp as ever, my friend, which is why I so value your coun-sel. But forgive my diplomatic jargon. I did not mean to be so cryptic. I was simply referring to the new government of Gogolov. 'Gog,' in Mossadspeak. Do let me know as soon as you are ready to meet. I fear storm clouds are building on the hori-zon, and I could use a good weatherman. DD."

So there it was.

GOG.

Mordechai shuddered. The prime minister *didn't* have any idea what he was really saying. David Doron knew only what everyone knew: that Russia had a new dictator—a former intelligence officer with a violent past, an expansionist ideology, close ties to Iran, and ten thousand nuclear warheads at his disposal. That was bad enough.

But there was something else. Something Mordechai knew that few others did. Something that rattled him to his core.

Was it really true? Could he prove it? And even if he could, who would listen?

25

★ ★
★

Bennett was exhausted.

Up since 4 a.m. and in the office since six, his eyes were bloodshot, and his medication was wearing off.

"Jon, it's late; go home."

Bennett looked up from a stack of classified State Department and CIA cable traffic to find Indira Rajiv standing in the doorway of his West Wing office.

"Hey, Raj, what's up?"

"You are. You want to get me fired? The president gave me strict orders to make sure you don't overdo it. If he finds out you're still here, he'll kill me."

Bennett highly doubted Rajiv's job was in any jeopardy. She was a rising star, a Langley prodigy. The American-born daughter of immigrants from India, Rajiv had been recruited into the CIA by McCoy while both were at Wharton getting their MBAs. She'd gone on to earn two doctorates, as well: one in Islamic history from Princeton University, the other in Persian history from Oxford, both paid for by the U.S. government.

Now, at the tender young age of thirty-six, she had already worked her way up to director of the NAMESTAN desk. She was fluent in Arabic, Farsi, and Urdu, the language of Pakistan (though, ironically, she spoke none of India's hundreds of dialects), and within the U.S. intelligence community, Rajiv was rapidly becoming known as one of their leading experts on radical Islam.

And if that weren't enough, though she dressed modestly in Western fashions and rarely wore makeup, she was a head turner—large brown eyes, pale mocha skin, and wavy jet-black hair that touched just below her shoulders.

"I'll be fine," Bennett muttered and went back to his work. He had no time for small talk, and if Indira Rajiv couldn't help him find his fiancée, he wanted nothing to do with her.

Rajiv didn't take the hint. She came over, sat down across from him, and asked, "Any news about Erin?"

Bennett looked up, annoyed. *Was that pity in her eyes?* It made his stomach turn. He'd had enough of everyone stopping him in the halls, asking him the latest word on McCoy. The only thing worse than not having an answer—*any* answer—about her whereabouts, much less her condition, was having to acknowledge that fact twenty or thirty times a day.

"No, not yet," he said, looking back at the cables spread across his cluttered desk.

Dozens of intelligence and military officials were engaged in the hunt for Erin McCoy, but they were looking for a needle in a haystack while the barn was on fire. If Rajiv was so smart, why wasn't she more help? What was she doing at the White House at almost eleven o'clock on a weeknight anyway?

"You hear about Gogolov?" Rajiv asked.

"No, what?" said Bennett, his mood suddenly changing.

"Costello has a source that says he's holding a press conference tomorrow."

"Why?"

"There's a rumor going around that Gogolov wants to address the U.N. General Assembly next week."

"Is it true?"

"I've got different sources from Ken, but I'm hearing the same thing."

"You've got to be kidding me," said Bennett. "The president will never give him a visa."

"Maybe he should," Rajiv countered. "The FBI could put him in cuffs the minute he touches down at JFK."

"Right, and have his minions back in Moscow launch Armageddon?"

"Actually, I hear Gogolov may already have a majority of the General Assembly wired up."

"To do what?"

"To pass a resolution calling on the president to let Gogolov have his day in court, in the spirit of world peace, as it were."

World peace? Gogolov? How could anyone keep a straight face using those three words in the same sentence? But the world wasn't laughing.

Bennett's phone rang, startling them both.

His car was ready. He thanked Rajiv, said good night, and put his papers in his safe. Then he turned off the lights in his office and headed out to West Executive Avenue to meet his driver. Maybe Rajiv was an asset after all.

Ten minutes later Bennett was home.

He said good night to the DSS agents stationed outside his door and entered his town house. He lived on a shady street in Georgetown, about three blocks from the university campus where he had studied as an undergrad. Locking the door behind him, he threw his keys on the shelf, hung up his suit coat in the front closet, and flipped on the news.

Details of Gogolov's meeting with the European and Asian ambassadors were beginning to leak to the public. Bennett had known about the meeting for weeks, first via a tip from Israeli intelligence, then from a lengthy phone conversation with E.U. foreign minister Salvador Lucente. But there had been no mention of a U.N. speech by Gogolov.

What struck Bennett now as the news broke was how differently each side of the Atlantic was reacting. The White House had spent the last weeks behind the scenes urging the U.N. to condemn Gogolov's coup as a breach of international law and a threat to global security. The administration had floated the possibility of applying economic sanctions against the Russian Federation until a legitimate, democratically elected government was restored to power.

But the Europeans weren't playing along.

Lucente, for one, was now on CNN warning that such moves were *"more appropriate to an old Hollywood Western than modern diplomacy."* He said several members of the European Union were concerned that the U.S. was overreacting to events in Moscow.

"Look," the E.U. Foreign Minister told his interviewer, *"all of us mourn the loss of innocent life in Moscow, and we condemn in the strongest possible terms the way President MacPherson's senior advisor Jonathan Bennett was treated. Furthermore, we join the White House in calling on the Gogolov government to disclose the whereabouts and condition of Erin McCoy, another senior advisor to President MacPherson."*

Bennett reached for his remote and turned up the sound.

"That said," Lucente continued, *"it would be completely irresponsible to try to isolate a country as important as Russia or to treat it as some kind of rogue threat. As I have said to the U.S. secretary of state and to Mr. Bennett, Pakistan's General Musharraf seized the reins of that nuclear nation in a military coup a number of years ago. But neither the U.S. nor the E.U. tried to isolate him. To the contrary, Washington, Brussels, and the international community sought to work with General Musharraf, and to good effect. All I am saying is that we should not rule out the possibility that we can all work with Mr. Gogolov as well."*

Who were these people? thought Bennett. *What was it about European leaders that made them blind to demagogues and dictators rising in their midst? Marx, Lenin, Hitler, Mussolini, Stalin, Khrushchev, Ceausescu, Milosevic— how could they have been blind to them all? How could they now be so blind to the Gogolov threat?*

Disgusted, Bennett clicked off the set and went to the kitchen to take his medicine. But something made his blood run cold.

Every muscle in his body froze.

He strained to hear another sound. All he could hear was the hum of the refrigerator. But he was sure.

Someone else was in the house.

26

★ ★
★

Bennett's eyes darted to the left.

No one was there. He calculated the odds of racing to the door but decided against it. It was more than twenty yards away. If someone was in the house—if they were determined to kill him—he'd never make it out alive.

His heart was racing. He could feel beads of perspiration on his upper lip.

Was his mind playing tricks?

Four DSS agents were stationed outside. One was posted there even when Bennett was at work. It was impossible for anyone to be in the house, wasn't it? Why didn't he just pick up the phone and call them? But what if someone was listening in? Then again, what if they weren't? Was all this just his imagination gone wild? How stupid would it look if he called for help and it was just a case of fatigue mixed with paranoia?

The chance that anything was wrong was about a thousand to one, Bennett calculated. He had enough troubles without making the DSS think he'd gone nuts. Still, he couldn't shake the fear rising within him.

He slowly opened a kitchen drawer and rummaged around until he felt the Beretta 9 mm McCoy had given him after they had narrowly escaped an Al-Nakbah attack. His fingers wrapped around the cold steel.

In one clean motion he swung around, holding the pistol with both hands.

But no one was there.

Bennett slipped off his shoes and began creeping out of the kitchen, the gun leading the way, elbows bent slightly, just as McCoy had taught him.

Sweeping side to side through the living and dining rooms, looking for any sign of movement, listening for anything out of the ordinary, he reached the stairs.

He was still ten or fifteen yards away from the front door. But it was locked—dead bolted. His back would be to the stairs leading up to the second floor.

He glanced left. The door to the basement was slightly ajar.

Bennett pressed his back against the wall. He opened the door slowly with his right foot. Nothing.

Moving quickly, he flipped the light switch on, turned the corner, and breathed a sigh of relief. No one was on the stairs.

But if someone was down there, they knew he was coming now.

He looked back at the front door, his heart pounding. He was being ridiculous, wasn't he? He stood there for a moment. The odds were good that if someone really was lying in wait, he'd be upstairs—in the hall, in the bathroom, in one of the bedrooms, waiting for him to sleep. The basement featured a walkout exit to the rear of the house. He'd have a better chance of getting away by going through the sliding glass doors downstairs to the backyard.

Bennett began working his way down to the basement he rarely used. Built in the 1940s, the town house was relatively young for Georgetown, where many homes dated back to the nineteenth century, some even to the late eighteenth century. But that didn't mean the stairs wouldn't creak.

Though it was finished and carpeted and he had a home office down there, the basement was mostly stacked with unopened boxes of books and files and clothes he'd never wear again.

His hands were sweating. He gripped the Beretta so hard his knuckles turned white. Any minute he expected someone to pivot around the corner and double-tap him to the head. It would be a silencer, of course. How long would it be before the agents found him? He couldn't imagine they'd come looking for him before morning.

Bennett turned the lights off.

It took a moment to adjust to the darkness.

Only the moonlight coming through the sliding glass doors at the far end of the room provided any illumination. Again Bennett pressed his back against the far wall of the basement and held the gun out in front of him, approaching the door to his office and trying to stay quiet.

The phone rang. It was so shrill, Bennett almost yelled out.

A shiver ran through his body.

On the next ring, Bennett made his move. He kicked in the door of the office. Someone was in his swivel chair, his back to him. Bennett pressed the Beretta to the man's head.

"Hands, show me your hands!" he yelled, and the man complied instantly.

It was too dark for Bennett to see his face.

Should he shoot now and ask questions later?

The phone rang again.

"Are you going to answer that?" the stranger said slowly.

Bennett knew that accent.

"Dr. Mordechai?"

"Shalom, my friend."

Bennett's heart was still beating hard. It took a moment for his breathing to return to normal. *What was his old friend doing in his house?*

He flipped the switch on the wall, turning on a small lamp on the desk and booting up the computer.

"Dr. Mordechai, what are you doing here? I almost killed you."

Mordechai's eyes twinkled.

"I just happened to be in the neighborhood, so I thought I would drop by. May I put my hands down now?"

"Of course, sorry," said Bennett, starting to breathe again. He set the Beretta on the desk. "How long have you been here?"

"Not long, but I am afraid I do not have time for small talk, Jonathan. I had some meetings at the CIA today. I head to Brussels on the first flight out. But where are my manners? It is good to see you again."

He stood and smiled and gave Bennett a hug—sensitive to Bennett's injuries and careful not to squeeze too hard—and then the two sat down. Bennett wiped his hands on his slacks. He'd been on edge for weeks. Yet there was something about this old man that put him at peace.

Mordechai was an acquired taste, of course. Who but a retired Israeli spymaster could consider it "small talk" to explain why and how he'd broken into the house of a senior White House official guarded twenty-four hours a day by trained professionals? But he was here now, and Bennett had a thousand questions.

Mordechai beat him to the punch.

"So, what's the latest with Erin?"

It had to be the twentieth time Bennett had been asked since breakfast. But this time he didn't feel annoyed. Bennett told him all he knew, which wasn't much.

"I still have a few sources in the old country," Mordechai offered. "Let me see what we can come up with. In the meantime, I will keep praying. The Lord knows exactly where she is. We just need Him to tell us."

Yeah, right, thought Bennett, but he kept quiet. This was not a conversation he wanted to have right now. He didn't know why exactly. It just wasn't. He wasn't looking for a miracle to rescue the woman he loved. A CIA extraction team or the 82nd Airborne would do fine, followed by a cruise missile down Gogolov's throat.

The phone rang again.

"You should answer that, Jonathan," said Mordechai. "It could be important."

"Let them leave a message," said Bennett. "I'm not in the mood."

"What if it is about Erin?"

Bennett shot Mordechai a quizzical look, then grabbed the phone and stepped out of the room. He instantly recognized the voice on the line. *You've got to be kidding me,* he thought.

"Mom? What's the matter? For crying out loud, it's almost midnight."

Ten minutes later Bennett was back.

"Everything all right?" Mordechai asked with a gentle, understated concern that reminded Bennett of his late grandfather.

"I don't know," said Bennett, running his hands through his hair and sitting down in the overstuffed chair across from Mordechai. "Ever since my dad passed away and I took this job with the White House, my mom's just been, I don't know—not herself."

"What do you mean?"

"I mean it's almost midnight and she just called—to say hi? No. To get an update on Erin? Not exactly. Don't get me wrong. She loves Erin like a daughter, but . . ."

"But what? What did she want?"

Bennett hesitated. "You're not going to believe me."

"Try me," said Mordechai.

"She wants to know if Yuri Gogolov is the Antichrist."

He expected the old man to laugh out loud. Instead, Mordechai asked, "Why does she want to know?"

"Good grief," said Bennett. "Don't get me started on my mother. I love her to death, don't get me wrong, but sometimes . . ."

Bennett stopped and seemed to drift off for a moment.

Mordechai repeated his question. "Why does your mother think Gogolov might be the Antichrist?"

Bennett slumped back in one of his office chairs and sighed.

"She was getting her hair done today, and her hairdresser said something about a story she'd read in the *National Enquirer* about how all these prophetic signs are converging—the discovery of oil in the Holy Land, the Iraqis moving their capital to Babylon, wars and rumors of wars in the Middle East. You name it, the UFO people are worked up about it."

"So why did she call you at midnight about it?"

"She can't sleep. I don't know what's going on. She's never wanted to talk about anything spiritual. She won't come to church with Erin and me when she comes up to visit. She's convinced a bunch of 'religious fundamentalists' have taken over the government. But now she wants to know if Yuri Gogolov is the Antichrist. Go figure."

"What did you tell her?"

"I told her to take a Valium and go back to bed."

"That's it?"

"No, no, of course not. I told her not to worry. Yuri Gogolov is evil personified, but he isn't the Antichrist."

"Did that satisfy her?"

"Hardly. She wants me to talk to some experts and get back to her with a definitive answer. Got one?"

27

★ ★
★

It wasn't hard to pick up.

The moment the conversation had turned spiritual, Bennett's discomfort had become palpable, and Mordechai worried about his young friend.

The man had almost lost his own life, and it wasn't the first time. The woman he loved was probably dead. He was in constant physical pain. The pressures of serving as a senior aide to the president in the current political environment put him under almost inhuman levels of stress. From what Mordechai heard, Bennett refused to see any of the counselors on staff with the CIA or State Department. And on top of it all, Mordechai was reluctantly coming to the conclusion that this young man's faith was faltering.

He didn't blame Bennett. On the contrary, he felt compassion for him.

In some ways, Bennett was at the top of his game. In others, he was enduring traumas few outside the military or intelligence world could fathom. He was not fully cognizant of the times in which he lived or the supernatural power that was his for the asking. And he was running on empty.

"You seem distracted, Jonathan," he said finally, hoping Bennett would confide in him as he had over the years.

Instead, Bennett turned the conversation back toward Gogolov. "What do you think he wants," Bennett asked bluntly, "and how can we take him down?"

Mordechai was disappointed, but he would not press too hard. "Doron is asking the same question. I am not entirely sure I have an answer for either of you yet. But I am working on it."

"I'll take whatever you've got so far," said Bennett.

Mordechai lit up his beloved pipe and leaned back in the leather chair. "Remember when I called you from Babylon? You were on the way to meet with Vadim."

"Of course. You warned me there might be a coup. I thought you were crazy."

"I am sorry I could not warn you sooner."

"How did you know?"

"I did not know for certain—not that it was imminent, anyway. But the files Al-Hassani gave me were a treasure trove. Truly unbelievable. I—"

Mordechai suddenly stopped in midsentence.

"What is it?"

"Jonathan, there is something I must ask you first," said Mordechai. "Why did you send me to Iraq?"

Bennett seemed surprised by the question. "President Al-Hassani told Erin and me that he wanted to meet with an Israeli, someone in intelligence—former intelligence, actually."

"Someone close to Doron, but deniable if the press caught wind of it?" Mordechai asked.

"That's my guess. Erin and I were in Iraq at the beginning of June. We had a private audience with Al-Hassani. President MacPherson wanted us to poke around the Arab world and see if there was anyone who might be willing to publicly back the Oil-for-Peace deal once we got it all nailed down."

"Besides Egypt and Jordan?"

"Exactly. Secretary Warner was working with Cairo and Amman to keep them in the loop and make sure they were on board. But the president wanted someone else. He wanted a surprise. Kuwait seemed like a possibility. So did Morocco. But neither would sign on unless the Saudis were on board. So we went to see the Saudis."

"Let me guess," said Mordechai. "It did not go well."

"No, it didn't," Bennett conceded.

"Whose idea was it to talk to the Iraqis?"

"Erin's, actually."

"Gutsy."

"The guys at State hated the idea, Secretary Warner especially. He thought our relationship with Iraq was already complicated enough without asking them to kiss and make up with the Israelis. Erin held her ground. Her take was that Al-Hassani was already looking to break out of OPEC restrictions on how much oil Iraq could pump and sell. Maybe he'd be interested in a tacit alliance with the other new kids on the oil block."

"And Al-Hassani was open to the idea?" asked Mordechai.

"Let's just say he wasn't opposed. He was willing to meet with someone close to Prime Minister Doron, but it had to be outside the normal diplomatic channels."

"And I fit the bill."

"You did, especially given your obsession with Babylon, the End Times, and all that."

Obsession? The word cut into Mordechai's heart like a knife. He wanted so badly to reengage in the conversations he and Bennett used to have. He wanted to share with his young protégé everything he'd seen and heard in Babylon.

The Scriptures were coming alive. He was now convinced the ancient prophecies were, in fact, coming true before their very eyes. For the past few weeks—ever since Doron's e-mail concerning "GOG"—he'd been studying everything he could get his hands on. He needed to understand the signs, the timing, the sequence of events that would climax in the Rapture of the church, the rise of the Antichrist, and the beginning of the Tribulation. His head was still full of questions, and he was convinced the window for finding answers was rapidly closing.

But it was clear Bennett had no interest in joining such a quest, and it grieved him. Mordechai was tempted to have it out with him right now. Bennett was playing with fire. He was increasingly at risk of becoming a casualty, of getting himself picked off in a supernatural war he hardly knew he was in. But now wasn't the time.

"Well, I appreciate you thinking of me," the old man said gently. "It was a very profitable trip, and I have a great deal to tell you, more than we can cover tonight. Let me start by saying that I believe Al-Hassani was willing to consider endorsing your peace deal."

"*Was?*"

"Whatever interest he had has been overtaken by events, Jonathan. At this point I'd say the entire treaty is DOA."

Bennett said nothing. He looked crestfallen. *He had to have known the treaty was dead*, Mordechai told himself. *Perhaps no one had actually said it out loud yet.*

"I am sorry, Jonathan. I know you have worked very hard on this."

Bennett shook his head. "Still, you said the trip was profitable. Why?"

Mordechai had thought he'd never ask.

Drudge had the story.

The full article was not yet posted on the *New York Times* home page, but Gogolov devoured every word he could.

It was 8:27 a.m. in Moscow, 12:27 a.m. in Washington. President MacPherson was, no doubt, asleep. But he would awake to another crisis.

According to Drudge, the front-page story by Chief White House Correspondent Marcus Jackson was to be headlined "AL-NAKBAH ATTACK IMMINENT; WHITE HOUSE HAS KNOWN OF IMPENDING STRIKE FOR WEEKS BUT CHOSE NOT TO TELL PUBLIC."

The twelve-hundred-word article cited two unnamed "senior administration officials" and an array of other "diplomatic and foreign intelligence sources" describing the concern that three or four "Al-Nakbah terror squads" were currently seeking to penetrate the Mexican and Canadian borders to attack various American population centers, including shopping malls, supermarkets, nuclear power plants, and elementary schools.

Senior U.S. Homeland Security officials who "insisted upon anonymity" said they "could not be sure" whether the threat was real or part of "an elaborate disinformation plot." Nevertheless, thousands of federal, state, and local law-enforcement officers, as well as intelligence agencies from at least a dozen countries, were engaged in the hunt for the terror squads.

One high-level—though again unnamed—FBI official told the *Times* that the FBI was engaged in "the most expensive and manpower-intensive counterterrorist effort in the history of our country, and all based on a rumor none of us can substantiate."

What Gogolov savored most was the detailed description of the raging debate within the White House about whether to raise the terror alert level to Red or to wait until there was more evidence that the terror-squad rumors were true.

Better yet, White House Press Secretary Chuck Murray refused to comment on the story for the record, and at least one senior Democratic senator was accusing the administration of "playing games with national security and the country's right to know."

All this, thought Gogolov, *and the Kremlin's fingerprints were nowhere to be found. Everything was going better than even he had expected.*

It took several hours.

Bennett listened carefully as Mordechai described the files President Al-Hassani had given him.

Saddam Hussein's private diaries of his meetings over the years with various Russian ultranationalists.

Signed contracts between Russian oil companies and the Iraqi government worth tens of billions of dollars in Iraqi oil-field concessions.

Audiotapes of Saddam granting Mohammed Jibril access to Iraqi terror training camps, such as Salman Pak.

Copies of wire transfers funneling Iraqi funds through a series of French and German front companies and Swiss banks to Al-Nakbah operatives scattered throughout Europe and the former Soviet republics.

And that was just the beginning.

The breadth and depth of the information was extraordinary. *Why had Al-Hassani given it to Mordechai in the first place?* Bennett wondered. But there was a more important question to be answered first.

"Why exactly was Saddam so wired into the subversive world of Russian ultranationalists?" Bennett asked. "Wasn't Moscow a staunch ally of Saddam's?"

"They had been; that is true," Mordechai agreed. "The Soviets sold Saddam most of his military hardware during the seventies and eighties. But things changed. By the time the first Gulf War was over, Iraq owed Moscow billions of dollars Saddam couldn't repay, especially given the U.N. sanctions, and relations grew icy. Then one by one, Yeltsin, Putin, and Vadim began playing footsie with Iran—Saddam's mortal enemy. They started selling Iran tanks and submarines and missiles and even nuclear power plants, something for which Saddam had begged the Russians for years."

"Saddam must have been livid," said Bennett.

"He was, and according to the files Al-Hassani gave me, that is when Saddam vowed to help Al-Nakbah overthrow the Russian government. He began funneling money to Zhirinovsky, and then to Sergei Ilyushkin, which could be used to buy the allegiances of disaffected Russian military officers and create a fifth column capable of overthrowing the politicians who had turned against Saddam."

"But we took Saddam out," said Bennett.

"By then it was too late," Mordechai responded. "The damage had already been done. Using the cash flow from Saddam, Gogolov and Jibril had already built an enormous network loyal to them. What is more, Ilyushkin built an alliance between Saddam and Boris Stuchenko, opening up a whole new source of funds and accelerating the process of buying anyone and everyone upset with Vadim."

"That's why you suspected a coup was coming?" asked Bennett.

"It was only a matter of time," said Mordechai.

"So what does your crystal ball say is coming next?"

28

⭐⭐
⭐

It would soon be daybreak.

Mordechai had a plane to catch. But Bennett's question was the entire reason for his visit. There was just one problem: Bennett wasn't ready to hear all that Mordechai had to say. Neither was Prime Minister Doron, for that matter. This wasn't something you could just spring on people. You had to prepare them. You had to win their confidence and ease them into the pool. Or you ran the risk of losing them forever.

"You heard that Andrei Zyuganov is alive, right?"

"I did," said Bennett. "Lucente told me. I couldn't believe it. All I can figure is that at the last minute Jibril must have shot Ilyushkin instead of Zyuganov."

"That is my guess, too," said Mordechai. "So did you hear where Zyuganov showed up yesterday?"

"No, where?"

"Berlin."

"Why?"

"Your friends over at Langley think Zyuganov was probably reassuring the Germans that Moscow was not about to send the Red Army to take over the Reichstag."

"But you don't buy it?"

"Not quite, Jonathan. Gogolov has something up his sleeve. And whatever it is, I suspect Zyuganov was there to get Chancellor Strauss and his government to sign on. As far as I can tell, Zyuganov has been working his way through each member of the Security Council—minus the U.S. and Great Britain, of course—harvesting the easy votes and buying the rest."

"To what end?"

Mordechai hesitated. Bennett liked him, trusted him. He wasn't ready for the full story—not yet—but Mordechai could at least point him in the right direction. He checked his watch. His plane left for Brussels in less than two hours.

"Jonathan, I believe Yuri Gogolov is trying to build Russia into a new global superpower. I think he is creating a strategic alliance with Iran through Jibril. And I think he is in the process of forcing most of Europe to get on board with his agenda."

"What are you talking about? How?"

Mordechai had to tread carefully. He had to be honest with Bennett without saying too much too fast. "I am not sure what Gogolov's next move is. Not exactly. But he is clearly trying to split the Europeans away from Washington. Just look at his moves over the past few weeks. Whatever his ultimate objective, he wants the Europeans on board. And behind the scenes he is playing hardball to make it happen."

"I'm still not following you," said Bennett, who had been exhausted five hours ago and was now almost completely out of gas.

"Let me put it this way, Jonathan," said Mordechai. "How much oil and gas does Germany import every year?"

"What do you mean?"

"How much? You know the figures."

"About ninety percent of her oil, and eighty percent of her natural gas," said Bennett.

Three years of working on the Oil-for-Peace deal had made the man an expert, thought Mordechai. The numbers just rolled off Bennett's tongue.

"And who is Germany's number one *supplier* of natural gas?"

"Russia."

"How much does Berlin import from the Russians?"

"Almost forty percent."

"How about France?"

"The French get nearly a quarter of their natural gas from Russia."

"Italy?"

"About the same."

"Austria?"

"They get about two-thirds of their natural gas from Russia."

"And Turkey?"

"With the new Blue Stream pipeline, they get almost eighty percent of their gas from Russia."

"You see where I'm going with this?" Mordechai asked.

"You think Europe's about to be blackmailed," said Bennett.

"*About to be?*" Mordechai responded. "My friend, the die has already been cast. Moscow could shut down Europe's economy in a matter of days if it wanted to. How long would it take for chaos to erupt from the moment Russia turned off the flow of gas into Europe? And think about it, Jonathan. What did Gogolov say to you in Moscow? 'Russia no longer believes in the efficacy of an East-West conflict. . . . A new day has dawned, a day of unprecedented peace *and* prosperity for everyone of goodwill.' "

Bennett looked stunned. The press in recent weeks had reported Bennett's release, but no one except the president and the NSC was supposed to know he'd met personally with Gogolov, much less the substance of those meetings. Yet Mordechai knew.

"How . . ."

"Jonathan, *how* I know is not your concern," Mordechai responded. "*What* I know is. And I am telling you, that line is the key to deciphering Gogolov's intentions."

"Meaning what?"

"Meaning Yuri Gogolov wasn't simply a disciple of Zhirinovsky. He was the man's brain. Very few people know that Gogolov was the ghostwriter of many of Zhirinovsky's speeches as well as Zhirinovsky's 1993 autobiography, *The Final Thrust to the South*. Few in the West have ever read it. But I believe it is a road map to where Gogolov is about to take us. Gogolov believes what Zhirinovsky believed, that Russia's last great imperial expansion will not be to the west but to the south. See for yourself."

Mordechai handed Bennett a plain brown folder.

"Read it," he said. "Then call me. I have a plane to catch."

☆　☆　☆

A moment later Mordechai was gone.

Bennett poured himself another cup of coffee and opened the folder. Inside was an English translation of Zhirinovksy's book. Key pages were marked with yellow Post-it notes. Occasionally a note from Mordechai was scribbled in the margins. Key passages had been marked with a yellow highlighter. Bennett skimmed the highlighted sections.

> *All Russia's troubles lie to the South. . . . Until we resolve this southern knot there will be no getting out of this extended crisis with its interminable exacerbations. . . . Russia reaching the shores of the Indian Ocean and Mediterranean Sea is a task that will be the salvation of the Russian nation.*
>
> *[I am proposing] a solution to a global problem, a solution with planetary implications. . . . We must permanently calm this [Middle Eastern] region. Resorts, youth camps, sanatoriums, and preventive health clinics will be established on the shores of the Indian Ocean and Mediterranean Sea. Great spaces can be acquired for relaxation. The entire South can become one large zone of resorts and rest homes for the industrial north and all other peoples.*
>
> *We must change our border. We must have an outlet on the Pacific and Indian Oceans, or set up a 'wall of China' to separate us from the South. But building a wall would interfere with our trade with Iran, Turkey, and Afghanistan. That would impoverish us. So we probably shouldn't do that. So there is only once choice. The operation should be carried out using the code-name "Final Thrust to the South."*
>
> *All this will be a stimulus to the economy, transportation, and communications and provide raw materials for food production and light industry, cheap labor, and the possibility of establishing new rail lines to Delhi, Tehran, and Baghdad, new air routes, roads. The Silk Road should be reestablished, running from China and India into Europe. It will run through Russia. Russia will grow rich.*
>
> *The Russian army needs this. It will let our boys flex their muscles instead of sitting around the barracks, worn out by hazing, in the depths*

of Russia, not knowing who and where the enemy is and what moral and physical preparations they should make.

Millions of people [will be] grateful to Russia. . . . The Germans want this. . . . This is also profitable for France. We would help them extricate themselves from American and Zionist influences. . . . Europe needs our help. . . . Only America would not be pleased, but she won't interfere. The alternative to the development of this situation is too grave for her if she interferes. There would be too many negative results if she tried to prevent the establishment of Russia's southern borders.

Let Russia make its final "thrust" to the south. I can see the Russian soldiers gathering for the final expedition southward. I can see Russian commanders in Russian division and army headquarters, mapping out the route for the military formations and the endpoints of those routes. I see aircraft gathered in air bases around the southern regions of Russia. I see submarines surfacing near the coastline . . . and amphibious assault ships nearing the shore where Russian soldiers are already marching, armored infantry vehicles are on the move, and great masses of tanks are rolling through. Russia will finally make her last military expedition. There will never be another war from the South for Russia, and it has long since been impossible for war to come from the North. In the West they understand, and in the East they will find out.

A chill ran through Bennett's exhausted body. Mordechai was right. Gogolov was preparing for war.

29
★ ★
★

The press conference started precisely at twelve.

Foreign Minister Andrei Zyuganov stood before a bank of microphones in the lobby of the United Nations Building in New York and requested that the new leader of Russia be permitted to address the General Assembly on September 11, the opening day of the fall session.

"We seek the opportunity to reaffirm Russia's desire to be a member in good standing of the international community and to discuss the great issues of our time," Zyuganov told the assembled reporters. "From protecting the environment from the threat of global warming to protecting our children from the threat of weapons of mass destruction, Russia has a new voice that should be heard by all people of goodwill."

As Zyuganov continued, it became clear that he also wanted assurances that the U.S. government would not impede Gogolov's movements during his eight-hour visit to New York City but would grant him the full measure of diplomatic immunity and protection—including Secret Service protection—afforded any visiting head of state.

Within minutes, the French ambassador stepped out to the microphones to voice his country's support for the proposal as "in the best interests of international diplomacy." Germany and China quickly voiced their support as well, as did the Arab League and half a dozen African states, including Ethiopia and Libya.

☆   ☆   ☆

A political firestorm was building in Washington.

The Justice Department was on the verge of appointing a special prosecutor to investigate the president's handling of the Aeroflot 6617 disaster. The Russian jet's black box had finally been found over the weekend, but was too badly damaged to be useful. Moderates were distancing themselves from the White House, and even a number of conservative Republican senators had voiced concerns on the weekend news shows about the administration's handling of foreign affairs.

The cover of the latest *Time* magazine asked, "Who Lost Russia?"

A new NBC News/*Wall Street Journal* poll found that 56 percent of Americans disapproved of the president's conduct of foreign policy in general, while 63 percent believed he was "mishandling" the Moscow crisis in particular.

Coverage of the Gogolov gambit dominated the news.

White House aides were sharply divided over how to respond.

Israeli prime minister Doron was the first foreign leader to call President MacPherson, imploring the U.S. not to issue the Russian dictator a visa. Bennett joined the president, Bob Corsetti, and Marsha Kirkpatrick in the Situation Room to sit in on the call.

"Mr. President," said Doron as the nine-minute conversation was winding up, "Yuri Gogolov is using the levers of democracy to preach hatred and advance Fascism. Would FDR have allowed Hitler to address the United Nations on the eve of World War II?"

Bennett found himself echoing Doron's sentiments.

He reminded the group of Aleksandr Golitsyn's warning that at that very moment forces loyal to—or directed by—Gogolov might actually be targeting the U.S. with terror squads. Providing him a forum would create legitimacy for a tyrant who deserved none.

Bob Corsetti countered with a vehemence that stunned Bennett in its intensity.

"Mr. President, this is no time to look intransigent," Corsetti argued. "The American people want you to be a peacemaker. I say let's hear the man out. It's not like he's going to declare war on the United States while he's standing on American soil."

Marsha Kirkpatrick's case was more strategic.

The U.S. desperately needed to shed its trigger-happy image and regain the moral high ground, she said. If Gogolov was foolish enough to challenge the United States and give MacPherson a home-court advantage at the same time, the White House shouldn't be foolish enough to decline.

The phone rang in the Sit Room. It was Chuck Murray with breaking news. AP was about to report that senior aides to the U.N. secretary-general were discussing the possibility of opening the U.N. General Assembly's fall session in Paris or Brussels instead of New York if the U.S. resisted Gogolov's "eminently sensible request."

MacPherson hung up and relayed the news to the others.

Corsetti reacted first. "Look, Mr. President, I'll be honest—my heart is with Bennett on this one. If it were up to me, I'd let Gogolov into the country just to have an FBI sharpshooter put a bullet in the guy's head as he stepped off the plane. But that's emotion talking, not good policy and certainly not good politics. We cannot afford to battle against granting a world leader a one-day visa to talk about peace. We simply don't have the political capital to burn."

Six hours later, the visa was granted.

30
★ ★
★

Yuri Gogolov finally rose to speak.

"Mr. Secretary-General, distinguished delegates, and ladies and gentlemen: As we gather together on September eleventh, the anniversary of the attacks upon this great city, let me begin by assuring all Americans—and reassuring each of you—that the Russian Federation is fully committed to being a member in good standing of this global community and to helping the world win the war on terror once and for all."

The General Assembly erupted in thunderous applause.

"The new Russia shares this great body's commitment to human dignity, eradicating poverty, and conquering disease," Gogolov continued. "The suffering of our fellow brothers and sisters around this planet is great, and our responsibilities are clear. Whether it is confronting the threat that AIDS could literally wipe out fifty, sixty, seventy percent of the population of some African countries in the coming decades—or the threat that by 2050 global warming could literally melt much of the Swiss Alps, radically altering climates and subjecting Europe to the most devastating heat waves in human history—the Russian people, from St. Petersburg to Vladivostok, stand ready to face these issues together, tackle them together, solve them together, lest together we suffer a thousand years of darkness."

Again the hall burst into applause.

☆ ☆ ☆

Bennett watched the speech in his West Wing office.

Joining him were Indira Rajiv of the CIA's NAMESTAN desk and Ken Costello, the U.S. undersecretary of state for political affairs. Bennett had invited them both to help him analyze the Gogolov speech and European and Islamic reaction to it.

Gogolov's English was flawless, as was his diction, and Bennett found himself at once impressed with the Russian political neophyte's command of his material. He worried that the audience was warming to him far too quickly.

☆ ☆ ☆

"Many issues confront us," Gogolov continued.

His pace was measured, confident; his proficiency with using a teleprompter intriguing given that this was his first international address.

"Some are regional. Some are economic, cultural, or social. But I believe we can all agree that the most pressing issue of our time is ridding the world of weapons of mass destruction and keeping them out of the hands of terrorists."

More applause.

"Regretfully, some would seek to divide the great powers. Some would seek to pit the United States against Russia on the great issues of our time, but they must not be allowed to succeed. Yes, we have our differences. Yes, the debate over whether the United States should have gone to war against Iraq was one of them. And yes, there is much work to do to repair relations strained so badly by the unfortunate U.S. response to the perceived threat of Aeroflot flight 6617.

"But let there be no confusion: the Russian Federation never disagreed with the objective of the United States to rid Iraq of weapons of mass destruction. To the contrary, we have always shared the vision of making the Middle East a nuclear, chemical, and biological weapons-free zone. Our disagreement with the United States was never over vision. It was over the strategies and tactics needed to bring it to pass.

"Those in Moscow who preceded me took issue with the aggressive, unilateral approach the United States took, and what seemed to many in the international community to be Washington's hyperaccelerated timing.

"Perhaps they were wrong. Perhaps we were all wrong. Perhaps it is time to concede that regardless of our differences, the world is much safer now that Saddam Hussein is no longer in power and can no longer threaten the peace."

The great hall was silent for a moment. The delegates were too stunned to know how to react.

"Where's Gogolov going with this?" Bennett asked.

Neither Rajiv nor Costello had a reply.

The U.S. was right in going to war with Saddam? What would provoke Gogolov of all people to make such an admission?

Gogolov adjusted his glasses and continued.

"Today, however, I would submit that another Middle Eastern country is known to possess weapons of mass destruction. She operates in defiance of multiple U.N. resolutions. She has repeatedly attacked and invaded her neighbors. She has repeatedly violated the human rights of the people entrusted to her care. And she is widely seen as a threat not only to regional peace but to world peace. Regretfully, of course, I speak of the modern State of Israel."

The General Assembly had never been so utterly silent.

"I say 'regretfully' because history records the great support the Russian people have given to the Jewish state from its inception. On May 17, 1948, the Kremlin officially recognized the newly born State of Israel. Russia was one of the first nations to do so. By August 9 of that year, the first diplomatic delegation from Moscow arrived in Tel Aviv. By September, Israel's first ambassador to Russia, the legendary Golda Meir—a remarkable woman who of course went on to become an Israeli prime minister—landed in Moscow and was welcomed by more than half a million Soviet Jews.

"In the years since, Russia has allowed more than a million Jews to emigrate to Israel, despite strong opposition from our Arab and Muslim friends. We have also been a consistent partner for Middle East peace, helping Egypt and Jordan and the Palestinians work toward peace with Israel, and we will continue to play such a role in the future.

"But we must be honest. Only one country in the Middle East refuses to become a signatory to the Nuclear Non-Proliferation Treaty—the State of Israel.

"Moreover, only one country in the Middle East is known to actually possess nuclear warheads—the State of Israel. They are not dreaming of them, designing them, or developing them. Israel has already deployed nearly three hundred nuclear warheads.

"Which begs the question: if the United States was able to persuade this body that Saddam Hussein was a threat worthy of international action, how can we allow a double standard for Israel?

"Some will argue that India, Pakistan, and Cuba have not joined the NPT either. They are right, and this is a great concern of mine. I am determined we can make tremendous progress in these areas if we work together. Indeed, we have already done so.

"I have the great privilege of announcing to you that over the past few days I have been in talks with the Cuban government. I have been able to convince Havana to drop her long-standing concerns, and for the good of the global community and in the interests of world peace, I can now announce that the esteemed president of Cuba will join me immediately following this speech to officially become the NPT's 188th signatory."

The General Assembly exploded with a standing ovation.

"And this is just the beginning," Gogolov continued, raising his hands and asking for everyone to please retake their seats. "I am also pleased to announce that the presidents of India and Pakistan have agreed to a summit in Moscow in January. Together, we will discuss a de-escalation of tensions between the two countries. We will also begin work on a strategic-arms-reduction treaty—similar to the START I and START II my predecessors negotiated with the United States during the waning years of the Cold War. And it is my personal mission to persuade both India and Pakistan to become members of the global community of NPT signatories within the next twelve to eighteen months."

This brought the house down—another standing ovation, which lasted for almost four minutes.

And now the Russian shifted gears. "Which brings us back to Israel— a rich country; a country living more securely than at any other time in her people's history; a powerful country with a strong army, an impressive air force, and the strength of the American superpower at her side. With all these assets, I ask you: why should such a country refuse to sign a treaty aimed solely at making the world a more peaceful and prosperous place for all mankind?

"When the United States went to war in Iraq, she did so, in part, because the regime of Saddam Hussein had defied sixteen U.N. Security Council resolutions. What, then, shall we say of Israel, which has defied *ninety-seven* such resolutions since 1948?

"Permit me to reference an article in the American newsmagazine *The Nation*. This article, entitled 'U.S. Double Standards,' notes that *'the most extensive violator of Security Council resolutions is Israel.'* The article goes on to point out that the U.S. has reached *'a new low in double standards'* by vetoing thirty-nine of the last forty-three Security Council resolutions directed against Israeli violations of international law. In the only four resolutions not vetoed, the U.S. abstained.

"In the General Assembly as well, the U.S. consistently seeks to shield Israel from being held accountable for her illegal actions. At the turn of the millennium in the year 2000, for example, the U.N. General Assembly dealt with twenty-nine separate resolutions condemning Israeli violations of international law. Five were adopted without a recorded vote. But of the remaining twenty-four resolutions, the U.S. voted *no* nineteen times and abstained three times. Only twice did Washington deign to vote *yes* to hold Israel accountable.

"Let me describe just one resolution that was considered that year: United Nations General Assembly Resolution 55/36. It warned that 'the proliferation of nuclear weapons in the region of the Middle East would pose a serious threat to international peace and security.' It called for a 'nuclear-weapon-free zone' in the Middle East. Furthermore, the resolution called upon Israel 'to accede to the Treaty on the Non-Proliferation of Nuclear Weapons without further delay . . . and to renounce possession of nuclear weapons, and to place all its unsafeguarded nuclear facilities under [the safeguards of the] International Atomic Energy Agency.'

"A reasonable request, one would think. Yet the U.S. voted *no*. Why?"

An instant message popped up on Bennett's computer.

It was from Dr. Mordechai in Jerusalem.

"This is unbelievable. Jonathan, do you see where he is headed?"

Bennett glanced at Rajiv and Costello. They had no idea.

But he did . . . all too clearly.

The Russian leader moved in for the kill.

Astonishingly, he did so echoing the very words the American president had once used to justify a previous war in the Middle East.

"Can the world morally justify one standard for Iraq and another for Israel? Is it right for the world to take action against a nation that defies *sixteen* Security Council resolutions, but do nothing against a nation that defies *ninety-seven*?

"Israel has answered decades of U.N. demands with decades of defiance. And now the world faces a test. The United Nations arrives at a difficult and defining moment. Are these resolutions to be enforced, or cast aside without consequence? Will the United Nations serve the purpose of its founding, or will it be irrelevant?

"Russia helped to give birth to the United Nations. We want the United Nations to be effective, and respectful, and successful. We want the resolutions of the world's most important multilateral body to be enforced. And right now those resolutions are being unilaterally subverted by Israel. Our partnership of nations can meet the test before us by making clear what we now expect of the Israeli regime.

"If the Israeli regime wishes peace, it will immediately and unconditionally foreswear, disclose, and remove or destroy all weapons of mass destruction, long-range missiles, and all related material. Further, the Israeli regime must immediately allow IAEA and U.N. inspectors into its nuclear reactor at Dimona as well as all other nuclear, chemical, and biological research facilities.

"Toward this end, this afternoon Russia will introduce U.N. Security Council Resolution 2441, giving the State of Israel thirty days to comply with the steps I have just outlined. If Israel does comply fully, a new era of peace and prosperity will sweep the region, and the world will be more secure.

"But let there be no doubt: if Israel continues to go down the road of defiance, the international community will have no choice but to join together to enforce the U.N. resolutions related to Israel, just as the United States and her allies enforced the U.N. resolutions related to Iraq."

Bennett watched as Gogolov left the platform.

For a moment an awkward silence filled the great hall, but then the General Assembly erupted in a standing ovation that went on minute after minute. Nearly all the delegates were on their feet, applauding wildly. Then the camera caught the Israeli ambassador storming up the center aisle. As he exited, the view switched to the U.S. ambassador, who sat in stunned disbelief.

Bennett, too, sat motionless. The gauntlet had just been laid down, and the White House was in shock.

31

★ ★
★

MacPherson gathered his team in the Situation Room.

Jack Mitchell weighed in first.

He conceded Gogolov was a thug with blood on his hands but reminded his colleagues that Washington had dealt with such thugs before using diplomacy. What's more, he argued, Gogolov's real objectives were financial, not military.

"In the last three years, oil prices have plunged from over $60 a barrel to near $20 a barrel at the beginning of this year, in large part because of Israeli, Palestinian, and Iraqi oil flooding the markets," Mitchell reminded the president. "This has caused tremendous economic hardship for Russia. Their GDP is falling. Unemployment is rising.

"And let's not forget that forty percent of the Kremlin's budget comes from the tax revenues paid by Russia's oil and gas sector. Every $1 drop in the price of oil costs the Kremlin $1 billion in lost tax revenues. Gogolov is no doubt green with envy at all the wealth the Israelis are enjoying at the moment. But do we really think he's going to go to war over it? Most likely Gogolov is simply making a play to drive up the price of oil, and so far he's succeeding. Oil just hit $41.69 a barrel."

MacPherson hoped he was right. "If that's the case, what would you recommend we do?" he asked.

"For starters we need to shine a spotlight on Russia's hypocrisy on the

WMD issue. For crying out loud, they've been shipping nuclear technology to Iran—a card-carrying member of the Axis of Evil—for years. I think the public has a right to know just how complicit Russia is in the Iranian nuclear program. And believe me, Mr. President, my team at Langley has everything you'd ever need to make that case—satellite photography, audio intercepts, videotaped confessions by Iranian intelligence operatives we've captured, you name it.

"Second, the secretary of state and secretary of energy need to reassure our NATO allies that we won't let Gogolov blackmail them by shutting off their gas and oil supplies. The Israelis and Palestinians can certainly supply Europe with what they need, so long as the Russians don't start filling the Mediterranean with warships.

"Third, let's remember that Zhirinovsky and Ilyushkin were ideologues. Gogolov, I believe, is driven by greed. That could be to our advantage, if we handle this right. We have an entire arsenal of economic carrots and sticks we can use if we need to. Russia wants to join the WTO. Let them. They want to become part of OPEC. Let's talk to the Saudis and the Gulf states and see if we can make that happen. They want to sell us more grain. Fine, it's a small price to pay to avoid a war."

"You want me to accede to blackmail?" asked the president.

"It's not blackmail," Mitchell countered. "It's diplomacy. Nick Warner does it every day. And nobody does it better."

The secretary of state was visibly flattered. "How do we know if your analysis is right, Jack—that Gogolov's real objective is money, not power?" Warner asked.

"We ask him," Mitchell responded. "Let's put some direct questions to Gogolov on the table and see if we can flush this guy out."

"What kind of questions?" asked the president.

"Mr. Gogolov, are you open to an honest, peaceful discussion of ways to expand Russia's economy and ways to further integrate Russia into the global economy? Are you interested in a new round of diplomacy regarding Russia's desire to be accepted into the World Trade Organization? Are you open to finding ways to reduce American and European tariffs on Russian products as well as ways to promote peace in the Middle East? Or are you gathering an international coalition to loot the Israelis, to carry off silver and gold, and to seize as much plunder as you possibly can?"

✩ ✩ ✩

"What took you so long to get back to me?" asked Doron.

Mordechai wiped his mouth with his napkin and looked up at his old friend. He wished he could tell David Doron exactly what he knew. They went back a long way. And now Mordechai was sure. He'd been doing his homework for weeks, poring over books and articles and every bit of research he could find, dotting every i and crossing every t. But just as with Bennett, the time was not right. Not yet.

"You have many advisors giving you much advice, Mr. Prime Minister," he replied. "I did not want to intrude."

Doron set down his glass of wine, and Mordechai noticed his hands were shaking slightly.

"I would not have asked if it was going to be an intrusion. I will be blunt with you, Eli. This is not like any crisis Israel has ever faced before. We have taken on the entire Arab world, but never Russia. Never a nuclear power. This is different. And just between you and me, I have to confess I am scared."

"You should be."

"I keep reaching out to the French, the Germans, the British. Nobody in Europe seems willing to stand by us. The atmosphere is poisonous, as bad as it was in the thirties when Hitler was rising. Lucente is the worst, always sounding so sympathetic and understanding on the phone, but I swear it seems he is working with Gogolov."

"Forget Salvador Lucente. Forget the E.U. They are a waste of time."

"I cannot just forget them, Eli. We need them."

"Of course we need them. But we are not going to get them."

"Then short of a miracle, tell me what am I supposed to do."

Every molecule in Mordechai's body was shaking. The temptation to lay it all out, right then and there, was almost overwhelming. Yet something held him back.

"Mr. Prime Minister, I recommend you put all of your efforts into securing full American backing—public statements from the president and Congress, an emergency arms package, and the U.S. Seventh Fleet parked off the coast of Tel Aviv, if you can get it."

"I am on the phone with the State Department and the CIA every single day. Nothing is happening."

"Go through Bennett," Mordechai counseled. "No one is closer to MacPherson than Jon Bennett. The president listens to him. He trusts him. I think he is your best shot at the moment. He may be your only shot."

Bennett's blood was boiling.

He couldn't believe what he was hearing. Gogolov was evil incarnate. The president couldn't negotiate with him. He had to be destroyed before he consolidated his power and began issuing ultimatums to Washington and London, not just Jerusalem.

"Jon, you want to say something?" asked MacPherson.

Bennett was the president's "point man for peace." As much as he wanted to exact vengeance on Gogolov and Jibril, it was not exactly in his job description to become an advocate of war with Russia. But he simply couldn't contain himself.

"Mr. President, I don't know any other way to say this, so I'll just be candid."

"Please."

"First of all, I shouldn't have to remind anyone in this room that Israel is a strategic ally. Or that Israel has long been recognized as a 'major partner' with NATO. Or that the Israelis played a crucial role in helping us thwart the expansionist ambitions of the Kremlin during the Cold War. And let's not forget, in the secrecy of this room, that we are the ones who helped Israel establish a nuclear-weapons program as a strategic counterbalance to Moscow and her radical Islamic allies."

Mitchell moved to cut him off. "Jon, really, I don't think we need—"

"Jack, I think I've earned the right to be heard at this table, and I'll let you know when I am finished," Bennett shot back, glaring at the CIA director.

"The strategic argument for defending Israel should be more than enough, but there's a moral case as well," Bennett continued. "How many times have we delivered speeches at the Holocaust Museum here in

Washington and to Jewish groups around the country denouncing the do-nothing attitude of the Western powers during the wholesale slaughter of the Jews at the hands of the Nazis? How many times have we joined with Jewish and Christian leaders to declare, '*Never again*'? How can we now turn our backs on Israel as it faces another Holocaust?

"And would we even be having this discussion if it was Great Britain or NATO, rather than Israel, that was in Moscow's crosshairs? Of course not. Think about it. In 1990 we sent a half a million troops to the Persian Gulf to protect the corrupt kingdom of Saudi Arabia from the threat of Saddam Hussein. Are you really telling me we are not going to move heaven and earth to protect Israel from the threat of Yuri Gogolov?"

Bennett looked around the room at the faces of his colleagues.

All were silent.

"With all due respect, Jack, yesterday's speech by Gogolov wasn't a move to drive up the price of oil. It was a pretext to move Russian forces into the Middle East. Why? To seize control of the Persian Gulf. To dominate the world's oil supply. To bring the American people and our allies around the world to our knees. Gogolov and his forces tried to attack Washington with a civilian airliner. They seized control of a country with ten thousand nuclear warheads. They attacked an American embassy. They have either murdered or taken hostage a senior advisor to the president. They have terrified the American people with the notion that terror squads may be on their way. . . ."

Again Mitchell tried to cut him off. "Come on, Jon, you can't possibly base a decision like this on a rumor of terrorist activity. For all we know, it's nothing but a hoax. You can't really believe—"

Bennett pushed back. "I hope it *is* a hoax. But does anyone here have any doubt that Gogolov is probing for gaps in our homeland security, looking for weak links? He now controls the FSB, *Spetsnatz*, and Al-Nakbah. He has an entire arsenal of suitcase nukes at his disposal. How soon before he tries—again—to decapitate us?"

Bennett looked around the room. He certainly had everyone's attention. But was he winning his argument?

"Look," he concluded. "Yuri Gogolov has a record. He's got an objective. He's got a plan. And he is banking on our indecision. You all have copies of Zhirinovsky's manifesto, *The Final Thrust to the South*, that I distributed earlier this morning. Read it. Study it. Gogolov's loyalties are not a mystery, and neither are his intentions. He and his regime pose a clear and present danger to U.S. national security, and I believe we need to seriously consider the option of launching a preemptive strike to take him out."

MacPherson was stunned.

No one was going to contemplate taking preemptive military action against Moscow. There were too many risks. The stakes were too high.

Was Bennett serious?

Maybe it had been a mistake to bring him back in the loop so quickly. Gogolov had almost killed him. He was still on heavy medication. He was desperate to find Erin. His judgment was impaired, to say the least.

MacPherson felt sorry for Bennett. He loved him like his own son. He hated to see Bennett suffering like he was. Perhaps a weekend at Camp David together would give them a chance to relax, catch up, and get back on the same page. For now, though, MacPherson had a decision to make, and it wasn't one Bennett was going to like.

He directed his secretary of state to fly to Europe with the goal of keeping NATO and the E.U. from jumping into bed with Gogolov and to reassure them they would not be subject to economic blackmail.

He directed Bennett to go to Jerusalem to coordinate with Doron on a response to the Gogolov offensive and to get Mordechai's take on the crisis.

And then he ordered his national security advisor to draft a prime-time address for him to deliver the following Tuesday night.

Jack Mitchell was right. It was time to challenge Gogolov on Russian hypocrisy. It was time to let the world know that Russia was, in fact, *introducing* dangerous nuclear technology to the Middle East, not trying to create a nuclear-weapon-free zone in the region, as Gogolov claimed.

He just prayed it would work.

The country didn't have the stomach for another war.

32

★ ★
★

Bennett stared out the window.

Cruising up Highway 1 toward Jerusalem in a bulletproof Chevy Suburban, he would arrive at the King David Hotel in less than an hour.

By noon he'd be in a closed-door meeting with Israeli prime minister David Doron, despite the fact that it was the Jewish Sabbath.

He knew the first question that would come out of Doron's mouth: *Was the U.S. prepared to stand by Israel militarily if Moscow pressed for war?*

He just wished he had a good answer.

Bennett's thoughts inevitably tried to turn to Erin, but it was too painful. There was still no word, no leads, nothing at all to go on. He couldn't afford to let himself become emotionally paralyzed. There was too much to do.

He blinked hard and tried to refocus. He stared out the window and shook his hand in wonder at all the changes the last few years had brought. Where there were once villages and farmland stretching out on either side of Highway 1, there were now oil wells as far as the eye could see. It was ugly. But with so much money pouring into the country, few Israelis seemed to care at the moment.

What a revolution Israel had been through. It had all begun in 1999 when a marine geologist working for *National Geographic*—the same geologist who'd located the sunken *Titanic* in the North Atlantic—was trolling the floor of the Mediterranean with high-tech sonar equipment near the Israeli city of Ashdod, just north of Gaza. He was looking for the shipwrecks of ancient Phoenician vessels, and he found them—two of them, in fact—dating back to 750 years before the time of Christ.

But that wasn't all.

The geologist had also stumbled upon the most spectacular energy discovery in the history of the Holy Land—enormous, hidden, under-water reserves capable of producing 30 million cubic feet of natural gas per day, *every day*, for decades, perhaps centuries.

Bennett could still remember the jolt of adrenaline he felt on September 15, 2000, when he'd read a startling front-page headline in the *New York Times*: "GAS DEPOSITS OFF ISRAEL AND GAZA OPENING VISIONS OF JOINT VENTURES."

That story was quickly followed on September 28, 2000, by another dramatic headline in the *Times*: "ARAFAT HAILS BIG GAS FIND OFF THE COAST OF GAZA STRIP."

And that, it turned out, was just the beginning.

Soon the *Jerusalem Post*, Israel's English-language daily, ran a head-line declaring, "NATURAL GAS, OIL FOUND IN DEAD SEA."

By May 4, 2004, *Haaretz*—one of the largest Hebrew daily news-papers in Israel—ran a story headlined "OIL VALUED AT $6 BILLION DISCOVERED EAST OF KFAR SAVA," reporting that an Israeli com-pany had first found traces of oil at the site the previous September but that new tests were leading to a stunning new conclusion: "There could be reserves of 980 million barrels of oil at the Meged-4 well east of Kfar Sava." And maybe more.

The prospects were tantalizing. *What if there was more?*

With McCoy at his side, Bennett had moved quickly, positioning Global Strategix to take the biggest gamble of his career: a billion-dollar bet on a joint venture between Medexco—owned by Dmitri Galishnikov, a Russian Jewish émigré to Israel—and the Palestinian Petroleum Group, run by Dr. Ibrahim Sa'id.

Bennett hit the jackpot.

When the final test results came in, Bennett could hardly believe the stunning news: the Israelis and Palestinians were sitting atop the second-largest oil reserves in the world, and GSX had cornered the market. In the blink of an eye, the geopolitical landscape—and Bennett's entire life—had changed forever.

Bennett was drafted by the White House to design the administration's new Middle East peace plan. McCoy was allowed to come clean as an operative of the CIA. And the Oil-for-Peace plan they crafted soon became front-page news. If both the Israelis and Palestinians agreed to put behind them centuries of violent hostilities to sign a serious peace agreement, develop a joint petroleum industry, and integrate their two economies, then—and only then—the United States would help underwrite the billions of dollars of loan guarantees needed to turn the dream into reality.

Polls quickly found a majority of Palestinians ready to give the Oil-for-Peace plan a chance. Did they still want to throw Israel into the sea? Polls found many did. But the same polls also found the vast majority of Palestinians were exhausted by violence, sick of the grinding poverty, desperate for a ray of hope, and ready for the first time in their lives for a strategic course correction.

The key, as in every successful deal, was timing, and in Bennett's estimation, the timing could not have been more perfect.

Ariel Sharon had been replaced by Prime Minister David Doron, a hard-core, right-wing *Likudnik* who preached the doctrine of "reciprocity"—an eye for an eye and a tooth for a tooth—but did, in fact, have a pragmatic streak.

Osama bin Laden and his Al-Qaeda terror network were finally out of business. Saddam Hussein, his sons, and his regime had waged their last jihad.

Yasser Arafat had seen his last days, and his regime had eventually been replaced in a dramatic turn of events by Ibrahim Sa'id, the world's wealthiest Palestinian and a man with whom the U.S. and Israel could finally do business.

Within months, an interim three-year peace agreement had been struck. The U.S. provided loan guarantees to help finance the drilling platforms, pipelines, and refineries needed by Medexco (now a joint Israeli-Palestinian petroleum consortium headed by Galishnikov), and Prime Minister Sa'id kept his word. He cracked down on radical Islamic terror cells, cut off their money, rounded up their shock troops, threw hundreds of militants into prison, and destroyed dozens of terror tunnels coming into Gaza from Egypt.

When Israel hadn't seen a single suicide bombing in more than twenty-six months, Doron had no choice but to reciprocate.

All Israeli troops were now out of the West Bank and Gaza. The policy of assassinating top terrorist operatives was mothballed, made easier by the fact that most were now either dead or in jail anyway. Palestinian assets—frozen in Israeli banks—began to be released. Permits allowing Palestinian day laborers to reenter Israel were again being issued, subject to background checks.

Israel was even beginning to tear down sections of the so-called "security fence," and Doron was publicly suggesting that upon the signing of a full treaty with the Palestinians, he would tear the rest of the wall down as well.

As a result, foreign investment was pouring into Israel, the West Bank, and Gaza. Tourism had once again begun to surge. Housing starts on both sides of the Green Line were at a record high. Refugee camps were being replaced by gleaming new apartment complexes, new schools, playgrounds, shopping centers, and malls.

And, of course, as Israeli and Palestinian oil and gas flowed out, hundreds of billions of dollars in foreign currency began flowing in. An IPO on the New York Stock Exchange drew millions of investors to Medexco, but only after every Israeli and Palestinian family was given shares. As the joint venture's share price soared, so did the fortunes of every Muslim, Jew, and Christian in the Holy Land.

How, then, could the U.N. so readily accept Gogolov's blatant lies? Bennett asked himself.

Israel wasn't defying the international community. Just the opposite. Never before had Israel been so willing to grant such concessions to the Palestinians. All that was needed now was a final status agreement that would lock in these gains and pave the way for an even more extraordinary era of peace and prosperity. *Had it all been in vain?*

33

★ ★
★

Slowly Erin McCoy opened her eyes.

The room spun. The light from two naked bulbs, each hanging by bare wires from the cement ceiling, was almost blinding.

She felt groggy. She could tell she was under heavy sedation and felt an IV in her left arm. Her mouth was dry. Her lips were chapped. She had no idea where she was. Guessing would take too much energy.

But she was alive. And as that fact sank in, McCoy began to cry, thanking God for saving her. And then it hit her: *Where was Jon? Was he dead or alive?* She looked around the room, but she was alone.

The door opened.

Out in the hall stood a burly, unshaven man in fatigues, toting an AK-47. A woman entered, pushing a cart stacked with medical supplies of all kinds—bandages, gauze, cotton balls, needles, and small bottles filled with various pharmaceuticals. She was a young woman, in her mid-to late twenties, about McCoy's height and build.

Though her nose and mouth were covered by a surgical mask, her eyes were not cruel. In fact, they looked terrified, as though she had no desire to be in this room one second longer than she had to be.

Good, thought McCoy, *at least we've got something in common.*

The woman's skin was pale, as if untouched by sunlight. She wore no makeup, no jewelry of any kind, just a simple watch with a nondescript black band, and an ID of some sort dangling from her neck.

McCoy tried to read her name but couldn't.

The woman nodded to the guard, who closed the door, remaining in the hallway. She then proceeded to pull back the covers and check McCoy's wounds.

McCoy realized her hands were cuffed to the sides of the bed.

And then she saw the needle, just before the sharp pain as it jabbed into her thigh. She would be out cold again in a matter of seconds, but even in her medicated haze, McCoy realized her training was kicking in.

She strained to take in every detail of the woman, the room, everything. She knew she could process it later, her eyes closed, even in her sleep. But she desperately needed a visual layout if she were ever to escape.

If it was the FSB holding her, she was in trouble. She knew how the Russian intelligence service worked. The sooner she recovered, the sooner they would torture her—until she broke or they put a bullet through her skull.

✯   ✯   ✯

Bennett was checking into the King David when his phone rang.

It was Mordechai. "Anything new on Erin?" he asked.

"No," said Bennett. "What about you?"

"I have the Mossad on the case, and I have contacted nearly a dozen sources I have used in and around Moscow over the years. Nothing yet. But I wanted you to know I am doing everything I can."

"Thanks," said Bennett. "I appreciate it."

"Of course. Oh, by the way, I do have an answer for your mother."

At first, Bennett had no idea what Mordechai was talking about.

Then it came back to him.

Mordechai's midnight drop-by in Georgetown. The phone call from Bennett's mother in Orlando. The *National Enquirer* story: Was Gogolov the Antichrist? It was an increasingly hot topic on the Internet, but hardly one Bennett wanted to talk about now.

"Look, I'm a little busy," Bennett demurred. "Can I get a rain check?"

It wasn't a question. It was a lie. Bennett had no intention of talking about the Antichrist with Mordechai. Not on this trip, at least. Immediately following the meeting with Doron, he was meeting Ibrahim Sa'id's widow and sons and then having dinner with Dmitri Galishnikov, still devastated by Sa'id's death and terrified of what Gogolov was going to do to Israel. After that, he was heading home.

Bennett's BlackBerry beeped.

He scrolled through a secure flash traffic e-mail from Marsha Kirkpatrick at the NSC. In coordination with six former Soviet republics, including Georgia, Armenia, and Azerbaijan, Russia was about to announce a massive series of naval and ground-forces exercises—code-named "Black Star"—in and around the Black Sea and the Mediterranean. The story would break over the weekend. The exercises would commence in four days, on the day of the U.N. vote on Resolution 2441.

Bennett's stomach tightened.

Gogolov was about to pre-position a quarter of a million troops and half the Russian fleet within striking distance of Israel's borders.

The Rubicon had just been crossed.

34

★ ★
★

Doron got right to the point.

Having offered his condolences regarding Erin McCoy and the DSS agents killed during the coup, he described the rise of Yuri Gogolov as "a massively destabilizing event," one that Israel now had to consider "an existential threat."

And he made it clear that the Jewish state would not be blackmailed into forfeiting her trump cards.

"Israel does not now—nor will it ever—discuss the details of its defensive-weapons systems," the prime minister continued. "Moreover, Israel is not now—nor will it ever be—a signatory to the NPT, not as a tacit admission that we possess nuclear weapons but to keep all of our options open, and to keep our enemies guessing."

Bennett knew full well that Israel had between one hundred and three hundred nuclear warheads and enough Jericho-I, Jericho-II, and newly completed Jericho-III missiles to deliver them as far as Moscow, Tehran, and Berlin if need be.

What's more, Doron knew Bennett knew.

But such was the *Kabuki* dance of Middle Eastern diplomacy, and Bennett tried to keep step with the music.

"Strategic ambiguity?" Bennett asked, with a wry smile.

"Call it what you will," said Doron. "We are not about to bow to the demands of a Fascist Russian dictator."

"Just to be clear, then," Bennett said, "the Israeli government has no intention of complying with Resolution 2441?"

"I do not think it would be appropriate to comment on hypotheticals," said Doron. "The resolution to which you refer has not even been voted upon, much less passed."

"But if it is?"

"The U.S. will veto it, will it not?"

"My government isn't prepared to take a position until we've seen the final language," Bennett said, seeing the concern in Doron's eyes suddenly intensify.

"You are saying there is a chance the president will not veto a resolution that is tantamount to a declaration of war on a strategic ally of the United States?"

"Mr. Prime Minister, I'm saying it's a long way until we get to that point."

"It is not as far away as you think," Doron shot back. "Do not fool yourself, Jonathan. The creation of a Russian-Iranian alliance poses danger not just to Israel but to American and European security and economic interests as well. Did Eli give you the excerpts from Zhirinovsky's book, *The Final Thrust to the South*?"

"He did."

"Did you read them?"

"I did."

"Then how can you sit there and tell me Gogolov does not have a knife to my throat?"

Bennett said nothing.

"Jonathan, you and I have been friends for many years. We have been through much together, but nothing like this. So listen to me very carefully. You need to go back and tell the president three things. First, it is critical that the U.S. veto this resolution before events spin out of control. Second, I need him to reiterate publicly Israel's right to self-defense and approve an emergency weapons and military aid package for us. And third, the president needs to mobilize NATO and beef up U.S. forces in the Middle East—and not only in the Mediterranean but in the Persian Gulf as well."

Doron suddenly lowered his voice.

"You know as well as I do that this is not just about Israel, Jonathan. Gogolov is not just coming for us. He is coming to seize control of the world's oil supply. He is coming to bring the world's economy to its knees and to make Russia a superpower again. He has delusions of grandeur, Jonathan. And like a Hitler or a Stalin, Gogolov cannot be appeased. He cannot be contained. He must be stopped—now—at all costs, and your president must lead the way, or . . ."

Bennett waited, but Doron never finished.

Instead, the prime minister got up, walked to the window, and looked out over the Holy City.

"Or what?" asked Bennett.

Doron was clearly reluctant to say, but Bennett didn't care. He could not go back to the president and the NSC with his own assumptions. He had to hear it from Doron's lips, and then he did.

Doron came back from the window, leaned down, and spoke softly in Bennett's ear. "Or we may have to resort to The Samson Option."

McCoy heard the jangling of keys and a lock opening.

She opened her eyes only to be blinded again by the two bulbs hanging over her. She instinctively turned her head to the side and tried to refocus. It was the same guard pacing in the hall, and with him the same nurse. This time McCoy caught her name off the dangling ID card.

Tatiana Grizkov.

Who was she? Could she become an ally? If so, how? And how quickly?

Time, McCoy knew, was not her friend.

"Today you must use the toilet."

The brusque order in Russian surprised McCoy. The woman's voice was tougher than McCoy had expected, but her hands trembled as she unlocked the handcuffs and helped McCoy to her feet.

With the pain medication wearing off and the new booster shot not yet jammed into her badly bruised thigh, McCoy could, for the first time, actually feel the bullet wounds in her stomach and abdomen. Curious, she stepped into the bathroom, pulled back the bandages, and saw the two small holes, oozing blood and pus.

McCoy felt her forehead. It was hot and clammy. She had a fever. Whatever antibiotics they had her on were only barely fighting back the infection.

Still, she felt surprisingly strong, considering the trauma she'd been through. Her legs weren't as shaky as she might have thought. She was making progress, though she wondered if that was such a good thing.

It was now clear she was in a Russian military prison. Solitary confinement. An armed guard with her around the clock. No windows. No fresh air. Just a damp, disgusting, cinder-block cell, and a cold metal bed frame to which she was chained twenty-three hours and fifty minutes a day.

Apparently she would be allowed at least a periodic bathroom break, but there was no sink, and the toilet was nothing more than a hole in the muddy porcelain tiles.

And this, she knew, was the best she could hope for. What lay ahead would be far worse.

☆　☆　☆

The Samson Option.

Mordechai had explained it to him three years earlier.

It was the last option in the Israeli defensive arsenal—the Armageddon option—named after the last desperate act of a Hebrew warrior. And to Bennett's surprise, he could suddenly recall the biblical story with striking clarity.

Samson was a fierce and effective Israelite warrior, blessed by God with supernatural strength. But he turned his back on God. Becoming involved with a prostitute named Delilah, he suddenly found himself surrounded by his mortal enemies, the Philistines.

The Philistines seized Samson, gouged out his eyes, and threw him into a dungeon. Later, they bound him in bronze shackles, brought him into their temple, put him on display for all of the rulers and some three thousand people to see, and prepared to sacrifice him to Dagon, their god.

But Samson was not about to go peacefully into the night.

"O Lord God, please remember me," he prayed, "and please strengthen me just this time, O God, that I may at once be avenged of the Philistines for my two eyes."

Blind but determined not to go down alone, Samson braced himself against the two central pillars upon which the temple stood and prayed once more.

"Let me die with the Philistines."

Then he pushed against the pillars with all his might. The pillars gave way, bringing the roof of the temple crashing down. Samson, the rulers, and all the people in the temple were crushed. The mighty Samson had killed more Philistines in his final, fatal attack than he had during his life.

Was Doron really contemplating such a move?

Was he really prepared to unleash all of Israel's nuclear fury to take as many of his country's enemies with him to the grave as possible, knowing that such a move would ensure Israel's own complete destruction?

He couldn't be serious. It was madness.

Bennett put the question to the prime minister point-blank.

"I will give no official comment," Doron responded without hesitation. "I will simply promise you this: Israel will never suffer another Holocaust alone."

35

★ ★
★

Bennett was going to need that rain check after all.

The Gogolov crisis was now spinning dangerously out of control. The president of the United States was running scared, unable or unwilling to stop a tyrant in his tracks. The prime minister of Israel felt cornered and hinted at a nuclear Armageddon. Perhaps a retired Israeli spymaster could help him navigate the minefields that lay ahead.

Bennett followed the cobblestone path and arrived under an immense, jagged limestone cantilever jutting out like a cliff over a spectacular view of the Old City of Jerusalem. As he approached the arched, cavelike front entrance, he remembered how intrigued he'd been the first time he had ever come to this Frank Lloyd Wright-ish home built into the side of the hill. McCoy had been with him. He could almost see her ringing the doorbell, almost hear the echo of chimes as beautiful as those in the Church of the Holy Sepulchre in the valley below. Even now, so many years later, he still had the sense that Dr. Mordechai's home was somehow a reflection of the man inside, a man shrouded in mystery and murkiness and a hint of magic.

Three years before, Bennett, McCoy, and Dr. Mordechai had almost been killed in this house; tonight, the dozen DSS agents with him were taking no chances. They set up a perimeter as Bennett rang the bell.

Bennett was quickly greeted by two armed Mossad agents, neither of whom had any idea he was coming. They required him to present his driver's license and put his thumbs on an electronic touch pad that was tethered to a notebook computer. Bennett couldn't see the well-hidden security cameras, but he assumed they were still in place, running his image through facial-recognition software that scanned eighty different facial landmarks, measured pixels on his eyes and lips, analyzed his cheekbones and skull structure, then cross-checked his three-dimensional "face-print" against a Mossad database of thousands of international spies, criminals, and terrorists.

Seconds later Bennett was cleared to proceed down a long, dark hallway, almost like a tunnel, covered by the limestone that jutted right through the external wall and ended where a wide, circular staircase began.

The great room into which he ascended was as stunning as ever. Thick, rich, gorgeous purple-and-gold-and-maroon Persian rugs covered the polished brown hardwood floors. Lush young palm trees—at least half a dozen of them—rose out of huge reddish clay pots positioned here and there. Large brown Italian-leather couches and chairs surrounded a glass and wrought-iron coffee table adorned with ancient archeological artifacts from all over the Near East along with the latest newsmagazines from Israel, Europe, and the U.S.

A sleek, black baby grand piano occupied one corner of the room. A collection of Jackson Pollock paintings adorned the walls. He could smell roast lamb and the ginger and turmeric and coriander of an Indian curry that was one of Mordechai's specialties.

Bennett loved this house, but there were memories here that still haunted him. The fire damage had been repaired. The shell casings had long since been removed. But as Bennett closed his eyes for a moment, he didn't hear the trickle of a water fountain or the roaring fire in the great stone fireplace; he heard explosions. The gentle strains of a Bach violin concerto seeping from small Bose speakers hidden all over the house were replaced by gunfire and the screams of those hit when bullets found their marks. He no longer smelled the sumptuous dinner cooking in the kitchen; he smelled the stench of gunpowder hanging in the air.

Bennett scanned the cavernous room.

The air was cool and soft. Thunder rumbled outside. A rare September storm was building, as were the flashbacks of that grisly December night.

The images still haunted him. Perhaps they always would. But they also brought back vivid memories of the woman who'd saved his life. He could still see Erin firing at a man in the shadows. He could see her rushing to his side. He could hear her begging him to stay with her and pleading with God to save his life and his soul.

Bennett was suddenly overcome with shame. Was he on his knees before God, pleading for her life every day? Why not? What was wrong with him?

And then Mordechai startled him with a tap on the shoulder.

"Hungry?"

Bennett had never eaten so well.

Roast-lamb kebabs. Couscous. Mixed vegetables sautéed in butter and some kind of Middle Eastern spices. It was almost as if Mordechai had been expecting him after all.

By ten, dinner was over. The two men relaxed in the living room beside the fire, sipping Turkish coffee and eating baklava. They'd covered the lack of news on McCoy, and the latest news from Moscow and Washington, and the meeting with Doron. And as they did, Bennett suddenly realized how much he had missed his old friend, the man who had led him to Christ, this brilliant, fascinating man who always seemed to have time for him.

He knew Mordechai was worried about him. He *was* running on empty. Life on the political bullet train hurtled by so fast he barely had time to breathe much less pray. But there was something about being back in this home, with logs crackling in the fireplace, that made Bennett ache for things that mattered most.

"So," he said finally, "about my mother's question."

Mordechai raised an eyebrow. "I thought you were not interested."

"Inquiring minds want to know." Bennett smiled.

"Very well, then. Let us begin. Grab that copy of the Scriptures."

On the coffee table in front of him, Bennett found an old, leather-bound volume and carefully opened the brittle, yellowed pages. It was a

side-by-side Hebrew-English edition of the Jewish Scriptures known as
the Tanakh. It included the Torah—the five books of Moses—as well as
the books written by the Hebrew prophets and the *Ketuvim*, or other sacred writings, such as the Psalms and Proverbs.

"Where are we headed?" asked Bennett.

"Daniel chapter 9, verses 26 and 27."

Bennett found the passage.

כו   וְאַחֲרֵי הַשָּׁבֻעִים שִׁשִּׁים וּשְׁנַיִם יִכָּרֵת
מָשִׁיחַ וְאֵין לוֹ וְהָעִיר וְהַקֹּדֶשׁ יַשְׁחִית עַם נָגִיד
הַבָּא וְקִצּוֹ בַשֶּׁטֶף וְעַד קֵץ מִלְחָמָה נֶחֱרֶצֶת
שֹׁמֵמוֹת

כז   וְהִגְבִּיר בְּרִית לָרַבִּים שָׁבוּעַ אֶחָד
וַחֲצִי הַשָּׁבוּעַ יַשְׁבִּית זֶבַח וּמִנְחָה
וְעַל כְּנַף שִׁקּוּצִים מְשֹׁמֵם וְעַד־כָּלָה וְנֶחֱרָצָה
תִּתַּךְ עַל־שֹׁמֵם

Knowing no Hebrew but *shalom*, Bennett began reading from the
column in English.

> *Then after the sixty-two weeks*
> *the Messiah will be*
> *cut off and have nothing,*
> *and the people of the prince*
> *who is to come will destroy the city*
> *and the sanctuary.*
> *And its end will come with a flood;*
> *even to the end there will be war;*
> *desolations are determined.*

And he will make a firm covenant
with the many for one week,
but in the middle of the week he will
put a stop to sacrifice and grain offering;
and on the wing of abominations
will come one who makes desolate,
even until a complete destruction,
one that is decreed,
is poured out on the one
who makes desolate.

It all seemed like gibberish to Bennett, an ancient riddle he had no capacity to decode. He was no Bible scholar. Erin had a strong working knowledge of the Scriptures. Mordechai was a master. But Bennett was a novice, and he was lost.

"You have to understand, Jonathan, that Daniel was one of the most extraordinary prophets in Scripture. He wrote a great deal about the End Times, and though he never used the term *Antichrist*, Daniel's meaning is crystal clear.

"He tells us the Antichrist will be a prince—a ruler, a demonic dictator the likes of which mankind has never seen before and will never see again. The sixty-two 'weeks' Daniel mentions are literally 'sixty-two sevens.' The term can also be translated 'sixty-two weeks of years,' or sixty-two periods of seven years. So sixty-two weeks means 434 years. A 'firm covenant with the many for one week' refers to a peace treaty the Antichrist will sign with Israel, 'the many,' for seven years. But after half that time—three and a half years—he will break it. We also learn that he will put an end to Jewish control of the holy Temple and desecrate the Temple with some sort of 'abomination.'"

Bennett wanted to take notes, something he could e-mail to his mom. He'd never remember all this. For now, however, he had the sense he should just listen.

"In Daniel 11:39-45," Mordechai continued, "we learn this enemy of God will be a ferocious conqueror. He will invade and conquer many countries. He will invade Israel, which Daniel describes as 'the Beautiful Land.' And 'with great wrath,' this global dictator will 'annihilate many.'

"Now, when you add these clues to all the others in Scripture, the picture is very sobering: the Anti-Messiah—or Antichrist—will be the most powerful ruler the world has ever seen. In 2 Thessalonians 2:3 he is called the 'son of perdition' or 'man of lawlessness,' which many scholars believe means that he will be indwelt by Satan himself. He will be a master deceiver. And he will be on the warpath against God, God's followers, and anyone who will not bow down and worship this king who calls himself a god."

"Wait a minute," Bennett said. "You're saying that Daniel predicted that Gogolov would invade Israel and annihilate the Jews—three thousand years ago?"

"He predicted that the Antichrist would, yes."

"But *is* Gogolov the Antichrist?" Bennett pressed.

"That is the million-dollar question, is it not? OK, now go back to Daniel 9:26. There is a critical clue for how to identify the Antichrist."

Bennett read the verse twice. Then a third time. "I'm not seeing it."

"Do you see where Daniel says that at the appointed time Messiah will come to Israel and then be 'cut off,' or killed?"

"Yes."

"And after that, see how Daniel says that Jerusalem—'the city'—and the Temple—'the sanctuary'—will be destroyed?"

"Yeah."

"All right, stop there for a minute. What is amazing is that this part of the prophecy has already come true. *Yeshua HaMashiach*—whom you call Jesus the Messiah, in English—has already come to earth. He has already come to Israel, as recorded in the Gospels. But the Romans cut Him off. They killed Him. And what happened next? Jerusalem and the Temple were burned to the ground. The 'city' and the 'sanctuary' were destroyed, just like Daniel said would happen. The big question for our purposes is, by whom? Who destroyed Jerusalem and the Temple?"

"The Romans."

"Exactly," said Mordechai, a gleam in his eyes. "It was the Roman army under Titus who destroyed Jerusalem, beginning in AD 70. The Roman legions killed over a million Jews at the time. This is important, because Daniel specifically prophesied that Jerusalem and the Temple would be destroyed by 'the people of the prince who is to come,' that is, by the nation out of which the Antichrist will one day arise."

"You're saying the Antichrist has to be of Roman origin?"

"Exactly. Daniel 8:8-9 also says the Antichrist will be a king who emerges from the ashes of the Greco-Roman Empire and gathers enormous powers as his military forces move south and east toward the land of Israel, to surround and eventually conquer it. The apostle John in Revelation 13:1 calls the Antichrist 'a beast coming up out of the sea,' referring to the Mediterranean Sea. Bottom line: the scriptural evidence strongly suggests the Antichrist comes from somewhere around the Mediterranean and has a Roman bloodline."

"Not Russian."

"No, not Russian."

"So it can't be Yuri Gogolov."

"No. No scriptural indication exists to suggest that the Antichrist will be from Moscow. Now it is true that Moscow has long been known by Russians as the *Third Rome*, and was built on seven hills like Rome. And it is true that Russia was ruled for three hundred years by a dynasty known as the Romanovs. Nevertheless, when Daniel says the Antichrist will have a Roman bloodline, he means *Roman*, not Russian. That said, the Scriptures also indicate that for much of his reign of terror, the Antichrist will be based in Babylon."

"Babylon, like in Iraq?" said Bennett.

"That's the one."

"How do we know that?"

"The prophet Isaiah describes the Antichrist as 'the king of Babylon.' And the book of Revelation makes it clear that the city of Babylon is the epicenter of the evil in the last days. What's eerie is that Babylon all but disappeared off the face of the planet hundreds of years ago. Only the Bible predicts Babylon will rise again to play a central role in the End Times. For centuries, that seemed ludicrous. But now that you Americans have overthrown Saddam Hussein's regime and the U.N. sanctions have been lifted, is it really so difficult to see Babylon rapidly emerging as one of the world's wealthiest and most powerful cities?"

"I guess not."

"Of course not, and the rest of the world does not seem to notice or care. And why should they? They are just glad that Saddam is gone, and that Iraq is finally quiet, and that you Americans have pulled out. They have no idea what prophetic forces have been set in motion. But think about it. If the Antichrist is going to reign in Babylon, then Babylon must rise again in the last days."

"Aren't you forgetting something?" Bennett asked. "You said a minute ago that the Antichrist will put something offensive in the Temple. There's just one problem."

Mordechai smiled. "The Temple no longer exists?"

"Yeah. How do you get around that?"

"Simple. If the Antichrist is going to desecrate the Jewish Temple in Jerusalem, then the Temple has to be rebuilt in the last days. Are you aware that some Orthodox Jewish groups are already preparing the priestly clothing and sacrificial implements in anticipation of the Third Temple?"

"And you think all this means what exactly?" Bennett asked.

"I think the last days are upon us, Jonathan. Which means I think the rise of the Antichrist is imminent."

"But wait a minute," Bennett said, trying to make sense of it all. "If the Antichrist is going to be the king of Babylon, doesn't that mean he could actually be some kind of Arab-Muslim dictator from Iraq, sort of a Saddam Hussein on demonic steroids? I mean, Al-Hassani, for example. He seems like a charming, mysterious, charismatic guy now, but couldn't he suddenly emerge as the Antichrist?"

"Some Bible scholars think so," Mordechai said. "Personally, I have my doubts. Racially, ethnically, the Antichrist will be Roman. Geographically, he will emerge from southern Europe, near the Mediterranean. Politically, he will resurrect the ancient Roman Empire and extend its reach across the entire globe. Militarily, he will wage war against Jews and Christians. He will seek to take over the Holy Land and the Holy City, and he will declare himself to be God. Operationally, he will run his empire from Babylon."

"All right," Bennett said, "so all the Internet buzz notwithstanding, Yuri Gogolov cannot possibly be the Antichrist; that's what you're saying?"

"That is what I am saying," said Mordechai. "That is the good news. Now the bad news."

36
★ ★
★

"Are they ready, Mohammed?"

Yuri Gogolov stood staring out the window of his palatial and newly refurbished Kremlin office as Mohammed Jibril briefed him on his trip to Tehran.

"Almost, Your Excellency. The warheads arrived at the base in Iran safely and on time, and we have no reason to believe the U.S. or Israelis have detected their arrival. They are being fitted into the nose cones of the *Shahab*-3 missiles even as we speak, under the guise of routine maintenance. I expect the work to be completed by the first week of October."

"And the other details we discussed?"

"They have all been taken care of, Your Excellency."

"Good. Then schedule the press conference here in the Kremlin for eight o'clock Tuesday night. That will be noon in Washington, just hours before MacPherson delivers his big speech. Then contact Tehran. Make sure President Kharrazi is here, along with a large delegation of Iranian legislators and dignitaries. I want them standing at my side when I make the announcement. But make it clear to Kharrazi—there must be absolutely no leaks. We must have the element of surprise."

✩ ✩ ✩

"Bad news?"

Bennett wasn't sure he could handle any more.

Mordechai nodded. "Yuri Gogolov is not the Antichrist. But I am afraid we have a different problem with Mr. Gogolov."

"What problem?" asked Bennett.

"A little over twenty-five hundred years ago," Mordechai began, "a Hebrew prophet named Ezekiel had a vision in which he foresaw a conspiracy that could have been ripped out of this morning's headlines. He saw modern countries then unborn, modern alliances yet unformed, and a day of unspeakable terror, all driven by a tyrant from the north.

"For centuries, scholars have argued over the meaning of Ezekiel's cryptic vision. Some have said it is merely an allegory of sin and judgment and the spirit world. But others believe what Ezekiel saw was, in fact, a glimpse into the future, that what he saw was the rise of an actual flesh-and-blood leader who would one day take over Russia, form an alliance with Iran and the radical Islamic world, and take up arms against a modern State of Israel—and in so doing unleash an apocalyptic nightmare leading to the Rapture of the church and the return of Christ.

"Now, for years, I will admit, I did not know what to believe. And to be honest, I did not much care. But recent events have changed everything for me, Jonathan. It gives me no pleasure to say it, but I must tell you that I believe Ezekiel's prophecy is coming true before our very eyes."

Bennett wasn't sure how to react.

Before him sat one of the most brilliant men he had ever met, a man who had predicted Iraq's war with Iran eighteen months before it began, a man who had predicted Iraq's invasion of Kuwait in 1990 when nearly every other Middle East analyst said Saddam was just "saber-rattling" and trying to drive up the price of oil.

Mordechai's understanding of the Islamic world did seem eerily prophetic, and it had earned him the top spot in the world's most effective intelligence agency. But how was Bennett supposed to process something like this?

Mordechai pointed to the old leather Bible still in Bennett's lap. "Please open to *Yechezchiel*—Ezekiel—chapter 38," he said softly.

Bennett quickly found the page and scanned the first two verses.

א וַיְהִי דְבַר־יְהוָה אֵלַי לֵאמֹר
ב בֶּן־אָדָם שִׂים פָּנֶיךָ אֶל־גּוֹג אֶרֶץ הַמָּגוֹג
נְשִׂיא רֹאשׁ מֶשֶׁךְ וְתֻבָל וְהִנָּבֵא עָלָיו

"Go ahead," said Mordechai, "start reading in English."
Bennett did.

> *And the word of the LORD*
> *came to me saying, "Son of man,*
> *set your face toward Gog*
> *of the land of Magog,*
> *the prince of Rosh, Meshech and Tubal,*
> *and prophesy against him and say,*
> *'Thus says the LORD God,*
> *"Behold, I am against you, O Gog,*
> *prince of Rosh, Meshech and Tubal.*
> *And I will turn you about,*
> *and put hooks into your jaws,*
> *and I will bring you out,*
> *and all your army, horses and horsemen,*
> *all of them splendidly attired,*
> *a great company with buckler and shield,*
> *all of them wielding swords;*
> *Persia, Cush, and Put with them,*
> *all of them with shield and helmet;*
> *Gomer with all its troops;*
> *Beth-togarmah from the remote*
> *parts of the north*
> *with all its troops—*
> *many peoples with you."*

He had no idea what he was reading, but he continued, curious to see where the old man was taking him.

"Be prepared, and prepare yourself,
you and all your companies
that are assembled about you,
and be a guard for them.
After many days you will be summoned;
in the latter years
you will come into the land
that is restored from the sword,
whose inhabitants have been gathered
from many nations to the
mountains of Israel which had been
a continual waste; but its people
were brought out from the nations,
and they are living securely,
all of them. You will go up,
you will come like a storm;
you will be like a cloud
covering the land,
you and all your troops,
and many peoples with you."

Bennett stopped for a moment and looked up for guidance, but Mordechai simply motioned for him to go on, so he kept reading.

'Thus says the LORD God,
"It will come about on that day,
that thoughts will come into your mind,
and you will devise an evil plan,
and you will say,
'I will go up against the land
of unwalled villages.
I will go against those
who are at rest, that live securely,
all of them living without walls,
and having no bars or gates,
to capture spoil and to seize plunder,

> *to turn your hand against the waste places*
> *which are now inhabited,*
> *and against the people*
> *who are gathered from the nations,*
> *who have acquired cattle and goods,*
> *who live at the center of the world.'*
> *Sheba, and Dedan, and the*
> *merchants of Tarshish,*
> *with all its villages, will say to you,*
> *'Have you come to capture spoil?*
> *Have you assembled your company*
> *to seize plunder,*
> *to carry away silver and gold,*
> *to take away cattle and goods,*
> *to capture great spoil?'"'*

Mordechai poured Bennett another cup of piping hot, thick Turkish coffee. He handed one across the table.

Grateful, Bennett carefully took a sip and felt the caffeine surge through his system almost immediately.

Mordechai had warned that Ezekiel's vision was cryptic—and it was that and more. But to his surprise, Bennett was beginning to catch glimpses of meaning in the murky passages. Evidently some king named Gog was going to attack a nation "whose inhabitants have been gathered from many nations to the mountains of Israel." That was clear enough. The number of Jews who had returned to the nation of Israel since its re-birth in 1948 was in the millions. And the text further described these people as being "at rest" and living "securely." Bennett himself had had a hand in establishing security in Israel in recent years. When before now could Israel be described as a nation at rest?

He had to admit that he found himself increasingly intrigued by the notion that an ancient prophecy was coming true in their lifetime. *Was it?*

The idea seemed ludicrous on its face. But even Bennett had to admit *something* bizarre was unfolding around them. He set down his coffee and continued reading.

"Therefore, prophesy, son of man,
and say to Gog,
'Thus says the LORD God,
"On that day when My people Israel
are living securely, will you not know it?
And you will come from your place
out of the remote parts of the north,
you and many peoples with you,
all of them riding on horses,
a great assembly and a mighty army;
and you will come up against
My people Israel
like a cloud to cover the land.
It will come about in the last days
that I shall bring you against My land,
in order that the nations may know Me
when I am sanctified through you
before their eyes, O Gog."'

"OK, Jonathan, you may stop there," Mordechai said finally, then set down his own coffee and looked Bennett squarely in the eyes. "I know this may be hard to accept at first, but what you just read was not the scribblings of some ancient lunatic. It was an intercept from the mind of God."

A chill suddenly ran down Bennett's spine.

"Almost a third of all Scripture is prophecy," Mordechai continued, his gaze still fixed on Bennett, "and half of all the prophecies in the Bible—some five hundred of them—have already been fulfilled. The rest deal with what the Hebrew prophets called the 'last days'—the count-down to Messiah's return, Messiah's reign on earth, and God's plan to destroy the heavens and the earth and to create them anew.

"Now, notice in verse 8 that Ezekiel refers to 'the latter years.' And in verse 16, he says this prophecy 'will come about in the last days.' Whenever the Hebrew prophets wrote about the last days, they were always referring to the last days *before* Messiah would come to set up His kingdom on earth, or what Revelation 20 teaches us will be the *millennial,* or thousand-year, reign of Christ. So we know that Ezekiel 38 is what's called an End-Times prophecy. It refers to events that will occur *before* the return of Christ.

"The big questions are, *who* are the major players in this apocalyptic drama, and *how soon* is all this going to happen?"

37

★ ★
★

Mordechai reached into a briefcase and removed a notebook.

"Here," he said, handing it to Bennett.

Bennett took it. Then, at Mordechai's request, he made a list of the bizarre-sounding names in the chapter's first six verses.

* Gog
* Magog
* Rosh
* Meshech
* Tubal
* Persia
* Cush
* Put
* Gomer
* Beth-togarmah

Bennett stared at the list for a few moments. Were these names of people? cities? countries? Were they a code of some sort? They clearly described forces that would one day "come like a storm" against Israel to wipe her off the face of the planet. But he hadn't a clue how one could break a code 2,500 years old.

"Let me see if I can make some sense of all that," Mordechai offered. "The first thing we need to understand is that the first word on the list, *Gog*, is not a name. It is a title, like *czar* or *pharaoh*. In this case, Ezekiel tells us that Gog is a 'prince' who will arise in a land called Magog. Which begs the question, where is Magog? One clue comes from Voltaire."

"The French philosopher? Hero of secular humanists?" Bennett asked.

"*Exactement*," said Mordechai with a smile. "Voltaire was hardly a religious man. Indeed, he was a self-declared enemy of Christ. He once wrote a letter to Frederick the Great, the eighteenth-century king of Germany, arguing that 'Christianity is the most ridiculous, the most absurd, and bloody religion that has ever infected the world.'"

"Doesn't sound like your kind of guy."

"True," Mordechai said. "But for some reason Voltaire was intrigued with solving the riddle of Gog and Magog. Here . . ."

Mordechai stood up and crossed to a tall bookshelf, covered with ornate carvings and filled with beautifully bound volumes. He ran a finger along a row of books, then selected one and pulled it out. He handed it to Bennett.

Bennett looked at the cover. It was a translation of *The Philosophical Dictionary* by Voltaire.

Bennett opened to the page Mordechai specified, then scanned the short essay he found there. Within seconds he saw what Mordechai wanted him to see. Voltaire had written: "There is a genealogical tree of the events of this world. It is incontestable that the inhabitants of Gaul and Spain are descended from Gomer, and the Russians from Magog, his younger brother.'"

Bennett looked up. "Voltaire thought Magog was Russia?" he asked in disbelief.

"He did, and remember, he was writing nearly one hundred fifty years *before* the rise of Russia as a major world power. Even more interesting, the genealogical tree to which he refers actually finds its origin in the very Bible for which he had such little regard."

"What do you mean?"

"The first place the world ever heard of Magog was in the Bible. Genesis 10—Magog was a son of Japheth, who was a son of Noah. Three of his brothers were Meshech, Tubal, and Gomer. I will get to them shortly, but let us stay with Magog for the moment.

"The Bible lays out Noah's entire family tree. It shows how Noah's descendants migrated to Africa, Europe, and Asia, establishing the first civilizations on those continents. In trying to decode the Gog and Magog prophecy, Voltaire studied Noah's genealogical tree, then compared it with the histories of these different continents in hopes of determining where each of Noah's descendants ended up. Wait a moment; I have something else for you to read."

Mordechai went back to the bookshelf and searched for several seconds before finding the book he wanted.

"Here it is. Ever hear of Josephus?"

"The Roman historian?"

"Yes."

"Sure. Why?"

"Here," Mordechai said, handing Bennett the large book. "This is a compilation of *The Antiquities of the Jews*, a twenty-volume classic written in the first century after Christ. Look in book 1, chapter 6."

Bennett began reading and found the reference to Magog almost immediately. He read aloud: "'Magog founded those that from him were named Magogites, but who are by the Greeks called Scythians.'"

"OK," Mordechai said. "Now the Scythians, we know from history, were absolute barbarians—expert horsemen but fierce, bloodthirsty killers. They actually used skulls as mugs to drink the blood of their victims. And genetically, they were Aryans."

Surprised, Bennett looked up from his notes. "The same Aryans that Hitler called the 'superior race'?"

"From the same gene pool, yes, but the Scythians did not live in Germany."

"Where did they live?"

"Russia and Islamic Central Asia."

"You're kidding."

"I am not," said Mordechai. "Ever been to the Hermitage Museum in St. Petersburg?"

"Can't say I have."

"Next time you go, check out the exhibit of Scythian artifacts found in southern Russia. And next time you are in Moscow, take the tour of the State Historical Museum on Red Square. I was just there last year, and I found case after case of Scythian artifacts, all dug up by Russian archeologists, and all on display in Russia's official museum."

Bennett knew he wasn't likely to be back in Moscow anytime soon. But Mordechai now had his full attention. He glanced back at chapter 38 and asked, "All right, Ezekiel says this Gog character is 'the prince of Rosh, Meshech, and Tubal.' What does that mean?"

"The word *Rosh* in Hebrew can mean 'head' or 'chief,' leading some scholars to the conclusion that Gog is the *chief prince* of Meshech and Tubal, not the prince of *Rosh*, Meshech, and Tubal. But both the Masoretic text and the Septuagint translate *Rosh* as the proper name of a geological place."

"Hold on a minute," Bennett said. "What's the Septuagint and the Massa-something?"

"The Septuagint," Mordechai explained, "is the oldest Greek translation of the Hebrew Scriptures. It was translated in Alexandria, Egypt, a few hundred years before Christ. The Masoretic text, or Masora, is the full Hebrew text of the Tanakh or Old Testament, upon which most Jewish Bibles are based. Ironically, one of the oldest and best-preserved copies we have of the Masoretic text—the one giving us a complete version of Ezekiel's vision of Gog and Magog—is called the Leningrad Codex. It is housed in the Russian National Library in St. Petersburg, Russia."

"Why do you say that's ironic?" Bennett asked.

"Because if you scour ancient history and languages," Mordechai said, "you will find the name *Rosh* is linguistically related to the words *Rhos*, *Rus*, and *Ros*, all of which were ancient names for Russia."

"That *is* ironic," Bennett said, his curiosity growing.

"Take Wilhelm Gesenius, for example," Mordechai continued. "Gesenius was a nineteenth-century German professor who died in 1842, but to this day he is considered the father of modern Hebrew lexicography. In his seminal work, *Gesenius' Hebrew-Chaldee Lexicon to the Old Testament*, he concluded that the *Rosh* to which Ezekiel refers is 'undoubtedly the Russians, who are mentioned by the Byzantine writers of the tenth century, under the name *the Ros*, dwelling to the north of the Taurus.'"

"Incredible," said Bennett, trying to take it all in. "Then what about Meshech?"

Mordechai didn't miss a beat. "Bible scholars say Meshech is Moscow," he replied. "Gesenius, for one, wrote that 'Meshech was founder of the Moschi, a barbarous people, inhabiting the Moschian mountains.' He went on to conclude that the Greek name *Moschi* was, in fact, the city of Moscow."

"And Tubal?"

"Ever hear of a Russian city called Tobolsk?"

"In Siberia, right?" said Bennett.

"The heart of Russian oil country, that is right," said Mordechai. "And do you know what river it is on?"

"No idea."

"Tobolsk is actually a port city at the confluence of the Irtysh and Tobol rivers."

"*Tubal*," said Bennett in disbelief.

"Correct," Mordechai confirmed.

"But wait a minute," Bennett said suddenly. "Aren't you actually from Tobolsk?"

"You have a good memory, young man. I was born there, yes. Fortunately, my family got out when they did. For a long time, Tobolsk was the capital of Siberia, but eventually it became a place of horror. Czar Nicholas II and his family were exiled there during the Russian Revolution, just before they were murdered. And Stalin built a gulag there in the 1930s, where he butchered some fifty thousand political prisoners. My grandfather was among them."

"I had no idea," said Bennett, stunned.

"It is not something I talk about. You have to understand, Jonathan, the satanic brand of Communism practiced by Moscow was not just another *ism*. Reagan was right. The Soviet Union was an *Evil* Empire. The Soviets were responsible for the deaths of a hundred million souls during the twentieth century—twenty million within their own borders. It is no wonder the Soviet flag was red. The whole history of the Kremlin is soaked in blood. For seventy years, the rulers of Russia waged war against God, against Christians, against the Jews, and—by proxy at least, through the Arab League—against Israel.

"But they lost. The Soviet Union collapsed, and Israel survived and flourished, just as the Bible predicted. More than a million Jews fled Russia for Israel during the 1990s, just as the Bible predicted. The gates of hell did not prevail against the church in Russia. Indeed, the church there is growing again, just as the Bible predicted. And now the Russian government is on the verge of a terrible judgment. 'The one who curses you I will curse' the Lord said to the Jewish people. 'Vengeance is mine, says the Lord.' A day of reckoning is coming, Jonathan. God will not be mocked. A country reaps what she sows, and the judgment of Russia is at hand."

The cell door burst open.

The lights came on, but there was no nurse. Two armed guards unshackled McCoy, ripped the IV from her arm, and forced her to her feet. They dragged her through a long, dark hallway and down three flights of stairs before strapping her hands, feet, and neck to a pole in the center of what appeared to be a large, empty basement.

The air was dank and smelled of mold and sweat and stale cigarettes.

There were few lights, no windows, and only one door. The floor was cold concrete. What caught her attention most were the bloodstains on the floor.

When the guards finished securing her, they stepped back, and a man entered the room. His face and head were covered by a hood, like someone in the Ku Klux Klan, except that this hood was black. He walked toward her, carrying something behind his back, though she couldn't tell what. Seconds later McCoy felt a baton smash into her stomach.

She couldn't breathe.

Again she felt the full force of the wooden club, this time across the face. She gasped for air as blood and tears blurred her vision.

"*Jesus!*" she tried to cry out, but the words would not form.

Blood streamed down her face.

She gritted her teeth and braced for more. *They would stop soon*, she told herself. *If they'd wanted her dead, they would have killed her by now. With a bullet to the forehead.*

No, she told herself, *these people want something.*

Which meant she was too valuable to kill. They wanted information. But it didn't matter. She would not give up her friends. She would not betray her country or her God. She didn't care how hard they beat her. She would tell them nothing.

But the questions never came.

The interrogation never began. The beating just continued mercilessly. This man was possessed. He was shouting at her, but she couldn't understand the words.

It wasn't Russian. It wasn't English or French.

The words were similar to Arabic but none that she knew.

What was it? Urdu? Farsi?

The blows rained down harder, on her face and arms, and across her chest and legs. Maybe she was wrong. Maybe she wasn't as valuable as she'd thought, or hoped.

Then let them kill me, she decided.

Other believers had suffered in this country. Others had died at these hands, and hands like them. Jesus had suffered far worse. He had suffered and bled and died for her. For her sins. To set her free. To adopt her as a child into His family. To bring her into His Kingdom. Forever. How could she not be willing to suffer and bleed and die for Him?

If that's what He asked, she would do it. With the strength He gave her. By the grace He provided. And maybe she would see Him soon, face-to-face.

"I don't know," said Bennett.

"What do you mean?" asked Mordechai.

"You're really saying that five hundred years before Christ, this guy Ezekiel predicted the rise of Russia, Moscow, and Siberia when none of those places were known to him or had any historic importance at the time?"

"That is what I am saying."

"But how can you be so sure all this stuff *really* refers to Russia? What if Ezekiel was writing about South America or Asia? I mean, how do we really know that over the centuries the name *Meshech* didn't evolve into *Moschi* and then into *Muskogee* or something?"

Mordechai smiled. "You think Oklahoma plans to invade Israel?"

"I don't know; I'm just saying, how can you—?"

"No, no, it is a fair question," Mordechai conceded. "Turn over to Ezekiel 39, and read verses 1 and 2."

Bennett flipped the page and began reading:

> *"And you, son of man,*
> *prophesy against Gog*
> *and say, 'Thus says the LORD God,*
> *"Behold, I am against you, O Gog,*
> *prince of Rosh, Meshech and Tubal;*
> *and I will turn you around,*
> *drive you on, take you up from*
> *the remotest parts of the north,*
> *and bring you against*
> *the mountains of Israel."*

"From that passage, where are Rosh, Meshech, and Tubal located?" asked Mordechai.

"'The remotest parts of the north.'"

"In relation to what?"

"To Israel?"

"Exactly," said Mordechai. He turned to one of the Jackson Pollock paintings hanging on the far wall, picked up a small remote off the coffee table, pointed it at the wall, and pushed a button. A huge map of the world lowered from the ceiling, completely covering the painting. Mordechai pushed another button, and the map was lit by small spotlights hidden in the ceiling.

"Impressive," said Bennett.

Mordechai just smiled. "So, what country is located to the *remotest* parts of the north of Israel?"

It was unmistakable, even from where Bennett sat.

"Russia."

"And what city is located due north of Jerusalem?"

That, too, was unmistakable.

"Moscow."

38

★ ★
★

"Erin, can you hear me?"

Someone was calling her name.

Gently, like a father. Like a friend.

"Jon . . . is that you?"

It took all the energy she had, but McCoy forced herself to open her eyes. But the face she saw was not Jon Bennett's. It was Mohammed Jibril's.

Instinctively, she recoiled—emotionally at least. She was still tied to the pole. For the first time, she knew exactly what she was up against. If Jibril was the one torturing her, she was not long for this earth. Her hands began to shake behind her.

There was no place to run.

"Erin, I want you to listen very carefully to what I am about to tell you."

McCoy shut her eyes. She tried to shut out the voice, but she could not. It was still there—first on her right side, then on her left. Jibril was circling her.

"Jon Bennett is alive—barely."

McCoy gasped.

"He is not here—not in this facility, anyway. But we have him. As you know, he was shot and severely wounded in the Kremlin. We almost lost him a few times, but we needed him, and he survived."

Jibril's voice was but a whisper.

"Now, Erin, you will be glad to know your government and your friends back home are anxious to get you both back. For the moment, our public position is that you were both wounded in the cross fire and are on life support. But I am prepared to send you both home, *if* you cooperate. Not Jon, mind you. We do not need his cooperation. We need yours."

Here it came—the offer she couldn't refuse.

They were kidding themselves. There was no way she was going to tell them anything. They'd have to kill her first. She was ready to die. At this point, she was almost looking forward to it.

"During the coup, we were able to capture a very interesting piece of equipment from the embassy vehicle that brought you to the Kremlin."

McCoy's heart began racing faster.

"You know which piece I am talking about. And you know something Bennett does not—the encryption codes."

Could that be true? Had Jibril gotten his hands on her laptop? If so, he and Gogolov could access the entire U.S. intelligence grid, including communications servers carrying classified cable traffic between the CIA, NSC, State Department, and the White House Situation Room. Giving up the codes would mean giving Gogolov and Jibril unrestricted access to everything the president and his senior advisors were saying, thinking, doing.

It was probable, of course, that the codes had been changed following the coup. And they were supposed to be changed on the first of each month anyway. But how could she take such a chance? Cooperating at all would make her guilty of treason even if the codes had been changed.

Jibril had to be bluffing. There was no way their driver would have allowed those laptops to be compromised—unless . . .

"You think I am lying, yes?" Jibril said softly, as if reading her mind. "Very well, I will show it to you."

She couldn't resist. She had to know. She opened her eyes and looked at him. And sure enough, he was holding her laptop—booted up and awaiting her password. Jibril set it on a small table, then walked over to her. His face was just inches from hers. She had one chance. She might as well take it.

"Drop dead," she screamed and spit in his face.

Jibril didn't move. He didn't even blink. He stared calmly at her for a moment, then slowly removed a handkerchief from his pocket and wiped his face. He didn't seem angry. He was even beginning to smile.

"Erin, Erin—come—you did not even let me finish. We both know what you really do for a living. And we both know whom you really work for. So here is the deal— every day you refuse to give us the correct codes, we will torture Jon Bennett without mercy."

McCoy could barely breathe.

They were bluffing. They had to be.

"It is as simple as that, Erin. Obviously, you will be tortured, too, though I do not think that really bothers you. You are a trained CIA operative. You know what it takes to survive, or at least to hold out for several weeks. But really, how could you live with yourself knowing that you alone were responsible for the suffering of the man you love?"

The question hung in the air for a moment, and then Jibril began to beat her again.

"Who is left on our list?" Mordechai asked.

Bennett flipped back through his notepad and read off the remaining names: "Persia, Cush, Put, Gomer, and Beth-togarmah."

"Of course," said Mordechai. "These are Gog's allies. Historically, Persia is the easiest to identify. Until 1935, *Persia* was the name of the country we now call Iran, one of the founding members of the Axis of Evil and the epicenter of modern terrorism. The Cushites, according to Josephus, settled in Africa, south of Egypt. Josephus called that area Ethiopia, but it included what we now call Eritrea and Sudan as well. Sudan, of course, has become a base camp for radical Islamic terrorism, armed for years by the Soviets and more recently by Iran. And, as you know, the Sudanese jihadists have waged a campaign of genocide, particularly in the Darfur region, killing some three hundred thousand people in recent years."

Mordechai used a laser pointer to direct Bennett around the map on the far wall.

"Which brings us to Put. Josephus wrote that '*Phut* also was the founder of Libya.' Now, I know that Libya claims to have given up their weapons of mass destruction and support for terrorism. But personally, I do not believe it. And you should know that ancient Libya actually included Tunisia and Algeria, both of which have long histories of hatred toward Israel and close ties to Moscow and Tehran. What is more, notice the reference Ezekiel makes in 38:13 to Sheba and Dedan. Those are ancient names for Saudi Arabia and the Persian Gulf region."

"So what are you saying, exactly?" asked Bennett.

"I am saying that when you add up Ezekiel's references to central Asia, Iran, Saudi Arabia, the Persian Gulf, and North Africa, you get a coalition of modern radical Islamic countries working closely with Russia."

One by one, the pieces of the puzzle were coming together. There were only two holes remaining now: Gomer and Beth-togarmah.

"These are a little trickier," Mordechai admitted.

He dug into the briefcase again and this time pulled out a thick file folder stuffed with pages of notes. He opened the file and selected a page as if at random, though Bennett figured Mordechai could probably identify every piece of paper simply from its location in the stack.

"Let me start with Beth-togarmah, which means 'the House of Togarmah.' The best evidence I have read for the identity of Beth-togarmah is in a book called *Things To Come* by Dr. Dwight Pentecost, a professor of Bible exposition at Dallas Theological Seminary. He concluded that Togarmah 'is generally identified as Turkey or Armenia.'"

"What was the evidence?" Bennett asked.

"Dr. Pentecost cites two primary sources," said Mordechai, consulting his notes. "One was Dr. Harry Rimmer, a prophecy scholar who wrote a book in 1940 called *The Coming War and the Rise of Russia*. According to Rimmer's research, 'Togarmah has always been the land which we now call Armenia. It is so named in the records of Assyria. . . . Indeed, all Armenian literature refers to the land and its people as The House of Togarmah.'

"The second source was Dr. Louis Bauman, one of the founders of Grace Theological Seminary. Bauman wrote a book in 1942 called *Russian Events in the Light of Bible Prophecy*. Based on his research, Bauman also concluded that Togarmah is 'the Turkoman tribes of Central Asia, together with Siberia, the Turks, and the Armenians.'"

Bennett wasn't sure he bought any of that. The Turks—from the Ottoman Empire onward—had maintained a fairly benign relationship with the Jews over the centuries. And of all the countries in the modern Muslim world, Turkey was without question the most moderate. Thousands of Israeli tourists flooded Turkish resort towns each year. Trade between the two countries was growing, and the Turks—who imported nearly all of their energy needs—were now exploring the prospect of buying Medexco gas and oil.

To Bennett, who had dined with Turkish president Kuzemir in Ankara a few months earlier, it was almost inconceivable that Turkey could join a Russian-Islamic invasion of Israel. But it was a question he would have to explore later, he decided.

For now, he just wanted to finish the list.

"Last one," said Bennett. "Gomer."

"Gomer is the toughest, I fear. I have been wrestling with it for a long time."

"And?"

"We know from Genesis 10 that Gomer—like Magog, Meschech, and Tubal—was a son of Japheth, which puts them all into one big, violent clan. Josephus writes that 'Gomer founded those whom the Greeks now call Galatians, but were then called Gomerites.' Galatia, of course, is in modern-day Turkey. But there's evidence that some of the Gomerites drifted northward over the centuries."

"To where?" asked Bennett.

"That is where it gets a bit murky. Voltaire, as I mentioned earlier, believed Gomer migrated to France and Spain. That may be partly true, but I believe most of Gomer's tribe headed northward into Europe. Genesis 10 identifies one of Gomer's sons as Ashkenaz. We know for certain that the Ashkenazi people migrated to central and northern Europe, where they lived in the Rhineland Valley and the region we now know as Germany and Austria. In fact, Israelis actually call European Jews—specifically those from Germany—*Ashkenazis*, to distinguish them from *Sephardic* Jews who come from Spain, North Africa, and the Middle East.

"Now, it is true that Ezekiel does not mention Ashkenaz by name. But in 38:6, he refers to 'Gomer with all its troops' and then adds that 'many peoples' will join with Gog in his campaign, suggesting there are other nearby members of the coalition.

"Dr. Pentecost from Dallas writes that 'there seems to be evidence to support the view that *Gomer* refers to modern Germany.'

"He cites a book called *The Prophet Ezekiel*, written in 1918 by a man named Arno Gaebelein. A leading Bible scholar, and one of the editors of the *Scofield Reference Bible*, Gaebelein wrote that 'valuable information is given in the Talmud; *Gomer* is there stated to be the Germani, the Germans. That the descendants of Gomer moved northward and established themselves in parts of Germany seems to be an established fact.'"

"Back up a step," said Bennett. "What's the Talmud?"

"The Talmud is a collection of ancient rabbinic writings and commentary," Mordechai said.

"And it says that Gomer is Germany?"

"It seems to, Jonathan. Look, if you are asking whether I can say with absolute certainty that Germany and Austria are part of this prophecy, the answer is that I cannot. But I must tell you that I believe they are about to face God's judgment for the evil they did during the Holocaust, when they murdered six million Jews and unleashed their bloodthirsty storm troopers upon the world."

"And what do you think is going to happen to them?" Bennett asked.

"Take a look for yourself," Mordechai said, pointing him to Ezekiel 38:18-23.

Bennett found the text and began reading aloud.

"It will come about on that day,
when Gog comes against the land of Israel,"
declares the LORD God,
"that My fury will mount up in My anger.
And in My zeal and in My blazing wrath
I declare that on that day
there will surely be a great earthquake
in the land of Israel.
The fish of the sea, the birds of the heavens,
the beasts of the field,
all the creeping things that creep on the earth,

and all the men who are on the face of the earth
will shake at My presence;
the mountains also will be thrown down,
the steep pathways will collapse,
and every wall will fall to the ground.
I will call for a sword
against him on all My mountains,"
declares the LORD God.

"Every man's sword will be against his brother.
And with pestilence and blood
I will enter into judgment with him;
and I will rain on him and on his troops,
and on the many peoples who are with him,
a torrential rain, with hailstones, fire, and brimstone.

"I will magnify Myself, sanctify Myself,
and make Myself known in the sight of many nations;
and they will know that I am the LORD."

When he was done, Bennett sat silently, reading the passage again to himself. Certain phrases seemed to leap off the page at him. *My blazing wrath. A great earthquake. Pestilence and blood. A torrential rain of fire and brimstone.*

At Mordechai's direction, Bennett then read 39:12, where Ezekiel predicted it would take seven months for Israel to bury all the bodies. Reading further, he found Ezekiel's prophecy that vultures and carnivores would swarm the region to feast themselves on the corpses of the slain. "You will eat fat until you are glutted, and drink blood until you are drunk, from My sacrifice which I have sacrificed for you," the Lord God said through his prophet to the birds of the air and the beasts of the fields. "You will be glutted at My table with horses and charioteers, with mighty men and all the men of war. . . . And all the nations will see My judgment which I have executed. . . . And the house of Israel will know that I am the LORD their God from that day onward."

Was it real? Was it coming?

The magnitude of it all was almost too much for Bennett to process.

Had a twenty-five-hundred-year-old prophecy actually warned that a modern master Aryan race—led by Russians, Iranians, and Germans—would one day try to destroy the State of Israel? If so, was the rest of the prophecy true? Was fire going to fall from heaven to consume the enemies of God?

How was he supposed to take any of this seriously? He was a senior advisor to the president of the United States. He was paid to develop political strategy in the real world, not shadowbox with dead saints and ancient riddles.

Yet Bennett had to admit the parallels between what Mordechai was describing from Ezekiel and what was happening in Russia and the Middle East currently were eerie, to say the least.

And there was something else.

Something deep inside Bennett *wanted* to believe there was justice in the universe, that the atrocities committed by the Communists and the Nazis and the horrors committed by followers of radical Islam would be avenged in his lifetime.

But did any of this make sense?

Were the hammer and the sickle really about to fall on the Kremlin and Red Army?

Was the world really about to witness the end of radical Islam as we know it?

Bennett shuddered at the implications and was suddenly overcome with thoughts of Erin. He was desperate to see her, to hold her, to comfort her.

He needed fresh air. He needed to stretch his legs and clear his head.

He got up and excused himself, stepped onto the stone porch, and stared out over the twinkling lights of Jerusalem. His mind raced through a million disparate thoughts, but all of them came back to this: *Could any of this be true? And if so, what did it mean for Erin? What did it mean for him?*

39

⋆ ⋆
⋆

McCoy awoke in a filthy shower stall.

She was naked and shivering, her body bruised and bleeding.

Her left eye was nearly swollen shut. She tried to shield her face from the searing pressure of the frigid water raining down upon her only to have fierce pain shoot through her right arm. It, too, was swollen and discolored. McCoy feared it was broken.

She shifted her legs—the skin was ripped open in several places, and she was losing quite a bit of blood, but she could still feel them, and she took that as a good sign.

How long had she been here? She had no idea.

The skin on her fingers was wrinkled and slightly blue. She used her left arm to prop herself up against the back of the stall, looking down toward the drain so her face would be protected, if only a little, and suddenly she realized how good the cold water tasted to her parched lips and throat.

It was a blessing, she decided—a small one, but a blessing just the same.

But what about Jon? She couldn't bear to imagine him suffering what she was. He wouldn't survive. She wasn't sure she could.

Maybe it was better just to tell Jibril what he wanted to know and pray that Langley was not so stupid as to have left those codes unchanged. If she ever survived this nightmare and got back to America, she could face the consequences then. For though it made her sick to her stomach to admit it, Jibril was right—she would never forgive herself for causing Bennett to suffer. It had been less than twenty-four hours, and it was already eating away at her.

Bennett awoke unrested.

He forced himself to shower, shave, and dress, then checked his voice mail before joining Dr. Mordechai out on the stone porch. The sky was a pale, cloudless blue. The air was cool for September, and there was a light breeze blowing from the north. It was the kind of glorious day for which Erin McCoy lived, and once again he could think of nothing but her.

"Morning," he said to Mordechai, almost in a whisper, as he sat down at the table.

"Good morning, Jonathan. How did you sleep?"

"Like a baby," Bennett admitted. "Woke up every few hours and cried."

And then, somewhat awkwardly, he said, "If you'll forgive me, Dr. Mordechai, I'll be right back." Then he bowed his head, folded his hands, and prayed silently.

Good morning, Father. I love you so much, and I thank you for your mercy, for saving my life, and saving my soul, and being a God of second chances. And Lord, I beg you this morning to forgive me—for the selfishness that's been consuming me, for the thoughts of revenge I've been harboring, for not spending time with you these past few weeks, for not being as faithful in prayer for Erin as I know she's been for me.

Lord Jesus, please have mercy on Erin this morning. Wherever she is—whatever she's going through—please take care of her, Father. Protect her. Give her peace. Give her courage. And bring her back to me, Lord Jesus, please. I know I don't deserve her. But your Word says it's not good for a man to be alone, and I don't believe you brought us together just to rip us apart forever. Did you? Is that what you're asking of me? I can't believe that. And I don't think I could handle that. But not my will, Lord, but yours be done. Thank you so much for this food, for this home, for Dr. Mordechai's friendship. I pray that you would lead me and guide me in the way I should go, and please counsel me, Lord, with your eye upon me. In Jesus' name I pray, amen.

Bennett took a deep breath, opened his eyes, and looked up.

"Welcome back," said Mordechai.

"Thanks, it's good to be back," Bennett sighed, and somehow the heaviness began to lift. His worries about Erin, at least for the moment, seemed to fade.

A breakfast of eggs, hash browns, and fresh fruit awaited him, and he suddenly realized he was famished.

"Well, Jonathan, what do you think about our conversation last night now that you have had a chance to reflect on it a bit?" Mordechai asked as he poured Bennett a cup of Turkish coffee.

"You've got to admit, it's pretty hard to swallow," said Bennett.

"What, that God is about to punish His enemies with earthquakes, hailstones, hellfire, and brimstone?"

"It sounds like something out of *Independence Day* or *Raiders of the Lost Ark*."

"I picture Tolkien's *Return of the King*, but yes, it is going to be dramatic, to say the least."

"And you *really* believe all this is about to happen?"

"I do," said Mordechai, looking out over the city he loved. "I am not going to lie to you and say it was not a leap for me at first. It was. But I no longer have any doubt that we are living in the last days before the return of the King of kings and the Lord of lords."

"How can you be so sure?"

"I am an old man, Jonathan. I have seen wars and rumors of wars. Revolutions, famines, earthquakes, tsunamis, persecution of unimaginable proportions. The Holocaust. The rebirth of the State of Israel. The Jewish people pouring back into the Holy Land from all over the world. Jerusalem back in the hands of the Jewish people. The rise of a dictator in Russia. A Russian alliance with Iran. It is happening, Jonathan. All around us, every day, the ancient Scriptures are coming alive."

"But you're talking about an apocalypse on the order of Sodom and Gomorrah."

"No, no. Much bigger—and far more visible. Sodom and Gomorrah were two small cities in the Jordan Valley. Ezekiel 38 speaks of the most dramatic day in human history since the resurrection of Jesus Christ."

"The beginning of the judgment against God's enemies."

"Yes, it is about judgment, to be sure, but it is about more than that. Do you remember the last verse of Ezekiel 38? God says, 'I will magnify Myself, sanctify Myself, and make Myself known in the sight of many nations; and they will know that I am the LORD.'"

Mordechai looked Bennett in the eye. "Do you see it, Jonathan? Can you hear the heart of God calling to us through the centuries? Yes, He will judge His enemies, those who have killed and persecuted Jews and Christians and waged war against His name. But for the first time since *Yeshua HaMaschiach* walked this earth, the God of the universe is about to reveal Himself to a world that has long forgotten Him.

"The apostle Peter said, 'In the last days mockers will come with their mocking, following after their own lusts, and saying, "Where is the promise of His coming?" . . . But the present heavens and earth by His word are being reserved for fire, kept for the day of judgment and destruction of ungodly men. But do not let this one fact escape your notice, beloved, that with the Lord one day is as a thousand years, and a thousand years as one day. The Lord is not slow about His promise, as some count slowness, but is patient toward you, not wishing for any to perish but for all to come to repentance.'

"Judgment is just one part of God's plan. But so is salvation. God wants to catch people's attention, Jonathan. He wants to awaken them from their slumber. I have no doubt a day of great terror is coming. But a great spiritual awakening is coming as well. And it is possible that more people could become followers of Christ through this single event than at any other time in history. Millions. Possibly tens of millions, if not more.

"Think of it, Jonathan—true followers of Christ have always dreamed of the Rapture, when in the blink of an eye Christ will snatch them away from the suffering of this life into the glories of heaven. But what if there was a great spiritual awakening first? Would it not be just like God to do something like that first—*before* the Antichrist is revealed, *before* the Tribulation begins, *before* billions suffer and perish forever?

"God doesn't *have* to do anything before the Rapture, of course—He could come this very instant—but what if He wanted to give the world one more chance before Satan is unleashed upon the earth? What if that is what we are about to see happen with our own eyes?"

Bennett loved Mordechai's passion, but his own emotional circuit breakers were about to blow. He wasn't an evangelist. He was a political strategist without a strategy.

"Bob Corsetti called this morning. The president wants me back in Washington. Something's up."

"Good or bad?"

"I don't know. But you can be sure the president is going to ask me about our time together. And what am I supposed to say? *'The end is near'?*"

"Tell him the truth," said Mordechai.

"Yeah, right. You want me to sit down with the president of the United States and the National Security Council and say, 'Look, I know the situation looks bad right now. The world is on the verge of another Holocaust. Russia is poised to seize two-thirds of the world's oil supplies. But don't worry. At the last possible second God is going to supernaturally annihilate the Evil Empire and destroy radical Islam as we know it'? They'll think I'm nuts."

Mordechai looked at Bennett for a moment. Then he said, "Here, I have something for you. This may help."

He handed Bennett a spiral-bound brief and a CD.

"What's this?" Bennett asked. He took the brief from Mordechai and leafed through the pages.

"It contains everything we talked about last night, plus a list of recommendations—some for the president, some for the prime minister," Mordechai replied.

"What recommendations?"

"As you know, the Israeli nuclear doctrine is called 'The Samson Option.' It says when all hope is lost, Israelis should put their trust in nuclear weapons. What you hold in your hands is my alternative. It says when all hope is lost, Israelis should put their trust in the God of Abraham, Isaac, and Jacob. I call it 'The Ezekiel Option.'"

"And just what do you want me to do with this? Give it to the president?"

Mordechai looked into Bennett's eyes, as if silently evaluating him.

"Jonathan, do you know the story of Queen Esther?"

"Vaguely, why?"

"You will know in a minute," Mordechai said. "Somewhere between

486 BC and 465 BC, most of the civilized world was controlled by the Persian Empire, stretching from India in the East to Ethiopia and Sudan in the West. The ruler of this empire was a king known in Persian as *Khshayarsha*—King Xerxes in Greek, King Ahasuerus in Hebrew.

"One day the king issued orders to all of his regional commanders, 'to destroy, to kill, and to annihilate all the Jews, both young and old'—men, women, and children—all in one day, 'and to seize their possessions as plunder.' What the king did not know was that his beautiful wife, Queen Esther—*Hadassah* in Hebrew—was Jewish, a fact that she had kept hidden from the king.

"Esther's uncle secretly sent word to her, urging her to tell the king that she was Jewish and to plead for mercy for her people. But Esther was paralyzed with fear. She sent word back to her uncle that he could not possibly expect her to risk her position, her status—perhaps even her life—by interceding on behalf of the Jewish people.

"The clock was ticking. The day of destruction was near. Esther's uncle sent back one final message: 'Do not imagine that you in the king's palace can escape any more than all the Jews. For if you remain silent at this time, relief and deliverance will arise for the Jews from another place and you and your father's house will perish. And who knows whether you have not attained your royal position for such a time as this?'"

40
★★
★

"Is everything set?" Gogolov asked.

"It is, Your Excellency," Jibril replied.

"Very well. Proceed."

On Gogolov's command, the motorcade departed on schedule. It took a left at the Hotel National and proceeded up Tverskaya Boulevard toward the Sheremetyevo 2 International Airport, catching throngs of Muscovites by surprise in the process.

It was the first time the new czar had left the Kremlin's protective bubble since the trip to New York. Though the excursion had not been publicly announced, it had been in planning for several weeks.

The occasion was the arrival of a high-level diplomatic delegation from Tehran, led by Iranian president Ifshahan Kharrazi. On Tuesday, Gogolov and Kharrazi would sign a series of economic and military agreements and hold a press conference designed to stun Washington and her NATO allies.

But first there was critical business to conclude.

Gogolov waved to the gawking crowds as Jibril began his briefing.

"Kharrazi says his people are ahead of schedule."

"How soon can they be ready?"

"The engineers are working in round-the-clock shifts. Kharrazi expects all twenty-five *Shahab*-3 missiles to be outfitted with our nuclear warheads by October first."

"Six days ahead of schedule?"

"Yes, and a full sixteen days ahead of the U.N. deadline, should our resolution pass," Jibril confirmed.

"Then we must be on full alert for an Israeli first strike, Mohammed."

"Doron will not launch before the first of October, Your Excellency."

"Why not?"

"It would be suicide. The Americans are pressuring him to accept a diplomatic solution. Bennett passed the word to Doron on Saturday."

"That hardly seems like a message with which Mr. Bennett would agree."

"You are quite right, Your Excellency. Our sources say Bennett has been pushing for a major U.S. military buildup, perhaps even a preemptive strike."

"What kind of support does he have?"

"Almost none. Neither Congress nor the American public wants another war. But Bennett is shrewd. He is not arguing that the U.S. should defend Israel."

"Then what *is* he saying?"

"He is arguing that the U.S. cannot allow a Russian-Iranian alliance to seize control of the Persian Gulf and put the Western economies in danger."

Jibril was right, Gogolov thought. *Bennett was dangerous. Perhaps it was time to kill him.*

"The Israelis will become desperate when they realize that the White House has no intention of coming to their rescue despite all the president's talk of being 'pro-Israel,'" Jibril added.

Gogolov nodded. "Then perhaps we must strike first."

Bennett lay in his own bed, staring at the ceiling.

It was only two in the morning, but his body was still on Israel time, seven hours ahead. There was no way he was going to sleep. In a few hours, after all, he would see the president face-to-face. His stomach churned at the prospect.

MacPherson was waiting for a briefing on Bennett's meetings with Doron and Mordechai. He couldn't just lie and say the former Mossad chief had nothing useful to say about the crisis. It simply wasn't plausible. Besides, he'd already e-mailed an electronic copy of the brief to a number of the president's other advisors. He would find out about it sooner or later.

But was he really prepared to pass Mordechai's brief directly to the president? Every fiber of his being told him it was professional suicide, that he'd be written off as one of the "UFO people." Then again, "The Ezekiel Option" was Mordechai's view, not his own, right? He was just the delivery boy. Why should he be blamed for the message?

He got up and put on a pot of coffee. Then he sat down at the kitchen table, powered up his wireless laptop, logged on to the secure White House Internet server, and checked his e-mail. There were messages from Ken Costello at State and Indira Rajiv at Langley. Both confirmed they'd received the copy of Mordechai's brief he'd e-mailed to them. Both promised to read and review it overnight, as he'd directed.

Bennett checked his AOL account as well. There was a message from his mom—six, to be precise—none of which he had even seen much less responded to in the last two weeks. A wave of guilt washed over him. Why was he so standoffish? She was a widow, for crying out loud, and he was all she had in the world. Fine, so she hadn't been the greatest mom. She hadn't always been there for him. She'd put her husband's career above spending time with him. Was he going to hold it against her forever? The woman was lost and alone, and all she wanted was to keep in touch with him on a regular basis. Why was that so hard for him?

He hated feeling guilty every time he thought about her, every time her name popped up on his caller ID. But it occurred to him that maybe he *felt* guilty because he *was*. He had not been there when she had needed him most, and she deserved better. From her only son. From a follower of Christ.

He was tempted to call her right then, to tell her he loved her and to give Mordechai's answer to her question. But it didn't seem fair to wake her up in the middle of the night. He'd call in a few hours. He sent back a quick e-mail apologizing for not staying in touch, then found an online florist and ordered her three dozen roses. It wasn't nearly enough, but it was a start.

Bennett suddenly noticed that Mordechai's name appeared in bold in the list of regular contacts along the side of the screen. Mordechai was using his AOL account. Shifting gears, Bennett quickly tapped out an instant message.

"dr. m—it's jon."

A moment later came the reply.

"hello, jonathan. welcome home. how was your flight?"

"long and lonely . . . but quick question for you."

"shoot."

"how come i've never heard of all this stuff?"

"what, the gog and magog prophecies?"

"exactly. I mean, the rapture, armageddon, the return of Christ—everybody who watches the history channel knows about the big doomsday prophecies. how come nobody talks about what you're talking about?"

"what do you mean, nobody? read the dead sea scrolls. you will find all kinds of references to ezekiel's prophecy and coming salvation of israel. read ancient arab texts that call the great wall of china the 'wall of gog and magog,' built to keep the russians from invading china. read THE TRAVELS OF MARCO POLO. wait just a moment. . . ."

Nearly a minute passed before Mordechai continued. Bennett imagined him flipping through one of his hundreds of reference books.

Then Mordechai was back, having found the quote he was looking for.

"marco polo wrote of a province where 'the lord of the tartars and of all the neighbouring provinces and kingdoms' lived, a place 'which we call in our language gog and magog; the natives call it yng and Mungul.' who are the tartars? they're turkic-speaking people who live in Russia!"

"no, no, that's all fascinating, but you're missing my point," Bennett responded. *"i'm talking about now. something modern, something current. if some huge prophecy is about to take place in our lifetime, it seems a little hard to believe you're the only guy talking about it."*

"jonathan, my friend, just because you have never heard of this prophecy does not mean nobody has. . . . ever heard of the left behind series?"

"i remember a newsweek *cover story about it a few years back, but no, never read the books. . . . too busy making money."*

"how could i forget?. . . . well left behind is a series of novels by an evangelical prophecy expert named tim lahaye and a writer named jerry jenkins . . . it's about the last days, the rapture, the rise of the antichrist. . . . they sold over 60 million copies."

"and?"

"and the first chapter of left behind *refers to the gog and magog prophecy as having already taken place before the rapture. why? because lahaye believed ezekiel 38–39 might very well take place before Christ comes back for his church. in fact, in 1984 lahaye wrote a nonfiction book called* the coming peace in the middle east. *in it, he concluded magog was russia, meshech was moscow, tubal was tobolsk—everything we have been talking about for the past few days."*

Was that possible? Had the number-one best-selling fictional series in American publishing history been based on the notion that a Russian-Iranian alliance to attack Israel would foreshadow the second coming of Christ?

Before Bennett could even respond, a new IM popped up.

"ever heard of hal lindsey?" Mordechai asked.

"no, why?"

"he wrote a nonfiction book in 1970 called the late great planet earth. *it was about a coming russian-islamic attack on israel and the coming of Christ. sold over 15 million copies. the* new york times *called it 'the number one nonfiction best seller of the decade.' now, lindsey and lahaye differed on some of the specifics, like the timing of these events. but both were convinced that ezekiel referred to russia and iran and that the war of gog and magog was coming soon."*

Bennett poured himself a cup of fresh coffee. Perhaps he needed to broaden his reading habits beyond the *Wall Street Journal* and *Sports Illustrated*.

The motorcade passed the Marriott Tverskaya.

Gogolov picked up the car phone and speed-dialed his chief of staff. "Get me Andrei," he said, turning back toward the windows.

But the connection was never made.

Out of the corner of his eye, Gogolov saw it coming from the left, a city bus careening through a police roadblock and smashing full force into the decoy limousine ahead of them, triggering a massive explosion and a fireball that could be seen for blocks.

Gogolov's bodyguard pulled him to the floor of the car, but not before the shock waves from the blast shattered all of the windows in their vehicle.

Smoke and blood filled the interior of the car.

Machine-gun fire filled the air outside.

"Stay down, stay down!" shouted the lead agent, covering the czar's body with his own and ordering the protective detail to return fire at the snipers on the roofs.

Sirens began to wail in the distance.

A helicopter soon hovered overhead.

Gogolov could see the blood streaming down Jibril's face. He could hear the bullets smashing into the sides of his armor-plated car and ricocheting off the pavement. He could hear women screaming and the shock in his agents' voices as they shouted into radios, demanding reinforcements they obviously feared might not get there in time.

41

Bennett thanked Mordechai and signed off AOL.

What should he do next? There had to be more out there, something beyond Mordechai's brief and six pages of endnotes referencing books on prophecy and ancient linguistics he'd never heard of.

He clicked over to Google and typed in "gog and magog." He was stunned by the results—thousands upon thousands of entries.

He wasn't sure whether to laugh or cry. There was no way he could wade through any of that even if he wanted to. He didn't have the foggiest notion where to begin, nor the time to do a doctoral thesis. At best he had four or five hours before he would walk into the Oval Office and seal his fate one way or the other.

Maybe more research wasn't the answer.

He needed to run, to clear his head. He threw on a T-shirt, shorts, and running shoes and took off down Pennsylvania Avenue, his DSS detail in tow. The cool, predawn air felt good, as did the pavement beneath his feet. He was used to running four or five miles a day, but it had been weeks since he'd been out. He was grateful that the injuries he had sustained during the coup were largely healed. He was still a bit sore, but he knew how fortunate he had been.

When he reached the White House, he took a right down 17th Street, rounded the Washington Monument, and headed up the Mall toward the

Capitol, almost aglow from floodlamps encircling the grounds. A few minutes later, he glanced at his watch. It was a few minutes before five, time to turn back. He needed to get home, take a shower, and get into the office. But when he looked up, he found himself at the 2nd Street entrance of the Library of Congress, and a crazy idea popped into his head.

A bleary-eyed guard met him at the door and spoke to him through the glass. "I'm sorry, sir. We're closed."

"You don't understand," said Bennett. "I just need to—"

"I understand better than you think, young man," the guard shot back. "You think you're the only one? You think you're so special, just 'cause your momma and papa keep paying through the nose to get you a good education. Now look, I don't know what paper you have due today, and I don't care what your professor's name is. The answer's the same: we're closed. C-L-O-S-E-D. You do know how to spell, don't you?"

Bennett was not amused.

He flashed the man his White House badge and demanded to be let in. It took a few minutes of yelling, a conversation with the DSS security team, and a call to his supervisor, but the guard finally relented and unlocked the door.

Bennett sprinted up the steps from ground level to the Main Reading Room on the first floor, under the great rotunda made famous in the Robert Redford–Dustin Hoffman film *All the President's Men*. No one was at the service desk, of course, so Bennett found a computer terminal, pulled up the online catalog, and hit "Basic Search." From there he entered "gog and magog," chose "Keyword," and hit "Begin Search."

9,976 entries.

This wasn't getting any easier. Or maybe it was. Perhaps Ezekiel's prophecy wasn't as obscure as he thought. Maybe clues were hidden throughout the literature of the ages. Bennett scrolled through the first few hundred entries, jotting down titles and authors that caught his eye:

★ *Gog and Magog: A Novel* by Martin Buber
★ *Dead Souls* by the great Russian novelist Nikolai Vasilevich Gogol
★ *Dutch: A Memoir of Ronald Reagan* by Pulitzer Prize winner Edmund Morris

* *United States: Essays 1952–1992* by National Book Award
  winner Gore Vidal
* *In My Father's Court* by Isaac Bashevis Singer, winner of the
  1978 Nobel Prize in Literature
* *Souls on Fire, All Rivers Run to the Sea,* and *Elie Wiesel:
  Conversations,* by Elie Wiesel, survivor of Auschwitz and
  winner of the 1985 Congressional Gold Medal and the 1986
  Nobel Peace Prize

Bennett checked his watch again. He had only scratched the surface, but he was out of time. He summoned the guard.

"I need copies of these immediately."

The man just stared at him.

"Yeah, right. Young man, it's 4:30 in the morning."

"And?"

"And in case you hadn't noticed, hotshot, we're *closed*! C-L-O . . ."

"Yeah, yeah, you're hilarious. Now look, I'm standing here, aren't I?"

"Well, you ain't getting no books—not right now—I don't care who you think you are."

Bennett was about to unload, but thought better of it. Instead, he flipped open his cell phone, pushed speaker so the guard could listen in, and hit a speed-dial button.

A moment later, the voice of a young woman came on the line. "White House Operations."

"Yeah, hi, this is Jon Bennett."

"Good morning, Mr. Bennett. Please enter your access code now, sir."

Bennett punched the seven-digit code into his phone and hit the pound sign.

"Yes, Mr. Bennett, how can I help you this morning?"

"I need the home number for the chief librarian at the Library of Congress."

The hapless guard's eyes went wide.

"Yes, here it is, Mr. Bennett. Would you like me to connect you, sir?"

"That'd be great."

"Absolutely. And is there anything else I can do for you, sir?"

"No, that's it. Thanks."

"You're welcome, one moment."

Bennett could hear the DSS agents trying valiantly to suppress laughter. He could imagine what they were thinking: *This poor security guard had obviously never run into Jon Bennett before.*

"Yeah, hello?" came a very groggy voice at the other end of the line.

"Good morning, sir. I'm calling from the White House. I need a little favor."

And then Bennett's pager went off. It was from Ken Costello at the State Department—and it was urgent.

McCoy finally awoke.

She was back in her cell, chained to the bed, handcuffs cutting into her wrists. Through the closed door she could hear the occasional rustle of the guard's newspaper as he turned pages. The only other sound in this wing of the military hospital came from someone screaming for mercy.

Was it Jon? Had Jibril been telling the truth? Was he really here? Did he know that he was suffering because she wouldn't talk?

She closed her eyes again, blinded by the bulbs hanging over her head. Her mind strained through the fatigue. But one thing was clear. She either had to give in, die, or get herself free.

Ten minutes later Bennett reached the White House.

Costello briefed him as they headed upstairs.

"The CIA confirms somebody just tried to assassinate Gogolov."

"*Tried?*"

"He survived. No one's quite sure how badly he was injured. Jibril was bloodied up, but he's likely to pull through. No one has ID'd the perps yet, but Radio Moscow says at least a dozen attackers were killed."

"Any suspects?"

"Three rebels were captured," Costello continued as they reached Bennett's West Wing office. "A half dozen—maybe more—are on the run. Zyuganov has declared martial law. Troops are back on the streets.

They've closed the borders and shut down the Internet, and long-distance phone service in and out of the country has been suspended."

Still in jogging shorts and a T-shirt soaked with sweat, Bennett wiped his face with a towel and flipped on the news. FOX had a feed from Russian television, and the images were gruesome, particularly the shots of Gogolov's bullet-ridden limousine and the smoking wreckage of burned cars nearby.

"Where's Rajiv?"

"I paged her right after you. She's on her—"

Rajiv burst through the door. "Sorry I'm late. What've we got?"

"A disaster," said Bennett. "He survived."

The phone rang.

"Bennett . . . yes? . . . Fine, just let me know. I'll be ready."

He hung up the phone and slumped down in his chair.

"Who was that?" asked Rajiv.

"Corsetti. The president wants to see me in a few minutes."

"What are you going to tell him?"

"I don't know. I was hoping I had some more time."

"And a shower?" asked Costello.

Bennett just sighed. "Yeah, that would have been nice. All right, where are we? You guys read the thing from Mordechai?"

Costello and Rajiv nodded.

"Well?"

"Well what?" asked Rajiv. "You're not seriously going to take that thing to the Oval Office, are you?"

"Why not?"

"What are you, nuts? The president needs options, Jon, not a bunch of hocus-pocus."

Bennett could see the cynicism in Rajiv's eyes. He wanted to be angry, but could he really blame her? He was still wrestling it through for himself. Why shouldn't she? She'd had less time to process it, and she didn't share his faith. She didn't see the world the way he did. Her grandparents had been Hindus, killed in Kashmir by radical Islamic jihadists from Pakistan. It's why her parents had fled India for the United States in the first place. And why she'd immersed herself in understanding the major religious movements of North Africa, the Middle East, and the Indian subcontinent.

Indira Rajiv prided herself on *not* being religious, on *not* being swayed by mystical or spiritual beliefs of any kind. And maybe she was right. Had his grief over McCoy clouded his judgment? In Jerusalem, Mordechai's case had sounded so compelling. In the West Wing, it suddenly reeked of lunacy.

"What about you, Ken?"

Bennett braced for Costello to pile on.

"You sure you want my opinion, Jon?"

"Of course I do."

"Well, it seems pretty cut-and-dried to me. Dr. Mordechai *was* head of the Mossad. He's known the president for years. The president sent you over there to get the man's take. Seems to me you've got to give it to him. Besides, you've got to admit, it's a pretty interesting theory."

Indira Rajiv couldn't contain herself. "*What?* You're both out of your minds. Why don't you just hand the president a copy of the *National Enquirer* and tell him Gogolov is the Antichrist, while you're at it."

Costello just laughed. "Raj, come on, don't be ridiculous."

"No, I'm perfectly serious. What's the difference?"

"A lot, actually, but that's not the point."

"Then what is?" Rajiv demanded.

"Look, don't get me wrong," said Costello. "I'm a lapsed Catholic. I haven't gone to church in ten years, maybe more. So I don't have a stake in this thing theologically. But you've got to admit it's pretty amazing to think that some guy writing twenty-five hundred years ago could nail this crisis so closely. I mean, look at page six of Mordechai's brief. Look at the countries listed in this anti-Israel coalition. Besides Russia and Germany, it's practically the who's who of the radical Islamic world, right?"

Bennett flipped open his copy as he and Rajiv scanned the names and nodded.

"Doesn't it strike you as strange that two longtime mortal enemies of Israel are missing from the list?" Costello asked.

Both looked at the list again. Both drew a blank.

"Egypt? Babylon? *Hello?*" Costello said finally. "Think about it. If any group of countries was about to attack Israel, historically speaking you'd have to expect Egypt and Iraq to be at the front of the line, right? But they're not. The question is, why? The Egyptians and the Iraqis were part of the 1948 war against Israel. And the '67 war. And the '73 war. But then what happened? The Egyptians signed a peace treaty with Israel in '79. And then we brought about our little 'regime change' in Iraq. Which means that for the first time since the rebirth of the State of Israel—i.e., the fulfillment of Ezekiel 36 and 37—the Egyptians and the Iraqis are not in the mix. I'm not saying it proves anything. But you've got to admit, it's interesting."

It was. Bennett was impressed that Costello had taken Mordechai's case so seriously.

"You're saying that if it were up to you—with everything going on right now, and everything on the president's mind and plate—you'd give him the brief?"

"Of course," said Costello.

"And if the president asked you why he should ever listen to Mordechai again, what would you say?"

"Well, that's a different question."

It certainly was.

The phone rang again.

"Bennett . . . yes, sir . . . I'll be right there."

He was out of time. The president was waiting.

42

✦ ✦
✦

"Jon, tell me this wasn't the Israelis."

No *hello*. No *good morning*. No *how dare you enter this office without a suit and tie*. The president was all business, and Bennett had rarely seen him so angry.

"I can only hope it was," said Bennett. "Unless it was us. Tell me that's why the Secret Service calls you Gambit."

"It *wasn't* us, Jon. And you'd better pray it wasn't the Mossad."

"I'm praying just the opposite."

"Then you're about to get a whole lot of people killed," the president shot back. "Look, Jon, I know this thing is personal for you, and Lord knows I'm praying for Erin's safe return. But you don't seem to get it, do you? If Doron or I order the assassination of Yuri Gogolov, what exactly do we gain? What assurances would we have that Andrei Zyuganov or some other madman won't take over and decide to retaliate with ten thousand nuclear warheads? Or maybe with just one. Have you seen the DOD estimates of death tolls from one Russian ICBM hitting New York or L.A.?"

Bennett shook his head.

"You should. And while you're at it, take a look at the computer model for a U.S. preemptive strike against Moscow and what that triggers—a hundred million Americans dead in the first few hours, another seventy-

five million dead in the next few weeks. I'm not about to play Russian rou-
lette with a bunch of nuclear-armed psychopaths."

Bennett asked if the president had read his report on his meeting with
Doron.

"I have," said MacPherson.

"Then you know Doron is seriously considering The Samson Option."

"It's a mistake."

"Nevertheless . . ."

"Jon, look, I'll do everything I possibly can to help make this turn out
right. But you've got to understand we simply do not have a realistic military option right now."

"Mr. President, it doesn't need to come to war," Bennett countered.
"Gogolov is a bully. No one's ever said no to him. Why not you? Veto his
resolution in the Security Council. Build a coalition to fight him in the
General Assembly. Park some warships off the Israeli coast. And sell the
Israelis the weapons they need to defend themselves."

"It's not that simple, Jon. Most of the world already believes I'm a
trigger-happy warmonger. You don't seem to appreciate how critical it is
that I not reinforce that image right now. Too much is at stake."

"So what *is* the plan?"

MacPherson handed Bennett a leather portfolio, embossed with the
presidential seal. Curious, Bennett opened to a draft of the president's
address to the nation, scheduled for the following night. Attached was a
draft of a Security Council resolution the administration planned to introduce at the U.N. on Wednesday.

Bennett scanned the speech first.

It made a compelling case of Russian collusion and hypocrisy in building nuclear-power reactors and research facilities in Iran. It also detailed
Iran's belligerent and consistent refusal to abide by IAEA safeguards.
What's more, it was accompanied by dramatic satellite photographs of
new construction at several Iranian nuclear facilities, and an audiotaped
intercept of two Iranian generals talking about enriching uranium into
weapons-grade materials.

The resolution formalized the charges. It called for full economic
sanctions against Russia and Iran—including the cessation of all oil and
gas exports from each country—until Iran's nuclear program was entirely

dismantled and subject to aggressive inspections by the U.S. and the IAEA.

It wasn't a bad start.

And it was backed up with more hard-hitting intelligence on the Russian-Iranian nuclear connection than any American administration had ever made public. It would immediately put Moscow and Tehran on the defensive and help the president recapture the moral high ground.

But Bennett wasn't ready to let the president off the hook. Not yet. At the end of the day, no American diplomatic offensive, no matter how shrewd, would ultimately be successful unless it was backed up—at least implicitly—by a credible threat of force.

"Mr. President, I just keep thinking of your hero, Teddy Roosevelt."

" 'Walk softly and carry a big stick.' Is that what Eli recommends— playing chicken with Yuri Gogolov?"

So this was it.

Bennett could feel his heart pounding in his chest. He wasn't at all convinced this was a good idea, but Mordechai's voice kept echoing through his thoughts. Perhaps he *was* in the White House for such a time as this.

"Not exactly, Mr. President."

"Then what?"

Bennett took a deep breath, reached into his briefcase, and handed the president "The Ezekiel Option."

"What is this?" MacPherson asked, visibly confused.

Good question, thought Bennett, now convinced his days at the White House were numbered.

43

★ ★
★

WEDNESDAY, SEPTEMBER 17 – 3:56 A.M. – GEORGETOWN, D.C.

Bennett awoke in a cold sweat.

He checked the clock beside his bed, then stumbled to the bathroom to splash some water on his face. He'd been asleep for less than an hour.

How could so much have gone so wrong so quickly? The last forty-eight hours had been a nightmare, and there were no indications that today would be any different.

Bennett made his way downstairs, turned on a few lights, and made a pot of strong, black coffee. He checked through the peephole of his front door. He could see the night shift of DSS agents in a car parked out front. The early editions of the *Washington Post* and *Washington Times* had not yet arrived.

Powering up his TV and satellite system, Bennett slumped into an easy chair and flipped through FOX News, CNN, and MSNBC for the latest news from Moscow.

It was all bad.

Gogolov's preemptive press conference the day before had been a masterstroke for the Kremlin—and a disaster for the White House.

Bennett was still in shock, as were his colleagues.

With Iranian president Ifshahan Kharrazi at his side, Gogolov had made a stunning announcement "in the name of world peace."

Under intense pressure from the Russian government, Iran had publicly announced that she had agreed to completely abandon her nuclear ambitions. Effective immediately, Tehran would begin dismantling all of her nuclear reactors and research facilities and would account for—and promptly return to Russia—all of the uranium Iranian officials had been enriching since the late 1990s.

Moreover, Kharrazi said, he would welcome international inspectors to both monitor and assist in the denuclearization of Iran. "We will even allow American and Zionist experts to be part of any U.N. and IAEA inspection teams, so long as such teams also include Russian, French, and German experts."

Gogolov had just fired a shot heard around the diplomatic world.

By accomplishing what no other world leaders had been able to—including successive American administrations going as far back as the Clinton-Gore team—Gogolov had effectively checkmated the White House's leading line of attack: Russian hypocrisy. And he had done so mere hours before President MacPherson was scheduled to deliver his speech to the nation.

Caught completely unprepared, MacPherson's national security team had scrambled to come up with its own internal analysis. *Was the Russian-Iranian deal legit? Was it verifiable? Was Iran really abandoning ambitions of building an "Islamic bomb" after decades of effort? If so, what was the quid pro quo? If not . . .*

Bennett, for one, didn't believe Gogolov or Kharrazi for a minute. Nor did the president. But what could they do? How could the president deliver a prime-time speech to the country detailing Russia's nuclear collusion with Iran if Iran now said it would scrap its entire nuclear program, *with American and Israeli assistance*?

In the end, MacPherson's speech was replaced with a formal prime-time press conference in which the president conceded that the Gogolov-Kharrazi compact could, in fact, be "a positive step forward toward building a more peaceful Middle East," similar to Libya's decision to abandon its pursuit of weapons of mass destruction.

Asked repeatedly if Iran's decision to give up its WMD program increased pressure on Israel to do the same, the president had refused to answer directly.

"I would remind you all that Israel was born out of the ashes of the

Holocaust," MacPherson said in the sound bite that kept repeating on all the cable news programs. "She has endured repeated attempts by her neighbors to drive her into the sea. She has signed peace treaties with Egypt and Jordan. And she is prepared to sign a treaty with her Palestinian neighbors in close cooperation with the U.N., the E.U., and Russia.

"If Iran, Syria, Lebanon, Saudi Arabia, and the rest of the Arab and Muslim world who have been in a state of war with Israel since 1948 are ready to sign formal peace treaties with Israel, I have no doubt Israel would no longer feel the need to stockpile the wide array of weapons she maintains for defensive purposes only."

It wasn't a bad answer, thought Bennett. But he doubted it provided enough moral firepower to block passage of Resolution 2441 at the U.N. Security Council, scheduled for a vote in just a few hours. It now appeared as if the president, unable to defeat the Russian power play, would have to veto it instead.

The only bright spot in the past two days had been hearing his mother's tears when he called to see if she'd gotten the roses. But even that was followed immediately by the inevitable question, "When are you coming down to see me, Jon-Jon?"

To which, of course, he had no answer.

Mordechai was getting anxious.

He was dying to know how the president had reacted to his brief. But he didn't want to pressure Bennett. Not today.

He would have loved to provide Bennett with news about McCoy, and he'd been working his sources for weeks, but so far there had been no progress.

He logged on to his laptop. There was one source in Moscow he had been hoping to avoid. Unfortunately, that was a luxury he could no longer afford.

"Sashu—I need help."

Moments later, an IM came back.

"anything for a friend."

Mordechai gritted his teeth. *Yes, a very good friend as long as I pay you. . . .*

"Need information on an American MIA in Moscow."

"the mccoy girl."

Mordechai was surprised. *"How did you know?"*

"rumor mill is going wild."

"Is she alive?"

"couldn't say."

"I need to know—fast. And I will pay handsomely."

"you always do. . . . i will check. . . . you will hear from me soon."

MacPherson rubbed his eyes and glanced at his watch.

It was almost 5 a.m. The First Lady was still asleep. The Residence was quiet, but for the ticking of the grandfather clock in the corner of their bedroom.

He slipped out of bed, donned a bathrobe, and sat down in his private study, where he fumbled for the lamp and put on his reading glasses.

"The Ezekiel Option."

Bennett hadn't said much about it other than that it was Dr. Eliezer Mordechai's take on the current crisis. This was MacPherson's first chance to read it, and he was curious. He picked up a phone and got a White House steward.

"Yes, Mr. President?"

"Tom, could you bring some breakfast up to my study?"

"Absolutely, Mr. President. The usual?"

"That would be fine, thanks."

He settled back in his chair and opened the brief, wholly unprepared for what he was about to read.

44

★ ★
★

The vote was about to begin.

MacPherson gathered with his National Security Council in the Situation Room to monitor the proceedings and provide final instructions to the U.S. ambassador to the U.N. in New York.

"Where's Bennett?" the president asked as on the large-screen video monitor the Argentinian ambassador finished his prepared remarks.

"On his way," said Corsetti.

MacPherson turned back to the video display, where the Italian ambassador—currently serving as president of the Security Council—cleared his throat and said, *"As to Resolution 2441 to compel the State of Israel to fully disclose and subsequently to destroy any and all stockpiles of weapons of mass destruction within thirty days, how does Argentina vote?"*

"Argentina votes aye."

"Argentina votes aye. How does the People's Republic of China vote?"

"China votes aye."

"China votes aye. How does the French Republic vote?"

"France votes aye."

Bennett's car pulled onto West Executive Avenue.

His driver pulled within a few feet of the entrance to the West Wing, but Bennett couldn't get out. He was glued to the radio, desperate not to miss a single moment as the U.N. vote transpired in Manhattan.

The Federal Republic of Germany was next, and not surprisingly, the German ambassador voted in favor of the resolution.

One after another, Indonesia, India, Japan, and Libya all cast their lots with Moscow as well.

The vote was now eight in favor, none opposed.

Bennett knew all too well that according to the rules of the U.N. Charter, the Russian Federation needed only nine votes of the nonpermanent members of the Security Council, so long as all five of the permanent members—China, France, Russia, Great Britain, and the U.S.—voted unanimously in favor as well.

There was still a chance to avoid a veto, but Bennett knew it was slim, at best. Over the past week, the president and Secretary of State Warner had been putting extraordinary pressure on five countries—the Philippines, Poland, Turkey, Italy, and Great Britain—to vote against the resolution. But since the Gogolov-Kharrazi press conference, their resolve had been weakening.

The Italian ambassador continued his roll call.

"How does the Republic of the Philippines vote?"

"This is a travesty against the Jewish people, and the people of the Philippines vote no."

"Yes!" Bennett shouted, pounding his fist on the seat beside him. Had the dam begun to crack?

"How does the Republic of Poland vote?"

"The Republic of Poland will have no part of another Moscow-inspired pogrom. The Jewish people have suffered too long, too much, and they have every right—indeed, they have a solemn responsibility—to defend themselves as they see fit. The people of Poland will do nothing to infringe upon that right. Noting that Article 51 of the United Nations Charter affirms every nation's right to self-defense, the Republic of Poland votes no on this insidious resolution."

Bennett could almost hear Doron and his cabinet cheering. Indeed, he could almost hear the cheers of an entire country as Israelis were glued to their televisions and radios now, even as they prepared for yet another war.

Bennett wondered if MacPherson was cheering.

He felt guilty for doubting his mentor of nearly two decades. James

"Mac" MacPherson had taught Bennett everything he knew about research, the markets, politics, and the art of the deal. He was one of the few
men Bennett admired. He was a man of convictions, a man willing to take
risks for peace, even if that meant war.

The code name Gambit was befitting.

But something was different. Something had changed. Bennett
couldn't put his finger on it. Somewhere along the way fissures had begun
to develop in their relationship, a distance that had never been there before.

It was uncomfortable, disorienting even. Bennett hated himself for
the suspicion—*distrust* might be a better word—he felt toward the president. He wasn't sure where such feelings were emanating from, but they
were real, and they were growing.

Suddenly his phone rang.

"Bennett."

"Jonathan, thank God you answered."

"Dr. Mordechai?"

"No, no, it's Dmitri—Dmitri Galishnikov. Are you listening? Of
course you are listening. Can you believe it?"

Bennett hadn't spoken to Galishnikov, his partner in the Oil-for-
Peace deal and the president of Medexco, in several weeks. It was good to
hear from him. Unfortunately, this wasn't the best time.

"We're not there yet, my friend."

"No, no, but it is happening, Jonathan. I can feel it."

"I hope you're right, Dmitri. But I'm afraid I need to keep this line
open."

"Yes, yes, of course," said Galishnikov, trying to contain himself. "I
just had to talk to someone, to share the good news, and I thought of
you."

"I appreciate it, Dmitri. Believe me, you and your family are in my
prayers."

"Thank you, Jonathan. Thank you for all you are doing for peace.
God bless you, my friend. We will pray for you, too—and Erin as well."

That was odd, thought Bennett.

Galishnikov and his wife didn't even believe in God.

☆ ☆ ☆

MacPherson felt his chest compressing with every "aye" vote.

He had tried everything to avoid having the final decision rest on him. *Was it all in vain? Was he going to have to make the call?*

He had read Eli Mordechai's brief cover to cover. "The Ezekiel Option." He had been stunned. Was it possible his old Israeli friend—a man he respected deeply—was actually recommending that the president of the United States base his foreign policy on theology that MacPherson felt was at best dubious and at worst downright insane? *How should he respond?*

Should he veto the resolution, risking all-out war with Moscow, in the hope that Eli was right and God was going to intervene at the last moment? Impossible. But how could he abandon Israel to fend for herself against the rest of the world? Was there any chance that diplomatic measures could still bring a peaceful solution even if the resolution passed?

On the monitor, the Italian ambassador stood. *"Italy votes aye."*

MacPherson knew he was running out of time. He had to make a decision.

☆ ☆ ☆

The next one was no surprise.

Bennett listened as the Russian ambassador cast his ballot.

"The Russian Federation votes aye."

The Turkish ambassador was next. *"The Turkish people share a long and deep respect for the Jewish people and the State of Israel in particular,"* he began, *"and we stand second to none in support of any effort to bring peace to the Middle East. That said, however, we cannot allow a double standard to exist. We cannot allow the world to require Iraq, Libya, and now Iran to give up their weapons of mass destruction but give Israel a free pass. Therefore, while we hope for a peaceful resolution, nevertheless, the Republic of Turkey votes aye."*

Bennett was stunned.

And when the British ambassador voted "aye" as well, he felt as though the wind had been knocked out of him. Britain was the final blow. Only hours before, the British and Turkish prime ministers had each separately told MacPherson by phone that they would "do the right thing." What had gone wrong? Had they been bought off? blackmailed?

The vote was now twelve to two, including nine nonpermanent members. Gogolov had all but won.

Only MacPherson could stop this war now.

Or—at the very least—delay it for several weeks.

But to do so required casting a veto that would isolate the White House and could tear an already fragile NATO alliance to shreds.

Either way, a global nuclear showdown was coming.

It was just a matter of time.

"And how does the United States of America vote?"

The moment of truth was at hand.

All eyes were now on the American ambassador.

MacPherson's entire presidency was on the line. He had prayed for this cup to pass from him, but it had not. He had prayed for wisdom, but it had not seemed to come. He had begged the God of the universe to speak to him in his weakest hour, but the heavens seemed silent.

MacPherson looked down at the laptop screen before him, at the blinking cursor waiting for his instructions.

Slowly, he typed and sent over a secure server his one-word decree, then looked up at the TV screen to see the ambassador read the message on his BlackBerry.

He could see the ambassador flinch momentarily, then look up at a waiting Security Council and a billion viewers on the edge of their seats.

The American ambassador cleared his throat.

"Mr. Secretary-General, the United States chooses to . . . abstain."

And then a bitter thought came to her mind. She had married a workaholic. Had she raised one as well? It was painful to think how much like his father Jon had turned out to be. Sol Bennett had been a man consumed by his job, convinced that finding "all the news that was fit to print" was some sort of divine calling under which all other things on heaven and earth had to be subordinated. Birthdays could be canceled, holidays missed, anniversaries forgotten, simple manners completely tossed out the window if, heaven forbid, news should break. Worse were the times when no one Sol was covering was making news. It was like living with a man in need of a heroin fix.

She'd played that game for almost forty-one years, and she'd resented it for nearly all that time. But she had never really thought about the effect an absentee father would have on Jon. Until now.

There was a restless, driven, frenetic quality about her son that unsettled her. He was, to put it mildly, a man in a hurry. He wanted to play the "big game." He wanted to prove that he could win. On Wall Street. In the White House. On the world stage. He didn't love money or fame or power per se, though he had attained them all at such a young age. *Influence* was what he craved. A sense of mission. A sense of destiny, of accomplishment that would prove his worth beyond a shadow of doubt.

Just like his father.

It was why Jon ran so hard, she had concluded. Why he almost never took vacations. Why he pushed himself and his team past the limits of normal human endurance. Because he wanted so much for his life to matter, because he wanted to be noticed, to be important.

But to whom was he trying to prove his worth? To a dead father who had rarely spent time with him and never would again?

Erin McCoy was the best thing that had ever happened to Jon. She, too, had a voracious drive to succeed, but it was different somehow. There was a warmth to Erin, a genuine kindness and love for people that too often seemed to elude Jon. What's more, anyone who had seen those two together knew that Erin absolutely adored Jon. Head over heels didn't even come close to capturing the passion and intensity of her love for him. And as someone once said, love covers a multitude of sins.

There was no question that Jon was a different person—a better person—since he'd found Erin and found God. Erin called him "the George

45

★ ★
★

Nothing was going to stop this war now.

That much was clear. If there was one thing Ruth Bennett had learned from her years in Moscow, it was this: when the Kremlin decided to go to war, nothing was going to stand in its way. The only exception she'd ever seen was the Cuban Missile Crisis. It was one of the few times she had ever gone to church. And when Khrushchev had backed down, she had cried like a baby and wondered, for the first time in her life, if there really was a God in heaven.

She wanted to talk to Jon and get his thoughts on all that was happening. What's more, she wanted him to tell her that it was all going to be OK, that there was a secret plan being cooked up in the White House to defuse this crisis the way Kennedy had done.

But what was the point? There was no way Jon was going to take her call. Not now. Not for weeks. By her count it had been more than two weeks since she had called Jon and asked him if Yuri Gogolov was the Antichrist. She knew he was busy. She knew he had the world on his shoulders and was agonizing over Erin. Maybe he thought it was a stupid request. And maybe it was. But it was important to her. The world was lurching to the brink of nuclear war, and she was scared. True, he had apologized when he'd sent all the roses. He'd promised—again—to get back to her soon. But that was two days ago, and still no word.

Bush Jon," and it was true, as far as it went. He was kinder and gentler than he'd been in college or at GSX. Except to her. "Mom" always seemed to be at the bottom of Jon's to-do list. Maybe it was her own fault. After all, Naina Petrovsky had practically raised him when they lived in Moscow.

Maybe Ruth was just reaping what she'd sown.

She just wondered if she'd ever have the chance to say she was sorry.

46

★ ★
★

Bennett stormed into the Oval Office.

"*Abstain?* You want the world to think we're cowards?"

The president was alone, just back from the Situation Room.

"Get off it, Jon," MacPherson shot back. "I did what I had to do."

"Which was what, exactly? To tell our allies if they're ever in mortal danger they're on their own?"

"Our *allies*—in case you hadn't noticed—are siding with Gogolov. And have you forgotten that a quarter of all the oil we use comes from the Persian Gulf? Do you really think we could afford an oil embargo right now if the Saudis and the United Arab Emirates decide to take a stand against Israel? With the U.S. on the verge of a recession? With the world moving toward war?"

"Medexco could easily make up whatever imports we lose from the Gulf," Bennett countered.

"And how would we get them here? The next step is a naval blockade of Israel."

"So you're just going to pull the Seventh Fleet out of the Med? You're just going to let this thing happen?"

"You don't get it, Jon. My hands are tied. There is absolutely no support for another war. Not against Russia. Not against Iran. Which means there is *nothing* I can do. How many ways can I make that clear to you?"

"You promised you'd do the right thing, you—"

"I *am* doing the right thing, Jon. And it's time you started helping me rather than throwing a tantrum and accusing me of abandoning the moral high ground."

"You *are* abandoning the moral high ground, Mr. President. It gives me no pleasure to say it, but it's true. Wasn't it you who taught me the only thing necessary for evil to succeed is for good men to do nothing?"

"I'm not doing *nothing*, Jon. I'm trying to be an honest broker. I'm trying to keep the world from going up in flames. And I don't appreciate you accusing me of being a coward. I brought you into this administration for one reason: to help me make peace in the Middle East. You've done an exceptional job, and I'm very grateful. But unlike you, I don't think it's unreasonable to believe that peace in the Middle East should mean the absence of weapons of mass destruction."

"And you're prepared to say that to Doron?"

"I already have."

"What do you mean?"

"I talked to the prime minister right before the vote. I told him if Israel is willing to give up her nuclear weapons the United States is prepared to create a formal security alliance with her, including bringing her into NATO. I was working the phones most of yesterday, and the British and French and even the Turks are open to bringing Israel under the NATO security umbrella. Secretary Warner has been talking to European leaders all morning about the idea, and he's getting a very warm reception."

Bennett tried to steady his nerves.

He couldn't believe what he was hearing. He felt betrayed, but most of all he felt disoriented. He didn't know the man standing in front of him, not like he thought he had.

"So let me get this straight," said Bennett. "First, you're accepting Yuri Gogolov's position that the Israelis aren't entitled to weapons—weapons we gave them; weapons that would only be used for self-defense; weapons that haven't ever been used, even during the Yom Kippur War when Israel was, at one point, just hours away from being overrun by Arab armies advancing on every side.

"Second, you're proposing that Israel unilaterally give up such defensive weapons in exchange for a couple of pieces of paper promising that the next time Israel is threatened, Washington, London, Paris, Berlin, Ankara, and the rest of NATO will come rushing to her aid, even though she's being threatened *right now* and Washington, London, Paris, Berlin, and Ankara are taking *Moscow's* side. Am I getting this right, because if I've missed something here, please let me know."

"Sarcasm doesn't become you," said the president.

"Neither does appeasement," said Bennett.

"This conversation is over, Jon. I would have thought after all these years you'd have a little more faith in me."

"Faith? Mr. President, one of the reasons I'm a believer today is because of the faith I've seen in you and the First Lady—faith in God, in me, in doing the right thing even when everyone said I was wrong. I'd never met someone who had such a deep faith yet didn't come across as a religious fanatic until I met you two, and Erin. And I thank you for that because I have no doubt that God used you to change my life.

"But, Mr. President, I don't see you operating in faith right now. I see you operating in fear. And with all due respect, sir, I don't believe it's an act of faith to stand on the sidelines and do nothing as a Russian dictator and a bunch of radical Islamic extremists light a match that could end with the death of six million Jews. What if God has put you in this office for such a time as this, to protect the Jews from another Holocaust in their hour of need? Are you ready to stand before Him face-to-face and tell Him that when His chosen people were in the crosshairs of a madman, you did nothing?"

Bennett spoke out of sorrow, not anger, but he braced himself for the president to lash out defensively.

Instead, MacPherson just shook his head. "Jon, I know you've been through a lot in recent weeks. Erin. The peace process. The coup. I understand all the pressure you've been under, and I—"

"Mr. President, please don't patronize me or psychoanalyze my motives."

"I'm not patronizing you. I'm not psychoanalyzing you. I'm just stating the obvious. You need some rest. You need some time alone, to clear your head."

"Actually, I've never felt more clearheaded, Mr. President."

"Well, frankly, you're sure not acting like it. You have the gall to accuse me of turning a deaf ear to the Jews, of betraying my own faith, of not being macho enough to threaten a nuclear war that could annihilate mankind as we know it? You're out of line—and out of your league.

"This is the White House, Jon. I'm the president of the United States. I don't have the luxury of dabbling in fringe theology—not to mention letting it influence my foreign-policy decisions—and quite frankly, neither do you. I've always had the greatest respect for Eli, and for you. But what happened to the go-to guy I hired? What happened to that steely-eyed strategic thinker I recruited to be my right-hand man? Because I don't see him anymore. I'm grateful that Julie and I have been able to serve as some kind of example for you. But you need some rest, my friend, and you need some serious, professional help before you become something you'll regret."

Bennett couldn't believe it had come to this.

"I'm already something I regret, Mr. President—a member of an administration that would so easily sell out a friend."

"What are you trying to say?"

"I'm resigning, Mr. President—effective immediately."

47

★ ★
★

Back in his office, Bennett called Mordechai.

"How soon until the judgment hits Russia?"

"Jonathan, I am so glad you called. Doron is furious. I just got off the phone with him. He is convening his Security Cabinet tonight. He wants me to be there."

"Good. You should go. But I need to know right now. How soon until the judgment hits Russia?"

"Why? What is going on?"

"How long until it hits?"

"I don't know. Soon. What are you getting at?"

"I need your best guess—*now*."

"Well . . . I don't know. . . . I suspect it will be toward the end of the U.N. deadline, perhaps just after. The prophecy is not precise about the timing."

"Will *all* of Russia be destroyed? I mean, will everyone be killed?"

"I don't know, but I do not think so."

"Based on what?"

"Well, some of the verses toward the end of Ezekiel 38 and much of chapter 39 suggest a great spiritual awakening. But Russians, Iranians, Germans, and others cannot decide to follow Christ if they are all dead. So no, I do not think the judgments are complete annihilations of these countries."

"Can you give me anything more precise than that?"

"Why? What are you looking for?"

"Is there any evidence that suggests there are survivors after the judgment?"

"Well, there is one thing."

"What?"

"It is not conclusive. Some scholars disagree."

"About what?"

"Something in the Masoretic text."

"That's the Hebrew Old Testament, right?" asked Bennett, remembering Mordechai's explanation from their previous conversation. "Most Jewish Bibles are based on it."

"Right. The King James Version is based upon it as well. And when you read Ezekiel 39:2 in that version, you will find that the Lord God says to Gog, 'I will turn thee back, *and leave but the sixth part of thee*, and will cause thee to come up from the north parts, and will bring thee upon the mountains of Israel.' God then goes on to vow to destroy 'all thy bands.' Now, some scholars believe this indicates that five-sixths of Gog's forces and his coalition's forces will be destroyed but that one-sixth will remain behind and survive."

Bennett needed clarification. "You're saying that God vows to wipe out roughly eighty-five percent of the military and security forces and leaves the other fifteen percent relatively untouched?"

"It seems that way," said Mordechai, "but there is something else, too."

"What?"

"Ezekiel 39:6 says God is going to send 'a fire on Magog, and among them that dwell carelessly in the isles.' So it seems as if the firestorm is, in fact, going to hit Russia and perhaps her allies. That could mean extensive collateral damage. Many civilians, particularly those living near government or military bases in those countries, may very well be at risk, though it is not entirely clear."

Bennett finally exhaled. It was clear enough for him.

"Jonathan, please, you must tell me what is going on."

So Bennett did, one piece at a time.

He told Mordechai about his blowout with MacPherson, about his resignation. And then he told his mentor that it was time for him to get off the sidelines and into the game.

"Meaning what, Jonathan?"

"Meaning if God is about to move, I don't plan to sit still. I need your help, Dr. Mordechai."

"Of course, what do you need?"

"Two fake passports—different names, different aliases. Access to large amounts of Russian currency. And contacts in Eastern Europe who can smuggle me into Russia."

"Are you crazy?" said Mordechai.

Bennett knew the old man wasn't often stunned, but he sounded so now.

"You are planning to assassinate Gogolov and Jibril? That is lunacy, Jonathan."

"No, no, that's not it."

"Then what? You have never been trained in covert operations. You would never get close to them. Not now. And if the Russians capture you, they *will* kill you this time. Jonathan, you do not know what you are up against."

"Actually, I do. Look, you're convinced this prophecy is real, right?"

"Right, but—"

"OK," Bennett said. "And if you're right, that means there's nothing I can do to persuade the president to stand by Israel, because the prophecy makes it clear no one is going to stand by Israel. The only thing I can do now is try to rescue Erin."

"Jonathan, I am grateful you agree with me, but your plan is suicide."

"Maybe, but what am I supposed to do? If she's not already dead, they're going to kill her soon. And even if she lives a few weeks longer, she's most likely being held in a military prison or a military hospital somewhere in or near Moscow. Which means she's at risk of being consumed by the very firestorm you say is coming. I can't just sit back and do nothing. I'm going to get her back, Dr. Mordechai. Or I'll die trying."

The other end of the line was silent for what felt like several minutes. Then he finally heard Mordechai say, "OK, I will help you. Meet me in France in three days. You know where?"

"Yes," said Bennett. "And three days is fine. There's something I need to do before then."

48

★ ★
★

The doorbell rang.

Ruth Bennett stopped folding laundry and glanced at the clock on the kitchen wall. It was only 3:30 in the afternoon. She wasn't expecting anyone. She didn't even want to see anyone. But there it was again.

She got up, smoothed down her dress, checked her hair, and carefully peeked out from behind the living-room curtains to see who it was.

Her heart almost stopped. She raced to the door and yanked it open.

"Jon? What are you doing here?"

"Good to see you, too," he said. "Can I come in?"

The moment was surreal. Jon had no suitcases or DSS agents. He was wearing blue jeans and a polo shirt rather than one of his trademark Zegna suits.

"Jon, of course, come in," she said, unlocking the screen door and giving him a hug. "I just can't believe it's you. Ever heard of a phone?"

Jon smiled, a bit sheepishly. "I wanted to surprise you."

"Mission accomplished. You want something to drink?"

"I'd love some coffee."

They went into the kitchen, where Ruth put on a pot of water and got out two White House mugs he'd sent her for Christmas.

"Actually, got something besides those?" Jon asked.

"Like what?"

"Anything; it doesn't matter."

"Why? What's going on?"

"How much time do you have?" he asked.

"How much time do you need?"

And for the next hour, he told her the entire story, from Mordechai's answer to her question, to the Ezekiel prophecy, to his sudden resignation from the president's staff. When he was finished, he gave her his copy of "The Ezekiel Option" and asked if she had any questions.

"I wouldn't know where to begin, Jon," she said, glancing through the pages of Mordechai's brief. "You really believe all this?"

"I think I do," he said. "But that's not even why I'm here."

"It's not?"

Jon shifted in his chair. "This is kind of hard to say, but maybe you could just let me get through it first and then we could talk about it. Is that okay?"

Ruth nodded. *Where was he going with this?* There was a long, awkward pause. She wasn't used to seeing her son at a loss for words. But as uncomfortable as he looked, she decided to keep quiet.

"I know I've disappointed you over the years," he said. "I know after Dad died I promised to come down more often, to call, to keep in touch—to be there for you . . . and I never really was. The truth is, I haven't been a very good son. I've been stingy with my time, with my love. I'm not married. I haven't given you any grandchildren. I just . . . I don't know . . . I don't want to sit here and give you a bunch of excuses. I just want to say I'm sorry. I'm *so* sorry.

"That's not enough, I know. It doesn't even begin to scratch the surface, but . . . it just seems like everything's been spinning out of control over the past few days, and I guess it's made me take a long, hard look at my life and what I've really accomplished, and how much of it has been just so worthless—useless—self-centered.

"I was reading in the Bible on the flight home from Israel on Sunday, and I came across a verse I'd never read before, or at least I'd never noticed it before—1 Timothy 5:8, where Paul basically says if a man doesn't love and care for his own family, he's denied the faith and is worse than an unbeliever. And I've got to tell you, Mom, that for the first time in my life it began to dawn on me how much pain I've been causing you. I felt so ashamed, and I started making plans to come down here."

Jon paused a moment, seeming to steady his emotions. He was looking at the floor, but then, suddenly, he looked up and stared straight into her eyes.

"Mom, did you know that Jesus, when He was dying on the cross, said to one of His best friends, 'Take care of My mother'?"

Ruth shook her head, trying to steady her own emotions.

"He did, which is more than I can say for myself. But that's what was so amazing about Jesus. He never became fogged, even in death. He loved His mom like He loved everyone else. All the time. Sacrificially. Even when it hurt. He wanted to take care of her, to make sure she was okay, even when He couldn't be with her. And He said to His friends, 'This is My commandment, that you love one another, just as I have loved you. Greater love has no one than this, that one lay down his life for his friends.'

"That's why Paul said in Romans, 'God demonstrates His own love toward us, in that while we were yet sinners, Christ died for us.' We don't deserve God's love. I certainly don't. But the amazing thing is that God loves us anyway. No matter who we are. No matter what we've done. If we accept His free gift of salvation through faith in Christ's death and resurrection, then God promises to forgive us, adopt us into His family, and let us go to heaven. He gives us the power to start living like He did and loving like He loved.

"Mom, I know you thought I was crazy for becoming a Christian. I know that's not what you and Dad brought me up to believe. But I just need to sit here and confess to you that just because I'm a Christian doesn't mean I get it all. I don't. Obviously, I don't. I have no idea how to love like Jesus loved. I don't know how to love you that way. I don't know how to love Erin that way. But I want to learn. Mom, I want to learn. I want to change. I want God to change me. And I had to start by coming here."

Ruth Bennett had no idea what to say. Her hands trembled. Her head was spinning. She was afraid if she moved she might just wake up and find Jon gone and all this a dream. Fortunately, Jon cleared his throat and wiped his eyes. Apparently he was not quite done.

"The best I can do right now is ask you to forgive me, Mom, and to ask you to pray that God would accelerate what He's already started in me. But I'm afraid I can't stay here. There's something I need to do."

Why? What was he talking about? Where was he going? The expression on her face obviously gave her away, and Jon began to explain.

"I believe 'The Ezekiel Option' is going to come true, but the prophecy only tells us so much. Things may get a lot worse before they get better."

"What are you saying, Jon?"

"I'm saying there's a chance to get Erin out of Russia alive, before all hell breaks loose. It's a slim chance, but I'm going to take it."

"Meaning what?" Ruth demanded, the fear once again rising within her.

"I wish I could tell you, but . . ."

"Don't tell me you're going to *Russia*."

"Mom, I can't say what I'm doing. But I don't want to lie to you. There's a real chance I won't be coming home. And I didn't want to leave without asking your forgiveness, and telling you how much I love you."

She wasn't sure whether she was going to cry or scream at him. But one way or another, she was about to lose it. She reached over, grabbed Jon, and wrapped her arms around him.

"I forgive you for what you've done in the past, Jon, and I can't tell you how much I appreciate what you've said. . . ." It was all she could do to finish her sentence. "But I don't know if I can forgive you if you walk out that door right now. I mean, what am I supposed to do? How am I supposed to go on? You're all I have, Jon. Your father's dead. My sister's dead. Without you, I'm all alone."

Her tears began to soak into Jon's shoulder. But she couldn't stop.

"I hear you, Mom, and I wish there was another way," Jon said softly. "But I have to do this."

"Why? It's suicide, Jon. Does being a Christian mean committing suicide?"

"Mom, it's dangerous—I concede that—but it's not suicide. It's love. I love Erin. I don't know what's going to happen over there. Neither do you. But I wouldn't go if I didn't believe there was a real chance of getting her out alive. And when you're doing what God wants you to do, there's always hope.

"And that's what I want for you, Mom. To have that kind of hope. To know that God loves you and has a wonderful plan for your life. To know that you're forgiven through what Christ did on the cross *for you*. To know beyond a shadow of a doubt that you're part of God's family and that you're going to be with me and Erin in heaven for all of eternity, no matter what happens.

"Believe me, Mom, there's nothing Erin and I would love more than for you to give your life to Christ. Jesus said, 'Behold, I stand at the door and knock; if anyone hears My voice and opens the door, I will come in to him, and will dine with him, and he with Me.' Jesus wants to be part of your life, Mom. To give you a hope that never disappoints. As a gift. Because He loves you. But only you can make that choice. Only you can decide to ask Christ to save you and give you eternal life. And time is running out."

49

★ ★
★

"Mr. President, you need to see this."

Marsha Kirkpatrick turned up the television in the Oval Office. A press conference was just under way in the Kremlin with Russian foreign minister Andrei Zyuganov.

"I can now confirm what many of you in the media have been speculating on for the last few hours," Zyuganov began. "As you know, for the past several days our security services have been engaged in a massive investigation into the plot to assassinate Czar Gogolov. I am pleased to report that we finally have a major break in this case.

"After intense questioning by the FSB, the three suspects being held in connection to this horrific crime have confessed to being agents of the Israeli intelligence service known as the Mossad. Thus far they have only given us their names and their levels of seniority within the Mossad. They refuse to cooperate further until they have a meeting with legal counsel from the Israeli government."

A buzz rippled through the press corps.

"About an hour ago," Zyuganov continued, "the Russian Federation made official contact with the office of the Israeli prime minister, passing along the Mossad officers' request for legal counsel. We have given the government of Israel seventy-two hours to respond. If they fail to respond, the Russian Federation will have no choice but to give the Israeli agents fast-track trials, which, given the enormity of the evidence already compiled against them, would likely lead to *rasstral*—execution by firing squad."

Zyuganov's aides then distributed copies of signed confessions by each of the alleged Mossad agents.

"The CIA got a heads-up on this about twenty minutes ago," Marsha Kirkpatrick told the president after muting the television. "I just spoke to Prime Minister Doron. He denies that any of the three men are Israeli, much less Mossad."

"You believe him?" asked MacPherson.

"I don't know. It could be a tactic by Gogolov to justify his military buildup. But I doubt we'll ever know for sure. And even if the three really are Israelis, Doron can't possibly admit it without handing Gogolov the trump card."

David Doron was furious.

The Mossad had not tried to assassinate Gogolov. They didn't have enough resources in Moscow to begin with. Nor would Doron have been so stupid as to authorize an act of war at such a delicate moment. Very likely the whole assassination attempt had been a farce, a clever ploy designed to turn world opinion against Israel.

This was classic Soviet-era disinformation. It was designed to give the Russians a pretext for war. And Doron and his senior aides had to admit it was as effective as it was insidious. Denials—while true—would merely sound like a smoke screen to a world that seemed increasingly determined to subject Israel to the same fate as Iraq.

Doron had no clue as to the identity of the three poor souls Gogolov had arrested and forced to confess to crimes they hadn't committed. But they were dead men. Of this he had no doubt.

Bennett landed at Charles de Gaulle Airport.

It was just before noon. He had no checked bags. He'd brought no security detail with him. He was no longer a VIP, and though fear for Erin's safety consumed him, he'd never felt so free. He quickly cleared through Passport Control, rented a car in his own name, and hit the open road.

It felt good to drive again.

With a mixture of clouds and sunshine and no rain in the forecast for the next few days, the late-September air was crisp and cool. Bennett jammed the two-seater into fifth gear and headed north out of Paris, following A13 to Caen and passing through Versailles. He was soon proceeding north by northwest on N13 toward Bayeux and Saint-Lô. By late afternoon, Bennett had reached Château de Balleroy.

Pronounced "bell-*wah*," the sprawling, seventeenth-century French castle was about twenty minutes from the beaches of Normandy. Until recently, the exquisite property had been owned by the sons of Malcolm S. Forbes, the late American publishing magnate. So far as the locals knew, it was now owned by an eccentric Belgian widower who'd made his money in pharmaceuticals and was often scuba diving at a Club Med or somewhere in the Caribbean. No one had the faintest clue it was actually a Mossad safe house.

The "widower" met Bennett at the door with a bear hug.

"Jonathan, I am so pleased to see you."

"Good to see you again, Dr. Mordechai. Thanks for your help."

"My pleasure. Please, please, come in. We do not have much time."

A giant mounted boar's head greeted the two in the foyer, as did a six-foot figure wearing a hand-forged suit of French armor from the Middle Ages. And that was just the beginning. As Bennett and Mordechai headed up the cantilevered staircase, the first of its kind in France, Bennett caught glimpses of room after room of untold treasures. Mordechai pointed out a few of them. There was the Salon Louis XIII, decorated with oak paneling and paintings by Count Albert de Balleroy, the late Parisian aristocrat who'd once shared a Paris studio with Manet. There was the Queen Victoria's Suite, decorated in the style of Louis XVI. There were formal dining rooms, exquisitely appointed guest rooms, and an English-style library whose shelves were stacked to the ceiling with thousands of tomes of European literature.

But Bennett had no interest in the history or a tour. He had one mission and one mission only: to find McCoy, whatever the cost. Nothing else would get in his way.

He followed Mordechai through the old servants' kitchen, where Mordechai pushed aside several dusty trunks, uncovering the entrance to a hidden staircase. The stairs descended into a narrow, dimly lit shaft that appeared to go all the way to the basement of the château.

Mordechai went first, instructing Bennett how to replace the trunks in the kitchen and close the door behind them. As they descended, they swapped the latest news. Mordechai assured Bennett that the Mossad had nothing to do with the attempted assassination of Gogolov. Bennett described more fully how badly his meeting with the president had gone.

"Your job is not to convince anyone the prophecy is true, Jonathan," Mordechai assured him. "Just to make sure they understand what it says—and what it means."

From there the talk was all about McCoy.

Mordechai explained he'd been working his sources for the past few weeks to track her down. There were still no leads, but he was hopeful.

The two finally reached a subterranean antechamber, where they faced a steel door with a state-of-the-art security system. Mordechai punched in his access code, and ten seconds later Bennett found himself staring into a high-tech Mossad operations center, comparable to the one under Mordechai's own home in Jerusalem.

"Welcome to the French underground," the old man smiled.

"*Après-vous*," Bennett replied.

Inside the room, Mordechai introduced Bennett to two Israeli operatives from the Mossad's Caesarea Unit, Carlos and Claude. Bennett assumed these were not their real names. The elite of elites of the Israeli special services, the Caesarea Unit had been responsible for capturing Adolf Eichmann in the 1960s and hunting down radical Islamic terrorist leaders since then. They were masters of infiltrating enemy territory and carrying out lightning-quick operations without leaving a trace.

Carlos spoke first. "I must make two things clear from the beginning: First, this is not an official Israeli mission. We are doing a favor for Dr. Mordechai, an old friend, nothing more. No Israeli government official above us has any idea what we are doing, and given the current situation, we would be court-martialed if they found out.

"Second, we will help you get into Russia, Mr. Bennett, but we cannot help you get out. And I must be candid. For someone with no training in

...tions, your chances of survival are minimal. Your chances for
 worse."

...nett swallowed hard but said nothing. He had no illusions about
...nay ahead, though he'd have appreciated some encouragement, at
lea...

...mission would be called "Operation Rahab." Rahab, Mordechai
...Bennett, was a woman in the Old Testament who was rescued
...oomed city of Jericho.

...hai opened a folder and pulled out a map of Russia and its

...et get you in through Europe, Jonathan," he began. "Those
...losed. We looked at sending you to Japan and getting you
...ivostok, but crossing Siberia and the Urals is out of the
...oment. You cannot fly. The airports are filled with Rus-
...rts preparing to fly to Beirut, Damascus, and Riyadh.
...rain. The rail lines are full of freight cars transporting
...tillery."

...ugh China?" Bennett asked.

...se border is the one border the Russians are actu-
...w, prompting the Chinese to reinforce their side
...e blood feud between the Russians and the Chi-
...What do you know about the Golden Hordes?"

...d. The Mongol forces were known as the Golden
...led *Rus*—it was not even called "Russia" yet—in
...the Russian heartland for almost three hundred
...most of what we know as the Great Wall of China
...Dynasty. What most people do not know is that the
...o prevent an invasion by the Russians. Arab writers
...e Wall of Al Magog.'"

...cinated. The clues about Gog and Magog were far
...an he'd thought. Still, none of this solved the problem

...ou propose I get into Russia?" he asked.
...e's turn to speak. "The only way is through Iran."
...es widened. *"What?"*

"There are only two Russian borders open right now," Claude continued. "One is north of the Caucasus, directly across from Turkey. But that is too dangerous. The Black Sea is completely clogged with naval ships coming south, bringing Russian military forces toward Israel.

"The other open border is along the Caspian Sea, directly across Iran. Almost all the shipping traffic is coming from the north, and mostly Russian naval vessels bringing troops, tanks, and other equipment to Iran to be loaded onto trains and shipped to Turkey, Lebanon, and Jordan. But for the moment at least, it is not nearly as congested Black Sea, which makes it our best shot. Besides, it is unlikely anyo suspect that you, of all people, are trying to get into Russia at all, mu through Iran."

"No, I guess not. But how do you propose we do this?"

"We will fly you to northwestern Turkey, where you and I w HALO jump," Claude answered. "Once we hit the ground, I will p off to a man named Hamid Mehrvash. Hamid is Persian. Grew up Fluent in Farsi and Turkish. Used to be a Muslim. Used to smugg ish, cocaine, vodka, caviar—you name it—into Iran. A few years found Jesus. Today he is the pastor of some underground chur Tabriz. Dr. Mordechai has known him for years."

Bennett was starting to get cold feet. No wonder Mordec called it a suicide mission.

But Claude didn't miss a beat. "If the two of you can cross th into Iran without getting caught—and that's a big *if*—you w through the Iranian mountains until you get to the Caspian Sea you will board a ship Hamid's old smuggler friends still use on ru trakhan on the Volga River. If you make it through all that—an *if*—we have a vehicle there you can use to drive to Moscow."

"In the meantime," Mordechai added, "I will be doing eve can to get a lead on Erin's whereabouts. In addition to false do sidearms, and enough Russian currency to buy your way out of will give you a secure satellite phone. If I find out something on E

"Another big *if*," Bennett added.

"Either way, I will call you and give you the best I have. Any qu

Bennett had dozens, but he started with one.

"What exactly is a HALO jump?"

50

"Two minutes."

Wearing his helmet and oxygen system, Bennett could barely hear Mordechai over the roar of the specially modified twin-engine Super King Air.

But the hand signal was clear. He was about to free-fall from thirty thousand feet into northern Turkey. Just under three minutes later, if all went well, he'd hit the earth traveling at well over twenty miles per hour, hoping to God he didn't break every bone in his body. And that was the *best-case* scenario. If something went wrong, he'd smash into the ground at roughly 120 miles per hour.

For the past hour an oxygen console had been pumping 100 percent pure oxygen into the cabin. Claude now did a final check of Bennett's heart rate (it was racing but acceptable). He also checked Bennett's blood-oxygen level, as well as his own.

It was critical that all of the nitrogen be flushed out of their systems. That would minimize—though not eliminate—the chance of experiencing violent decompression sickness, similar to ascending to the surface too quickly from a scuba dive. Without the prebreathing, nitrogen bubbles would explode into Bennett's bloodstream and trigger any number of reactions ranging from vomiting to paralysis to death.

Bennett checked his watch.

It was 3:37 a.m. local time.

When Bennett got the thumbs-up, he opened the valve on his portable air bottle, adjusted his regulator, and disconnected himself from the onboard oxygen console.

Next, he pulled down and tightened his goggles, then triple-checked his clothing to make sure that none of his skin was exposed.

At thirty thousand feet, the air temperature outside was thirty-five degrees *below* zero. Any skin exposure at all would lead to instant and irreparable frostbite.

And it wasn't unheard of for damaged or improperly adjusted goggles to freeze and shatter, causing eyeballs to freeze instantly and inducing a usually fatal heart attack.

Bennett was already soaked in sweat, in part from anxiety, in part from all the clothing he had on, layered though it was. Under a black, military-grade jumpsuit, he wore a long-sleeved turtleneck, a black T-shirt, thermal underwear, and blue jeans. On his head he wore a black balaclava that was also now soaked with sweat. On his hands he wore thermal inserts under Nomex flight gloves. It was all "Made in the USA," untraceable to the Mossad. As it had to be.

What unnerved Bennett was that for all his equipment, there was one thing he wasn't wearing: *a parachute.*

Claude held up four fingers.

He proceeded to clip Bennett to himself in four different places. They would jump, free-fall, deploy a single parachute, and land as one package—a tandem jump, it was called—unheard of in the world of the special forces but increasingly popular with civilian sport jumpers.

Bennett still hated the plan, but he had no choice.

In another day or two, Turkish airspace would be completely closed to civilian aircraft. The last door into Russia was closing. He would put his life in the hands of men whose real names he'd never know and try not to die in the process.

Mordechai climbed out of the copilot's seat and opened the cabin door.

He and Carlos both wore full jumpsuits and chutes, just in case, but their plan was to land at the airport northwest of Dogubayazit, retrieve Claude, and hightail it back to France before they were spotted by Turkish intelligence or overrun by Russian and Iranian forces now massing by the thousands.

A blast of frigid air rushed into the cabin and chilled Bennett to his core. Mordechai pointed Bennett and Claude to a white *X* on the carpet.

Ten seconds.

Bennett could feel his heart racing. He checked the rucksack strapped to the front of him for the umpteenth time. It would be his life for the next few weeks.

Inside were an Iranian passport and a Russian one, the satellite phone Mordechai had promised, two Berettas—one for him and one for Mc-Coy—ammo, power bars, bottles of water, a first-aid kit, several changes of clothes, and a beat-up old backpack to carry everything in once he ditched his jumpsuit and gear.

Five seconds.

The two inched their way to the door. Bennett moved his toes to the edge and fought the urge to look down in the icy blackness.

Three, two, one . . .

Mordechai gave the go sign.

Claude tapped Bennett on the shoulder, gave him a bear hug, and lunged forward.

They were airborne.

Bennett felt his stomach rise to his mouth.

He was in danger of hyperventilating. He tried to breathe deeply. He tried to remember the Scripture Mordechai had given him on a slip of paper just before they'd taken off, but his mind went blank.

"My God, my God, why hast Thou forsaken me?"

For the moment, it was all he could remember.

Bennett felt a tap on his shoulder and suddenly remembered to spread his arms and extend his legs. As he did he glanced at the altimeter on his wrist.

They were falling a thousand feet every six seconds.

They were hurtling through the atmosphere at terminal velocity. But in the pitch-blackness and thick cloud cover with no lights, no night-vision goggles, no geographic reference points to depend upon whatsoever, it was impossible for a novice to have any sense of how long they'd been out of the plane or how far they'd fallen.

He checked his altimeter again.

5,000 feet.

He couldn't believe how fast the dial was counting down. And it suddenly occurred to him that from the moment he'd quit the White House staff and decided to follow Christ no matter what the cost, his whole life had become a HALO jump. He no longer controlled his life. A strategic optimist and a tactical pessimist, his very survival was now in God's hands.

4,000 feet.

It had to be time for Claude to pull the chute.

3,000.

2,000.

Twelve seconds to impact.

Bennett tried to scream but no sound emerged. He craned his head to see Claude's eyes, but the man was literally right on top of him. Bennett tried to get his attention, waving his hands, tapping his watch furiously, anything to indicate the time was up.

1,500 feet.

Nothing.

1,000.

Just six seconds to impact.

Was Claude dead? Had he passed out? It had happened to other jumpers. Mordechai had told him stories, warned him of the risks. But Bennett wasn't ready to die. Not here. Not like this.

Bennett could see the ground now, hurtling toward his face. He could see the lights of a cottage on the other side of a field. He could see a VW van.

Five seconds . . . four . . .

Bennett's eyes went wide. Sweat poured down his back and legs. He wanted to pray a final prayer but all he could get out was *"Jesus."*

A HALO jump. He finally understood what it meant—High Altitude, Low Opening. He just hoped there *was* an opening.

Then suddenly—without warning—he felt the chute eject. He felt the harness tighten under his armpits and groin.

Claude kicked the back of his legs, and Bennett raised his feet and prepared to land. They hit the soft grass and rolled right.

Not a moment too soon.

51

★ ★
★

MONDAY, SEPTEMBER 22 – 25 DAYS TO THE U.N. DEADLINE

The world awoke to a *Washington Post* exclusive.

> *A senior advisor and close friend to President James T. MacPherson was fired over the weekend after urging the administration to either assassinate Russian leader Yuri Gogolov or launch a preemptive military strike against him, and then threatening to go public with his advice if the president did not immediately comply.*

The story was full of lies and mistakes, but it certainly made for good copy.

> *High-ranking administration aides, speaking on condition of anonymity, told the* Post *that Jonathan M. Bennett, the architect of and chief negotiator for the president's Oil-for-Peace plan, may be suffering from "extreme post-traumatic stress disorder" or some other form of stress-induced illness. Bennett was seriously wounded during the recent coup in Moscow. His fiancée, Erin Christina McCoy, a fellow White House official, is missing in Russia and presumed dead.*

White House Press Secretary Chuck Murray vigorously denied the story. But given its front-page prominence in the country's paper of record, and the fact that Bennett was nowhere to be found, the story quickly sparked an international firestorm.

Was the White House considering a preemptive strike against Gogolov's regime?

Insisting the answer was no, the White House press shop went into damage-control mode while Bob Corsetti quietly demanded that the CIA find Bennett at all costs.

McCoy stared at the lightbulbs above her.

One was now burned out.

How long would the other one last? she wondered. *How long would she?*

She closed her eyes again. She couldn't afford to be seen as recovering, much less awake and alert. Every time she began to regain her strength they came for her again and beat her within an inch of her life. And after spending some unknown amount of time in the cold shower, she would pass out again.

She feared for Bennett's life. Was she being selfish? Should she give in to Jibril's demands? Her head said yes. She couldn't bear to think of Bennett suffering as she was. But every time she was about to give in, something inside her said no.

Wait a little longer. Endure a little more. My grace is sufficient.

She clung to her only source of solace, the Scriptures her mother had made her memorize as a young girl, particularly the Twenty-third Psalm. She might not be in green pastures or beside quiet waters, but the Lord *had* made her lie down. And there was no question in McCoy's mind that He was restoring her soul.

She could feel the prayers of thousands back home lifting her spirits, giving her strength. How else could she explain the strange sense of peace she felt? She was walking through the valley of the shadow of death, yet she feared no evil. She was mentally and physically exhausted. Yet her spiritual tanks were full, and she was not afraid. How else was that possible without the help of a Messiah who had once suffered far more than she?

They were behind schedule.

But there had been no choice. A ferocious storm was battering the whole of Turkey. It had rained—driving, relentless sheets of rain—nonstop during the hours since Claude had handed Bennett off to Hamid. Bennett hoped Claude had managed to get to his rendezvous point to be picked up. Bennett and Hamid, meanwhile, had been stuck in this cottage for hours, unable to drive on the treacherous roads. Visibility was almost nil. Mud- and rockslides made several key mountain roads virtually impassable. Flash floods were reported throughout the country.

Yet Hamid was now convinced it was time to move.

It was just after 9 p.m. *Why the urgency?* Bennett wondered. But Hamid was insistent, so the two of them packed the VW bus and wiped down the cottage of fingerprints or any sign they'd been there at all. Fifteen minutes later, they were on the move as lightning flashed around them and thunder crashed across the eastern skies.

Progress was slow, and what they saw over the next ninety minutes terrified them both. A convoy of Russian and Iranian troop transports and flatbed trucks carrying tanks, gasoline trucks, and other military vehicles passed them, heading south, with no end in sight.

As they finally entered the border town of Bazargan and approached the frontier—freshly cleared from mudslides by a bevy of military bulldozers—only three cars stood in line ahead of them at Passport Control.

No one in his right mind would be going *into* Iran. Not on a night like this.

"Nervous?" Hamid asked, gulping a can of cola as the windshield wipers worked furiously to give them at least a meager view of the road ahead.

"A little, yeah," Bennett admitted, wiping the perspiration from his hands.

"Here, take this," Hamid said, pulling a pill from his pocket.

"What is it?" asked Bennett.

Hamid laughed. "It is not illegal, if that is what you mean. Believe me, my drug-running days are long behind me."

So Bennett swallowed the capsule.

He liked Hamid.

They'd spent a day and a half together conspicuously avoiding any talk of themselves or the dangers that lay ahead. The less they knew about the other, the less that could be forced out of them if either was captured. Still, Bennett was curious about Hamid's story, and how he'd met

Mordechai. There was something about this man—no more than thirty years old—that suggested Bennett could trust him.

So he did.

Mordechai typed another e-mail.

"Sasha—haven't heard from you—any news at all?"

He hit Send, then got back down on his knees to pray. Bennett was counting on him to get some answers—and get them soon.

It was Gogolov's first TV interview since the coup.

And it wasn't even with a Russian network.

A German news network was airing the program, which would be retransmitted throughout the world over and over again for the next twenty-four hours.

Gogolov sat in a red velvet chair by a crackling fireplace in his cere-monial office within the Kremlin. He was dressed in a charcoal gray suit, a crisp white shirt, a gold tie, and the trademark round, gold wire-rimmed glasses that made him look far more like some sort of scientist or professor than the ruler of a rising new Russian Empire. But for a small bandage on his forehead and some scabs on the left side of his neck, one might not have had any evidence he'd just nearly been killed.

"Czar Gogolov, first of all, you look remarkably healthy for a man who was almost assassinated."

"I was very fortunate," Gogolov replied in a firm, measured voice. "Sadly, a number of agents in my protective detail were not so lucky. There are grieving widows in Russia tonight, and I believe they deserve justice."

"Foreign Minister Zyuganov indicated at Saturday's press conference that you have three suspects in custody and that all of them have confessed to being operatives of the Israeli Mossad. When you speak of Russia's grieving widows deserving justice, are you referring to the kind of punish-ment these men will receive if they are found guilty?"

"Yes, in part. The case is a very serious one. It is about far more than the individuals we captured. This assassination attempt was, in my view, an act of war."

"By Israel?"

"Who else? We have no one else in custody but three Israeli hit men."

"Does this account for the mobilization of Russian forces?"

"There is no correlation. The U.N. vote triggered the mobilization of our forces so that we and our coalition will be in position to enforce the wishes of the global community, if such action is required."

"Would you say the actions of the Israeli government over the past few days, particularly if they were behind the plot against your life, have made war more likely?"

"They certainly have not improved the situation. The Israelis should take a serious look at Saddam Hussein's miscalculations in the days leading up to the U.S.–led war. No one is interested in war with Israel. We are all interested in peace. Only peace. But the decision is not ours to make. It is Israel's alone."

It was time.

The closer they got to the border crossing, the more Bennett's pessimism rushed to the fore. He pulled out his new passport—the Iranian passport—and glanced at it one last time before handing it to Hamid.

Nadia Mehrvash.

It was crazy. How in the world was he supposed to pass as Hamid's twenty-eight-year-old wife? A pregnant wife, at that? It was madness.

He wiped the fog off his window and caught a glimpse of himself in the side mirror. For the first time in weeks, he was grateful Erin couldn't see him now.

Over a false pregnant belly made of rubber—under which were hidden the Berettas and ammo, his satellite phone, and Russian cash—Bennett wore a traditional Persian dress. His face was nearly covered by scarves more suggestive of a religious Saudi woman than one from rural northwestern Iran, but who was he to argue?

Mordechai and Hamid had said it would work, and there was no backing out now. They couldn't exactly shoot their way through the border with fifty thousand heavily armed troops passing by.

"Ever read *God's Smuggler* by Brother Andrew?" Hamid asked.

Bennett shook his head.

"Ever hear of the smuggler's prayer?"

Bennett shook his head again.

"It goes like this," said Hamid. "Lord, when you were on the earth, you made blind eyes see. We pray now, Lord, that you would make seeing eyes blind. Amen."

"We're going to die, aren't we?" Bennett said, feeling his stomach cramp up.

"Hopefully not. Just keep quiet, and whatever you do, do not make eye contact with the guards. Remember, you are an eight-and-a-half-months-pregnant Muslim woman. If any of these guards touches you, I will cut his throat."

Bennett looked at Hamid, not sure if he was serious. He'd know in a moment.

The line continued to move. Only one more car to go, a filthy white Toyota with Turkish plates. Bennett tried to remember what kind of plates the VW had, but just then he felt a series of intense pains shoot through his stomach and doubled over.

What was wrong with him?

Bennett looked over at several soldiers standing by the guardhouse ahead of them. They seemed to be looking at the VW. One of them checked a clipboard and pointed in their direction.

Hamid jammed the stick shift into first.

Bennett winced in pain again.

"Good, that is good," Hamid said as the lead guard waved them forward. "Pretend you are having contractions."

"That pill," Bennett groaned as the pain increased. "*You* did this to me."

"Shut up and pray," Hamid shot back. "And for heaven's sake, do not go into labor."

Bennett felt like his appendix was about to burst.

He glanced in the side mirror. A large truck had pulled in behind them. Even if they wanted to escape, there was no way out now.

Suddenly, there was commotion ahead.

The Toyota ahead of them wasn't moving. The truck behind them inched forward, blocking them in. Was it a trap? Bennett looked at the guards again and saw the concern on their faces turn to alarm as one of them got off a cell phone and drew his weapon.

"Get out! Get out of the car! Get your hands up!"

Bennett didn't understand the words, but the tone was unmistakable. He looked up to see guards with machine guns racing in from all directions.

Desperate, he began to pray as the most intense pain set in. This was it. They weren't going to make it into Iran, much less Russia. They weren't going to be able to save Erin. They couldn't even save themselves.

And then, ahead of them, the driver of the Toyota hit the gas and raced for the border.

"Stop! Stop!" one of the guards shouted.

The night erupted with gunfire.

The windows of the Toyota exploded as the body of the car was riddled with bullets. Moments later, the car plowed into a Russian fuel truck and erupted into flames.

People were shouting furiously. Bennett couldn't understand a word but assumed they were calling for fire equipment. A border-patrol agent ran to their car and shouted something at Hamid, who quickly handed over their passports.

"We're trying to get to Tabriz as quickly as we can," Hamid said, "before the pain gets any worse."

The guard peered into the VW.

Bennett turned his face away and groaned.

"May Allah be with you," the man said.

"And with you," Hamid replied.

The guard returned their passports and waved them through. Hamid gently stepped on the gas, trying to clear through the frontier without attracting any attention but before the fuel truck blew.

Seconds later, they turned the bend and picked up speed as an enormous explosion lit the night sky behind them.

52

★ ★
★

Mordechai found a letter waiting for him.

His post-office-box information had been carefully typed on an old IBM Selectric. There was no return address and no postmark.

Perhaps it was from Sasha with news of Erin.

Mordechai's pulse quickened. His Mossad security detail assured him it had been thoroughly screened for explosives and toxins. It was clean.

The old man took it to his balcony and sat down with a cup of hot *chai* to read it. But the moment he tore the envelope open, he knew it was from Bennett.

Dear Dr. Mordechai,

I have only a few minutes, so I'll be brief. By now I am either in or dead. Either way, this may be my last communication with you before I meet you on the other side. If that's the case, I want you to know how grateful I am for your friendship and wise counsel. I thank God for you, for bringing me to Christ and teaching me so much. I'm sorry I'm so slow at this. Thanks for your patience.

I have something to say that I'm too much a coward to say in person. Thus, this letter. I am not the only one positioned for such a time as this. God has positioned you as well, my friend. First, to tell Prime Minister Doron about "The Ezekiel Option." And second, to go public. The world needs to know what God is about to do. The church at large does not seem prepared to share this message. Few have studied the prophecy closely. Now events are moving so rapidly that few will have time—or take the time—to decipher its meaning. But the lives of millions hang in the balance.

Jesus commands us to pray for our enemies, because we, too, were once enemies of God. What of the millions of Russian, German, and Islamic soldiers massing on Israel's borders? What of the thousands of intelligence operatives and government officials who are now just days away from divine judgment? Christ died for them, too, didn't He?

You must explain the prophecy to anyone who will listen. You must share the good news of Christ's saving love to those who will soon perish in the firestorm, to their families and friends and loved ones, and to those who live in fear of a nuclear holocaust, especially your Jewish brothers and sisters in Israel and in the Diaspora.

I am young, and perhaps I am foolish for trying to save the woman who saved me. But even if I stayed, I would never have had the platform—or the standing—you have to be God's spokesman. I know He doesn't need mere mortals to speak on His behalf. But wasn't it you who taught me that He chooses us to speak for Him? Wasn't it you who taught me the words of the apostle Paul?

"For there is no distinction between Jew and Greek; for the same Lord is Lord of all, abounding in riches for all who call on Him; for 'Whoever will call on the name of the Lord will be saved.' How then will they call on Him in whom they have not believed? How will they believe in Him whom they have not heard? And how will they hear without a preacher? How will they preach unless they are sent? Just as it is written, 'How beautiful are the feet of those who bring good news of good things!' . . . So faith comes from hearing, and hearing by the word of Christ."

On the back, you'll find the phone number and private e-mail address for Marcus Jackson at the New York Times. *I have a feeling he would love to do this story. Thanks again for everything, and may God continue to bless you.*

Your brother in Christ, JB.
(AMOS 3:7)

Ken Costello pored over the latest cable traffic.

Russian forces were streaming toward the Mediterranean. Iranian forces were pouring into Syria and Lebanon. German forces were being mobilized and would soon begin deploying to Saudi Arabia. France was still on the fence in regard to committing forces, but two new nations had joined the coalition against Israel over the weekend: Ethiopia and Sudan.

Mordechai's memo was playing out.

Talking about it with Rajiv, however, was pointless. By now she admitted that Gogolov's coalition looked a lot like the one Ezekiel had described. But every day she threw new objections at him. *Didn't Ezekiel say Israel's enemies were supposed to be armed with arrows and swords? Didn't he say the army would be mounted on horses? Did Costello see any cowboys and Indians out there? cavemen? Roman legions, even?*

That had bothered Costello for days. But wasn't it possible that someone writing 2,500 years ago might have described missiles as "arrows"? After all, the Russian R-37 air-to-air missile was code-named Arrow. The Chinese had an antitank missile known as the Red Arrow, now being deployed by the Iranians and Libyans. The Israelis themselves had an entire class of missiles called the Arrow, designed jointly with the U.S.

The horses, on the other hand, he had no answer for.

It was almost two in the morning.

But Gogolov insisted on an update.

"All in all, we are slightly ahead of schedule," Jibril reported.

"You do not take talk of an American first strike seriously?" asked Gogolov.

"No," Jibril replied. "Obviously, we must be vigilant, but look how quickly the White House distanced itself from the *Post* story. They are painting Bennett as a psychopath."

"Perhaps, but that ignores the larger point, Mohammed. If the United States really is planning to assassinate me or launch a commando operation of some kind, would you not expect them to deny it—especially in public?"

"Of course, Your Excellency, but there is no evidence of U.S. or NATO forces moving toward us, and our borders and airspace are effectively sealed."

Gogolov was not convinced. They weren't looking for a full-scale invasion, after all. Signs of American special forces preparing for a surgical strike would be harder to detect than perhaps Jibril was prepared to admit.

"Mr. President, you called?"

It was Jack Mitchell from Langley.

"Yeah, Jack, what's the latest on Bennett?"

"It's sketchy so far, Mr. President," the DCI began. "We know he took an Air France flight out of Dulles to Charles de Gaulle. He rented a car in his own name and took out three hundred euros from an airport ATM. He hasn't popped up on the grid since."

"Why Paris?"

"At this point we have no idea."

The president began to imagine the worst. Gogolov and Jibril had proven to be craftier adversaries than any of them had expected. They'd put both the Mossad and the CIA on the defensive. Could they now be luring Bennett into a trap?

MacPherson couldn't believe he'd let Bennett resign, much less sign a waiver allowing him to refuse further DSS or Secret Service protection. He'd been angry. They both had been. But the stakes were too high for either of them to let their emotions get the best of them. The last thing the country could afford was to have another senior White House official missing and presumed dead.

"Anything from McCoy?" Gogolov asked.

"Nothing so far."

"*We need those codes, Mohammed!*" Gogolov erupted. "We have no idea what the Americans are really up to. We are flying blind, and time is running out."

"I understand, Your Excellency. And I assure you, everything is being done."

"Perhaps Miss McCoy is tougher than you had thought," said Gogolov, changing tactics.

"Her psychological profile suggests she is a religious fanatic," said Jibril. "She believes her death will take her to heaven. We thought the threat of torturing Bennett would break her. So far, it has not."

"Give it another week," said Gogolov. "Then kill her."

Gogolov knew Jibril had been waiting for permission to do just that.

"And Bennett?"

"What do you recommend?"

"If it pleases you, Your Excellency, I would suggest you authorize my forces to track Bennett down, capture him, and videotape his beheading. Then I suggest we ship his body parts to the *Washington Post* or the *New York Times*. I guarantee the White House will get the message: do not even think about a preemptive strike, or more Americans will die like this."

Now Jibril was finally making sense, thought Gogolov.

"Just make sure I see the videotape before you send it."

53

★ ★
★

Someone was unlocking the door.

McCoy prayed it was the nurse, and it was. She heard the metal cart being rolled across the cement floor as the steel door closed and locked.

A verse suddenly came to mind—*"Thou dost prepare a table before me in the presence of my enemies"*—and then an idea.

McCoy could hear Nurse Grizkov begin her nightly ritual, preparing the heavy narcotics that would again plunge her into a deep and dreamless sleep. She heard her fumble for the right bottle. Then came the tearing paper, from which a new hypodermic needle was emerging. McCoy slowly opened her eyes and began to stir.

"You live," Grizkov said flatly.

"I need to use the bathroom," McCoy replied in Russian, suddenly wincing at the intensity of the light and realizing the second bulb had been replaced during the night.

"*Da*, but quickly. I am late as it is."

McCoy closed her eyes again, as if to rest, and heard Grizkov unlock her handcuffs. Then McCoy made her move.

With her left hand, she grabbed the ID around the woman's neck and smashed her face down into her pillow, cutting off Grizkov's oxygen. With her right hand, McCoy grabbed the needle off the cart and stabbed it into the woman's neck, depressing the plunger.

Stunned, the nurse struggled, but only for a moment until she fell limp across the bed. McCoy checked her pulse. She was still alive.

McCoy rolled her face away from the pillow, allowing the unconscious woman to breathe again. She knew she had only a few minutes. She stripped off Grizkov's uniform, ID, and wristwatch, donned them herself, then positioned Grizkov under the bedcovers and gave the woman another shot of sedatives to make sure there would be no surprises.

Next, McCoy took several pieces of gauze and carefully unscrewed the newly replaced lightbulb. Careful not to burn herself, she took hold of the bulb's metal base, put the bulb under one of her blankets, and smashed the glass as quietly as she could.

"You finished in there?" the guard barked in Russian.

"*Da, da,* let me out," she mumbled back, trying to approximate Grizkov's voice as best she could.

Keys jangled. The door began to open, but McCoy didn't wait.

Using all her strength, she pulled the door open and plunged the hot, jagged bulb into the man's throat. The guard never knew what hit him; he was dead even before he collapsed to the floor.

The hallway was clear. The cells up and down the floor were all empty. McCoy pulled the guard inside her own cell and rolled the medical cart over the pool of blood on the hallway floor.

There was no way she was going to make it out of the hospital carrying the guard's AK-47. Instead, she grabbed the man's pistol and radio and stuffed them in her pockets. Then she locked the cell door behind her and made her way toward the end of the hall.

Swiping Grizkov's ID through the electronic card reader, she gained access to the darkened stairwell. She realized she was on the fifth floor, but of what building she had no idea. She made her way down to the fourth floor, then the third. She saw no one.

When she finally reached the second floor, she suddenly saw a video camera mounted over the door. *Had there been others? Could she have been spotted?*

Her heart raced faster. She was now down to the first floor, and another security camera stared at her, threatening to expose her. She had to stay calm.

McCoy swiped the ID through the card reader and heard the electronic locks snap open. Her left hand pulled the steel door open as her right hand slipped into the pocket of her nurse's smock and rested on the sidearm.

The night staff was skeletal, but as McCoy entered the main floor and looked left toward the main doors, she saw three guards, all armed with automatic weapons. She prayed there was a back entrance, for staff perhaps, and turned right, ducking the glances of fellow comrades at the main nurses' station.

Suddenly she saw a group of doctors coming toward her. What if they saw her ID? What if they knew Tatiana Grizkov? Her eyes darted from side to side, and just as the doctors were coming within range she spotted a staff lounge and ducked inside, breathing a sigh of relief as she heard the doctors pass.

She poured herself a steaming hot cup of coffee, her first in weeks, then fished a half-eaten muffin out of the trash. She closed her eyes and thanked God for her food.

Two guards suddenly walked in.

"Who are you?" one demanded.

When she hesitated for a moment, he reached for his sidearm.

She threw her coffee into the face of the first guard, then kicked the second in the groin, knocking him to the floor and sending his gun flying across the room. She grabbed a chair and smashed it over the man's head, only to see the other guard going for his gun.

McCoy spun around. She grabbed the remaining pot of coffee, heaved it forward, and forced the guard to duck, buying her just enough time to dive to her left, grab her own pistol, and fire the first shot. Her aim was true, and the guard dropped instantly.

McCoy heard a siren. She feared a lockdown.

If that happened, she'd never get out alive.

She grabbed the first man's machine gun, burst into the hall, and raced for the nearest exit sign, spraying rounds at guards approaching from both directions.

She crashed through the internal exit but found the next exit door locked.

She tried Grizkov's pass. It didn't work.

She tried to go back. She might have to shoot her way out, but it was better than being trapped. But the door back into the prison was locked as well.

It was too late. She was already trapped.

The employee parking lot was inches away. But the lockdown had already begun. Her mind raced through her options. She could already see emergency vehicles racing to the front of the building. It would only be a matter of seconds before some units pulled into the back and she was surrounded.

McCoy pulled the radio from her pocket. It was alive with cross talk from guards trying to figure out what was going on. She found an open channel.

"Who's in charge here?" she growled in Russian.

"General Stupachkin," came the reply. "He's on his way."

"He's here, you fool. But he can't get in. Open the outer doors before he puts a bullet in your head, instead of the prisoner's."

"Da, da, one moment."

Six seconds later the outer doors released.

McCoy raced outside and ran headlong into a black Mercedes coming in from the north gate, bearing blue flashing lights. She immediately recognized General Stupachkin of the FSB in the backseat. The Mercedes screeched to a stop. The driver slammed on his horn and lowered his window, cursing at her to get out of the way.

McCoy pulled the .45 from behind her back and fired three shots through the windshield. The horn went silent, as did the driver. Two more shots and Stupachkin was dead too. Machine-gun fire erupted behind her.

McCoy ducked down, reached through the open window to unlock the door, then pulled the driver out and jumped in behind the wheel.

Jamming the car in reverse, she floored it and did a J turn as bullets smashed through the remaining windows of the vehicle. Crouching down and praying that she wouldn't be hit, she peeled through the closing gate only to slam into a Moscow police cruiser.

She fired six shots through the windshield of her car and into the windshield of the cruiser. She backed up far enough to get clear of the cruiser, then hit the gas again, fishtailing down the narrow street as the night filled with gunfire and sirens.

At the first intersection, McCoy took a hard left, then veered left across four lanes of traffic and cut across the deserted parking lot of a shopping plaza.

McCoy knew she had to ditch the shattered Mercedes. In a dark corner of the plaza parking lot she saw an old Volga sedan. She stopped the car, got out, and ran toward the Volga. It was unlocked. She got in, reached beneath the dashboard, and pulled a handful of wires down from inside the steering column. She had trained for this; she could do it blindfolded. Ten seconds later she had removed the protective coating from the battery lead and wrapped it firmly around the bare wire to the ignition switch. For a breathless moment, nothing happened. Then the car's engine roared to life.

Six minutes later, she eased through several alleys and onto a main boulevard. When she hit a straightaway, she glanced in her rearview mirror to see if any FSB agents were hunting her down. That's when she noticed the blood streaming down her face.

It was almost 4 a.m. when Gogolov got the news.

No one had wanted to wake him, including Zyuganov and Jibril.

Prison officials and the top FSB brass had been desperate to find McCoy before having to confess that they'd ever lost her in the first place. They'd found the Mercedes by now, with blood all over the steering wheel, dashboard, and front seats. They knew McCoy was wounded. They also knew she was too smart to seek medical attention.

Gogolov was furious. He cursed Jibril and threatened to murder Zyuganov's children if McCoy wasn't found quickly. He demanded a house-to-house, building-to-building search of Moscow and ordered that McCoy's photo be distributed throughout the city on flyers and nationwide over television. He no longer cared that the U.S. would know she was alive.

"Frame her as a serial killer," Gogolov directed. "Tell the press we never had her, that we believed she'd been killed in a cross fire on the night of the coup. Say she just resurfaced and has gone on a killing rampage. Tell them three innocent women are dead, including a pregnant woman and her child. Then give them pictures of the bodies—brutally slaughtered."

"But we don't have any pictures like that."

"Then kill a pregnant woman and take some."

"Y-yes," Zyuganov stammered. "Anything else, Your Excellency?"

"*Da*. Put a price on her head—ten million rubles, dead or alive . . . preferably dead."

An e-mail popped onto Mordechai's screen.

It was from Sasha. Mordechai's pulse quickened.

"*Old friend, you have caught a break,*" Sasha wrote. "*The police radios here are going crazy with reports that Erin McCoy has been spotted in Moscow and is on the run. Don't know more yet. Am monitoring every frequency I can. Send your first funds transfer to my account in Zurich. When I have more, you'll be the first to know.*"

Twenty minutes later, the phone rang in the Oval Office.

"Yes, Jack?"

"Radio Moscow reports a massive manhunt is under way for Erin McCoy," Director Mitchell reported.

"She's alive?"

"The Russians are saying she's CIA, and that she's killed three people, one of whom was a pregnant woman. They're about to release pictures. They say she's been spotted and is on the run somewhere in Moscow. And they've put a bounty on her head, Mr. President."

"How much?"

"More than three hundred thousand dollars, U.S."

"You think it's really her?" the president asked.

"It could be, but . . ."

"But what?"

"It could just be bait to catch Bennett."

McCoy stopped the car under a grove of trees in Gorky Park.

She'd been on the run for hours. She knew she could not last much longer, exposed on the streets. She was exhausted. She was losing blood. She had no way to contact Washington or Bennett, and now, as she listened to the breaking news on the car radio, she tried desperately to think of any of the CIA's dozen safe houses in Moscow. But her mind was blank.

It was strange to hear any news from the outside world, even if it was news controlled by the Kremlin. She'd had no idea, for example, of the assassination attempt against Gogolov. Nor of the U.N. resolution and deadline or of Russian and Islamic forces moving toward Israel.

Why? What was happening?

McCoy fought back tears at the thought of the men she'd killed or injured. She knew there was no other way, and she didn't believe that God wanted her to give up and die after all she'd been through in the past weeks. Still, she felt numb, hollow. She'd come so far. There was no point losing faith now, but she felt completely disoriented. Nothing seemed familiar.

Except, oddly, Gorky Park.

Why was being here of all places ringing a bell?

She hit the windshield wipers and looked out through the trees at the row of buildings across the river. *What was it?*

Her mind reeled. Across the river were row upon row of apartment buildings. New ones. She looked left, then right. She couldn't see it. *But it had to be there.* Somewhere along that street was the condemned apartment building where Naina Petrovsky, Jon's nanny, had once lived. It would be abandoned.

Could she find it? Would it be safe?

54

★ ★
★

Hamid began cautiously. "I have a question."

"Fire away, my friend," said Bennett.

"I do not understand, *fire-way*?"

"No, no, it's an expression, it's . . . never mind. What's your question?"

"Are you ready to leave for Russia? I believe it is time."

Bennett stared in disbelief at his new friend. Was he kidding? For almost two weeks, Bennett, Hamid, and Hamid's pregnant wife—the *real* Nadia—had been holed up in Hamid's home in Tabriz, Iran. A city of nearly one and a half million, Tabriz was about three hundred kilometers east of the Iranian-Turkish border. It was the provincial capital of East Azerbaijan, not to be confused with the former Soviet Republic of Azerbaijan. Now it was a transit point for the Great Mobilization.

So far, they'd been unable to move as continuous caravans of Russian and Iranian shock troops and their supplies used every available lane of every major road—as well as all available rail lines—to get to Turkey and then into Syria and Lebanon, ostensibly to enforce U.N. Resolution 2441. Bennett was beside himself. Local TV and radio were useless for details from the outside world. Hamid had no shortwave radio, and satellite calls were too risky, making it impossible for Bennett to stay in contact with Mordechai.

Local police commanders had banned townspeople from making any international calls—or even calls beyond Tabriz—during the troop movements to maintain "operational secrecy," despite the fact that Tehran and Moscow knew full well that Washington and Jerusalem were monitoring everything from geosynchronous spy satellites hovering in the stratosphere.

As far as Bennett was concerned, every day in Tabriz was a day closer to a death sentence. The U.N. deadline was only twelve days away. McCoy's life was in danger, as were his, Hamid's, and Nadia's. It was time to move. Yes, he told Hamid, he was ready.

"So am I. I have fasted for two days. I have peace. We must go quickly."

They could not, of course, use the main roads or railroads. They would have to head through the volcanic Sabalan mountain range, a treacherous journey at any time of year but unthinkable at night during the beginning of the rainy season. But they had no choice. Nadia quickly packed food and bottles of water for their trip.

"May I pray before we leave?" Bennett asked.

He had rarely prayed out loud, certainly not with people he barely knew. But he had no intention of heading into the mountains of Iran without God's blessing.

"We would like that a great deal," said Hamid.

Nadia covered her head with a scarf, and the three got down on their knees and bowed their heads to the floor. Bennett's mouth went dry, but he did the best he could.

"Father, we love you and praise you, and we are on our faces before you tonight asking for your mercy. On each of us, and most of all on Erin, your child, whom you love. Give her strength, Lord. Tell us where she is. And help us find her and set her free, Lord. For your glory, not for our own."

Bennett began to choke up. A lump formed in his throat.

"Lord Jesus, I thank you for Hamid and Nadia, for their love and hospitality. Please guard Nadia and her baby and protect them while Hamid is away. I pray for the congregation of Muslim converts who meet in their home, and for the dozen other churches they have planted from Tabriz to Tehran. Bless them, Lord Jesus. Protect them from the evil one. Give them the courage to live for you in dark times and the boldness to share their faith with anyone who will listen.

"I pray too for the peace of Jerusalem, and for the salvation of many souls through these dark hours. For Dr. Mordechai, that he might be willing to tell the world what he knows before it is too late. For President MacPherson, that he would be the right man in the right place at the right time. And I pray for my mother, Lord Jesus—that you would open the eyes of her heart, that you would love her and bless her and draw her into your Kingdom and into your family. Please, Lord Jesus. Have mercy on her . . . and on Erin. . . . Have mercy on these two women who . . ."

But Bennett couldn't go on. He broke down and began weeping uncontrollably. Hamid and Nadia put their arms around him and began praying in Farsi. Bennett couldn't understand a word they were saying, but he had no doubt they were praying for him, for Erin, for his mother, for a great salvation, and a great reunion. And the tears flowed even harder. He knew it was time to go. He knew it was time to get into Hamid's beat-up Renault and start climbing into the torrential rains and forbidding Sabalan Mountains that lay ahead. But inside a dam was breaking. He was HALO jumping, and he suddenly knew beyond a doubt that God was really with him all the way.

On Monday, millions took to the streets of Tehran.

As Bennett and Hamid continued driving, they were glued to the radio as a reporter described a scene of marching, chanting, screaming crowds burning American and Israeli flags and effigies of MacPherson and Doron. Bennett could only imagine how terrifying it must be for his friends Dmitri Galishnikov and Dr. Mordechai, and all the other Israelis huddled around their TVs and radios.

"The world must understand—the Zionists must be humbled," shouted one of Tehran's leading Imams. *"Death to Israel. Death to America, the Great Satan. The hands of the Zionists are covered in blood. Crimes against the Muslims. Crimes against the Russians. This cancerous Jewish tumor is the most dangerous threat on the face of the earth. But the Night of the Jews is almost over. Allah, we beseech thee, annihilate them with your wrath. Make their blood flow like a river through your holy city of Al Quds."*

☆ ☆ ☆

On Tuesday, Doron met with his Security Cabinet again.

He was not a man given to fear. He had fought and bled for his country in four wars—the Six-Day War in 1967, the Yom Kippur War in 1973, the 1982 invasion of southern Lebanon, and the first Palestinian *intifada* in 1987 and '88. He had once been held as a prisoner of war. Now, as Israel's prime minister, David Doron commanded one of the world's most powerful militaries. Yet anxiety was gnawing a hole through his stomach.

Gathered around the table were the most senior members of his national security team, the men he'd once dubbed the Sons of Issachar, "men who understood the times and knew what Israel should do." He welcomed their counsel. But he knew this was a decision only he could make.

"Gentlemen, before you is the Mossad's latest intelligence estimate of enemy forces in place or on the way," Doron began. "The first tier represents the bulk of Gogolov's military muscle—countries committing one hundred thousand or more troops and support personnel into the theater. For brevity, the forces of the former Soviet Union have been grouped together, as they are operating together through a central command structure.

"At present, we see no Egyptian mobilization, and the Sinai is clear, though we continue to monitor that front. Iraq has not mobilized. Nor has Jordan. And the king of Morocco, to his great credit, appears for the moment to be unwilling to lift a hand against us. Good news all, but I am afraid these are the only pieces of good news.

"The U.S., I believe, has abandoned us. Most of NATO is against us, though only the Germans and Turks are actually committing troops to fight against us. And I trust all of you have seen the latest reports out of Tehran, Tripoli, Riyadh, Khartoum, Addis Ababa, and so forth, to say nothing of Mecca and Medina. The Islamic world is aflame, gentlemen. The Arab and Islamic world now believes that Israel is facing her last days."

He paused as the Security Cabinet members reviewed the threat estimate in stunned silence.

```
************ NATIONAL INTELLIGENCE ESTIMATE *************
22 Tishri ** 06:00:16 ** Ops Center ** 0761-049TLV-0000917
```

To: Prime Minister Doron
From: Director Avraham Zadok
Subject: Current Threat Assessment

* Russia -- 807,000 troops -- 12,989 tanks -- 2,691 combat
  aircraft
* Former USSR Republics -- 493,000 troops -- 1,266 tanks --
  66 combat aircraft
* Iran -- 487,000 troops -- 1,581 tanks -- 335 combat aircraft
* Turkey -- 403,000 troops -- 4,271 tanks -- 523 combat aircraft
* Syria -- 210,000 troops -- 3,817 tanks -- 627 combat aircraft
* Saudi Arabia -- 131,000 troops -- 1,101 tanks -- 447 combat
  aircraft
* Germany -- 103,000 troops -- 2,300 tanks -- 246 combat aircraft
----
* Algeria -- 97,000 troops -- 996 tanks -- 176 combat aircraft
* Austria -- 21,000 troops -- 41 tanks -- 23 combat aircraft
* Bahrain -- 8,000 troops -- 99 tanks -- 37 combat aircraft
* Ethiopia -- 367,000 troops -- 104 tanks -- 31 combat aircraft
* Kuwait -- 13,000 troops -- 401 tanks -- 93 combat aircraft
* Lebanon -- 65,000 troops -- 319 tanks -- 12 combat aircraft
* Libya -- 72,000 troops -- 1,121 tanks -- 478 combat aircraft
* Oman -- 12,000 troops -- 152 tanks -- 53 combat aircraft
* Qatar -- 8,000 troops -- 39 tanks -- 23 combat aircraft
* Sudan -- 52,000 troops -- 1,657 tanks -- 21 combat aircraft
* Tunisia — 31,000 troops -- 100 tanks -- 66 combat aircraft
* U.A.E. — 62,000 troops -- 105 tanks -- 119 combat aircraft
* Yemen — 63,000 troops -- 316 tanks -- 103 combat aircraft
```

```
********************* EYES ONLY **************************
22 Tishri ** 06:00:16 ** Ops Center ** 0761-049TLV-0000917
```

"What this estimate does not cover, of course, are the naval forces steaming toward us," the prime minister continued. "Nor does it cover the strategic and tactical nuclear forces arrayed against us. Those
```

estimates are still being developed, but suffice it to say that while Moscow still has a good deal of its strategic nuclear forces targeted at the U.S., Western Europe, and China, IDF intelligence informs me that upward of one-quarter to one-third of Russia's tactical nukes are currently arrayed against Israel.

"Gentlemen, we must acknowledge that the threat we now face is existential. We are in danger of losing all that our fathers and their fathers bought for us with their blood and sweat and treasure. Therefore, as much as it pains me to say it, I believe we now have no choice but to discuss The Samson Option."

McCoy was famished.

She had managed to scrounge up a half-eaten loaf of bread and some vegetables several days before. But they were gone now. Never in her life had she ever really meant it when she'd prayed, "Father, give us this day our daily bread." But she meant it now.

McCoy refused to succumb to fear. She was alive. She was free. She had a loaded pistol, a police-band radio she'd lifted from the Mercedes, and shelter from the storm clouds coming over the horizon.

True, the abandoned apartment was filthy, crawling with cockroaches and other assorted creatures she was not yet desperate enough to eat. But it had a seventh-floor view of the Moskva River and of the changing autumn leaves of Gorky Park.

Dayenu, Mordechai would have said, as he'd taught them when she and Jon had celebrated Passover at his home in Jerusalem. "This alone would be enough." It was a hard message to learn in Washington, with the world at her fingertips. But the privilege of learning it here was almost more than she could bear.

Suddenly there were sounds in the hallway.

They weren't voices. They were boots, and they were approaching quickly.

She turned off the police radio and reached for the pistol. She got up and moved toward the door, the gun aimed in front of her. Counting the footsteps, she guessed there were four men. No wait, there were five. Wait—what was . . .

It didn't make sense. More and more people were massing in the hall-way. None spoke, nor did they move with the speed and stealth of Russian special forces.

Beads of sweat formed on her forehead and slid down the sides of her face. She could taste the salt, and it intensified her hunger pangs.

A door opened nearby, but not hers. The small crowd was moving, and in a moment, she could hear the door shut, and it was quiet again.

McCoy checked her pulse. She had to avoid hyperventilating. How could God let her come this far only to be recaptured or killed? Who would even know that she was dead? The good news was that word of the manhunt had to have been picked up by Langley. They knew she was alive and on the run. But if she died here, alone, would that news get out? Or would Gogolov and his thugs hold it back, hoping to lure in a CIA extraction team as a pretext for war against the United States, as well as Israel?

The handle to her door began to turn.

McCoy held her breath. The door creaked open. She waited two beats, then slammed it forward, crushing the intruder's fingers. As the man howled in pain, McCoy pulled the door open and grabbed the man by the hair. She pulled him forward and smashed his face to the ground, then pulled him back to his knees and drove the gun into his right temple. She had her hostage. It wasn't much leverage, but it was something.

Yet when she looked up, the faces staring back at her weren't those of *Spetsnatz* or a Russian SWAT team. They were the horrified faces of chil-dren, dressed for church.

"Please, please, do not kill him," cried a young woman in Russian. *"I beg of you, please . . . please . . . do not kill him. . . . I . . . he . . . he is . . . he is my husband."*

The woman, probably in her twenties, was sobbing.

The children froze like statues.

Startled, McCoy loosened the pressure of the pistol against the man's head.

That's when he made his move. In a single swift motion, he knocked away the gun with his right hand and, pivoting, drove his left hand into McCoy's face, sending her flying back. The gun skittered across the floor, landing several feet from McCoy. The two lunged for it, but the man was quicker.

Before McCoy realized what was happening, the man was behind her. His arm was around her throat. The .45 was pressed against her temple as his wife and a group of parents now stood by their terrified children, staring on in disbelief.

She begged the man to wait, to listen to her.

She was running from Gogolov. That was true. But she was not an enemy of Russia. She was an American diplomat and a friend of the Russian people, trying to make peace until she'd been taken hostage by the new regime and tortured.

"So, today must be my lucky day," the man said in passable English. "You must be the ten-million-ruble lady everyone's talking about."

Mordechai had avoided the subject for days.

He was a man who had spent his whole life in the shadows. He felt at home there. But as the U.N. deadline steadily approached, a gloom the likes of which he had never felt before settled over the house of Israel—and his own.

Mordechai was having trouble sleeping. He couldn't get Bennett's letter out of his mind. What haunted him most was the verse scribbled at the bottom of the note.

Amos 3:7.

He feared it would say something he didn't want to hear. But he could no longer hide from the God of Abraham, Isaac, and Jacob. Not with judgment so close at hand. He opened the Tanakh and looked up the passage.

ז כִּי לֹא יַעֲשֶׂה אֲדֹנָי יְהוִה דָּבָר כִּי אִם־גָּלָה
סוֹדוֹ אֶל־עֲבָדָיו הַנְּבִיאִים

Instantly, Mordechai knew in his soul that Bennett was right.

> *Surely the Lord God does nothing*
> *unless He reveals His secret counsel*
> *to His servants the prophets.*

It could not be more clear. He reached for the phone.

The man ordered the room cleared of all but his wife.

After the door to the hallway closed, he released McCoy's throat and stood up.

"Welcome to Gorky Bible Church, Miss McCoy. I am the pastor. I, too, am considered an enemy of the new Russian regime. So I will make you a deal. I won't turn you in if you won't turn me in. Fair?"

McCoy wanted desperately to believe him. She nodded carefully.

"Good. My name is Mikhail Zorogin. And this is my wife, Karenna."

Karenna leaned over and whispered in his ear.

"Yes, yes, Karenna is right. It is not safe for us to stay here. We may have been heard. Come, you must stay with us. It is not far. We live in the building next door."

55

WEDNESDAY, OCTOBER 8 – 9 DAYS TO THE U.N. DEADLINE

Zyuganov burst into Gogolov's office.

"The Israelis just put their nuclear missile forces on full alert."

Gogolov finished lighting up a cigar and stared out over a rain-drenched Moscow.

So, the great chess game had been joined at last. Didn't Doron know he was already in *check*? Soon it would be *mate*, and then it would be the Americans' turn.

"Very well," Gogolov said calmly. "Do the same. But first, hold a press conference accusing Israel of pushing the world toward another Holocaust."

Bennett turned off the radio.

The notion of another couple of hours, much less days, thinking about the magnitude of enemy forces now converging on Israel made him sick.

"By the way," he asked abruptly, looking for a new topic, "what's in all those boxes in the backseat?"

They were now winding their way through the high-peaks region, along narrow, muddy roads, around too many hairpin turns to count.

Only a native of these parts would maintain such speeds unless he was crazy.

"Farsi New Testaments," Hamid replied, driving with one hand, taking another swig from a water bottle with his other. "I get them from Turkey every few weeks and distribute them among the house churches. You are wondering why I brought them with us?"

"We don't have enough to worry about?" asked Bennett.

"It was Nadia's idea, actually. She was worried the government might force her to let troops stay with her overnight while they are passing through. She just thought it would be safer not to have so much contraband in the house."

"So you thought it'd be better for us to have them, in case *we* get pulled over?"

"There is nothing to worry about. I do it all the time, and I have not had any trouble yet."

The car swerved. Hamid barely made the next turn.

If he was about to plunge off the side of the road into a gorge at least a mile deep, Bennett figured the Bibles were the least of his worries.

"So let me ask you something, Hamid."

"Fire-way, my friend."

Under other circumstances, Bennett might have laughed. But not now. "All this Ezekiel stuff I've been talking about. What do you think?"

During the last few days at Hamid's home, Bennett had explained Mordechai's theory in great detail. Thus far, however, neither Hamid nor his wife had given him much of a reaction.

"It is fascinating; I will grant you that," Hamid said. "And it rings true. But honestly, Nadia and I never paid much attention to those passages before. So much of Ezekiel is hard for us to understand, and we have very little access to commentaries or the kind of research Dr. Mordechai used."

"That's OK," said Bennett. "I was just wondering."

But Hamid was not finished. "I wonder if what Ezekiel wrote could be a parallel to the prophecy against Elam?"

"I've never heard of it," said Bennett.

"You would if you lived in Iran."

"Why?" Bennett asked.

"I do not know if you are aware of it, but the number of secret followers of Christ inside Iran has exploded in the years since the revolution of 1979 and the rise of the Ayatollah Khomeini."

"No, I had no idea," said Bennett.

"Few people outside Iran know the incredible spiritual awakening going on here, which is probably just as well. We live under tremendous persecution and spiritual warfare. And the more intense the persecution becomes, the more people become followers of Christ. It is incredible. Before the revolution, we estimate there were only two to three hundred Iranian believers in Christ. Today, we say there are more than sixty thousand, but that's just to confuse the secret police. The truth is there are far, far more than that, and the numbers are growing every day."

"You're serious?"

"I am. Just like the Lord said through Peter in the book of Acts and the prophet Joel in the Old Testament, 'And it will come about in the last days that I will pour out My Spirit on all mankind; and your sons and daughters will prophesy, your old men will dream dreams, your young men will see visions.'

"What Joel predicted is happening all over. Even the most radical Muslims are seeing visions that are turning them into followers of Christ. They are getting baptized. They are forming clandestine house churches. And not a few, my friend. I am talking about thousands of them. Never in the history of the church of Iran has anything like this happened."

"That's amazing," said Bennett. "But what was that about a prophecy against Elam?"

"Yes, yes, I am coming to that. As the numbers of Persian believers have surged, we have all looked to see if God has a message for us in the Scriptures. And that's when people began studying the prophecy against Elam in Jeremiah 49:35-39."

"Which says what?" asked Bennett.

Hamid proceeded to recite it from memory.

> *"Thus says*
> *the LORD of hosts,*
> *'Behold, I am going to break*
> *the bow of Elam,*
> *the finest of their might.*

> *I will bring upon Elam*
> *the four winds from*
> *the four ends of heaven,*
> *and will scatter them*
> *to all these winds;*
> *and there will be no nation*
> *to which the outcasts*
> *of Elam will not go.*
> *So I will shatter Elam*
> *before their enemies*
> *and before those*
> *who seek their lives;*
> *and I will bring*
> *calamity upon them,*
> *even My fierce anger,'*
> *declares the* LORD,
> *'And I will send out*
> *the sword after them*
> *until I have consumed them.*
> *Then I shall set*
> *My throne in Elam,*
> *and destroy out of it*
> *king and princes,'*
> *declares the* LORD.
> *'But it will come about*
> *in the last days*
> *that I will restore*
> *the fortunes of Elam,'*
> *declares the* LORD.*"*

Bennett was still confused. "What does that have to do with Ezekiel?"

"*Elam* is the ancient biblical name for Persia," Hamid explained.

"Elam is Iran?"

"Yes. This prophecy began to make sense in 1979. Before the revolution, there had never been a scattering of the Iranian people all over the world like Jeremiah predicted. But when the revolution began, Iranians who could flee the country did. Iranians working abroad feared for their lives and refused to come home. Iranians studying abroad refused to return as well. Many applied for asylum in whatever country they were in. That is why over the last several decades—for the first time in history—Iranians have been scattered all over the earth. At least four million Iranians now live abroad. Some say the number is closer to eight million. In the U.S. alone, there are more than a million Iranian expatriates."

Bennett was intrigued.

"And in the meantime, those stuck in Iran have been shattered, just as the Bible foretold. Persians used to be the envy of the world in art and literature and medicine and science, but look at us now. The mullahs have caused a spirit of fear to settle over the people. Our economy is horrible. Unemployment here is unbelievable. And the secret police are everywhere. This is all the judgment of God, but it is only part 1."

"What's part 2?"

"Jeremiah says that God, in his 'fierce anger,' is going to bring 'calamity' upon Iran until He has 'consumed' us. None of us know for sure what that means. But many believe it to mean two things: First, that God is going to destroy Iran's spiritual leaders once and for all—the ayatollah, the mullahs, and the teachers of radical Islam. And second, that God is going to 'destroy' Iran's government and military leaders—her 'king and princes,' as Jeremiah says.

"The good news is that God also says He will restore our fortunes and bless our nation. None of us take that to mean that He will make us rich. What would be the point? That is not the way God thinks. We think it means He will pour out His Holy Spirit on the people of Iran and bring millions more Iranians to Christ. I believe Iran will become a country of peace, a missionary-sending country, and thus a blessing to the whole world. And best of all, Jeremiah is clear about *when* this will all happen."

"When?"

"Verse 39 says it will happen *'in the last days.'* Which brings us back to Ezekiel, who also wrote about what will happen in the last days. Based on what you've told me, I wonder if Iran's alliance with Russia against Israel could actually be the trigger for Jeremiah 49 to be fulfilled in its entirety. Would that not be exciting? I have great sorrow in my heart about the suffering my people are about to go through. But when I think of the great spiritual awakening that will follow, would that not be worth it all?"

It would, thought Bennett. *But would they live to see it happen?*

MacPherson could not believe it had come to this.

He hung up the phone and looked out the window of the Oval Office. He stared at the brilliant oranges and reds and yellows of the autumn leaves tumbling through the Rose Garden in the afternoon breeze.

For a moment, he wished he were back in the Colorado Rockies of his childhood, with his wife and their two beautiful daughters, retired from public office and completely unaware of the nightmare unfolding.

Israel's nuclear forces were now on full alert. So were Russia's.

He had just gotten off an emergency conference call with his secretaries of defense, state, and homeland security, as well as the director of the CIA and the national security advisor. They were unanimous. MacPherson had no choice but to ready the country's strategic nuclear forces for the worst-case scenario.

He had just given the order. The United States was at DefCon 2.

The anxiety consuming him was almost unbearable.

And for the first time, he began hoping Bennett and Mordechai were right.

56

★ ★
★

The rains were growing more intense.

Bennett could barely see the next turn coming, but Hamid rarely slowed the car down. Both of Hamid's hands were on the wheel now, but he was becoming so engrossed in explaining how horrible he'd been before becoming a follower of Christ, Bennett was afraid they were going to see Christ face-to-face before the story was finished.

"I was not a good kid, Jonathan. I hated everyone, including myself. I hated my father, his job, his religion. There were many reasons, but I have no excuses. It was my fault. I was cruel, and I was spiteful. I got into drugs and alcohol. I slept with women and got into fights. I brought great shame to my Muslim family."

Though he still expected the car to go into free fall at any moment, Bennett was fascinated with Hamid's story. Until a few weeks ago, he'd never met a Muslim convert to Christ. Now he was hurtling through Persian mountains with a man who had already planted a dozen house churches before the age of thirty.

"By the time I was fifteen, I had run away from home."

"Where'd you grow up?"

"In a small town near the Afghan border, a few hours from Kabul . . ."

Hamid stopped talking. He was staring at something ahead.

"What is it?" Bennett asked. He looked out the windshield.

They were less than fifty feet away from another hairpin turn and approaching fast.

"*Hamid, turn!*" Bennett shouted.

"I can't, I can't; it's locked."

The car began to fishtail out of control.

Hamid pulled his foot off the gas and pumped the brakes, but despite the pressure he was applying, the steering wheel wouldn't turn.

The car slowed, but still it skidded toward the precipice.

Bennett unbuckled his seat belt and tried to open his door to jump, but the car smashed against the side of the mountain, pinning him in. He screamed for Hamid to stop or turn or do something, but there was nothing either of them could do. Both men shut their eyes, preparing to plunge into the abyss.

"Mr. Prime Minister, we have a new development."

Doron turned to the Mossad director. "What is it?"

"If you will turn your attention to screens four and five, you'll see a series of images gathered from the *Ofek*-3 satellite, from our unmanned Predator drones, and from assets on the ground inside Russia, Iran, and the other coalition countries."

What in the world? thought Doron. *What were those?*

"Mr. Prime Minister, now that most of the coalition troops, tanks, and other hardware are in place, every available ship, train, and truck now appears to be tasked to move horses to the front lines in southern Lebanon, southwestern Syria, and the western Saudi deserts."

"Horses?" Doron asked, not sure he'd heard correctly.

"Yes, sir."

"Why? What for?"

"We are not quite sure, Mr. Prime Minister," the director explained. "But it's not entirely without precedent. More than a million horses were used in battle in World War I. Nearly three-quarters of a million were used in World War II. And for good reason. Horses are an incredibly effective way to move ground forces in rough terrain and in rough weather such as what we are experiencing.

"Russian cavalry units were once the most feared ground force on the planet. Trotsky used his cavalry during the Russian Revolution. Stalin used horses against the Germans in World War II. Horses can move forces quickly and stealthily in any weather. Siberian ponies could withstand the subzero temperatures of the Russian winter, while Hitler's panzer divisions froze up and bogged down. Nazi General Manstein once claimed that a Soviet cavalry division could move a hundred kilometers in a night, even in terrain inaccessible by tanks and artillery. In the fifties, most Soviet cavalry units were disbanded. But the cavalries have a long legacy in the history of Russian warfare, and Vadim actually began rebuilding them a few years ago. U.S. special forces even used horses in Afghanistan, as did the Northern Alliance, to great effect."

"And you think Gogolov plans to overrun us with a million troops on horseback?"

"We are not certain what Gogolov is thinking, sir. We are simply telling you what we are seeing on the ground."

It was another bizarre twist to a Kafkaesque nightmare, thought Doron.

Up to now he had been in crisis mode, focusing tactically on the specific tasks at hand. But here, secure under thousands of tons of reinforced steel and concrete that separated his war room from the world outside, the full picture of the horror unfolding far above them was suddenly coming into sharp and chilling focus.

Would he be the only Israeli prime minister in history to lose six million Jewish souls in less than an hour?

Not without taking sixty million others with him, Doron thought. *Maybe more.*

The car lurched to a stop on the absolute edge of the cliff.

They had skidded 180 degrees so that Bennett's side of the car was nearest the drop-off. If Bennett's door could have opened, he literally could have stepped into eternity.

Both men were afraid to move. They could hear the gravel slipping out from under the right tires and down the sheer rock face. The car teetered for several moments as sheets of rain washed over it. Hamid shut his eyes, clasped his hands, and prayed in Farsi. Bennett followed suit in English.

Suddenly, there was a knock on Hamid's window.

Terrified, both men opened their eyes, only to find the face of an old man staring back at them. The old man knocked again and motioned for Hamid to roll down his window.

"Don't do it," Bennett whispered, his hand reaching below his seat for a gun.

"Why not?" Hamid whispered back. "Maybe God sent him to help us."

"Maybe Gogolov sent him to kill us."

"Out here? In the middle of nowhere?"

Again the mysterious man pounded on Hamid's window.

Something in the man's eyes flashed with an intensity that sent chills through Bennett. Though he was covered in an old robe of some sort, the bearded, wizened man was clearly soaked to the bone and shivering with cold. But even at his age, which Bennett pegged at north of seventy, he appeared to be in remarkably good shape. And one push was all it would take to send them to their deaths.

With a nod, Bennett relented, and Hamid opened the window.

The man muttered something in some dialect neither understood. Hamid shook his head and tried Farsi. When that worked, Hamid translated the conversation.

"Did you bring them?" the man asked suddenly.

"What?"

"Did you bring them?"

"Bring what?" Hamid asked again. "What are you talking about?"

"The books."

"What books?"

"The books about Jesus," the man replied.

Hamid turned and stared wide-eyed at Bennett.

Bennett's mind raced. *Was it a trick? a setup?* How could this man possibly know they were transporting Bibles? Bennett hadn't even known himself until just the day before.

Hamid turned back and asked the man why he wanted to know. And the man began to tell them a story that made the hair on the backs of their necks stand on end.

"Do you see that village up on the mountain?" the old man asked, pointing into the night.

Bennett craned his neck and was surprised to see lights twinkling about a quarter of a mile ahead and at least a thousand feet up.

"A week ago," the man continued, "my family and I were gathered to eat our evening meal. Suddenly a man appeared to us. His eyes were burning like fire. His feet glowed like molten lava. He said he was an angel of the Lord. He said that a man named Jesus was the way, the truth, and the life, and that no one could come to God except through Him. He said that this Jesus loved us with an everlasting love, and that now was the day of salvation. That night, my wife and my children and grandchildren and I bowed to the ground and wept as we worshiped Jesus and gave our hearts to Him."

Bennett shuddered, but not in fear. He was in awe.

"But then, when the angel disappeared, we were suddenly afraid. We were no longer Muslims. We were afraid we would be found out and killed. But as we emerged from our house, we discovered that the angel had appeared to everyone in our village. All of us had become followers of Jesus. And we have been celebrating all week.

"Then, early this morning, another man appeared to me in a dream, dressed in white clothes that seemed to glow like the sun. He told me to climb down the mountain—alone—and wait by the side of this road. He said two men would come and give me books for my people that would tell us more about Jesus. So I ask you, did you bring the books?"

Bennett and Hamid were speechless. For a moment they just stared at the old man. Then suddenly, as if on cue, they both reached into the backseat to uncover four boxes, each holding twenty-five small Farsi New Testaments.

Hamid handed one copy through the window. Taking care not to let it get wet, the old man read the first page, and then he began to weep. He pulled from his pockets wads of Iranian rials and thrust them through the window.

Hamid refused to take them. He shook his head and pushed the money back into the man's hands. "We are your brothers," he said in Farsi. "We do not want your money. We ask only one thing."

"Yes, yes, I will do anything."

"You and your people must tell the other villages about Jesus. You must teach them everything Jesus says in this book. For He is coming back to get us very soon."

"Yes, yes, we will do it. I have many sons. They are very strong. I will tell them, and they will listen." And with that, he stuffed the New Testaments into a large sack, swung it over his shoulder, and began his journey back up the mountain.

Overcome with emotion, Bennett and Hamid just sat there for a few minutes, staring into the darkness and thanking God for His mercy.

Then Bennett suggested Hamid try the steering wheel again.

It worked. Very carefully, Hamid steered the car back onto the road and turned it around. In a few minutes they were driving again—more slowly this time—amazed at what the Lord had done but wondering if there was any way to get to Moscow in time.

57

MacPherson had time for one more gambit.

He called in Bob Corsetti and told him to get in touch with one of the wire-service correspondents. He wanted to float the idea of a presidential trip to Jerusalem for one last round of high-profile diplomacy. Kennedy had gotten Khrushchev to blink during the Cuban Missile Crisis. Maybe somehow he could do the same.

Nadia Mehrvash woke up in a cold sweat.

It was barely four o'clock in the morning.

Was she dreaming? Was she going into labor?

Maybe it was Hamid, she thought. *Was he in danger? Did he need prayer?*

Disoriented and feverish, she stumbled to the bathroom to get a glass of water. Suddenly the bedroom window shattered. Nadia screamed. Someone was trying to break in the front door. The room began to fill with smoke. Nadia started to choke. She raced back into the bedroom to get her cell phone. Through the shattered window she could see men in black hoods in the backyard. Men on the front porch shouted in Farsi, *"Go, go, go."*

Nadia's heart raced.

Who were these men? What did they want?

She fumbled in the darkness to power up the phone. She feared for herself and her baby. She had to get word to Hamid. They had no more Bibles in the house. Her own was hidden under a plank in the floor. There was nothing that could incriminate her. Still, she secretly wished for a weapon, for some way to defend herself.

She knew full well that Jesus commanded her to turn the other cheek. But did that really include the jihadists and the secret police?

Six men burst through the door.

Nadia turned, the phone in her hand.

Two shots rang out, and Nadia crashed to the floor.

The diplomatic world was soon abuzz with anticipation.

The U.N. secretary-general had agreed to take MacPherson's suggestion for one last round of shuttle diplomacy under consideration, as had the Israelis.

The Kremlin signaled reluctance.

"We will, of course, review the suggestion of the American president," Foreign Minister Zyuganov told reporters. "But we suspect this is another Israeli attempt to postpone the inevitable. A nuclear-free Middle East is the only goal. Nothing less will do."

DRUDGE REPORT

XXXX DRUDGE REPORT XXXXX SATURDAY OCT 11 XXXX
22:23:59 ET XXXX

APOCALYPSE NOW

** WORLD EXCLUSIVE **
[CREDIT DRUDGE REPORT WHEN QUOTING]

With only six days left to the U.N. deadline, the *New York Times* is set to rock official Washington.

MORE

"As Russian and coalition forces surround Israel and bring the region to the brink of nuclear war, administration officials -- including the president -- have consulted prophecy experts about the possibility that the showdown could be the start of a biblical apocalypse, sources close to the White House tell the *New York Times*."

That's the lead sentence in an explosive, front-page story -- written, edited, proofed, fact-checked, and ready to roll.

But editors at the *Times* are holding it back for reasons yet unknown. It was supposed to run Thursday. Then Friday. And now it has been spiked again.

The story, written by *Times* White House reporter Marcus Jackson, is the subject of knock-down, drag-out fights inside the *Times*' newsrooms in New York and Washington. Jackson, who refused to return repeated phone calls, is basing his story on a 37-page brief called "The Ezekiel Option," written by former Israeli Mossad chief Dr. Eliezer Mordechai.

The brief -- the entire copy of which has been obtained exclusively by **THE DRUDGE REPORT** [and available in PDF format by clicking here] -- explains Mordechai's theory that the world is witnessing the fulfillment of ancient biblical prophecies found in Ezekiel 38 and 39 in which Russia [Magog] joins with Iran [Persia], Libya [Put], Germany [Gomer], and various other Middle Eastern allies to attack a newly prosperous and peaceful Israel.

According to Mordechai, at the last minute -- when all hope seems lost -- God will supernaturally intervene and destroy Israel's enemies with fire from heaven, like a scene out of Peter Jackson's *Return of the King.*

MORE

Then, writes Mordechai, huge numbers of Jews and Gentiles will experience "the most dramatic spiritual awakening in the history of mankind."

A top White House source tells **THE DRUDGE REPORT** that such talk is "absolutely nuts" and that no such brief has ever been given to the president.

"You're a liar, Drudge!" said one irate aide, demanding he not be named. "No one's talking to prophecy gurus or reading Nostradamus or calling psychic hotlines. You think we're complete lunatics? It's a hoax, Drudge. You're getting spun. Take it from me: no one in the White House is basing U.S. foreign policy on the book of Ezekiel. Period."

But **THE DRUDGE REPORT** has learned that Jackson's story quotes two unnamed but very senior U.S. government officials saying the brief does exist, and has, in fact, been read by the president.

THE DRUDGE REPORT has also learned that MacPherson is not the first U.S. president to be intrigued with Ezekiel's prophecy.

On page 1001 of his book *United States: Essays, 1952-1992,* Gore Vidal describes a 1971 banquet that Ronald Reagan, then governor of California, attended to honor State Senator James Mills. After the main course, Reagan asked Mills if he was familiar with "the fierce Old Testament Prophet Ezekiel." Mills said he was, so Reagan -- "with firelit intensity" -- told him Russia was the Magog in Ezekiel's prophecy and was thus doomed to destruction.

On pages 1001-1002, Vidal quotes Reagan as saying:

* "In the thirty-eighth chapter of Ezekiel it says God will take the children of Israel from among the heathen

MORE

when [sic] they'd been scattered and will gather them
again in the promised land. That has finally come about
after 2,000 years."

* "For the first time ever, everything is in place for
the battle of Armageddon and the Second Coming of
Christ."

* "Everything is falling into place. It can't be too
long now. Ezekiel says that fire and brimstone will be
rained upon the enemies of God's people."

* "Ezekiel tells us that Gog, the nation that will lead
all the other powers into darkness against Israel, will
come out of the north. What other powerful nation is to
the north of Israel? None. But it didn't seem to make
sense before the Russian revolution, when Russia was
a Christian country. Now it does, now that Russia has
become communistic and atheistic, now that Russia has
set itself against God. Now it fits the description
perfectly."

In his book, Vidal notes that ten years later, Reagan
was president of the United States, and points to the
"Evil Empire" speech Reagan gave in 1983. "That was the
year that Reagan decided to alert the nation to Gog,"
wrote Vidal.

On March 8, 1983, Reagan declared, "They [the Soviet
Union] are the focus of evil in the modern world,"
later adding, "I believe that Communism is another sad,
bizarre chapter in human history *whose last pages even
now are being written.*" [Vidal's italics]

A leading Israeli Bible scholar — offered a summary
of the brief over the phone — tells **THE DRUDGE REPORT**
it "is the work of a tired old man," has no merit,
and completely mischaracterizes the context of Ezekiel
38 and 39.

MORE

"No one in Israel thinks God is about to send fire from
heaven," he said, insisting on anonymity. "Israel has
a nuclear arsenal. This is why. How dare the prime
minister desecrate the memory of Auschwitz and
Treblinka by hesitating. No supernatural being is
going to save us. Only Jews can save the Jews. It's
time to push the button."

A scholar at Al Azhar University in Cairo told the
Times that any talk of "the end of radical Islam as
we know it" will merely intensify the wrath of the
Muslim world against Israel. "Allah is not on the
side of the Jews. He will not be mocked by claims
that he is. The world will know who the One True God
really is when Israel is wiped off the face of the
map **forever.**"

IMPACTING...

Reports are moved when circumstances warrant
http://www.drudgereport.com for updates

☆   ☆   ☆

Mordechai's unlisted phone started ringing off the hook.

By the time the AP and Reuters started moving wire stories on the
Ezekiel brief, the *New York Times* felt forced to run the full story and get
ahead of the pack.

By the time the U.S. woke up Sunday morning, Mordechai was at a
television studio in Jerusalem doing back-to-back satellite interviews on
NBC's *Meet the Press*, ABC's *This Week*, CBS's *Face the Nation*, *FOX News
Sunday*, and CNN's *Late Edition*, followed by a spate of interviews for Israeli and European networks as well as Al-Jazeera.

Mordechai knew the White House must be terrified at how the public
and the international community would perceive the story. But
Mordechai himself had never felt such exhilaration in his life.

☆　☆　☆

Gogolov cackled as Jibril read him the story.

The Jews were such a pathetic lot, he mused.

Let them pray to their gods. Let them cling to their false hopes. The only fire-storm coming was the one he himself would unleash on Israel.

58

★ ★
★

Bennett wondered if he looked as scared as he felt.

Forty-eight hours ago, he and Hamid had been driving through the Iranian mountains. Twenty-four hours ago they had reached the southern shore of the Caspian Sea in spite of the throngs of Iranian secret police and Russian military forces they saw everywhere. Since then they had traveled roughly seven hundred miles, taking a nerve-racking twenty-hour ride across the Caspian Sea on a fishing trawler typically used for smuggling caviar and hashish. They'd passed so many naval ships packed with soldiers and weaponry they had long since lost count. Now, with only four days left before the U.N. deadline, they had finally arrived in the Russian port city of Astrakhan.

The border guard stared at the Russian passport, then back at Bennett's face. "Why were you in Iran?"

"I was visiting my friend and his family," Bennett said in Russian, terrified his rusty accent would give him away. "They have a lovely little cottage on the coast. I go every—"

"Weren't you called up?"

Bennett froze. *What was he talking about? Called up for what?* "I'm sorry, I don't—"

"Everyone is being called up. Why not you?"

The reserves, Bennett realized. *The war.* Every able-bodied Russian male between the ages of eighteen and twenty-two was already serving somewhere in the military. How long did one serve in the Russian reserves? Bennett had no idea. Mordechai had never brought it up. Nor had Hamid.

"I, uh . . ."

Bennett began to panic. He was seconds away from being arrested. How long would it take to determine he wasn't really Russian? Ten minutes? Fifteen? He'd be shot as a spy, as would Hamid, and that was if they were lucky. And if Gogolov or Jibril realized they were holding a former senior advisor to the American president . . .

He needed an answer fast.

"I got a medical deferment."

The guard's eyes narrowed.

Bennett hoped he'd used the right word for *deferment*.

"You look fine to me," the guard said.

Bennett could see the man's hands move almost imperceptibly toward his revolver.

"I was wounded—shot, actually . . . during . . . an operation."

"What operation?"

"I cannot say."

"Your papers say nothing of a medical discharge."

"Yes, but, sir"—Bennett's mind was racing—"that passport is six years old."

Again the guard just stared at him. He didn't seem to be buying it.

"Where were you shot?"

This couldn't be happening.

"In both shoulders," Bennett said.

"No, no, I do not believe you. Take off your shirt."

"Sir, it's after midnight, and I—"

The guard gritted his teeth; his hand was squarely on his revolver now.

"Take . . . off . . . your . . . shirt."

Bennett did as he was told.

The man moved closer, staring at the ugly, jagged scars on both of Bennett's shoulders. The guard had no idea, of course, that Bennett had been wounded by Iraqi terrorists in the Jerusalem home of a former Mossad chief. Nor did he need to know. The very fact that the scars existed seemed to satisfy him.

"Fine," the man said at last. "Welcome back to the Motherland."

He snorted, stamped Bennett's passport, and waved him through.

MacPherson snatched the phone.

"Yes?"

It was Bob Corsetti. "I'm sorry, sir. CNN is reporting that the Kremlin has officially rejected your request for further diplomacy."

"I see," the president said simply. "Anything else?"

"No, sir."

His last-ditch plan had failed. All he could do now was wait.

McCoy lay in bed, listening to the police radio.

She was grateful for the Zorogins, the family who had taken her in. She appreciated their warmth and hospitality. But she couldn't get comfortable.

She knew the second she lost focus, she was dead.

The hunt for her clearly had the authorities on edge. But there was a new mission under way as well. By order of the czar, Jews were being rounded up and taken to local police stations throughout the country, where they were subjected to fingerprinting, mug shots, and background investigations.

Officially, it was all being done "to ensure the safety of the Jews" and to clear them of any involvement in the "Zionist conspiracy" to destroy Mother Russia. But it was clear from the graphic, racist comments of the officers talking to each other on the radios—and the beatings of Jewish families of which the officers bragged—that Gogolov was unleashing a new round of anti-Semitic pogroms that McCoy feared would make Russia's sordid past seem mild by comparison.

Astrakhan was an ugly city.

Bennett had been here with his father as a child, and it still looked the same. It was a gritty, polluted, industrial wasteland known for shipping petroleum and fish and shoes and fur, and it would soon be choked by ice that would refuse to melt for at least four months. The Mongols had loved the city they had conquered in the thirteenth century. But they were used to brutal winters. Bennett couldn't stand them.

He and Hamid took a cab to a shopping plaza on the edge of town. They tipped the driver generously, waited for him to disappear, then found the charcoal gray Mercedes minivan Mordechai's team had promised would be waiting.

Bennett would have given anything to take the two-and-a-half-hour Aeroflot flight into Moscow's Sheremetyevo Airport from Astrakhan. But that was out of the question. Instead, they had almost fifteen hundred miles to cover on the ground. Then they had to find their way into one of the most heavily guarded cities on the face of the planet.

Bennett did the math as he took the wheel.

Driving nonstop and averaging sixty miles an hour, it would take them at least twenty-five hours to get to the outskirts of Moscow. It was Monday afternoon. With stops to change drivers, refuel, stock up on food, and use the facilities, they'd be pushing it to get there by Wednesday morning. And they still had no idea if McCoy was alive or how to find her.

Bennett powered up the satellite phone for the first time and dialed Jerusalem.

Mordechai answered instantly. "Thank God. You had me worried sick. Are you well?"

"We are, but we can't talk long. We're on the move. Any news?"

"She is on the run."

"You found her?"

"No, no, not yet, but neither has anyone else. Every entrance to the city is blocked off and there is a bounty on her head." Mordechai briefed him on the manhunt.

"But she's alive?"

"That is all I know. I will call you when I have more," said Mordechai.

"Thanks."

"Oh, and one more thing."

"What's that?" asked Bennett.

"Hadassah three-one-four," Mordechai said. Then the line went dead.

☆　☆　☆

Mordechai awoke early Tuesday morning.

With two Mossad agents at his side, he headed into town to mail some letters and get a cup of coffee. But fear was palpable. He could see it on people's faces. He could feel it everywhere he went.

Few men were on city streets, or in office buildings, or in shops or factories. Every able-bodied Israeli male between the ages of eighteen and fifty-five had been deployed to the borders or to one of the support bases in the interior of the country.

Most Israeli women between the ages of eighteen and thirty had been called up as well, unless they had children. Those exempt from military service for religious reasons massed at the Wailing Wall in round-the-clock prayer vigils, asking for a miracle they were sure would never come.

Everyone else stayed home with gas masks close at hand.

They called family and friends around the world. They surfed the Internet, e-mailing each other with the latest news or gossip, anything to stay and feel connected. Israeli newspaper Web sites in Hebrew, English, and Russian saw traffic surge to all-time highs. Two of the smaller Israeli news sites crashed, but most were linked through massive server farms and huge broadband pipes that shipped their material to the uttermost parts of the earth with little or no disruption.

No discos were open, nor were theaters or most restaurants. The entire economy had basically come screeching to a halt. No oil was being refined. No stocks were being traded. Grocery stores were almost empty, cleaned out by a nation preparing for war.

By nightfall, air-raid sirens began going off constantly. Israeli fighter jets streaked across the sky.

It was almost midnight when Mordechai finally dropped into bed. He could sense the nation's tension mounting. His appearances on Israel's leading talk shows were big news. It seemed everyone in Israel was talking about Ezekiel's prophecies.

Most accused Mordechai of losing his mind.

Few breathed any easier.

☆ ☆ ☆

McCoy awoke early on Wednesday morning.

She hated sitting and waiting. She hated listening to police scanners and Gogolov-dominated radio news. She hated being away from Bennett. Was he still alive? Did Jibril really have him? How much did he know about what was about to happen?

The Zorogins had explained the Ezekiel prophecy to her during the past few days, but she had so many questions and so little time.

The U.N. deadline was just two days away. Russia and the world now braced for war.

McCoy desperately needed a phone line out of the country, but there were none to be found. Mikhail and Karenna Zorogin were risking their lives to give her food and shelter; she was risking her life by staying.

Suddenly the news she had been dreading was broadcast over the police scanner.

She jumped up and frantically knocked on the Zorogins' bedroom door.

"We can't stay here anymore," she said as loudly as she dared.

A moment later, the door opened.

"What's wrong?" asked Mikhail, his voice raspy with fatigue.

"The FSB just found the car I stole."

"*How? Where?*"

There was fear in Karenna's eyes.

"Doesn't matter. They're searching an apartment row two blocks from here. It's only a matter of time before they enlarge the perimeter. Do you have a car?"

Mikhail shook his head. "No."

"Can you borrow one?" McCoy pressed.

"No, no, almost every believer we know has left the city. They're going to their *dachas*, or to friends' or relatives' homes, anywhere so long as they're not in Moscow when the judgment comes."

McCoy studied Karenna. Her eyes seemed to plead with her husband, but for what? Mikhail looked away from them both and paced. He'd been the calmest of the three over the past few days. But suddenly something had changed.

"It's time, Misha," Karenna whispered. "We don't have a choice."

For a few moments the two were silent.

"You are right," the pastor finally said. "Come, we must hurry."

Hadassah three-one-four?

Even after a day's discussion, Bennett and Hamid were bewildered by Mordechai's mysterious sign-off.

The news about McCoy was encouraging. But if she was alive, Gogolov's forces were hunting her down. Or maybe it was all a lie. Even if it was true, how were they supposed to find her in time—if they could find her at all?

Bennett was convinced there was something Mordechai was trying to tell them. The question was, what? *Hadassah* was the name of a hospital in Jerusalem. Actually, there were Hadassah hospitals all over the world. Was there one in Moscow? Whom could they ask without giving themselves away?

Bennett told Hamid to power up the satellite phone again, tap into a wireless Internet account, and do a search for "Hadassah and Moscow." Over twenty thousand entries came up. A skim through the first few dozen led nowhere.

Hamid did another search for "Hadassah 314."

That brought up over two thousand entries, starting with St. Louis area phone numbers for former Hadassah Hospital personnel and grant recipients.

"What does *Hadassah* mean, anyway?" asked Hamid as Bennett pushed the minivan through mountain curves at speeds that made even Hamid nervous.

"I have no idea. Look it up."

A moment later, Hamid said, "It means Esther."

Esther 3:14? Could it be that simple?

Hamid logged on to an online Bible search site and entered "Esther 3:14." When the verse popped up, he read it to Bennett.

> *A copy of the edict*
> *to be issued as law*
> *in every province*

was published
to all the peoples
so that they should be
ready for this day.

"I don't understand," said Hamid. "What does that mean?"

Bennett couldn't help but smile.

So, the old man had taken his advice after all. He'd given "The Ezekiel Option" to Marcus Jackson. Bennett just wished he could see the expression on the president's face when the story broke. And on his mother's.

The couple worked quickly.

They straightened the small apartment, making it look as though they might be away on holiday. Then Karenna pulled out an already packed suitcase from underneath their bed, stuffed several duffel bags with boxes and cans of food from the pantry, grabbed a couple of flashlights from a drawer, and followed her husband into the hallway, motioning McCoy to stay quiet and follow close behind.

The trio took the back stairwell rather than the elevator.

Nineteen flights down, they pushed through a fire door and found themselves in the basement. All three turned on flashlights, communicating only through hand signals.

Mikhail led them down a narrow hallway, then into a musty storage room draped in cobwebs. As McCoy stared in amazement, the couple pushed aside an old soda machine, revealing a trapdoor that looked like the front of a bank vault.

"It is a bomb shelter," Mikhail whispered. "They built it in the fifties when they put up this building. No one knows it is here. I used to play down here all the time, and I never found it. But my father was in the politburo. He had all kinds of privileges. He never had to fear a nuclear war in the same way others did. Just before he died, he brought me down here. He told me I might need it one day and swore me to secrecy. I thought he was crazy."

McCoy descended into the steel and concrete cavern.

The walls held shelves fully stocked with foodstuffs and large bottles of water. There were three sets of bunk beds, clean sheets and towels, gas masks, and weapons, none of which looked more than six months old. There was even a Geiger counter, though it was by far the oldest item in the room.

"You've been planning for this, haven't you?" McCoy asked.

"The prophecy is very clear, Miss McCoy," Mikhail agreed, locking the vault door above them. "Ezekiel 38:7 says, 'Be prepared.' That should not just apply to Gog, should it? I have been teaching my congregation about this prophecy for months. I have been telling them to get ready. We need to be alive and prepared when millions of Russians become followers of Christ."

Then Mikhail opened a drawer, and McCoy's eyes went wide.

59

★ ★
★

Costello had devoured the *Times* and Drudge stories.

Now, sitting in Bennett's West Wing office, he sifted through the books that had been sent over from the Library of Congress. Had Bennett even seen them before he'd quit? They were all still neatly packed in the box in which they had arrived.

He picked up a copy of *Dead Souls*, written in 1842 by Nikolai Gogol. He'd read it a long time ago—along with *Crime and Punishment, Demons,* and *The Brothers Karamazov*—in one of his many graduate-school courses on Russian art, literature, and philosophy.

Clipped to the front was a note on stationery from the office of the chief librarian. It read simply "96, 397." Costello flipped to page 96. Sure enough, there was a reference to Gog and Magog, followed by a footnote leading him to page 397. Costello read: "In Ezekiel (38:2, 3, 18; 39:11, 15) Gog is named as prince of Meschech and Tubal, in some unclear relation with 'the land of Magog.' . . . But in the popular [Russian] mind, the rhyming names suggest two evil monsters."

The Gog and Magog myth permeated Russian children's books and folklore. *Was it more than myth?*

At first Bennett thought it was a dream.

Until Hamid shook him awake.

The satellite phone was ringing, and only Bennett was authorized to answer it. He glanced at his watch. He'd been asleep for less than two hours.

He stared at the caller ID. It was Mordechai.

"Tell me you have good news."

Mordechai's voice was sober. "How far away are you?"

Bennett had no idea. He turned to Hamid for their ETA.

"Two hundred miles, give or take," said Hamid.

Bennett passed the news along to Mordechai.

"Why? What's up?"

"You're not going to believe it."

"What?"

"I just heard from Rahab."

He certainly knew the man's reputation.

Holocaust survivor. Jewish philosopher and novelist. Winner of Congressional Gold Medal in 1985. Nobel Peace Prize winner in 1986.

But Costello had never read any of Elie Wiesel's work. What fascinated Costello now were the references to Ezekiel 38 and 39 he found laced throughout Wiesel's writings, similar in many ways to the work of the Jewish mystic Martin Buber, author of an entire novel called *Gog and Magog*, also sitting in Bennett's in-box.

Wiesel was a serious man, deeply respected in Jewish society. He certainly wasn't a right-wing, "born again," religious fundamentalist. Yet in *Souls on Fire*, he wrote of rabbis awaiting "the gigantic, apocalyptic war" of Gog and Magog as a prelude to the coming of the Messiah. What's more, in his memoir, *All Rivers Run to the Sea*, Wiesel wrote of his longing for the coming "climactic battle of Gog and Magog," the defeat of Israel's enemies, and "the Savior's triumph."

In *Elie Wiesel: Conversations*, a series of previously published interviews edited by Robert Franciosi, Wiesel was asked, "Is mystical Jewish thought unhappy?" To which he responded, "On the contrary, it is very happy since it develops a theory according to which history progresses, thanks to messianism, and leads us to redemption. Messianism is the gift of the Jew to the world, but in our tradition we believe that before redemption there will be a huge catastrophe. We call it the war of Gog and Magog."

"What have you got?"

Jack Mitchell and Marsha Kirkpatrick stood in the Oval Office, briefing the president. "NSA just intercepted a satellite call from a highway two hours south of Moscow," said Mitchell. "We think it was Bennett. The call cut off before we could get it all. But we've tagged the satellite account. Next time he makes a call, we'll know it."

MacPherson almost swore. "You've got to be kidding. Bennett's heading to Moscow? He's going to get himself killed."

"Actually, Mr. President, it could be worse than that," said Kirkpatrick.

"How?"

"We have to assume Russian intelligence intercepted the same call. Who knows how quickly they can process it, but it'll be flagged top priority because it was obviously coming from inside Russia, and Bennett and whomever he was talking to were speaking in English. I can't tell you how long it will take for Gogolov's people to determine the voice is Bennett's. But once they do, the danger is that Gogolov will suspect that Bennett's part of some kind of CIA or Mossad plot."

"Worst-case scenario?" the president asked.

Mitchell took that one. "Gogolov could suspect we're preparing for an assassination attempt or a preemptive strike."

"What would that mean?"

"There's no way to know for sure, sir, but it's possible that if Gogolov feels threatened he could move up his plans to strike Israel."

She was alive, and she was safe.

Bennett knew he should feel elated. But for the moment he simply felt numb. McCoy had escaped. She'd made contact with Mordechai. She knew Bennett was on his way to rescue her, and they had even roughed out the beginning of an extraction plan.

He had so many questions. How had she gotten away from Jibril's clutches? And how in the world had she gotten hold of a satellite phone?

As his mind reeled, Bennett's emotions forced their way to the surface, and his eyes welled up with tears.

"What?" Hamid asked. "Good news or bad?"

Costello knew he had to get back to work.

But he simply couldn't pull himself away. It was as if he had stumbled onto a secret code whose clues were hidden throughout the ages—from the Dead Sea Scrolls to the pages of great Russian and Jewish literature—that only now were coming together.

And yet, perhaps because he was a political animal by nature, it was the Reagan quotes that intrigued him most. Reagan's fascination with the End Times and the return of Christ was common knowledge. Costello vividly remembered Reagan telling a reporter during the 1980 campaign, "We may be the generation that sees Armageddon." But until the story on the Drudge Report, Costello had never heard of Reagan's fascination with Ezekiel.

Costello skimmed through the Gore Vidal book. Sure enough, Drudge's quotes were accurate. Now he flipped through *Dutch: A Memoir of Ronald Reagan* by Edmund Morris. On page 632, he found the story of Reagan telling Howard Baker, Colin Powell, and Morris that he believed Ezekiel 38 was going to happen, that Gog was the leader of Russia, and that Meshech was the "the ancient name for Moscow."

He flipped to the endnotes. There was more. On page 835, Morris described Ezekiel as "RR's favorite book of prophecy" and explained that Reagan's "reference to Meshech connotes Mushku, the ancient Phyrigian kingdom in Anatolia, from which the name Moscow might possibly be derived."

Was it really possible that the man who had rightly designated the Soviet Union the Evil Empire had been basing his conclusions on biblical prophecies?

Then something else caught Costello's eye. Under the pile of books there was a plain brown envelope. He opened it and pulled out a sheaf of papers. It was a photocopy of a speech of some kind, with a handwritten note from the chief librarian attached to it.

Jon—Sorry about the guard. Just doing his job. I'd better do mine, too. I see you're hunting for material on Gog and Magog. Thought you'd be interested in this address, delivered by the Rev. F. E. Pitts before Congress back in 1857.

Costello set the note aside and began reading.

It had to be a joke. Here was a nineteenth-century pastor warning Congress that Russia would emerge as a horrific new world threat—and doing so a full *sixty years* before the Russian Revolution, using only the book of Ezekiel as his source of intelligence. That wasn't possible.

Costello pulled out a pen and began to highlight key passages.

The voice of the prophetic Scriptures frequently and fully announces the warfare of the world. Preparation for ages has anticipated the struggle; while the clammor of its trumpets is almost heard marshaling its millions to the charge. It is true as destiny, and the gathering storm is rising. . . .

Who leads this invasion? . . . This overwhelming power we shall demonstrate to be Russia. . . . Russia, according to the Scriptures, is the headship or leading power around which the multitudinous armies of allied monarchy shall be gathered together. . . .

The more he read, the more impressed he was with this remarkable piece of oration. But Pitts had made one fundamental error: the target. He had ignored Ezekiel 36 and 37, in which God explicitly promised to draw the Jewish people back to their homeland, and had erroneously concluded that the United States must be the new Israel and thus the focus of a future Russian attack.

"Were all the Jews on earth restored to the small territory of Palestine," the pastor from Tennessee had told Congress, "what temptation or provocation could they offer to arouse the allied armies of earth to invade them? No, my countrymen, it is not ancient Jewry that will witness this invasion. There is another Israel, the Israel of America."

But Costello knew the rest of the story. It *was* unfolding before his very eyes. A modern, resurrected State of Israel *was* in the Russian crosshairs, precisely as Ezekiel had predicted. He picked up his cell phone and dialed the West Wing.

"It's Costello. I need to see the president."

60

★ ★
★

Jibril slid a black folder across the table.

"What have you got?" asked Gogolov.

"Iranian intelligence in Paris thinks the Mossad sent Bennett to Turkey in a private jet on September twenty-first from a small airfield near Caen. The plane landed in a small city in northeastern Turkey. The next day, there was an explosion in Bazargan when two people tried to crash the border into Iran."

"Were they caught?"

"They were killed, which made everyone think that was the end of the story."

"But there is more?" Gogolov asked.

"There is, Your Excellency. A border agent says a man and a pregnant woman carrying Iranian passports entered the country just after the explosion, headed to Tabriz. On a hunch, I asked one of my colleagues to check it out. We found the pregnant woman. Her neighbors say her husband left town with another man on the night of October fifth. They have not been back since."

"And you think it is Bennett?"

"It seems unlikely, I realize. But I thought you would want to know."

Jibril was right. He did.

Was it Bennett? How could it be?

Gogolov considered that. What if Bennett hadn't really quit the U.S. government? What if he hadn't been fired? What if he was working for the CIA, and with the Mossad? But to what end? Bennett wasn't a trained operative. He was more likely to be caught than accomplish anything of value. But what if that's what Langley wanted all along?

What if the CIA had sent Bennett on a mission to "rescue" his fiancée, only to serve as diversion from other strike teams preparing an attack against Moscow?

It was a clever play, thought Gogolov. But the CIA was unlikely to attempt it alone. The Mossad had far more experience running agents in and out of Iran and the Caucasus. They *had* to be involved. Which meant Eliezer Mordechai was involved.

After all, the old man thought Israel was invulnerable to attack.

"If Bennett and the Mossad are operating inside our borders," Gogolov said, "then we are out of time. We must strike first."

The thought of a Russian preemptive nuclear strike against the Israelis was delicious. Gogolov had already created the pretext—the assassination attempt he had ordered against himself in order to blame it on the Jews. It had worked perfectly. He'd even been injured, and the world's enmity against the Zionists had only intensified.

Gogolov turned back to Jibril.

"Send Bennett's photo to every police station, intelligence officer, and military unit in Russia. Send word that Bennett is believed to be inside Russia with another Mossad or U.S. intelligence agent. He is to be considered armed and extremely dangerous. I want him found, dead or alive."

"Of course, Your Excellency. Anything else?"

"What was done with the woman?"

"Which one?"

"The wife of the man helping Bennett?"

"She was shot twice and survived. She's scheduled to be executed on Friday."

The phone rang.

It had to be Bennett or McCoy, thought Mordechai. But it was neither.

"Eli, it's David."

Mordechai was stunned. Surely the prime minister had more pressing matters on his plate than talking with a man viewed by most of the nation as a heretic.

Instinctively, Mordechai sprang out of his living-room chair and stood to his feet. "Mr. Prime Minister," he said. "To what do I owe this honor?"

"You've become quite a celebrity in recent days," Doron said softly.

"A traitor, you mean?"

"Come, come, Eli. We've known each other too long. You know I'm not Orthodox, even if I sound like one in my campaigns."

It was true. David Doron had never been a religious man. It had always been one of the reasons the two of them had gotten along so well. They were realists, pragmatists. They loved science and statistics, things you could touch and hold and quantify and contain.

"Eli," Doron said again.

"Yes, Mr. Prime Minister."

"Come and have coffee with a weary old man."

They were less than sixty miles out.

Emotionally and physically exhausted, Bennett was tempted to ask Hamid to pull off the main road for a while. Both men desperately needed rest. They also needed some idea of how to get into Moscow without getting killed.

But they could not stop now. They were within striking distance of the Russian capital, and they'd continue even if they had nothing to run on but sheer adrenaline and the grace of God.

Bennett took out his pistol and made sure it was loaded as Hamid tromped on the accelerator.

A steel blast door opened electronically.

Mordechai had not descended into the prime minister's nuclear bunker in years, and the technological upgrades caught his attention immediately.

Gone were the plastic world maps covered with pushpins and erasable marker. The walls were now covered with flat-screen monitors showing real-time feeds from Predator drones patrolling Israel's borders and digital maps displaying Israeli forces in navy blue and enemy forces in crimson red.

And the world was now a wine-dark sea.

The two men shook hands and sat down alone.

"It is good to see you again, Mr. Prime Minister. You look well."

Doron managed a smile. "You always had a better poker face than that, Eli."

"I am praying for you, my friend. As are millions."

"Millions pray that I push the button. Millions more pray that I won't. I suspect you are all canceling each other out."

"I am praying for your soul."

Doron smiled again. "Now would be a good time for the Messiah to show Himself, would it not?"

Mordechai chose not to respond to the sarcasm.

"I assume you realize how close we are to it now," Doron sighed. "A matter of hours, I suspect. They will hit us, or we will hit them. I guess I just wanted a familiar face around. I hope you don't mind."

"To the contrary," Mordechai replied. "I am honored."

Doron stared into his eyes for a long while, as if he were searching for something but could not find it. "Eli, let me ask you a question."

"Anything."

"You really believe this, don't you—that God is going to supernaturally save us at the last possible second? Tell me this is an Andy Warhol moment, Eli, fifteen minutes of fame for a man who always lived in the shadowlands."

"No, I am a true believer."

"Why? I mean no disrespect, Eli. You have never come across as a religious fanatic, even when you first told me that you had become a follower of *Yeshua*. I have always considered you a serious man, a man of evidence and of extraordinary insight and wisdom. But you must admit, to many ears you do sound . . . well . . . not your usual self."

"Actually, many are listening quite carefully."

"They want hope. We all do. But false hope is no hope at all."

"Is that what you think Jesus is, Mr. Prime Minister—a false hope?"

"Please do not take it personally, Eli. I am glad you have found something that makes you happy. God knows I wish I could do the same. I read your brief. I even enjoyed it. It got me to pull out the Bible my wife gave me on our wedding day. I did not read it then. And I had not read it since, until yesterday. And this is why, my friend. Nietzsche was right. God is dead, or impotent. I am not sure it makes much of a difference."

61

THURSDAY, OCTOBER 16 – 1 DAY TO THE U.N. DEADLINE

"The president will see you now."

It was a few minutes after midnight in Washington. Two Marine guards opened the door. Ken Costello straightened his tie and stepped into the Situation Room.

His heart almost stopped. He had requested to see MacPherson alone, but the first person he saw was his boss, Secretary of State Nick Warner.

It was a full house. The vice president was there, as were Defense Secretary Burt Trainor, CIA Director Jack Mitchell, National Security Advisor Marsha Kirkpatrick, and Bob Corsetti.

Costello knew the situation was grave. The president had been working the phones all day with world leaders and the U.N. secretary-general, trying to find some way to resolve the situation, to no avail. Costello suddenly felt foolish for taking any of the president's rapidly diminishing time.

"You picked a bad night for a visit, Ken," the president said without looking up. "What have you got?"

☆   ☆   ☆

Thick, black clouds formed on the horizon.

Though barely eight o'clock in the morning in Russia, it was now so dark that every car on the road had its headlights on.

But no one was heading north. Instead, a sea of humanity was heading toward them, away from the city. Whether they believed the Ezekiel prophecies or simply expected an Israeli missile strike, Bennett had no idea. Either way, no one in his right mind wanted to be in Moscow at the moment. Thousands were escaping from the city they feared would soon be ground zero.

"How much farther?" Bennett asked.

At the rate Hamid was driving, they had to be close. Bennett glanced at the speedometer. They were clocking in at well over 140 kilometers per hour.

"We're about five or six miles out," Hamid said. "We should see Moscow after that next hill."

"What is it, Ken?" the president repeated.

Costello could feel the perspiration bleeding into his starched white collar. MacPherson didn't have any time to play games.

"Mr. President, I've been reviewing—"

"For crying out loud, Ken, spit it out."

Costello thought of himself as a careful, thoughtful man. He was a professional diplomat, after all. His whole life was built on delivering carefully chosen words at carefully chosen moments. He glanced around for a glass of water but realized he hadn't the time to drink it. It was now or never.

"Mr. President, I've been reviewing the research behind 'The Ezekiel Option.' . . ."

He could almost feel the oxygen being sucked from the room.

Hamid glanced in the rearview mirror and tensed.

"We have company."

Bennett looked to his side mirror and saw the blue flashing lights. A Moscow police car was bearing down on them. "Can we outrun them?"

"To where?" asked Hamid. "We are heading toward heavily armed roadblocks, and even if we could lose this guy for a few minutes, we would alert the entire Moscow police force in the process."

Hamid was right. Fatigue was clouding Bennett's judgment. He glanced back again as the patrolman turned on his siren. They had no choice. They had to stop.

"I believe the prophecy is real, Mr. President."

Costello heard the words come out of his mouth, but he didn't remember deciding to say them. His head was telling him to bolt. But somehow he kept talking.

"All of the intelligence we've been gathering and sifting through over the past several hours supports Dr. Mordechai's observations. It's logical for us to consider that his conclusions may, in fact, be accurate as well."

Hamid pulled the car over to the shoulder.

"Stall him," Bennett said, unlocking the passenger-side door and sliding off his seat to the floor. He wiped the sweat off his hands and clicked off the pistol's safety.

"What are you talking about?" said Hamid. *"What are you doing?"*

For the first time since the road through the Iranian mountains, Bennett heard genuine fear in Hamid's voice.

"Roll down your window and stall this guy," Bennett repeated. "And make sure the interior lights don't come on. I'm getting out."

"What? They will kill you."

"There's only one," Bennett shot back. "Now shut up and pray."

Hamid clicked off the interior lights and rolled down his window.

"Is he out of his car?" Bennett whispered.

"Not yet."

"Probably running our plates. Tell me the minute he starts walking toward you."

The DCI slammed down his phone.

"Mr. President, we've got a new problem."

All heads turned from Costello to Mitchell.

"What is it, Jack?"

Mitchell directed the president to two new feeds from two American spy satellites. "Screen one is the live image of a KH-12 spy satellite hovering over a Russian strategic missile base in the Ural Mountains," said Mitchell. "That one there."

MacPherson blanched. "The Russians are getting ready to launch?"

"They are, sir. You're looking down the barrel of an SS-18 Satan ICBM."

"How many warheads?"

"Ten, sir, all nuclear."

The single SS-18 could annihilate all of Israel in less than thirty minutes.

"Why are they readying two dozen more?" asked the vice president, looking at the other screen.

"They're not, sir," Mitchell responded. "What you're seeing on screen two is an Israeli missile base in the Negev, home of twenty-five Jericho missiles, all of which are equipped with nuclear warheads as well."

"They're fueling all of them?"

"Not just those, sir. The Israelis are warming up all 253 of their ICBMs."

"Who went first?" asked MacPherson.

"We're not sure, Mr. President. NORAD picked up warning signs on the Russian bird first, but it's not clear."

"How much time do we have?"

"Any one of these missiles could be airborne in a matter of minutes."

"Get me Doron and Gogolov on the line—*now*."

"He's out of the car," said Hamid.

"Good," said Bennett quietly. "Now don't forget . . ."

"I know, I know," whispered Hamid. "Cut the lights and stall him."

Bennett nodded, then cracked open his door, slipped out onto the shoulder, and gently closed the door behind him. It was dark. The mass of oncoming traffic was deafening, but he—

"*Stop. What are you doing?*"

Bennett froze. The words were Russian. He looked up and saw the patrolman coming around the passenger side of the car. He was reaching for his gun.

"Jonathan!" Hamid screamed.

The night suddenly exploded with gunfire. He heard the first shot smash through the window above him. Bennett squeezed off two rounds of his own and rolled left, down a small embankment. The officer fired again and ducked behind the car.

Bennett was five or ten yards from a wooded grove. His instinct was to bolt for cover, but he feared being shot in the back.

Another shot whizzed by him.

Bennett rolled left and fired, taking out the back window of the Mercedes in the process and keeping the Russian off balance.

Bennett couldn't stay where he was. He was out in the open and exposed. He aimed toward the car, feverishly looking for signs of movement. But the oncoming headlights were blinding him.

Where was Hamid? Had he been hit?

And then, to his left, Bennett heard a hammer cock.

"Drop the gun and don't move, or I'll blow your head off!" the man screamed in Russian, adding a string of curses along the way.

Bennett dropped the gun and froze.

The officer started moving toward him, a pistol in one hand, a flashlight in the other, now shining directly in Bennett's face.

The man started muttering excitedly, and Bennett knew instantly he'd been ID'd.

How long had they known? How many cops were hunting for him? If the price for McCoy was ten million rubles, how much would Gogolov pay for his head on a platter?

The officer was now three feet away. Bennett tried to think of options. If he struggled, he was dead. But wasn't he dead either way?

"Welcome to Moscow, Mr. Bennett," the officer said in English.

The man clicked off the flashlight and dropped it to the ground, then put both hands on his sidearm and took aim at Bennett's face.

Bennett closed his eyes. He couldn't believe he'd come so close only to lose everything. But for the first time in his life, he had no regrets. He only hoped the Lord would have mercy on Erin, on Hamid and his family, and on his mother. He was ready to die. He held his breath and heard the man say, "Sweet dreams, Mr. Bennett."

And the gun went off.

Bennett's heart seemed to stop. But he didn't feel any pain.

Was he dead?

Trembling, his body soaked with sweat, Bennett opened his eyes and couldn't believe what he saw. There, no more than ten yards away, stood Hamid, trembling as smoke rose from the barrel of the pistol in his hands.

BEEP, BEEP, BEEP, BEEP.

The door flew open. Mordechai's head whipped around as the general in charge of Israeli military intelligence burst into the war room.

"Mr. Prime Minister, a Russian missile just went airborne," shouted the general.

"Out of the Urals?"

"No, Siberia—a missile base near Tobolsk."

Mordechai shot a look at Doron—*Tobolsk?*—but said nothing as the rest of the prime minister's inner circle poured into the room: Defense Minister Chaim Modine, the IDF chief of staff, and the current head of the Mossad.

"Should I leave?" asked Mordechai, getting up to go.

"Where would you go, Eli? We have less than thirty minutes."

"Twenty-eight minutes, nineteen seconds to impact, sir," said the intelligence chief. "What do you want to do, Mr. Prime Minister?"

"You're absolutely sure?" Doron pressed.

"Yes, sir."

"There's no chance this is a satellite or computer error?"

"No, sir."

"Have the Americans confirmed it?"

Defense Minister Modine took that one. "I'm on it, sir," he said, already on the hotline to the National Military Command Center at the Pentagon. A moment later he nodded his head. "They confirm the launch, sir."

"Target?"

"Not clear, but it is definitely coming south."

Doron scanned the satellite feeds and a digital map showing the site of the launch and the trajectory of the inbound ICBM. "We have no choice, gentlemen. Initiate the countdown sequence, and get me the list of the final target packages."

"Sir, you don't have time to change them now."

"How much time do I have?"

"Twenty-six minutes."

62
★ ★
★

"Mr. President, the Russians just launched."

All eyes turned to the computer track from NORAD. Sure enough, an SS-18 was entering the atmosphere out of Siberia.

"Target?" MacPherson demanded.

"It's southbound, sir. Too early to say, but there's no doubt it's Israel."

"Is Doron on the line?"

"I've got Defense Minister Modine," Burt Trainor responded. "He says Doron's not available."

"They're going to unleash," said Corsetti.

"Wouldn't you?" asked Trainor.

"They've got ABM systems—the Arrow, the Patriot—they could shoot it down," said Marsha Kirkpatrick.

But MacPherson shook his head. "They're going with The Samson Option."

"What do you want to do, Mr. President?"

To misunderstand the nature and threat of evil is to risk being blindsided by it, MacPherson said to himself. *And evil, unchecked, is the prelude to genocide.* How many times had he heard Mordechai say it?

"We have no choice," the president said aloud. "Take us to DefCon 1."

Bennett grabbed his gun and the Russian's.

He checked for a pulse, but the man was dead.

He could hear sirens approaching from the distance.

"We can't stay here, Hamid; we need to move."

Bennett pulled the officer's badge, hat, and leather jacket off the body and shoved them into Hamid's arms. "Put them on and get in the car. You're driving."

Hamid didn't move. He just stood there shaking.

Bennett feared Hamid was slipping into shock. He grabbed Hamid and dragged him back up the embankment.

The body of the Mercedes was riddled with bullet holes. Its windows were shattered. Bennett turned to the police cruiser. It was still running.

"Hamid. Put them on and let's go."

Still nothing, and the sirens were getting closer. They were almost out of time.

Bennett turned and without warning reared back and punched Hamid in the face, sending him crashing to the pavement.

"What was *that*?" Hamid demanded, his lower lip now bleeding.

"I need you in the game, Hamid. Now, get in the police car. You're driving."

"What about you?"

"I'll be in the backseat."

"What?"

Hamid scrambled to his feet, but Bennett grabbed him again and slammed him against the hood of the cruiser. "I love you, Hamid, but I don't have time for this. If we're not out of here in the next sixty seconds, both of us are dead. So get in the car, hit the siren, and get us into Moscow. I'm your prisoner. *Now move.*"

⭐ ⭐ ⭐

"Move all strategic forces to Snapcount," Doron demanded.

"All of them?" Modine asked.

"All of them."

Mordechai's heart was in his throat. The Samson Option was no longer an *option*. It was reality.

Siren wailing, Hamid raced north toward Moscow.

Bennett speed-dialed Mordechai, but there was no answer. He hit redial, but again there was no answer. Then came an emergency broadcast over the police radio.

"All units, this is Moscow Base. We have reports of a multiple shooting on the northbound lane of the M2, about half a mile from the *Stroitelej* interchange. Be advised a CIA or Mossad hit team may be in play. Repeat, American and Israeli operatives or special forces may be on the ground. Proceed with caution."

Bennett was stunned. Were U.S. and Israeli forces really on the ground? Or were the police on to *them*?

There was only one way to find out.

"Hamid, give me the radio."

"Why?"

"Hamid, just give me the radio."

Reluctantly, Hamid pulled the handheld microphone off the receiver and stretched the cord to the backseat.

"How much time do we have?" Bennett asked.

"We are about a mile out from the roadblock. You only have a few seconds before they will see you."

Bennett took a deep breath, then pressed Send and started talking in rapid-fire Russian. "Moscow Base, this is Unit 225. Repeat, this is Unit 225. Can confirm shots fired along the M2, but be advised I have a suspect in custody."

Bennett saw Hamid glance back at him through his rearview mirror. His eyes were wide with fear, but for the moment, he said nothing.

"Unit 225, this is Moscow Base. Please repeat—you have a suspect in custody?"

"Affirmative, Moscow Base."

"We need a description."

"Male, about six feet, a hundred and ninety pounds, dark brown hair, green eyes. I found a Russian passport on him—stamped in Astrakhan—but he looks American. Repeat, he looks American. Please advise."

Bennett could only imagine the explosion he'd just caused. Would they take the bait?

"Unit 225, this is General Barovka of the FSB. *Do not* proceed to Moscow Base. Repeat, *do not* proceed to Moscow Base. Proceed directly to Lubyanka. We will have agents waiting out front. Confirm."

"Roger that, General. Request immediate clearance across the Krymski Bridge."

"Done."

Krymski Bridge?

They were coming through Gorky Park. They were coming right to her.

McCoy bolted to her feet. She turned her police scanner up, but there was no doubt in her mind that was Bennett's voice.

"That's him," she half shouted to the Zorogins, then caught herself and whispered, "That's him. That's Jon. He's coming."

She picked up Mikhail's satellite phone and dialed Mordechai. No answer. Desperate, she tried again. Nothing.

McCoy tried not to panic. They had less than twenty-four hours until the U.N. deadline, but they had less than fifteen minutes—maybe twenty—before the FSB realized Bennett was playing a con game.

So where in the world was Mordechai?

McCoy was an optimist by nature. She kept telling herself everything would work out. It had to. But they'd never finalized the extraction plans. Neither she nor Mordechai—nor Bennett, presumably—could afford to spend more than two minutes on the phone with each other without dramatically increasing the likelihood that the call would be intercepted—or worse, that their locations would be compromised.

It had been Mordechai's job to nail down an extraction point. It was Mordechai's job to manage this operation. She hit Redial.

He didn't pick up.

Doron scanned the target package.

One hundred nuclear missiles would be simultaneously launched at Russia.

Fifty would hit the former Soviet republics allied with Gogolov.

Twenty-five more would target Iran. Fifteen would be launched at Germany and Austria, eight at Saudi Arabia, and six each at Syria and Turkey. The remaining missiles would hit the capital cities of the rest of the coalition arrayed against them, and all the troops massing on Israel's borders.

The carnage to come was incalculable.

But so far as he could tell, he had no choice.

The Krymski checkpoint lay ahead.

Barbed wire and tire spikes lined the pavement as heavily armed soldiers walked patrols, backed by battle tanks and a phalanx of surface-to-air missile batteries.

"Last chance, Jonathan," Hamid whispered as they came around the bend and found themselves staring into the barrels of at least a dozen machine guns.

"Flip your lights on and off," Bennett replied through clenched teeth, his hands behind his back, gripping a pistol.

Hamid complied and slowed to a stop.

Mordechai felt for his phone.

But it was gone, of course—taken by the security team when he'd first arrived at the office of the prime minister. He glanced at his watch and bit his lip.

Bennett and Hamid had to be there, or close, and he had never tied off the details of the extraction. He'd been too surprised by Doron's call, too excited at the chance to talk to his old friend at this critical hour. And he had never expected to stay so long.

Now he was seven stories below Jerusalem. Even if he had his phone, there wouldn't be any reception anyway.

Bennett could feel every eye on him.

He watched as soldiers checked their license plates and removed the tire spikes from their path, as ordered by the top brass at FSB headquarters.

Still, they needed a miracle.

Hamid's Russian was passable, but far from perfect. Despite the dead officer's hat and jacket that Hamid was wearing, he had no uniform, no ID. *He was wearing blue jeans, for crying out loud! What if Hamid was asked to step out of the car for some reason? There was a bloodstained bullet hole in the back of the jacket.*

Bennett looked down the Moskva River to the left and right.

All tour boats were shut down. There were no tourists. The only vessels on the water now were some speedboats and a barge or two. Everyone in his right mind was heading for the hills as fast as he could. Except fools like them.

A soldier approached the driver's-side window.

Just then, the radio crackled to life.

"Unit 225, this is Lubyanka. You are cleared for immediate passage. Proceed to the Naina Petrovsky Center—back entrance—immediately. Repeat, proceed to the Naina Petrovsky Center—back entrance. You'll be met outside."

The blood drained from Bennett's face.

That was McCoy's voice. She was in Naina's old apartment? How was that possible? *Was* it possible? Or was it a trap?

A soldier tapped on the glass with the butt of his pistol. Another approached from the passenger side, his finger nervously tapping the trigger of his AK-47.

Bennett looked at both men, then at the road ahead. It was clear.

"Gun it, Hamid—go, go, go!"

Both soldiers looked startled as Bennett yelled and Hamid hit the gas.

The sudden acceleration thrust Bennett against the back of the seat. He could hear men screaming for them to stop, and as he leaned forward again, he heard the crackle of machine-gun fire. The back window exploded.

Bennett ducked, waited a beat, then popped up and fired back.

Skidding right, Hamid regained control just in time to avoid smashing headlong into a Russian battle tank.

"Take the second left," Bennett shouted as they came off the bridge.

Hamid's mountain-driving skills were coming in handy after all.

The city suddenly erupted with the sounds of sirens. The entire FSB force knew they were here and were mobilizing to take them down.

And now, air-raid sirens began to wail as well.

Hamid took a hard left, though the skid marks were leaving a trail that wouldn't be hard to follow.

He looked back to see how many were on their tail. For the moment, he could hear only the pursuing sirens. Bennett grabbed the radio.

"This is Unit 225, we are inbound for Petrovsky Center. Request immediate assistance. We have—"

From out of nowhere a black Mercedes broadsided Hamid, putting the car into a 360-degree spin and sending Bennett smashing into the passenger window.

Dazed and bleeding, Bennett saw an FSB agent rushing toward the car, firing wildly. Glass flew everywhere. Blood gushed from Bennett's head. He fished around on the floor of the backseat for his Beretta.

"Hamid, get down!" Bennett screamed as more rounds pierced their car.

With Hamid out of the way, Bennett fired five rounds through what was left of the front windshield. Two hit their mark. He pivoted hard and saw another agent coming from his right side, reaching for his weapon.

Bennett emptied his entire magazine until the man collapsed to the ground. The sirens were getting closer.

"Hamid, we need to move," Bennett said, ejecting one magazine and loading another. There was no response.

"Hamid, let's go; let's go!"

Still Bennett heard nothing. He looked up to find Hamid slumped against the steering wheel. He reached for Hamid's pulse. There was none.

"Unit 225, this is N.P. Center standing by. Where are you?"

It was McCoy on the radio, but Hamid was dead, and the entire police force of Moscow was bearing down on him.

Bennett checked Hamid's pulse again, just to be sure, but it was over.

As he closed Hamid's eyes and said a final rushed good-bye, he choked down the rage rising within him. Bennett scrambled over the front seat, grabbed Hamid's Beretta and his wedding ring, exited the passenger-side door, and raced to the running Mercedes.

The front grill was smashed in, but it would do. He slammed the door behind him, gunned the engine, and rammed past the police cruiser.

"Unit 225, this is N.P. Center—repeat—standing by. Where are you?"

Erin's voice startled Bennett until he realized that the FSB was, for the moment at least, using the same frequency. But he had no time to respond. He had both hands on the wheel and was weaving through side streets and back alleys to get to the apartment building in which he'd spent so much time as a child.

He still had no idea how she'd gotten there or why, but as he drove up to the back entrance he flipped his lights on and off and suddenly saw her bolt from the door and race to the car. He reached over and pushed the door open, and before he knew it she was in his arms, sobbing and kissing him.

The roar of a helicopter emerged overhead.

CRACK, CRACK, CRACK.

Someone was firing at them. Gasping for air, Bennett reluctantly pulled away.

"Miss me?" He smiled through blood and tears.

"Of course—now drive!"

63

SIXTEEN MINUTES TO IMPACT

Their chopper was waiting.

Gogolov and Jibril raced to the helipad and climbed in, with Zyuganov right behind them.

"All set, Commander?" Gogolov shouted to the pilot over the roar of the rotors.

"Yes, Your Excellency. Clear skies ahead."

"Good, let's do it."

The Israelis had not yet launched, but they would. That gave them a thirty-minute head start in which to leave Moscow behind and reach their nuclear-blast-proof command center deep inside the Ural Mountain range. From there Gogolov could watch the final devastation of the Jews on large-screen monitors and in full color.

He could hardly wait.

"Mr. Prime Minister, all systems are go."

So this is it, thought Mordechai.

The bunker was silent. Every eye was glued to the computer screens, where telemetry and tracking data updated in real time. There were only twelve minutes to impact. If Israel was going to launch a counterstrike, it had to be now.

But Doron said nothing.

"We can only launch on your command, sir," said Defense Minister Modine.

Still no reaction. Doron just stared at the trajectory of the inbound ICBM and shook his head.

"Sir?" Modine asked again. "We need a decision."

Every eye was now on him. Six million Jews were about to be inciner- ated. He had every right to retaliate. Indeed, it was his responsibility.

So why wasn't he giving the order?

Darkness completely engulfed Moscow.

Bennett hit his high beams and slammed the pedal to the floor. They were racing through Moscow with tracer bullets blowing out their win- dows and aiming for their tires. Bennett cruised through a side street and headed for the embassy. How safe they'd be he had no idea, but he didn't know what else to do.

"Jon, look out!" McCoy screamed.

As they came around a corner, a Russian battle tank sat two hundred yards ahead. Its turret shifted. The 125 mm smooth-bore cannon aimed right for them, and a second later they saw the tank rock back.

"He fired—break left, break left."

The embassy option was out.

Bennett took a hard left and smashed through a bus stop as 50-caliber rounds tore up the road behind them. He was driving as fast as he could while trying to maintain some measure of control. They had no hope of U.S. assistance and no plan B.

They also had no margin for error. The Moscow police and FSB were systematically cutting off all possible escape routes out of the city. And even if they could break free, cars and trucks filled with fleeing Muscovites jammed every major thoroughfare.

As they blew through another red light, they narrowly missed being broadsided by two police cruisers, both of which now opened fire.

Bennett hit the brakes and spun the car to the right. They spilled out onto Tverskaya Boulevard, and Bennett gunned the engine.

For the moment, they had no options to either side. Red Square was dead ahead. Perhaps they could make it to the river. It was a long shot, but . . .

McCoy's satellite phone rang. It was Mordechai.

"Erin, where are you?" the old man shouted.

"I'm with Jon, but we've got a little situation here."

"You've got to get out of Moscow now."

"Tell me something I don't know," she shot back.

"No, no, you don't understand. Gogolov just launched—"

But the call suddenly went dead.

"Sir, we have a problem."

With Gogolov on the phone with his generals, Jibril leaned forward.

"What is it, Commander?" Jibril shouted, barely able to hear himself.

The pilot pointed to the helicopter's radar display. "Sir, storm intensity on this radar system is displayed in four colors against this black background. That green to our south is light rainfall. The yellow represents a mild storm to our north. This red patch indicates heavy thunderstorms coming in behind us."

"What is the dark purple section straight ahead?" Jibril asked.

"I don't know, sir. I have never seen a storm that big."

They were heading straight into it.

"I thought you said we had clear skies ahead, Commander."

"We did, sir. Ten seconds ago, that storm was not there."

"This is CNN Breaking News."

Dmitri Galishnikov and his wife, Katya, huddled in the bomb shelter under their home. Desperate for the latest news, they were glued to three television sets all linked to the Medexco satellite system.

"CNN has received unconfirmed reports that Russian and coalition forces in Lebanon are beginning to advance toward the Israeli border. Israeli radio is reporting that a column of some five hundred Russian and Iranian battle tanks is heading south from Beirut and is expected to link up with another two thousand tanks positioned just east of Tyre and Sidon."

Katya began to sob.

She and Dmitri had left the Soviet Union to give their sons better lives, not this. Uri, their youngest, was part of an Israeli tank battalion on the border of Lebanon. Moishe, their oldest, was in a paratrooper unit guarding the Golan Heights.

She cursed herself for listening to Dmitri. He was the Zionist in the family, not her. When they'd finally been given exit visas out of Russia, she'd begged him to take her to the United States, "the true Promised Land." But he had refused. He'd insisted on making his life a Jewish life, and making his fortune in the land of Abraham, Isaac, and Jacob. In Israel, and nowhere else. And where had it gotten them?

It was a death sentence.

What she didn't know was that a Russian ICBM was already inbound toward Tel Aviv and only eight minutes from impact.

Suddenly the walls and floor began to shake.

One of the television sets slid off the table and crashed to the floor. The lights began to flicker, then went out, and Katya's sobs turned to screams.

MacPherson felt it first.

But an instant later everyone in the Situation Room was on his or her feet. The room was shaking violently. Files, coffee mugs—anything that wasn't bolted down—crashed to the floor. It felt like an earthquake, but that didn't make sense. Washington, D.C., almost never had earthquakes. Neither did Maryland or Virginia.

Was it an attack? Had a bomb just gone off?

Six Secret Service agents burst into the room. They grabbed MacPherson and Vice President Oaks and raced them down to the Presidential Emergency Operations Center deep underneath the White House. Costello and the NSC team were right behind them. But even there the room convulsed. Lights flickered. Several television monitors blew out. The sound was almost deafening, like the roar of a freight train.

"Get me NORAD," shouted MacPherson. "Find out what's going on."

Corsetti pressed a cell phone to his ear.

"Interior just confirmed," he shouted back. "It is a massive earthquake. The epicenter is just outside of Jerusalem, but it's being felt all over the world."

"That's impossible," said MacPherson, trying to brace himself against the conference table.

"That's what they're saying, sir. FEMA's getting reports from L.A., Chicago, Orlando—everywhere, sir. State's getting flash traffic reports from all our embassies. Everyone's getting hit, and damage is severe."

Mordechai's first thought was that they'd been hit.

The command bunker's ceiling seemed ready to collapse. Chunks of concrete and plaster fell like rain. The ground beneath them continued to heave and sway.

Though the overhead lights were gone, the backup generators kicked in immediately, keeping the computers running. The room now was devoid of light but for the eerie green and red glow of the computer displays and the video monitors displaying live satellite feeds from over the borders.

Mordechai uncovered his head and looked at the computer tracking the ICBM. It said they still had six minutes. Was it wrong? What else but a Russian nuclear warhead could have caused something like this in the most secure location in the whole of Israel?

But then he knew. It wasn't any man-made weapon.

He heard the prime minister calling out in the darkness. "Was that it? Did we just get hit?"

Modine had an open line to six of his top field commanders. On the speakerphone, Mordechai heard all of them reporting a horrendous earthquake and massive devastation, but none of them could see any signs of bomb or missile damage.

"No, sir," Modine said. "Not yet. We still have time. But you need to order the counterstrike now, sir."

"No!" shouted Mordechai. "Don't you see, David; it is coming true. The prophecy is coming true."

"Five minutes to impact, sir," Modine said. "There's no more time."

Mordechai tried to find his friend in the shadows.

"What are you talking about, Eli?" Doron shouted. "We're all about to die."

"No, no, this is Ezekiel 38:19 and 20 coming true—'In My zeal and in My blazing wrath,' says the Lord, 'I declare that on that day there will surely be a great earthquake in the land of Israel. . . . And all the men who are on the face of the earth will shake at My presence.' All men, sir, every-where—even you."

Costello stared at the monitors in disbelief.

It was happening. It wasn't a dream. This was real. Which meant Bennett and Mordechai *had* been right. Which meant that *he'd* been right. Which meant . . . *what?*

The world as he had known it all his life was about to change forever. Nothing would ever be the same again. He knew the prophecy cold by now. He knew what was coming next. The judgment of Russia. The de-struction of radical Islam. The realignment of nations and fortunes, un-precedented in human history. But what did it *really* mean—for him, for his wife, for the future they had planned for themselves?

Costello knew what he had to do, the choices he now had to make. He just didn't know if he had the courage he needed, or the stamina to see it through.

Ruth Bennett cowered under a table.

The walls were crumbling. Beams crashed down from the ceiling. Electrical wires sizzled and popped and sparked in the darkness. She screamed for help, but no one could hear her. She could barely hear her-self. Something smashed into the table right above her head.

Terrified, she cried out in the darkness, *"Lord Jesus, forgive me."*

For a moment she was startled by her own words. She had not said *Protect me.* Not *Save me.* She had cried *Forgive me.* And in that moment she suddenly knew beyond a shadow of a doubt that what Jon had told her was the truth. She knew the judgment of God had begun. And more than physical protection, more than a peaceful feeling of security, she knew she needed forgiveness. She suddenly realized she was in danger of dying without ever having accepted Christ's free gift of love and forgiveness. What's more, she knew that the only thing stopping her from getting right with God was her stubborn, foolish pride—and there was no more time for that.

Weeping now, as her world crashed down around her, Ruth Bennett opened her heart to God.

"Lord Jesus, I need you. I'm so sorry for not coming to you sooner. Forgive me, Lord, for everything. Thank you for dying on the cross to pay for my sins. And thank you for rising from the dead to give me eternal life. Please come into my life and be my Savior and my Lord. Have mercy on me, Lord Jesus. Show me how to follow you, and let me be with you forever. Please. Amen."

And in that instant, her life changed. The terror was suddenly gone. In its place was an overwhelming sense of peace that surpassed any possible understanding, and it began to dawn on her that nothing she knew would ever be the same.

64

TWO MINUTES TO IMPACT

The helicopter shook violently.

Gogolov hung up the phone. His eyes locked onto the Doppler display. They were engulfed by a raging electrical storm. He quickly buckled his seat belt and looked out the window, but there was nothing to see. Day had turned to night, but for the strobe effect of the lightning.

Zyuganov was hyperventilating, insisting they were all going to die. Every flash of lightning, every bone-crunching thunderclap drove the man deeper into panic.

"Commander," Gogolov ordered, "get us on the ground—now."

Before the pilot could react, the front windshield of the chopper shattered.

Zyuganov screamed.

Gogolov realized what had hit them—a hailstone the size of a small bomb. And when another bolt of lightning lit up the sky, it was clear the sky was full of them.

Freezing rain and winds poured into the cabin. Gogolov and Jibril tried to protect themselves with their hands, but suddenly a smaller chunk of ice came hurtling through space, impaling Zyuganov between the eyes.

"Erin, watch out," Bennett shouted.

It was almost too late. An FSB Mercedes swerved in behind them and was gaining on their right. McCoy grabbed a Beretta and lowered the window. She squeezed off six rounds. The windshield of the pursuing car shattered. The Mercedes spun out of control and smashed through the plate-glass window of the Hotel National.

Bennett blew through the intersection of Tverskaya and Mokhovaya. Smashed cars piled up behind him, but at least a dozen more were still in hot pursuit. They were coming in from either side now, leaving them only one path—directly into Red Square. But they had no choice. They had to find a way out of the city before they were completely surrounded and the noose tightened around their necks.

Bennett raced through the promenade outside the State Historical Museum, then through the floodlit Resurrection Gate and into the square that had come to symbolize the Evil Empire. He could see Lenin's Tomb and the Kremlin to his right. St. Basil's Cathedral lay straight ahead.

From the roof of the Kremlin, someone fired a rocket-propelled grenade.

Bennett saw the flash of the ignition but had no time to swerve. The RPG sliced the air directly in front of them, barely missing their front windshield and leaving a flaming white contrail in its wake.

The missile exploded inside the GUM Department Store. McCoy saw two more commandos race into the square ahead of them, preparing to fire. Bennett saw it, too. There was still nothing he could do. They weren't close enough to shoot the men down, and turning at these speeds would roll the car and kill them both instantly.

McCoy screamed. Bennett held his breath and prepared to die.

But then—directly ahead of them—the ground suddenly split open and seemed to swallow the men alive.

The walls of the Kremlin began to collapse.

The earth below them shook with fury.

Bennett hit the brakes. Behind them, too, a great rift suddenly ripped apart the pavement of Red Square, swallowing their pursuers and setting off a series of explosions that swallowed their screams as well.

And then, in the darkness, Bennett saw a fireball streaking through the sky. His mouth opened in horror but emitted no sound. He wanted to shield McCoy, but he could not move.

The first fireball hit the Presidential Administration Building inside the Kremlin and engulfed the whole complex in flames. Seconds later, one fireball after another began smashing into the buildings of the Kremlin, obliterating them before Bennett's eyes. Flames and smoke shot fifty, sixty feet into the air.

Then Lenin's Tomb was hit.

St. Basil's Cathedral exploded into a billion pieces.

The museum was ablaze.

Within moments, it seemed the entire sky was on fire. Bennett didn't know if they were missiles or meteorites or "hellfire and brimstone." All he knew for sure was that the firestorm predicted by Ezekiel had begun.

The earthquake had ended, but a new chapter had opened.

"Mr. President, Moscow is under attack."

MacPherson turned to Kirkpatrick, then to the live satellite feed. "You said the Israelis hadn't launched yet."

"They haven't, sir."

"What are all those inbound tracks?"

"They're not from Israel and they're not from us."

"Then where are they coming from?"

Kirkpatrick turned and looked MacPherson in the eye.

"They're coming from space, sir."

MacPherson had no reply.

Mordechai stared at the computer monitors.

In the blink of an eye, the computer track of the Russian ICBM just disappeared. Doron saw it, too, as did Modine and the rest of Doron's team. They were aghast, unsure what had just happened, unsure what to do next.

"Somebody tell me what's going on," Doron demanded.

Modine worked the phones, starting with the National Military Command Center at the Pentagon. "Sir, Moscow's been hit," he told Doron. "Tehran, too—we're getting reports from all over, sir."

"But how? What happened? We never fired."

"That's what the White House wants to know," said Modine. "The Pentagon's telling the president they've detected no launches out of Israel or anyone else in the world. Just the Russian launch out of Siberia. But everyone still thinks you ordered a massive nuclear counterstrike."

"But I didn't," Doron said, and then he turned and looked at Mordechai.

Ken Costello could not speak.

NORAD was now tracking thousands of "missiles"—*what else should they call them?*—striking Russia, Iran, and every coalition country. None of them had lifted off from Israel. The computers showed no heat plumes, no launch warnings of any kind, only fiery projectiles entering the earth's atmosphere and hurtling toward Asia, Africa, and Europe.

Costello watched in stunned silence as satellite feeds showed every Russian nuclear missile silo and military base being hit, one after another.

Iranian and Libyan military sites and government buildings were obliterated in front of his eyes. The same appeared to be true of every country allied with Gogolov. One by one, the militaries of the entire coalition were being decimated.

NORAD and CIA monitors translated each impact with blinding flashes of white light, causing a hypnotic, almost strobe-light effect within the dim setting of the Situation Room.

Mosques and national symbols were being hit as well. Live coverage from Al-Jazeera showed fireballs hitting Mecca and Medina. In a millisecond, hundreds of thousands gathered to pray for the destruction of Israel were incinerated on live television. Local coverage from Istanbul showed the seventeenth-century Blue Mosque now a smoldering wreckage. Berlin TV showed the Reichstag utterly destroyed. Casualties around the world were rapidly mounting into the millions.

As the world watched in horror, scorching fire rained from the heavens onto the coalition forces. Within minutes it seemed as if the whole of Lebanon, Syria, and Saudi Arabia was a blazing inferno.

And then there was the carnage occurring on the mountains of Israel.

Amid the chaos on the battlefield, coalition forces were now attacking each other, mistaking fellow tank and infantry units for advancing Israeli divisions. Meanwhile, several dozen fighter pilots had managed to take off from Russian aircraft carriers in the Mediterrean, but one by one their planes were consumed by the firestorm. A few MiGs unleashed their missiles at Israel, but their efforts were in vain. The heat-seeking missiles were simply drawn to the raging fires on the coalition warships behind them, killing what few sailors were left alive.

Everywhere Costello looked he saw more images of destruction.

On one small monitor he saw the thermal imaging from a U.S. spy satellite hovering over the Golan Heights. The screen was awash with hellish reds and oranges so intense Costello almost had to look away. In the lower left corner he could see the glowing outline of someone crawling through flames.

At first the body was a pale yellow—normal body temperature. But as Costello continued to stare, unable to avert his eyes, the image turned light orange, then dark orange, and then a ghastly, fiery maroon. Whoever it was had just cooked to death while he had watched in silence, half a world away.

What Mordechai saw next even he did not expect.

From the Mount of Olives, with the Old City of Jerusalem behind her, an Israeli reporter broadcast the latest stunning developments. The sound was muted, so Mordechai stared at her eyes. *Was that fear? joy? disbelief?* Perhaps it was all three.

Then suddenly the reporter looked up in the still-darkened sky and hit the deck as her cameraman followed. The camera itself rocked back and forth for a moment, then fell to the ground. The lens cracked. The camera was on its side. But the image it broadcast to the world was unmistakable.

Burning sulfur and massive meteorites rained down on the Temple Mount. One after another, seven balls of fire smashed into the Dome of the Rock, the Al-Aksa Mosque, and everything around them, shattering rocks and melting anything that would not burn. It was as if God Himself was cleansing the holy site.

Gogolov could see the fireball coming toward them.

But there was nothing they could do.

The pilot aimed the chopper for the ground, hoping to outmaneuver whatever this thing was. Within seconds, they had dropped from nine thousand feet to less than six thousand. Gogolov and Jibril tried in vain to grab hold of anything solid, but what was the point?

"Base Camp this is Black Star; we are going down. *I repeat, we are going down.* Three thousand feet and dropping fast."

There was no reply. All they could hear over the radio were the screams of men dying in the air and on the ground.

Another explosion of thunder and a burst of wind shear rocked the helicopter from side to side. Gogolov could see the pilot fighting for their lives.

And then it hit with a deafening roar.

Through his pain, Gogolov saw Jibril burst into flames. The man's flesh crackled and split open, melting from his bones as his eyes turned to liquid in their sockets.

Then all color drained away, as did the light of the flames. All noise faded, including the sound of his own screams. Gogolov could see nothing but a black, misty void, as if the spirits of the dead were rising from the abyss to take him away.

In that instant, Gogolov feared death. He could feel himself falling through the dark void of space. He was flailing and terrified and utterly alone. He braced for impact, but it never came. He cried for mercy he would never see. He felt the searing heat and the demons ripping at his eyes and face with claws like razors. And then, in a terrifying flash of clarity, he realized it would never end.

☆   ☆   ☆

Out of the hellish fury emerged Bennett and McCoy.

They were running for their lives. With the inferno at their backs, they raced down to the Moskva River only to find every bridge—and every tank that had guarded it—destroyed.

Even if they could find a car or truck and get it started, how would they get out of the city? Every street and boulevard was littered with the charred wreckage of Russian police and military vehicles and the still-smoking bodies of those forces who had tried to flee. Everyone else was gone. The city had become a ghost town.

"Jon, the boats."

McCoy was already running. Bennett scrambled to catch up.

There—about a quarter of a mile downriver—was a speedboat tied along the far bank. McCoy dived into the water as soon as she got close and swam to the other side, with Bennett right behind her. There was no one around, no one to stop them, so they clambered aboard, started the motor, and headed south.

Moscow burned as Rome once had.

Red Square was consumed by scorching winds. Explosions rocked the city, and a thousand years of bloodstained history went up in flames.

As he stared back at the smoke of her burning, Bennett felt sickened by all the death and destruction he had seen—and caused. He grieved for his friend Hamid, who had died that he might live. *How was that right? Why hadn't God taken him, instead?* thought Bennett. He grieved for Nadia. Who would tell her the terrible news? No one else knew but him, he realized. But the thought of facing her, the thought of telling her she would have to raise Hamid's baby all by herself, was almost more than he could bear.

He grieved, too, for his mother as it suddenly dawned on him: Had she lived through the earthquake? Was she hurt? Would anyone find her? His satellite phone had been destroyed. There was no way he could reach her, no way to send help, no way to tell her that he and Erin were alive, or find out if she had ever trusted Christ.

And yet amid the swirl of conflicting emotions, Bennett also felt humbled by God's protection. He had no food, no extra fuel, and no idea what lay ahead. Still, somehow he felt at peace. The great liberation of millions had begun. Across the hard soil of so many countries, the promise of new life was finally free to grow.

And he was in the arms of the woman he loved, the woman he'd feared he'd lost forever. He held her tight. He was home. The tears began to flow, and he had no idea when they'd stop, and he didn't care.

EPILOGUE

★ ★ ★

It was time.

As he sat in his palace in the heart of Iraq, watching the coverage of the events in Russia and Iran and Saudi Arabia and beyond, Mustafa Al-Hassani was a cauldron of mixed emotions. But one thought kept rising to the fore: *The leaders and forces of all of his enemies had just been wiped off the face of the earth.* He did not know how or why, nor did he care. He knew those answers would come in time.

For now it was clear that if he moved quickly, he could build the Babylon of his dreams—not just the city . . . his Empire.

IS IT TRUE?

★ ★ ★

To learn more about the research used for this book—and to track the latest political, economic, and military developments in Israel, Russia, Iran, and other countries described in *The Ezekiel Option*—please visit www.joelrosenberg.com.

You can also sign up to receive Joel C. Rosenberg's e-mail newsletter, >> FLASH TRAFFIC <<.

ACKNOWLEDGMENTS

* * *

King Solomon once wrote, "He who walks with wise men will be wise." I have been fortunate to walk alongside some wonderfully kind and insightful men and women in my life. To all I owe an enormous debt of gratitude. Thanks again to everyone mentioned in my previous acknowledgements, especially Lynn's and my families, and our dear friends from McLean, Frontline, and Syracuse. Thanks, as well, to Daniel and Susan Doron, who first alerted me to the rising threat of Iran back in the early 1990s and taught me so much about the Arab-Israeli conflict; Tim and Beverly LaHaye, whose book, *The Coming Peace In the Middle East*, first drew my attention to the prophecies of Ezekiel 38–39; Jerry Jenkins; Tim MacDonald; Capt. Jeff Donnithorne (USAF); Wes Yoder and his team at Ambassador Agency; everyone who gave me their time and insights on my research trips to Russia, Turkey, and Israel; everyone in our Tuesday night groups; June "Bubbe" Meyers, who always goes above and beyond the call of duty; and Edward and Kailea Hunt, who have become such dear friends and done so much to help us on this book, and this book tour.

A special word of thanks to Scott Miller at Trident Media Group, a great agent and a great friend; Ron Beers and Becky Nesbitt at Tyndale House, who got behind this project from the start and drove it with their enthusiasm; Jan Stob, Cheryl Kerwin, Bev Rykerd, and the sales, production, and marketing teams at Tyndale who have done such a wonderful, professional job of turning this dream into a reality; Jeremy Taylor, the best editor in the business; and Ken and Mark Taylor and the rest of the Tyndale family, with whom it has been such a pleasure to work.

Most of all I want to thank my wife, Lynn—my college sweetheart and best friend. Her love inspires me, her joy lifts my spirits, her wisdom blesses me, and her boundless energy and zest for life keep me going. If all I had was you at my side, *dayenu*, "this alone would be enough." But you have also given me four wonderful sons—Caleb, Jacob, Jonah, and Noah—of whom I could not be more proud. Thank you, Lynn. Thank you, boys. I love you each so much.

JOEL C. ROSENBERG

Joel C. Rosenberg is a *New York Times* best-selling author and a communications strategist who has worked with some of the world's most influential and provocative leaders, including Steve Forbes, Rush Limbaugh, former Israeli deputy prime minister Natan Sharansky, and former Israeli prime minister Benjamin Netanyahu.

His first novel, *The Last Jihad*, put readers inside the cockpit of a hijacked jet on a kamikaze attack into an American city, leading to a showdown between the U.S. and Saddam Hussein over weapons of mass destruction. Yet it was written nine months before September 11, 2001. Published in November 2002, *The Last Jihad* hit number one on Amazon.com and spent eleven weeks on the *New York Times* best-seller list.

Mr. Rosenberg's second novel, *The Last Days*, was about the death of Yasser Arafat and a White House push for peace. The first chapter put readers inside a U.S. diplomatic convoy heading into Gaza as part of the Middle East peace process. The convoy was attacked by a massive explosion. Three weeks before the book was published in October 2003, such an attack took place in Gaza, leading *U.S. News & World Report* to call Mr. Rosenberg a "modern Nostradamus." *The Last Days* quickly became a *New York Times* and *USA Today* best seller. A Hollywood producer optioned the rights for a major motion picture.

The *New York Times* has twice profiled Mr. Rosenberg, calling him "a Washington success story." He has appeared on more than three hundred radio and television programs, including ABC's *Nightline* with Ted Koppel, *CNN Headline News*, FOX News Channel, MSNBC, CBN's *The 700 Club*, *The Sean Hannity Show*, and the *The Rush Limbaugh Show*.

www.joelrosenberg.com

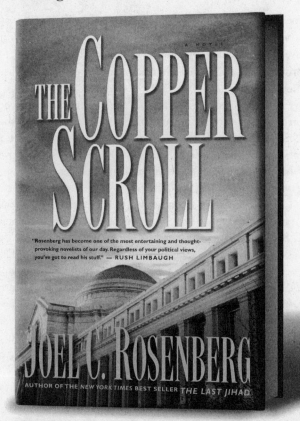